SYLVIA

INTRODUCTION
BY HOWARD FAST

IN 1959, THE NOTORIOUS BLACKLIST, OPERATIONAL UNDER THE auspices of J. Edgar Hoover and the House Committee on Unamerican Activities, was still functioning—close to the end of its unappetizing life, but still enforced. I had been blacklisted as a writer ever since Clark Clifford confessed to the Unamerican Committee that he had purchased and distributed as Christmas gifts fifty copies of my biographical novel *Citizen Tom Paine*. Pleading that he did so without being aware that he was handling "communist" propaganda, Mr. Clifford was let off the hook.

However *Citizen Tom Paine* was duly banned and ordered destroyed by J. Edgar Hoover's FBI. Librarians at the central branch of the New York Public Library informed me that my books had not been destroyed as per Hoover's orders, but had been hidden in the basement, to be brought out at a happier time.

In 1951, Mr. Hoover, as the head of the FBI, issued orders that any publisher dealing with my writing would be considered by the FBI as consorting with the enemy; and as impossible as it may sound today, most publishers believed him. I had just finished the writing of *Spartacus*, the novel upon which the film was based, and my publisher Little, Brown and Co. turned it down under pressure from the FBI. The situation was unprecedented in all the history of American letters, and following this event, seven major publishers refused to publish the manuscript. Finally, after Doubleday rejected it—stating nevertheless that it was the best manuscript they had received that season—Mr. George Hecht, head of the Doubleday chain of bookstores, telephoned me and suggested that I publish it myself. He was enraged at the cowardly reaction of the editorial board and he gave me an initial order for 600 books, considering that I would publish it.

Thus I did what no author should ever do; I published *Spartacus* myself. They say that the client who defends himself has a fool for a lawyer. Be it well said that the writer who publishes himself has a fool twice over for a publisher. Yet I was lucky beyond any reasonable expectation, and the self-published *Spartacus* became a best seller, and has since that time sold well over a million copies. But the small success of my initial printing of the hardcover edition—which had an almost immediate sale of 40,000 copies—went to my head, and I proceeded to publish not only several additional books of my own, but the books of a number of blacklisted authors. I hung on for the next few years, and then I went broke. I managed to pay off my debts without resorting to bankruptcy, and once and for all, I turned my back on publishing.

Yet out there in the real world was the blacklist, and here was a man who had to write. It was my meat and drink and wine; I either wrote or I could not live. There was no way I could turn off my thoughts and keep the stories from forming.

It began with a woman's name: Sylvia. I loved the name. I loved the song. "Who is Sylvia and what is she?" And the other sweet song, "Sylvia's hair is like the night." Dark hair, raven black, a tall woman and beautiful. I could envision her as I might a living person.

Meanwhile, I had found a new literary agent. My former agents, who had marketed four of my early best sellers, had fled before the FBI. Now I was introduced to a gentleman, Paul R.

Reynolds by name. He was an extraordinary man, slender, handsome, wise, and totally secure in his position as an American, a direct descendant of Paul Revere and someone who gave not a tinker's damn for either J. Edgar Hoover or the Unamerican Committee.

"I have a book in mind," I told him, "and it's seething there and driving me crazy."

"Write it," he said.

"And the blacklist?"

"We'll worry about that when we have the manuscript."

The book took shape, and some months later, I brought the MS to Paul Reynolds. He read it with delight and assured me that any publisher he decided to send it to would publish it.

"However," he added, "I've been talking to people, and the blacklist still intimidates. Suppose we were to publish under another name? How would that strike you?"

"It's been done," I admitted. "I hate the thought, but if that's what it means to get the book out, I'll go along with it."

I told Paul to pick any name he desired, and the name he chose was E. V. Cunningham. He used initials, as he told me afterwards, to avoid any lawsuit for invasion of privacy by the use of another's name. He then put it out for bids and accepted a 12,000 dollar advance from Doubleday, a very substantial advance thirty years ago. The book was published, very well received, reviewed with high praise and sold to Paramount Pictures for a film.

This was the beginning of a long relationship with Paul R. Reynolds, a man I came to treasure as a dear friend and a wise literary advisor. The success of *Sylvia* was such that I went on to write a second book of similar genre, suspense-mystery, and then another and still another. In all through the years since then, I have written twenty books under the name of E. V. Cunningham—and recently, I have come to regret that I ever agreed to a pseudonym.

In France, where they cared nothing about a blacklist, they

published *Sylvia* under the name of Howard Fast. It has sold well over a hundred thousand copies in France, and this year, 1992, another edition of 50,000 has just been printed.

All of the books written under the name of E.V. Cunningham have been brought out under the name of Howard Fast in France. *Sylvia* is the first of the E.V. Cunningham books to be published in America under my own name. Since *Sylvia* is one of my favorites, I am absolutely delighted that at this late date, while I am still alive and well, I can see it published under the name of Howard Fast.

PART 1

LOS ANGELES

MOST PEOPLE GO ON DOING WHATEVER THEY WERE DOING BE-
fore; if they were doing it yesterday, they're doing it today,
and the odds are that they'll be doing it tomorrow as well. It
applies to myself. I make a poor living in a rut and routine,
and my work is mean and miserable and routine. When I
have a buck, I can push aside the really filthy jobs and accept
the moderately filthy jobs, and then perhaps I feel a cheap
sense of virtue, as empty and meaningless as everything else
I feel. And always, like so many of my kind, I dream that the
improbable will come along.

What a senseless and passionless business life must be if
it never comes along! In that way, I am lucky, because it came
to me once, and once is almost enough. That was when Sylvia
West entered my life and I entered hers.

My own name is Alan Macklin. I am five feet eleven inches
tall, brown hair and brown eyes, and no better or worse looking than the next one. I was born in Chicago in 1923, did
most of the things that kids do, and was patriotic enough to
enlist in the army three days after Pearl Harbor. Five years
and four days after that I received an honorable discharge. I

returned to Chicago, enrolled at the University of Chicago, and found myself a part-time job at the Armour plant. I majored in ancient history and thought that I would like to teach at some small college after I got my degree, but that changed too.

By the time I got my degree I had saved enough money to bury my father and mother. The frame house we lived in on the North Side burned down and they both died in bed. I was working the night shift at the plant then, so I was lucky or they were unlucky, however you look at it. I suppose there are worse ways to die, and the police doctor said that they had breathed enough smoke and fumes to prevent them from feeling the flames, and since their bodies were in the bed I tried hard to believe him.

I had no family there, no brothers, no sisters, no aunts or uncles—just myself; and I thought of that when I heard about Sylvia. Herself alone and myself alone.

I remained in Chicago another month then, and after that I bought a train ticket to Los Angeles. Eight years later I was still in Los Angeles, older, not too much wiser, but with the knowledge of how to live with loneliness and boredom. I had a one-room office on Rodeo just off Wilshire, a 1956 Ford convertible, and a one-room apartment in West Hollywood. I had three suits, two pairs of daks, a sport jacket, a top coat, and an address in Beverly Hills. I had a marriage behind me that had lasted three months and left a minimum of bitterness, and there were half a dozen people I called my friends. I suppose you can do worse.

On the twelfth of August, 1958, I was sitting in my office— hot and without air conditioning—and trying to balance a checkbook with two months' rent, a month due and a month overdue, when the telephone rang. It was Frederick Summers. He asked me whether I could be at his office at three o'clock that same afternoon. I said that I could.

2

I was there at five minutes to three. The office was downtown in one of the older, substantial buildings. The lettering on the door read FREDERICK SUMMERS, nothing else, but the office was large, air-conditioned, and well furnished with pale Danish modern, pastel drapes, and vinyl floors. A good-looking blonde sat in the reception room; she was as pale as her pastel-colored desk and the two light gray telephones that flanked her, each equipped with its own bright set of buttons and lights. On either side I could see two smaller rooms, a man bent over some ledgers in one of them, a girl busy at a typewriter in the other. The lighting came from behind a ceiling of white glass, and the walls were covered with pearl-gray monk's cloth.

"We've just had it done over," the blonde said. "Do you like it, Mr. Macklin? You are Mr. Macklin, aren't you?"

"Yes, I'm Macklin." I pointed to the pictures on the walls. "Those are Mirós? They're real, aren't they?"

"Of course they are. Mr. Summers wouldn't have them there unless they were. Won't you go in? He said you were to go in as soon as you came." She admired the fact that I could guess at a Miró, but she didn't think much of my uncertainty. Anyone who knew Mr. Summers would know better, and she knew Mr. Summers. She picked up one of her telephones, pressed a button, and told Mr. Summers that Mr. Macklin had arrived. There was only one door facing the entrance, and Summers had it open before I reached it.

We shook hands, and I went inside and sat down where Mr. Summers nodded for me to sit. His personal décor was severe white paint and black leather, and a wide picture window behind his desk looked across the Freeway toward the hills. He was an inch or two taller than I and broad-shouldered—and perhaps ten or twelve years older than I was. Blue eyes, strong facial bones, and a wide mouth. His gray hair was cropped close, perhaps because he enjoyed it that way, perhaps because of the youthful appearance it gave him. His shirt had cost more than twenty dollars, his suit was tailored, and his shoes were black alligator. In all, he was a handsome, well-groomed, and expensively dressed man, poised and well spoken. He seated himself behind his desk, myself facing the window light, and we spent a quiet minute reading each other.

"This is a delicate matter, Macklin—you understand that," he said at last.

He had established the position and relationship. I was Macklin; he was Mr. Summers. I assured him that I was an old hand at delicate matters, and I guessed that he had already inquired and that my references, whoever had supplied them, were sufficient.

"Yes, that's so," he admitted. "And what do you know about me, Macklin?"

"Nothing."

"You looked for me in *Who's Who?*"

"Yes, I did."

"I am not that distinguished. Wealthy, but nothing to make me famous or infamous. Did you check me through Dun & Bradstreet?"

"Yes."

He raised an eyebrow. "Are you a subscriber?"

"A friend of mine is."

He smiled and pressed the fact that I did know something about him.

"I know that your credit is good."

"Outside—in here?" He motioned with his hand.

"You have an expensive office and two real Mirós. What should I conclude from that, Mr. Summers?"

"I suppose you're right." He smiled again. He had a controlled yet ingratiating smile. "Then let me tell you something about myself, and then we'll get to you. My father was Charles Summers, whose name you would have found in *Who Was Who*. He was the president of California General Petroleum, and when he died a very considerable estate was divided between my sister and myself. That was seventeen years ago. I became a rich man when he died, and I am a much richer man today. In the ordinary sense I have no business, but my affairs are large enough to require constant and intelligent management. I go into all this because, as you will see, it is pertinent to our own arrangements."

He paused to take a cigarette from a crystal box on his desk and to offer one to me—and to light it after I accepted it. Like his smile, his politeness was calculated and ingratiating.

"What are my affairs?" he continued. "Well—I have some property, ranch property, acreage leased for oil exploration, some commercial properties here downtown, and an apartment house in Brentwood. Also a good deal of undeveloped land in San Diego County—perhaps two million in equities all told. I have some common stock—I need not specify how much, but it runs well above ten million. My bond holdings are at least as much, and there are odds and ends of investments that I need not go into. My home is in Beverly Hills. I keep a beach house at Santa Monica and a lodge at Arrowhead Lake and a small yacht with a crew of four. I also own a stable of horses, which I find I can give no time at all to. I enumerate these factors, not to impress you with my wealth—many men are far wealthier—but to spell out the fact that I am a very rich man and that I command a considerable and growing fortune."

I nodded and told him that I was impressed.

"Of course you are." He smiled. He could be disarming as well as ingratiating. "I am impressed myself when I spell it out. Let me add a seventeen-year-old daughter to the list. Her name is Claire. She is a long-legged, good-looking, and spoiled brat, with most of the unpleasant qualities of a rich man's daughter. The blame for this and the reason for this lie with me. Understand me, I am very fond of her, but I see her clearly. I hope she will improve with age; some of us do. I say that the reason lies with me because my wife died twelve years ago of cancer. I have not remarried, and I had no intentions of remarrying until now. During those years I evaded boredom and lived an interesting and often amusing life. The empty, hollow life of the rich is a cliché; if one has sufficient money and a normal amount of intelligence and good health, life can be far from empty."

I listened to him and heard him. I was more interested in a job and a retainer than in his life history, but I listened attentively and nodded at the right places.

"That's myself," he said. "What about you, Macklin?"

"What about me, Mr. Summers? I'm a private investigator, and I make a sort of living at it."

"A private eye?"

"That's gauche, Mr. Summers. That's like calling me a shamus. Even a kid in the game wouldn't have the nerve to call himself a private eye."

"I'll remember that." Summers nodded seriously.

"Like calling you a plutocrat—or a king of finance."

"I see. What made you become an investigator?"

"I majored in ancient history——"

"Ancient history? That's a hell of a non sequitur. What college were you at?"

"Chicago, Mr. Summers. When I came out here I went to UCLA, and they thought there might be an instructorship for me if I took enough credits for my master's, but I also like to eat. I answered six advertisements for a job. The sixth was with the Jeffery Peters Agency, and they hired me. That's how I became an investigator."

"Never went back to get the master's?"

"No—I never did."

"Peters fire you?"

"You know he didn't, Mr. Summers. You don't get along in this tight and rotten business if you're fired out of a place like Peters."

"All right, Macklin. Why did you quit Peters? He paid you a hundred and fifty a week. You don't clear any hundred and fifty now."

"I look better in my other suit."

"I didn't mean that."

"Oh, the hell with what you meant, Mr. Summers. I left Peters because I like to be my own boss."

"Yes—that's what Peters said."

I looked at him for a little while before I told him that I didn't like games played with me. "I earn a buck the hard way," I said. "Don't play, Mr. Summers. Either you got a job for me or I put on my hat and go."

"You took a quick dislike to me, Macklin?"

"I'll be honest with you," I said. "It's not you, Mr. Summers. I don't admire the way I earn my living or the people who pay me to earn it."

"Then why don't you leave it?"

"I stay poor and dirty for the same reason you stay rich and clean, Mr. Summers. I'm used to it, and I always tell myself that next semester I'll start building up credits at UCLA. But it's late. I'm eight years in Los Angeles. Now tell me, if you know Peters, why didn't you give him the job? He has a large agency, over twenty men, and a lot of entree I'll never have."

"I wanted to give it to him, but I told him it had to be kept to one man and myself. He doesn't take jobs that way; he says he can't put a man on something and not know what it is."

"That's right."

"So I asked him to recommend someone, and he recommended you."

"Why?"

"He says you have brains and you can keep your mouth shut."

It was as much as Peters ever said about anyone, except in the way of slander, and I felt good with myself for the first time that day. "If you talk to him again, thank him for that," I said. "I'm not the most charming man you know, but I do my job. What do you want done?"

Instead of telling me, he took a picture from his desk and handed it to me. It had sat on the desk facing him, so I had not seen it before, but I had noticed the lovely filigree of the gold frame, a most unusual frame and like nothing I had ever seen before. The picture was of a woman in her middle or late twenties, a soft and gentle portrait of the head and shoulders. That was the first picture of Sylvia I looked at. I still have a copy of it.

Summers did not interrupt me. He let me look my fill at the picture, and he waited silently until I had looked enough and was ready to say so.

The picture was of a very beautiful woman, her head poised regally, her white shoulders broad and smooth and fine—but how does one say more than that? No object on earth is more rigged with weary sound than the face of a beautiful woman, and with Sylvia it was the quality of the face, not the measurement of it. She did not look like anyone else; she looked like herself. One might say that her full lips had just a trace of sullen discontent; but it was meaningless, because the lips, the nose, the broad brow, and the black hair had meaning only as a whole, as a mobile, living thing that even in a picture was restless, angry, demanding, and yet, in the deepest sense of the contradiction, content. I looked at her picture with the same pleasure that men must have experienced when they looked at her. In my mind I gave it color and emotion and warmth. I saw how the dark brows would narrow with perplexity or indignation. I knew that the slightly flaring nostrils of the strong, straight nose would contract with emotion, with pleasure or anger. She drew me to her, and I had to break from her with as much of an act of will as if she were alive and in the room with me.

I looked up at Summers, who was watching me curiously. "Well?"

"It's a remarkable frame," I said, running my fingers across the gold filigree. "Is it actually Sumerian—the goldwork, I mean?"

"So I was told. It was made for me in Baghdad. I was assured that the filigree work is more than four thousand years old."

"It probably is."

"And since you are knowledgeable among beautiful things, Macklin, do you recognize the woman as well?"

I shook my head. "No. I've never seen her before."

"What is your impression, Macklin?"

"It's only a picture. I'd like to meet her before I make up my mind."

"I'm afraid you won't."

"Oh? Well, she's a beauty—but that's obvious."

"I think so." Summers smiled.

"An unusual woman, I'd guess. Is that what this is? You want me to play a game—to guess?"

"You're touchy enough. I wanted you to look at the picture, that's all. Here's a copy of it. The rest of these are snapshots." He handed me a copy of the picture on his desk and half a dozen snapshots of the same woman. "Keep the pictures." He nodded. "The lady's name is Sylvia West. She has agreed to be the future Mrs. Frederick Summers. We are to be married on the twenty-sixth of October."

"You have my congratulations," I said.

"Thank you." Then he paused and waited, and I could see that he was turning over in his mind what he intended to say. I also waited for a while, until the silence became uncomfortable —and then I observed that he had not asked me here to listen to family history and look at snapshots.

"That's right, Macklin."

"Then what?"

After he had studied me a moment, uneasily and uncomfortably, he rose and walked to the window and said, his back to me:

"I want you to find out who Sylvia West is."

That was not the kind of statement I could comment on or reply to, so I said nothing and waited and looked at the snapshots. One was of Sylvia in a bathing suit, kneeling at the edge of a pool—his Beverly Hills place, I supposed. She had a good figure, but not the kind that wins contests; she was long-limbed, not thin but with a knife-like quality, if that makes any sense—full-bosomed, an able and strong and capable figure. There was a casual portrait, quickly taken and blown and clipped, the wind whipping her dark hair, and a glisten of sea spray on her face. There was a profile full-length as she stood and looked at something, a shot of her playing golf, another of head and shoulders with the upper rail of the yacht and the sea in the background, and the last was of Sylvia asleep, sprawled on the grass like a tired kid, her limbs loose and innocent, a lock of hair across her face.

He pulled away from the window and snapped at me, "Dammit to hell, Macklin—do you know what I'm saying?" It was the only show of temper or anger or annoyance he permitted himself, and it was gone as quickly as it flared.

"I'm afraid I don't," I replied.

"All right. Maybe I put it poorly." He sat down at his desk again and leaned toward me. "I met Sylvia West about a year ago—a little less, it was in October actually. At a party Bennett Hall gave. You know who he is?"

"He was a big star when I was a kid. His name always made me think of a dormitory at a Bennington type of college. It still does."

"You might like him if you met him. He's a pleasant, well-mannered, and decently informed person, and his parties are parties, not brawls. I enjoy the picture business, Macklin, and I like being with picture people. On occasion I have put some money into it and taken some out, but I tend to separate my investments and my pleasures. In any case, I met Sylvia West at his place, and after that I saw her more and more frequently. I found her delightful, that rare combination of beauty and intelligence, not an easy woman to know or understand, nor by any means an ordinary woman. She is clever—more than surface, far more—quick-tempered, moody at times, gay at times . . ."

I listened to the fleshless and toneless description, the nutshell image that a man like Summers must of necessity make of any woman, the pedestrian words that neither implied nor described but folded worn images into a space already full, a closet full of clothes and words and prejudice. I listened and watched Summers and wondered and anticipated.

". . . well read, literate. I don't read a great deal lately, but I did when I was in school. She has published a book of poems. Do you enjoy poetry?"

"Some."

"A *Moon without Light,* it is called. Don't you ever take notes, Macklin?"

"I have a good memory. I don't carry a gun either—I don't own one. That wraps me up. You were talking about Sylvia West."

"I'm sorry. Well, in the course of things, I fell in love with her. I asked her to marry me, and she accepted. I took it for granted that a person like herself would have roots, cords, threads at least, a structural past, some family, at least a second cousin somewhere, a place of origin, a home town, a city—a childhood friend—at least a birth certificate."

"It seems reasonable," I agreed.

"She has none of this."

"Oh?"

"Yes—exactly. I have told you enough about myself for you to understand my predicament. I am not an ordinary person. No very rich man is. How can I marry a woman in such circumstances?"

"Why can't you?"

"Who is she? Is she married? What has she been? What has she done?"

"Ask her," I suggested.

"I have."

"Did she explain?"

"Yes, she explained."

"But you don't believe her?"

"No, Macklin—I don't believe her."

"It's none of my business, but isn't that a hell of a basis for a marriage?"

"I wish I could like you, Macklin," he said slowly. "I don't suppose I have to, if you're as good as Peters says. We won't discuss moral issues or theories of marriage. It is enough for me to say that I want this woman for my wife unless it is impossible to make her my wife."

"I talked out of turn," I admitted. "I'm sorry. I would like to hear what she told you."

Without emotion, without resentment or any further trace of annoyance, Summers detailed the facts of Sylvia West's background, as put forth by Sylvia West. She told him that she had been born in China in 1931. Her father and mother were Methodist missionaries. Her father's name—according to her story—was John Wesley West, her mother Abigail West. The father and mother had come to China as young people. Abigail West passed away in 1937. When conditions in China became too unsettled for John West to continue his work, he and his daughter left for France, where he was given the pulpit of a small Methodist congregation in Paris. A year later the war came, and John West and his daughter crossed over to London, supposedly the place of John West's birth. They lived with John West's brother, a man of considerable means who had made his fortune out of Egyptian aromatic tobacco. His name was Elbert West. During the summer of 1944, when Elbert West was away on a business trip and Sylvia West was sleeping at a friend's house—a schoolgirl friend—Elbert West's residence was struck by a bomb and destroyed. John West and Martha West, his sister-in-law, were in the house at the time and both were killed. Sylvia's uncle then rented a cottage in Surrey, where they lived until Elbert West's death in 1952.

Sylvia West was his sole heir, and she came into an estate of something less than a hundred thousand pounds. She moved to a hotel in London, and then, after a few months, took a small apartment. She fell in love—a not too meaningful affair —and almost plunged into what would have been an unfortunate marriage. After that, there was travel—Greece, Italy, and a summer in the South of France. Eventually she decided to come to America, the country of her mother's birth. In 1956 she appeared in California.

Such was her story, her past offered in bits and patches during the time Frederick Summers knew her and courted her. It was not—according to Sylvia—a happy past or one that she was particularly eager to resurrect, and she spoke of it reluctantly and briefly.

"It could be checked," I said when Summers had finished.

"Not as easily as you might imagine, Macklin."

"Still, it could be checked."

"I checked it. Enough to guess that it is an invention from beginning to end."

"A very creative invention."

"And Sylvia West is a very creative woman, Macklin. My attorneys have a branch in London. There never was any Elbert West in the tobacco business. No city home was destroyed by bombing which had any connection with an Elbert West.

No will of an Elbert West was ever probated, nor is there any tax record of such property intestate. Our immigration department has no record of the entry of a Sylvia West. There is a Methodist congregation in Paris, but the church has no record or recollection of any John West. And while this is not conclusive, the Methodist Missionary Service has no record of him either. These were routine matters of inquiry handled by my attorneys, as I said—and sufficient to convince me that the entire background is an invention."

"Did you confront Miss West with this?" I asked him.

"I did not."

"Why?"

"Because, knowing Sylvia, I also knew that it would mean the end of our relationship."

"And suppose you find out the truth. That could also be the end, couldn't it?"

"I'm not afraid of the truth."

"Then why not let it lay?"

"I tried to explain that to you, Macklin. Sylvia lied to me. She had reasons, and I respect those reasons. But I am also a person with my own needs. I have to know the truth."

"And I am to find out who is Sylvia West. 'Who is Sylvia, and what is she, that all our swains adore her?'"

He observed me coldly and said that he had given me credit for distaste of the obvious.

"When it's that obvious——"

"Can you find out who she is, Macklin?" he interrupted. "That's to the point."

"I don't know."

"You should know. That's your job, isn't it?"

"Yes."

"Well?"

I placed the photographs in a neat stack on his desk, lit one of my own cigarettes, and told him the truth. "I said I don't know. That's all I can say, Mr. Summers. The tricks, talents, and capers of your *private eye*, as they would have it, are a product of literature, television, and the film. If the like of it exists, I have not seen any sign of it. Most private investigators are slow-witted boobs, a good many of them retired from the police force for one reason or another. That is why a person of normal intelligence and no particular grace, myself for instance, shines out. I can not only tail someone, but I can read the street signs while I do it. That's why Peters thinks I am singular. Now as to Sylvia West—I don't know. I can try."

"If a firm of lawyers can check her own story as easily as they did, then surely a man trained for the work——"

"Oh no," I interrupted him. "To check a story against public records is a pure mechanical process. Where do I start? Will you allow me to interview her?"

"No!" he said sharply. "That is out. I want your word that you will not attempt to see her or speak to her."

"Just to make it easier for me."

"No—just to make sense. Do you know how she would hate me, turn on me, if she even dreamed that this conversation was taking place?"

"I don't know. Let's put it all on the table, Mr. Summers. You took pains to impress me with your wealth and position. Will Sylvia West let a point of nicety come between her and twenty-five million dollars, give or take a few million?"

"She is not marrying me for my money, Macklin. We'll make that plain and accept it as a premise. Sylvia West has enough money."

"Oh? How much is enough?"

"She's not wealthy, but she lives well. She has a fine enough house in Coldwater Canyon, on the Beverly Hills side. Her investments are excellent, conservative, and intelligently chosen. She has an income of better than thirty thousand a year."

"If her story is phony, where did the money come from to begin with?"

"I don't know."

"Who chooses her investments? She must have a lawyer."

"She is represented by an excellent local firm. I don't want you to approach them. It would be a dead end in any case, but I don't want you to approach them."

"At least you simplify it, Mr. Summers. You realize, of course, that Sylvia West is not her real name."

"It has occurred to me."

"In other words, you hand me a few pictures of a woman. I don't know her name. I have never seen her. I am not to see her or question her or question anyone who might come back to her and tell her that a fellow called Macklin was asking questions. There are ten thousand cities and towns in this country, but I don't know which one she comes from or whether she comes from this country at all. It's a simple job. A simple straightforward job."

"I didn't say it was easy, Macklin."

"By the way—what about her speech? Does she have an accent?"

"No." Summers was watching me curiously; he was no fool; there are men who have the talent of observing thought in another, and he had that talent. I made the guess that he was better with men than with women, but that might have been only my own pettishness. "No accent that you could put a finger on, Macklin, but my own guess, for what it's worth, is that she's American-born. She'll throw in a trace of British,

not for display, but as if it were an accident of speech, care-
lessness of speech, throw the word away and repeat it, shake
her head, and even murmur that she's sorry."

"A good actor."

"A very good actor, Macklin, but not insincere, believe me.
She was offered an excellent part in a film. She refused. I don't
know why."

"It could be that too many people would see her," I said.

"Yes, it could be that."

"Does she talk French?"

"Some. Not very good French."

"Chinese?"

"I would have been disappointed if you hadn't asked me
that, Macklin. As a matter of fact, she does—not much, and
what she knows of Chinese is the vocabulary and tonality of a
child."

"How do you know?"

"At my house she met Simonson—oriental languages at
UCLA. He told me that her Chinese was delightful in its
simplicity and childishness."

"You arranged that?"

"Yes, I did."

"You're a suspicious man, Mr. Summers."

"Inordinately curious, perhaps. There is a difference, Macklin."

"I suppose so." I nodded, thinking for the first time of
Sylvia as a woman, a person known to me, connected with me,
and thinking of how easily she must have seen through him
and his silly scheme—and wondering again what his own concept of Sylvia was. "What does she do with her time?" I asked
him then. "She doesn't sound like someone who makes an
avocation out of our California sunshine."

"She writes—mostly poetry. About a month ago she mentioned something about a play, still in her mind. She will not talk about her writing. She's very diffident about it."

"Is she well read?"

"Better read than I am, Macklin. One evening at a party, we ran into one of those latter-day literary smart alecks, part of that Ventura crowd, beard and all, and he was taking Joseph Conrad apart. Sylvia was gentle and curious—the lure of 'please tell me.' In an hour he was naked mentally, and pathetic. He had read one book of Conrad's—*Typhoon*, I believe it was. I'm no Conrad reader. But Sylvia knew every book the man wrote, had not merely read them but knew them, just as, if the subject were to come up, she would know Mencius——"

"The Chinese?"

"Yes."

"I didn't know he had ever been translated."

"I couldn't tell you that." Summers smiled.

"She uses a typewriter?"

"No—she writes by hand and has it typed up afterward."

"She's not left-handed, is she?"

"No."

"You've watched her write?"

"I can't say that I have. But I've seen her manuscripts."

"Have you anything here that she wrote?"

"I'm afraid not——" Summers began, and then interrupted himself to say, "But I have. She left this note for me at her house yesterday. I was to pick her up for a cocktail before dinner."

It was a card that he now took from his wallet, slightly larger than an ordinary calling card, with *Sylvia West* printed in plain script—not engraved—on one side of it, and on the other, written in a tight and careful hand:

"I went for roses and will try to be back at five. Be a dear and wait for me in all good grace."

I asked Summers, "Does she always say something a little differently than the average person would?"

"More often than not."

"Does she try? Or is it part of her?"

"I don't think she tries too hard."

"What does she mean by roses?"

"She has a good garden and a passion for white roses. She had been talking about a nursery over in the valley that someone had told her about. Yesterday she drove there and bought three bushes."

"Climbers or tea roses?"

"What difference does it make?"

"Humor me. I am also curious." I smiled for the first time since I had entered his office.

"I believe these were climbers."

I nodded and asked him whether I could keep the card. He said that I could, and then I took the pictures and the card and put them in my pocket.

"What will you do," I asked him, "if I turn up nothing? Go through with the marriage in October?"

"Let me decide that, Macklin. I presume you are willing to take the case?"

"I'll take it," I said. "Not because I feel hopeful about it, but because I'm broke. I need the money."

"What's your fee?"

"Whatever the traffic will bear, but I never had one like this before. Today is August twelfth. Suppose we say sixty days. I'll either have something by then or know that I'll never have anything. Suppose you pay me a thousand dollars now, four thousand more if I bring in what you want, a thousand more if I come empty-handed. Fair enough?"

"Fair enough," he agreed.

"And expenses."

"What kind of expenses?"

"Most of what I get I'm going to pay for, Mr. Summers. Something like this is not nice and not cheap. I am going to have to pay cops and elevator men and hoodlums and maybe a judge or a mayor somewhere along the way, and maybe an assortment of upright citizens, and maybe a lady or two. I may also have to go to a number of places, and while I ride trains and buses with skill, it will be quicker if I fly."

"All right. How much?"

"Three thousand in cash to start—and no limit except common sense if I find something that has to be bought and if I call on you to buy."

"How much is common sense?"

"How much do you want?"

"I'll make the limit when the time comes," he said.

"Fine. Now I'm no paragon of virtue, but I'm not a cheap crook, Mr. Summers. If I want money, I ask for it in my fee; I don't chisel it out of expenses. I don't want to keep any accounting; I don't want to keep names or notations of money in my pockets."

"That's understandable. I'll agree to that."

"When do I start?"

"Now, if you want to. I keep about a thousand in cash here at the office, and I'll have the rest for you in the morning. If you want to see me, it's best that you see me here, and I'd appreciate it if you called for an appointment in advance. How and when do I hear from you?"

"When I've got something worth talking about, you'll hear from me."

"All right."

"Do you want any kind of a contract or agreement?"

"Not if you don't, Macklin."

"I don't," I said.

He was good at things like that. He handled money as if it wasn't money at all, not with disdain, but not with reverence either. He left me alone for a few minutes and then returned with a thousand dollars in cash and a check for a thousand dollars. But when I rose to go he didn't shake hands with me. I was going on a dirty errand, and I was a dirty man who did dirty work. He hired me, but he was clean.

3

The following morning I picked up the rest of the money, put the thousand-dollar check in the bank, and then drove over to Sunset Boulevard and along Sunset to the turnoff for Coldwater Canyon. It was cool and sunny and pleasant, and the morning air was sweet and clean and my pockets were lined. There is a lot of talk about money, but when you've been without it on and off for the best part of your life, you find the feeling of having it hard to match. It's a nice feeling to know that you can eat when you're hungry or when you're not hungry and drink when you want to drink, and take a girl to dinner—provided you've got a girl—and not worry about the check or the fact that you've drawn a thirsty tramp or a thirsty angel. If you can live and be happy without money, I've never learned how; at least with it I live, and I can relax a little and think about something else.

As I drove through Coldwater Canyon, I thought about Sylvia and looked at the high-priced houses and wondered which one was hers. Whichever it was, I agreed with her taste, because if I had to live in Los Angeles and had the money to do it right, there is no place I'd rather be than on the inside slope of Coldwater Canyon.

Now my wonder was an idle wonder and a lazy speculation. There were at least ten ways in which I could locate her house and ten more ways to get inside of it and talk to her. It was not integrity that held me back; no man who follows a stinking trade and makes his dollar out of peeping and listening and gumshoeing has any right to talk about integrity. If a shred of integrity belongs to a man, it shows in the way he earns his daily bread; and if I had no integrity, I have at least the objectivity to own up to that. I also had a rule of buy and sell; and if I sold dirty pictures, I gave value for the buck. When a man became my client, I worked for him and not against him. If he wanted something done, I tried to do it; and if there was something else that he didn't want done, I didn't do it. That was the way I did business, and that was why occasionally a man like Peters threw a job my way.

So I didn't know which house belonged to Sylvia West, and I didn't try to know. I drove up to the spine of the hills, and then I turned left into Mulholland Drive and followed it to where the pavement ended and along the dirt road past the army reserve. At a place where the eye meets nothing but tumbled hills and canyons as wild and lonely as they were a thousand years ago—all of it within the city limits—I pulled over to the side, cut the motor, lit a cigarette, and relaxed.

It was my own celebration, and I was celebrating the fact that I had paid my rent, that I had money, and that my own small, unappetizing place in the universe was accounted for and justified over the next sixty days. I have been known to drink, and on occasion a little more than is good for me; and on and off I have tried to celebrate something with a willing lady whom I neither liked nor disliked but who would be amiable enough to share a bed and allow me to rid myself of a normal amount of tension. But I don't think either of those therapies can hold a candle to the cool shank of the morning at this end of Mulholland Drive, the taste of a cigarette, and the sweet hum of insects in the sunlight.

4

The Dryden Bookshop, on Santa Monica, just around the corner from Roxbury Drive, is owned and operated by Mrs. Ann Goldfarb. The fact that it is as good as any bookstore in Los Angeles is due to the personal attention of Ann, who knows as much about books as anyone in the world; and it continues to be a profitable venture, because that part of Beverly Hills is as good a location as anywhere in the country for a bookstore. I take the liberty of calling Mrs. Goldfarb—her husband was killed in action on the *Boise*—Ann, because I have been a steady customer for a long time and because, on occasion, I take her to dinner and the movies afterward. She, in turn, will have me at her house now and then to talk to literate people. She is a small, plump woman, about forty, with bright blue eyes, a capable head, a pretty face, and graying hair that she does nothing to retard.

She is one of a few good friends I have made in Los Angeles, and as I came into her place she nodded to me, grinned, and with a motion told me that the place was mine, provided I had the money to buy it. I browsed until she finished with her customer, and then she came over, greeted me warmly, and informed me that she had just received the new Penguin on the Hittites.

"I wouldn't know."

"Oh yes, you would. So would I. I read some of them. I like them. Do you know Sylvia West?"

"Never met her. Have you?"

"I met her," Ann replied casually.

"In other words, she's good-looking."

"And intelligent. A tall, stunning brunette. She buys here occasionally—lives in Coldwater Canyon. I ordered the book originally because she was one of my customers, and then I had a number of calls for it—friends of hers, possibly—and I reordered it. That's why I still have four copies. Do you want one?"

"Yes, I'll take one," I said.

5

There are all kinds of cops, and some of them take and some of them don't. I have never been a buff for cops, but I have known other professions where everybody takes. I never had a cop for a friend, but how many friends does anyone make? On the other hand, I never had any kind of run-in with them. I never stumbled over a body in a dark room, or grabbed a gun to withhold evidence, or made any kind of vendetta for my own justice. A private detective who brooded about justice wouldn't last very long.

In other words, a cop was a cop, and I lived and let live. Sergeant Haggerty of the Los Angeles Police Department was a cop who took. I didn't put him on the take. When Peters wanted a cop who took, he sent me to Haggerty, and when I wanted a favor done, I went to Haggerty. I went to Haggerty now and told him that I wanted a make on a Sylvia West, if there was any, and that I wanted him to pull all the Sylvias under the age of forty that they had in their files. I had agreed with myself that West was just a notion, but for some reason that I find difficult to explain I was convinced that Sylvia was her real name.

Perhaps I wanted it to be that way. I had never known another Sylvia. I liked the name. I wanted it to be that way. On the other hand, there is a type of person who cannot surrender his given name—even if the risk of retaining it is very great. The name becomes an inner symbol, as necessary as heart and lungs, a hinge to the soul that assures the individual of his own being and continuity. If Sylvia was that, she had always been Sylvia.

"I can get you the make," Haggerty told me, "but to pull the Sylvias is going to cost."

"I expect it to cost. How much?"

"A yard," Haggerty said.

"You're out of your mind. Peters would pay you a yard to blow up City Hall. Where am I going to get money like that?"

"Find it."

"The hell with it," I said. "You play your games, I'll play my own."

When I walked away, Haggerty threw in, and we bargained until twenty dollars was agreed on. There was no Sylvia West on the record, here or in San Francisco. There were eighteen Sylvias within the age group, and I spent an afternoon at the Hall, going through the pictures and salient details. There was nowhere even a remote resemblance.

6

Four o'clock in the morning I awakened, and then there was no more sleep for the lame end of the night. I took a shower, shaved, brushed my teeth, opened a can of frozen orange juice, and then smoked a cigarette in front of my window

and watched the faint lights of downtown through the morning mist. When I am awake during the hour between five
and six in the morning, I am full of pity and sorrow for
myself. I look at myself from the wrong end of a very long
telescope, and I see a tiny, soft, quivering bit of matter that
is utterly without importance or meaning. The world is vast
and the universe is vaster, and if Alan Macklin turns on the
gas and puts his head in the stove, it will rate six lines in the
Times and a few words of casual regret on the part of half a
dozen people. At such a time I am usually as alone as any man
on earth, but this morning was different.

This morning I was there to greet the sun. The orange juice
tasted good and so did the cigarette. I had a thoughtful conversation with myself:

"It isn't a case of ethics or integrity or any other high-flown
word. As for your client, your business is to give him what he
wants."

"Fine. So you turn up at her house and tell her you are
selling vacuum cleaners. Or you rent Barney Adler's gas-com-
pany credentials and tell her you are checking the heaters. Or
you flash the Tri-City Real Estate stuff and tell her that you
have a customer for her house——"

"That's right. One way or another."

"Then?"

"Then I talk to her."

"Then what have you got?"

"I learn something."

"Or you lose something and the job is over. What are you
—some punk adolescent kid with his first crush? Have you been
nursing a dream of some dark-haired tomato who writes poetry, or have you had idiocy kicked out of you? Didn't a war, a
job in a slaughterhouse, a fire, and eight years in this lousy

fake town teach you anything? You were even married once
—a very great marriage."

"What does that have to do with it?"

"Think it over."

"I will. But don't make a fool of me. I have never seen
Sylvia West and, all things considered, I likely never will. I
am a practical man, and I have been burned by more things
than fires. I also have a chance to pick up five thousand dollars
for sixty days of work. With my expenses paid. Which is a
little more than I cleared over the past twelve months; and
when you wrap all that money around my heart, there is no
room left for sentiment. So get away from me and leave me
alone."

That finished the conversation, but not the way I felt. I
smoked another cigarette and watched daylight filter through
the smog and mist that covered Los Angeles.

7

Henry Ingleman was a cop who did not take. Danish-born, he
had gone in the hard way and had made something out of
himself against long odds. That's not a story for here, but now,
pressing retirement age, he was the best handwriting man on
the Coast. He did not take, but when I pressed it he let me
buy him lunch. Now he sat facing me in the Steak House and
eating the lunch I had bought him and telling me that it was
too expensive.

"My digestion is not flattered by a six-and-a-half-dollar lunch,
Mack, and when a penny-pinching Scot buys it for me I
cannot even enjoy it properly."

"I am not buying. It comes out of expense money."

"What do you want?"

"Information."

"Then why don't you join the force if you have such dedication to your work?"

"I hate my lousy work. The only thing good about it is that occasionally I meet someone like yourself."

"That is bullshit, as the Americans say."

"As you say."

"Yes. But before you squeeze me, Mack, tell me, did any of the ancient people develop a calligraphy?"

"If you mean simply a subordination of angles to curves and a curvous simplification—well, yes."

"Who were they?"

"Well, in Egypt, the demotic. The Jews developed a curvous script, in part from the Arabs. To some extent, the Greeks and the Romans were on the way——" He is impressed by that sort of thing, the way every self-educated man nurses a secret and nagging envy of the schoolboy learning and memory without comprehension of the college-trained. With gratitude and attention he listened to me exhibit my little bit of ignorance, and over our coffee and dessert he eagerly and diffidently told me what I desired to know. I gave him the card that Sylvia West had left for Summers, and he studied it carefully and thoughtfully. When he had examined it for at least five minutes, he said almost apologetically:

"Let me parade myself a little—yes, Mack? I will read you a fortune from this card."

I nodded and leaned forward eagerly, because I was now privileged to hear what few ever heard, not the dry comparison that comes out in court or in the police laboratory, but uninhibited analysis by the finest handwriting expert I knew of. Ingleman cocked his head, let his old-fashioned steel glasses slide down his nose, and tempered his words with self-conscious smiles whenever he glanced up at me.

"The lady's age, Mack," he began, "is between twenty-five and thirty years. Shall I lecture on the age-curve equation, or do you remember my last one?"

"I remember. Go on, lieutenant."

"She is a fine-looking woman. I come to that out of the strength and thickness of the line. The line faces the world as she does. But nevertheless, there is more in the woman than what you see, for she has created herself and a controlled and careful hand to go with that creation. West is her husband's name, not hers, or maybe a name she has taken a fancy to—but Sylvia goes far back to what she once was, and the old Sylvia was less attractive to her own notions than what she is today. But this is her own judgment, you see, Mack, and many a woman is far from expert with the problem of herself. If you wanted fiction, Mack, I could make some guess about what this woman goes through, but fiction is no use to you, is it?"

"I am afraid not," I agreed.

"She could be a dangerous woman, maybe a determined woman, maybe very hard, and maybe only strong—and maybe not so strong as she tries to be—any one of those, yes, Mack?"

"I don't know her. I never saw her."

"Oh?"

"A criminal, Lieutenant?"

"It is nonsense that criminals reveal themselves in their handwriting. Unless they are pathological, as some are. She is not. Not at all."

"And what was she once—before—say ten, fifteen years ago?"

"You ask me that seriously, Mack? Out of two sentences?"

"Just a stab in the dark." I shrugged. This was not the time to flatter him. "Another stab in the dark—where was she born?"

"America, I can say—yes."

"China, perhaps?"

He glanced at me shrewdly. "If she was born in China, I don't think she learned to write in China."

"Why?"

"A little trick of my trade." He smiled. "A very good guess. It is just barely possible that she learned to write at some American school in China—in the old China, you see."

"Or some British school? In China?"

"No—unless she had a strong-minded American teacher."

It was my turn to look at him, and he smiled at me. The old man was proud as a peacock. He was doing something that no one else in the state, maybe in the world, could do, and if a good deal of it was a parlor trick, he performed wonderfully.

"What city in America did she learn to write in?" I asked him slowly and carefully.

"Mack, do you know how many cities there are in this country?"

"I counted them. I know."

Now he leaned across the table and tapped the back of my hand with his finger. "Mack, Mack, listen," he said, grinning. "I do one of my best tricks just for you. But you tell no one, or they will kick me out and I lose my pension for being an old fraud."

"I forget what you tell me and you forget the name of Sylvia West. A bargain?"

"A bargain, Mack. Now I tell you some of the cities where she did not learn to write." He leaned back and closed his eyes. Then he said slowly, "New York, most of the state; Boston—no, we make a guess, all Massachusetts—Richmond, Virginia; Charleston, South Carolina; Chicago, Minneapolis, Omaha, I think Kansas City too——" He opened his eyes and looked at me with delight.

"That leaves a few cities. Anyway, I don't believe you," I said.

"Mack—am I a faker? I told you, I make a little excursion into fortunetelling. I will tell you my trick. Like all tricks, it is simple when you know how. Many years ago American children in a number of cities were taught to write with what used to be called the Palmer Method. This foolishness consisted of torturing the child by making him learn something almost impossible, to write script with the motion of his whole arm. You remember this barbarism?"

"I think I do." I nodded.

"So? Is it not simple? When they learn with the Palmer Method, some trace remains with them. But even school boards realize sometimes that children have been tortured enough by foolishness, and they stop teaching with the Palmer Method. Is it so hard for me to recognize the trace of Palmer Method? That was the way this woman learned to write, and I have only to try to remember when certain places discontinued it. So you should not call a man a faker so quick, even if you buy him a steak and good beer for lunch."

8

A moon without light,
It is other illumination

On the fat sow's belly,
Bleeding with child.

Confuse birth with vomit,
Spasm is spasm egocentric.

Porcus in labor divine, ecco,
Echoes with mama lullaby, ecco

Lend an ear for hearing, ecco,
And spin some of vomit my way

Across the bar in the stink of beer,
A shot glass full of immortal soul

And pious breakwind parting pea green
Or stool not restful sitting.

Suck the tits, swiggle it,
The milk of human kindness

Curdles—baby doll, never!
Make me whole, hole invitation,

And education, cool finishing school
Blady lady's smilographic function.

Thus thee ahwa onongo heeler,
Self-healing—cool man cool

This is my sermon today:
A little patience pays off.

Sitting in my office, I read it again. I read it for the sixth, seventh, or eighth time. I read it and tried to make pictures and images out of the words, as you do when you read something worth reading; but the pictures would not hold or conform to reason and the images blurred and slid away. I read it aloud as if I were not listening or judging or analyzing but only receiving pitch and sound and rhythm, and I felt the manipulated bitterness and horror as you feel music; but when I attempted to take it apart, it crumbled and refused.

I had no judgments or opinions. I felt something that could

have been poetry or perhaps not. I did not know whether it was good, bad, or indifferent. I tried to be Frederick Summers reading it. I tried to be the once-glamorous Mr. Hall reading it. I even tried to be Ann Goldfarb reading it—and to sense what it said to them, if anything. I sensed nothing.

I had read the little book of poems through, cover to cover, before going to sleep the night before. I read it again after my lunch. I came back to my office, paid some bills, folded a fifty-dollar bill, shank money, into a corner of my desk blotter, and read through the book a third time. Then I concentrated on this particular poem.

Finally I gave up and telephoned Professor Bertram Cohen at UCLA, and I was lucky enough to get him first try. Not only did he remember me—I had not seen or spoken to him for five years—but he seemed to be delighted to hear from me. He hoped that this meant I had decided to go on with my work at the university. He had met very few students with a talent like mine. Would I drop around and have a chat with him?

I told him that I would love to sometime, any time he could find for me—it was the truth. He is a brilliant antiquarian and a pleasure to talk to. But right now could he do a favor for me?

"Of course, Mr. Macklin. If I can."

"Is there anyone on the faculty, Professor, who is considered an authority on modern poetry? And if there is, could you arrange for him to give me an hour of his time?"

"Gavin Mullen, of course. And he is no inconsiderable poet in his own right, Mr. Macklin. It will be no trouble at all. Suppose I speak to him and call you back? May I say that it is in the line of your work?"

"It is."

"And where can I reach you?"

I gave him the number at my office and thanked him. A half hour later, he called back and said that Professor Mullen would see me at ten o'clock that same night if I could make it. At Professor Mullen's home.

"But, Mr. Macklin," he added, "remember what I said before. First chance, we'll have a bite of lunch together."

I said that we would, and I meant it.

9

It was a few minutes before ten when I reached Professor Mullen's home in Brentwood, an old-fashioned Spanish stucco bungalow, the type that was garish and cheap and impudent thirty-five years ago but has mellowed with time and taken on a patina of reality and gentleness among the flat roofs, picture windows, and aggressive angles of today. Mullen answered the doorbell himself, a small, thin man, no more than five feet four inches, with a big head, a mop of unruly hair that was streaked with gray, and eyes of such bright blue that they seemed to be lit from within. He was wearing a cotton-knit sport shirt and a pair of patched, faded blue denims. He gave me his hand, a strong hand, grinned, drew me into the house, and said in an amazingly deep voice:

"You would be Alan Macklin, am I right? The private eye with an interest in poetry."

I accepted it gracefully this time; it was only right, for he was giving me of his time, and a private eye was one thing, a private investigator who makes his dollar out of providing grist for the filthy mills of divorce something else entirely.

The living room of the house was chaos, the walls lined with books, the floor decorated with a playpen, a wet diaper, two toy trucks, a scooter, a panda (stuffed), a great pile of enormous unpainted wooden blocks, and two cats (not stuffed). Also other odds and ends of child rearing too numerous to specify.

He dismissed and explained it with a casual wave of his hand. "My wife and myself, we believe in large families, Mr. Macklin. Sit down, won't you?" (The large family consisted of six children, I learned.) "For they are less trouble than small ones," he added, "and more rewarding than the bitter catcalling of a man and a woman facing each other alone." He swept a stack of nursery books off an easy chair onto the floor. "Will you have Irish whisky or the Scotch? Myself, I prefer plain rye."

"Plain rye is fine."

"On a little bit of ice?"

"Just as you say. It's very kind of you—very kind of you to see me at all."

"Say no more of that," he began, and interrupted himself when his wife entered, and introduced us. His wife was at least a head taller than he, a handsome, slow-moving, unperturbed mass of woman, not fat, but massive and strong, with corn-yellow hair, a soft, gentle voice, and an air of affectionate tolerance toward men.

"Last one down," she said. "In its infinite wisdom, Mr. Macklin, nature rewards you after a day with six waking children by presenting you with six sleeping children. Are you hungry?"

I shook my head as I watched her circle the room, picking up about ten objects, and drift out as easily and gently as she had entered. Mullen handed me my drink and seated himself opposite me.

"Now what can I do for you, Mr. Macklin?" he asked.

"Tell me about poetry, if you would."

"In general? I have three separate courses at the university, and——"

"No—I'm sorry. One poet. Have you ever heard of Sylvia West?"

"Indeed I have." He popped up, went to a wall where hundreds of books were stuffed into their shelves, and miraculously emerged with Sylvia's book on his first try. (She had become Sylvia for me, not Sylvia West or Miss West any more.) I took my own copy out of my pocket.

"Have you read it?" I asked.

"Yes, I have. Now that's not unusual, Mr. Macklin. I try to read everything the younger poets produce. And not such a wearisome job with the trickle published these days. I do a poetry piece for the *Quarterly*, and a good many of the books are sent to me by the publishers."

"And what do you think of it, if I may ask, sir?"

"Ah, now—what do I think of it, Mr. Macklin? You know, there is no glib answer to such a question. We do not live in a time when you can say of this poet or that one that greatness or grandeur has kissed him. The poet is a tired, lonely lad, cast out of his father's house and looking for a proper door or reason to enter. Or else he sits under the bramblebushes in the back yard and coddles his precious gift and whispers it to the poet neighbor yonder under the other bramblebush. Once the poet was part of a grand orchestra, Mr. Macklin, and he made his sounds with great large brasses and whole banks of fiddles and big drums that boomed so loud and with such fine syncopation that the world cocked its ears and listened. But that is no longer, young man. Oh no. Not at all. Today the world listens only to the poor silly lyrics that the Broadway people write, and only those peculiar versemongers are rewarded, while the gift of poesy is booted away on its poor bleeding ass. The most the poet does today, having been labeled with queerness and that mortal American sin, poverty, is to twitter on his bit of a pipe and try with such thin music to portray the vast, idiotic and confusing world that once hailed him as his voice and song. Oh, he has splendid memories, all right, but poor lad, he is devoid of piss and vinegar, as are all those who whisper to themselves.

"Now here—this woman, Sylvia West, I will not say to anyone she is a good or a bad poet. How dare they ask? Let them first listen and feel the burning hurt and wild hatred inside of her. Now listen to this, Mr. Macklin."

And he opened the book and read:

> "I got those Jesus blues—
> My belly crawl with doses,
> Don't go way from me and leave me now
> Rolling and pitching—
> Oh I got such sin as no woman ever had,
> I got those Jesus blues—
> O preacher look me up and down,
> Don't stop at the knee, o there's more to see
> I got a long round leg and thigh
> I got pie in the sky and I got sin
> A belly full of sin,
> A dark blue syncopated sin—
> O child Jesus Christ, I got those Jesus blues."

He paused, and his blue eyes bored into me. His wife had come into the room silently, and she had stood still and silent, listening to his deep, rich voice. Then he smiled and shook his head.

"We become too serious over the small matter of poetry, Mr. Macklin. You want an opinion? This is not very good poetry, no, and it is good poetry, yes. Both. Did you ever hear Helen Morgan at her best? This Sylvia West has no formal education, none of the niceties or trained equipment of language, and in all truth she knows very little about the polite structure of verse. But she has something else, hurt and passion and necessity—and, above all, music. The pain in her is like Handy's pain must have been. When she finds peace, if she ever does, she will be a regal woman; but mother of God, if she learns to make poetry as she has the talent to, and learns it before she finds her peace, we will have something in America, believe me."

"Then you know her?"

"Devil's shame, I don't!" grinning at his wife, who said softly, "Listen to the little man, will you?"

"Then how do you know what she is and what's inside of her, Professor Mullen?"

"From her poems—how else?"

I nodded but said nothing. I felt a peculiar and not unpleasant uneasiness, and above all a desire for this evening not to end too quickly. Mullen's wife smiled at me, poured some whisky into my empty glass, and then sat down with us. From her every word and gesture, the way she moved, walked, spoke to her husband and looked at him, it was plain that she adored him, this big, handsome woman adoring a skinny little dwarf of a man with a basso voice. I was suddenly so bereft and lonely that I wanted to weep.

"What is poetry," Mullen said, not asking me, but the declarative of the teacher who must teach above all else. "The first men on this earth sang, for man is a creature of music as well as words. But when the words came, with all their images and colors and memories, there began to be a particular music of language itself. The poem was the beginning of all our literature and all our art. Homer sang poems, and the terrible preaching of the old Hebrew prophets, that was also in poetry, and who made music for old Ireland but the wild poets who wandered around the land with their fine voices and their stringed instruments. And even here at home the culture of the Indians was to play on their wooden flutes while their singers made poetry. It is an old thing that grew and flowered, but somewhere of late we danced a step too quickly and the world became strange. Now the poet looks for pictures and music and finds it hard hunting—so many is the one content with polishing his little apple forever and never giving a damn about the tree. Your Sylvia will win no awards for a long time, but she will learn. She has something to say and a clear voice."

"I don't find it so clear," I confessed. "Take the poem A Moon without Light. What is she trying to say? What does she mean? And if she does mean something, why can't she just come out and say it?"

"Ah, now," Mullen smiled, "you have put your finger on it. Is she trying to be obscure? No, not at all. We are simple folk, Macklin, as well as complex, and artists do not try to be obscure unless they are fakers. The obscurity comes from their being unable to say a thing in the inner way that they feel it. Your Sylvia is bursting with something that cannot be said in the plain meaning of words—a thing that time will cure. She will know better what must be said and say it better too.

"But in this poem she is seeking symbols and comparing. She writes of the place where she was a child, with loathing and with all the twisted horror of childhood nightmares. She cannot say, 'I was a child in such-and-such a place'; she must put down for adults what the child saw, and she uses an in-

tricate group of symbols and images out of her childhood. Do
you follow me?"

"I think so." I nodded. "Do you know where this childhood was?"

"I could make a good guess—the city, you mean?"

"Yes, the city."

"Probably Pittsburgh."

"Why Pittsburgh?"

"Well, let me put it this way. When people come to the
writing of poetry out of a formal and complete education,
often followed by years in the deep freeze of academic life,
they very likely gain in craftsmanship but lose the vitality and
inventiveness that would spur them to create symbols of their
own and their singular meaning. We are a careful race in
our universities, you can be sure. So old symbols are used
and curried and manipulated. Your Sylvia, it would seem to
me, has not much formal education behind her. She builds
her symbols out of what she has seen and experienced. When
she first heard the Spanish word for water, it made a phonetic
impression upon her. So she spells it *ahwa* to recall and convey
that first impact in terms of herself. Now Pittsburgh, as you
know, is at the junction of the Allegheny and the Monongahela
rivers, and furthermore it is the only city or town of any consequence upon the Monongahela. Now here again she is making
symbols and comparisons. The initial sound in Monongahela
is in the nature of a prefix in the highly inflected Algonquin
language. Onongahela would be a more accurate noun, although our transliterations of the old Indian names leave much
to be desired. Now where your Sylvia picked up this curious bit
of information, I can't say—yet oddities of knowledge are a
special virtue of the self-educated.

"So we have the *ahwa onongo heeler*, or Monongahela River. You note that she then breaks the word and spells the last two syllables *heeler*, water the healer, a slight play of words and symbolic reference to the second meaning. The river was the red man's god. The red men were destroyed and the hideous image of Pittsburgh as your child Sylvia saw it replaced them. But the river continues to flow. The river is eternal, patient, and cleansing. It flows, it cleans, and it heals the old ugly scars. There you are. I hate to do this with a bit of verse. It's a bagful of tricks to impress lowerclassmen——"

"It impresses me," I said.

"Well, now! Come to think of it, I have been doing a little bit of detective work on my own, have I not?"

"You certainly have, sir."

"And how do I rate as a private eye, Mr. Macklin?"

"Large enough to use the word, Professor Mullen, by all means."

PART 2

PITTSBURGH

THE SHORT, PUDGY, PINK-CHEEKED MAN WHO SAT NEXT TO ME
on the plane to Pittsburgh asked me for the second time what
my name was.

"Macklin—Alan Macklin."

"I thought you said MacLean."

"Macklin."

"Not in the movie business, are you?"

"No."

"Funny thing, twice on the plane out of L.A. I sat next to
folks in the movie business."

"It happens," I said. I have no local patriotism or pride, so
my distaste for people who call Los Angeles "L.A." and San
Francisco "Frisco" is simply a matter of prejudice. I also had
a copy of The New Yorker magazine that I was trying to read.

"Nice folks," he added.

"I'm sure."

"First trip to Pittsburgh?" he asked.

"First trip."

"Well, there you are! If that isn't typical of Americans, what
is? I bet you been to Paris, France."

"Yes."

"There you are! Time was, they used to say, 'See America first!' Not today. No, sir. See Timbuktu, see Casablanca, see Moscow. Regular parade going on to Moscow. I got a brother-in-law, he never laid eyes on the Grand Canyon, Yellowstone Park, or even them redwood trees back in your own state, but he got to Moscow, all right. Went in a businessman's party, and he was wined and dined like a king. They just couldn't make it good enough for him. Ever been to Moscow?"

"No," I said.

"Take Pennsylvania now—you know what it suffers from? Contentment, blessed contentment, and believe me, that can be a disease in these United States. Never learned to blow our own trumpet—never—not like you Californians and the Texans and the others. Did you ever come to ask yourself what state has the most churches and colleges and cities and towns in these here United States? Ever ask yourself that?"

"No," I said, "I never did."

"Pennsylvania. Largest iron and steel production in the nation, top production of coal in the nation, most miles of paved highway—most game. Ever go hunting?"

"No," I said.

"Talk about your Powder River country and Jackson Hole country! More game in one county of Pennsylvania than in the whole state of Wyoming! It's a fine sport. Tell you the truth, the President would rather hunt than play golf. It's his physical condition keeps him at the golf, that little bit of exercise that is just right. I got that from my brother-in-law, who played nine holes with him when Ike was at Pittsburgh last year. Now, look—I'm no name dropper. Not me, my brother-in-law. Going to Pittsburgh on business?"

"Yes," I said.

"Heart of the state. The absolute heart of the state. Ever ask yourself how many bridges there are in Pittsburgh? Now if I was running one of those large national quiz shows, I'd pop that one. How many bridges in the city of Pittsburgh? What do you think of that?"

"Yes," I said.

"Well, I mean that if you didn't know—it's just too far-fetched to answer. More than two hundred bridges within the actual city limits. Two hundred. And more than eight hundred in the county. Good heavens, I would say that's more bridges than there are in Venice, Italy."

2

At the William Penn Hotel, I paid fifteen dollars a day for a large and comfortable room; it required only that I keep my head and remember that I was not someone used to sleeping where I wanted to sleep and eating what I desired to eat. In any case, the expense-account luxuries of travel were nicely balanced by the alone quotient of my existence; that did not change.

Civilization has accepted the man who is alone. It has made his existence tolerable and has provided all sorts of diversions for him to pull between himself and boredom. In ancient times the man alone, without kith or kin, was outlaw and outcast. He did not have to commit any crime; his very existence was a crime. Anyone could enslave him, kill him, beat him—and not fear any punishment of law. The gates of most cities were closed to him, and even the robber bands of men like himself more often than not killed without questioning. So I was not one to forget that a room and bath in one of Pittsburgh's best hotels was an improvement. By the time I had bathed and shaved and changed my shirt, my mood was just about as good as it ever was. I could contemplate the three color prints of the Swiss Alps that decorated my walls without hostility; the twin beds looked comfortable and inviting under their bright yellow spreads; and I also was in temporary possession of two easy chairs, a high chest of drawers, a low chest of drawers, and a writing desk. A man can do worse.

It was after six now, and I was hungry enough to eat. I ate alone in the hotel dining room, and along with my steak and salad I went through a copy of the *Post-Gazette*. I smoked a cigarette and then went out to take a walk.

I walked down Liberty Avenue all the way to Point Park, and in the park I sat down on a bench and watched two kids, a boy and a girl of sixteen or so, stare at each other with eyes full of love, hope, and wanting. It was a cool, pleasant evening, with no smoke or smog in the sky, only the golden sun of twilight.

I walked back along the Boulevard, had a whisky sour at the hotel bar, bought some magazines and a new novel, and then went up to my room to read myself to sleep.

3

The next morning I put five ten-dollar bills in a plain white envelope and called on Inspector Garowski of the city police. Peters had given me his name but not any high hopes about co-operation, and when I walked into his office he looked at me from under a pair of shaggy brows and said:

"So your name is Macklin. What do you want, Macklin? You got a crime to report?"

His voice was like a rasp. He was a broad-shouldered, heavy-set man of fifty or so, his complexion yellow with some sickness inside of him, his big face lined with hatred, suspicion, and resentment.

"No, Inspector," I said quietly and politely, "I'm a private investigator from Los Angeles."

"All right. Go investigate."

"I got a job to do here in Pittsburgh."

"Go investigate here in Pittsburgh. Stay out of my hair."

"I thought perhaps I could get a little co-operation out of the city police, Inspector."

"You thought," he growled. "You do a lot of thinking?"

"Some."

"Then think yourself the hell out of here, Macklin."

The plain white envelope with the fifty dollars in it was in my back pants pocket. When I leaned over his desk and said, "Give me a break, Inspector," I slid the envelope onto the corner of his desk and left it there.

"Why?"

"I'm trying to do a job I get paid for."

"Go do it! You got a hell of a nerve walking in here and asking me to turn out the force for you."

"All I'm asking is a look at your records."

"Go fly a kite, Macklin. I'm a busy man. Now get out."

The envelope was among other envelopes and papers. The inspector was not meticulous in his desk habits. At the door I turned and said to him:

"If you change your mind and decide to give me a break, Inspector, I'm at the William Penn Hotel. Alan Macklin."

He didn't bother to answer, and I closed the door behind me and went down to the street. It was about ten o'clock now, and I began to walk at random, just drifting and trying to get some feel of the city.

I walked up a long high hill on a street that was lined with ancient and unpainted houses, leaning, tired houses; and some of the people who lived in them looked at me strangely, with no love in their eyes for a man in a business suit who strolled along at this hour of the morning.

It was a few minutes before noon when I returned to the William Penn, and there was a message for me to call Detective Sergeant Franklin at Headquarters. I telephoned him, and when I got through, a slow and tired voice said:

"I hear you need some help, Macklin, so the inspector said I should give you some help if it don't take all the time in the world."

I asked him if he could have lunch with me, and he said he could.

4

You grow older, and it is easy to lose the awareness that each and every human soul on this earth is locked inside himself and looking out upon the world—and knowing, too, that the world's existence depends upon the flicker of light against his eyeballs and that, when his eyes are closed, so far as he is concerned everything is over and done with. A man is a cop or a steelworker or a millionaire or a bum; he is still locked in for whatever he can make of it. No one is brave, and everyone is filled with hunger and doubt. Everyone hurts somewhere.

Detective Sergeant Franklin was forty-six and he had arthritis. He was full of hurt. His eyes were yellow with sleeplessness. He toyed with his food, ate little, and told me about a week he had spent in Florida, lying in the sun, and how for the first time in years he felt human.

"But it costs to go to Florida, Macklin," he said to me. "You got oil and gas and wear and tear on the car, and suppose you put up at one of them motels, it's still an arm and a leg for a guy like me. The wife don't put up any kick. 'You go to Florida if it takes the last penny we got,' she tells me. What am I supposed to do? See my kids eat beans and walk around busting out of last year's clothes just so I can go to Florida? I'm boxed in. Pittsburgh is no place for me, but I'm boxed in with a pension that I'm hooked to and with all the years of being a cop. Who says that a kid knows what to do with his life? Where's the kid that turned me into a lousy cop? He's dead and gone. I'm not that kid. Ah, the hell with it! What do you want me to do for you, Macklin?"

I told him what I needed, and he wiped his mouth and shook his head. "Chasing ghosts," he sighed. "You know her name ain't Sylvia West, so that's nothing. Sure we got a first-name file, if Sylvia's her real name, but who says she got to give her real name if she got in any trouble? You say maybe she was just a kid. Well, if we pick up a kid, thirteen, fourteen years old, we don't mug her and book her formally, even if it's a morals rap. It's lousy enough earning a buck here without doing that to kids. All I can see is that you got a hell of a problem. You're looking for a girl with the name of Sylvia who was maybe born here and maybe not, who maybe lived here as a kid and maybe didn't. You maybe know her date of birth, give or take a year, but you don't know anything else. That's no use. This is a big city. There's no first-name make on birth certificates, and this is a town sucks in men like a big mud dredge, rakes them over and throws them out. This is a steel town, and the men come and go, and how many kids were born here in the bad old days and never registered at all, I wouldn't even guess. You're a private cop, Macklin, but still you're cop enough to know that what you're trying to do is just a pipe dream."

I shrugged and said that it was a job—which is what it was.

"All right." Franklin nodded. "I'll do what I can, and we

can go over to the hall and I'll show you all the pictures and makes that we got."

"Do you take, Franklin?" I asked him bluntly and deliberately.

"No!"

"Don't look at me like I stuck a knife in your guts," I said. "I didn't shove any money at you, did I?"

"No."

"I asked you a plain open question."

"You guys make me sick."

"Why? I'm not asking anything illegal, no protection, no close your eyes, no slippery stuff. You're doing me a favor because the inspector asked you to."

"That's right."

"Well, I got an expense account. Take twenty from me."

"Go to hell!"

I folded a twenty-dollar bill and pushed it across the table, and his hand moved, hesitated, and then closed over it. I have felt worse, but it is not easy to remember when. He got up and said:

"Let's go down to the hall."

While we drove there in his car, I said to myself, "In this good life everything stinks, and wherever you touch, the dirt rubs off. So I humbled him with a lousy twenty dollars and made his hand move while his soul spit on it, except that I was never certain that anyone had a soul to begin with. Still, he will remember the twenty dollars because it's the only god that any of us see with our two eyes, and maybe he'll stretch a little to help me."

It turned out, in due time, that I was right.

Down at the hall I sat at a table while the makes and pictures were brought to me. I looked at thirty-seven Sylvias who had run afoul of the law in Pittsburgh, but none of them was even possible, and of course there was no Sylvia West. Then I went through the juveniles, and there too I came up with absolutely nothing. Beginning and end. I stopped at Franklin's office to thank him.

"Thanks for nothing," he replied sourly.

I left there and walked again. In Schenley Park I stood in front of the George Westinghouse Memorial and stared at the lily fronds and thought about Sylvia. Then I sat on a bench and smoked a cigarette, and two young hustlers who could not have been more than eighteen tried to do business. I walked back to the hotel, stopped at the bar for a whisky sour, and there was a lady who would not see fifty again, and she also tried to do business. It shows that I am attractive to all ages. I had some supper and went up to my room and watched television for a while.

Then I read poetry by Sylvia. I read:

> There's no place like home,
> You take it, mister,
> And shove it up your reet-pleet jeens,
> Be it ever so crumble,
> Frame it in bells,
> God damn god damn ding dong bells,
> And take me far away on my wedding day—
> Ah Wah wash me free of home, any home—

There it was again, a Spanish word stuck in her craw and mind and hope and bitterness. I was tired when I went to bed, but I couldn't sleep. I lay with my tiredness until the flickering doze of predawn settled my own whimpering thoughts.

5

If my memory serves me, Andrew Carnegie raised up out of his bushels of dollar bills twenty-eight hundred and eleven public libraries. Again, if my memory serves me, it was in one of them that I read the line of an old ballad that goes, "The king sat at court in Dunfermline Town, drinking his blude red wine." Time passed, and in the same Dunfermline Town, Andrew Carnegie was eventually born and eventually scattered broadcast across the face of America buildings with gray stone fronts. They are lonely places today—it is easier to watch television—but when I was a kid they were full of warmth and wonder, full of doors that you could open if you had a mind to.

Childhood places shrink. You go into them, and all the great size and space of long ago crowd in and sit upon your shoulders. There are still the bright pictures and appliqués tacked onto the walls, but you feel that you are looking at them through the wrong end of a telescope. And being a private detective, you feel twice the interloper, dirtied and out of place.

I tried not to feel that way. There was nothing in these quiet, saddened places that I desired to disturb or change. I sought for a ghost in a place that was full of ghosts. I asked a white-haired lady who glanced up at me with faded blue eyes:

"Could you help me?"

"Help you?" How could she or anyone like her help me? the eyes asked.

"I'm a private investigator."

"Yes?"

"Well, it may seem strange. These things usually do. I am trying to trace a woman who might have lived here in Pittsburgh as a child. I have very little to go on, but I am guessing that she was an avid reader. She would have spent a good deal of time in the libraries."

"How long ago was that——?"

"My name is Macklin."

"Mr. Macklin?"

"Oh—about fifteen, seventeen years ago."

"Mr. Macklin, that is a very long time."

"I suppose it is, yes."

"What was the child's name, Mr. Macklin?"

"Sylvia."

"Her family name?"

"I don't know."

"Really, Mr. Macklin! I mean, how can you expect——? I am sure this is not a joke of some sort, Mr. Macklin."

"No, ma'am. I am doing the best I can, and I hate to take up your time like this and be an irritant."

"I don't want to be impatient with you, Mr. Macklin, but you must admit that your request is a strange one. Fifteen years ago—a child whose name was Sylvia, no family name, just Sylvia. It's hard to believe that you are being serious, Mr. Macklin."

"I am being serious, ma'am. Look at it this way. Isn't it possible that an unusual child would impress herself on your memory? Isn't it possible that you would remember such a child, even after fifteen years?"

"I suppose it is possible, Mr. Macklin. Anything is possible."

"But you don't remember such a child?"

"No, I don't, Mr. Macklin."

"Would you have an associate I might speak to?"

And so it went, with one variation or another of the above. There are fourteen Carnegie libraries in the city of their founder, and by five o'clock that afternoon I had covered eight of them and I had a list of forty librarians missed, retired, or gone on to other fields of endeavor. I was tired, irritated, and almost ready to accept defeat—the more so when I thought of public school system and what might await me there if I tried it. Nor need that have been the end of it. Convinced that Sylvia had originated in Pittsburgh, I could have divided the city into neighborhoods, poked into old candy stores, the universal meccas of children, talked to established citizens, and done any number of other things. But I was by no means convinced that Sylvia had originated in Pittsburgh; I was proceeding through an obscure symbol in an obscure poem; I was chasing a ghost on a most ghostly trail.

That was the frame of mind with which I approached the ninth library and Irma Olanski.

6

From where I stood at the entrance to the children's room I saw a sign which said that this room closed for the day at five o'clock. There was another sign at the desk which told me that the librarian's name was Miss Olanski. A half dozen children were lined up at the desk to have their books stamped, and behind the desk sat Miss Olanski, who observed me with a quick glance as I entered. She was the kind of person who always observes, who never lets go of the world, but watches and sees and observes and reacts.

I guessed that she was my age, which is thirty-six, give or take a year or two in either direction, and with my first look I appreciated the clean-cut handsome planes of her face. Either you saw and recognized that immediately with Irma Olanski or you never saw it, and after that she would be to you a plain and rather severe woman, a tall, dry woman approaching a loveless and lonely middle age. Her brown hair, already streaked with gray, was drawn back tightly on the sides of her head and fastened in a large bun at the back. Her eyes were gray-green, her brows straight, her lips bare of lipstick, and only the width and the fullness of her lips suggested anything more than a colorless spinster librarian.

I waited until she was through with the children. By then another librarian was beginning to pull down the shades, and I walked over to Miss Olanski and asked her whether she had a moment to talk to me.

"You're an officer of some sort, aren't you?" she said.

"A private investigator. I didn't know it showed that plainly."

"Just the way you stood at the door." She smiled. Her face became different, younger, when she smiled.

"Can I talk with you?"

"Can you wait a few minutes?" she asked me. "It's just that after a day I don't feel good with myself until I wash and freshen up."

"Are you free then? My name is Macklin, Miss Olanski. Alan Macklin. I'm from Los Angeles." I took out my credentials and showed them to her. "Because if you're free maybe you could have time for a drink or a cup of coffee with me."

"I'll have the drink, Mr. Macklin." She nodded. "Why don't you sit down? I won't be five minutes."

I squeezed into an undersized chair at one of the low tables, while all around the place shades were lowered, hand trucks were pushed into position, and tables were cleared of books. This was done by two young men who eyed me curiously. The other librarians had disappeared with Miss Olanski. The two young men looked at me, judged me, and then whispered their judgments to each other. They were awkward, long-limbed and pimple-faced, full of cumbersome and frustrated desire. When she emerged, Miss Olanski did not look at them but walked over to me and nodded.

"We can go now, Mr. Macklin."

Still no lipstick. Her face had been washed. Her skin was good, but some face powder would have helped it. She wore a white blouse and a brown skirt, brown shoes, and a plain brown purse. She was a handsome woman, neatly dressed, but not trying to be a woman at all.

The two young men smirked as we walked out. We stood on the sidewalk in front of the library, and a cool wind blew down the street from the west. She told me that I was fortunate, her voice the precise, controlled speech of a woman who has worked where she worked for a long, long time.

"Yes," she said, "I don't remember such a summer in Pittsburgh for a long, long time, Mr. Macklin. The smog is gone —I guess you would know about smog, being from Los Angeles?"

"We have it."

"Well, it's a rare thing to have the sky so fine and blue over Pittsburgh. Where do you want to go for that drink you asked about? Yes, I like a drink in the evening," she said in explanation or in apology.

"How about the bar in the William Penn?"

"That would be very nice." Her comments were precise and plain and without any attempt at charm or ingratiation. She was trying to be perfectly natural but did not know how. My guess was that I was the first man to ask her out for a drink in a long, long time.

I stopped a cab, and we went down to the William Penn. When we were seated in the bar, she asked for a manhattan.

She was nervous now. I told her that a bar was not the worst place in the world, but I felt sad and foolish.

"You really do have something important that you must ask me? I can't imagine what it might be."

"Important to me, not to you," I replied. "It's part of my work. I am alone in Pittsburgh, the first time too, so it was very kind of you to come here with me. Just think of it as a kindness to a stranger."

"A very pleasant stranger, Mr. Macklin."

"That's the nicest thing that has been said to me in a long time. People don't go out of their way to say nice things to me, so I really appreciate it, Miss Olanski."

"Yes," she whispered, a flush spreading across her face.

"Very well. Now let me tell you what this is all about— if you have the time?"

"I have nothing to do until dinnertime, Mr. Macklin."

"And don't keep thinking I picked you up," I said. "I did nothing of the kind. Most people will answer questions and be polite to an investigator."

"How did you know what I was thinking? I wasn't think-ing—"

"Then we'll forget that completely. Now I am a private detective in Los Angeles, not a private eye, not a man with a gun—I don't own a gun—just a man who does the kind of investigation jobs—when he can get them—that people don't go to the police with. This is such a job. I am trying to trace a woman who may or may not have been born and brought up here in Pittsburgh. I don't know for sure. I think I know her first name, but I am not absolutely certain."

"How can I help you, Mr. Macklin?"

"Well, how do I work with a thing like this? I have to make

a series of assumptions and then state each assumption to myself as an operative premise. Assumption number one: she
comes from a city like Pittsburgh. Therefore, I make Pittsburgh my first premise. Assumption number two: she was poor,
underprivileged, and had a lousy time in her youth. This can
add up to trouble, so I make a police record my second premise. Then I try to operate logically out of each premise."

"That sounds fascinating, Mr. Macklin. May I ask where
each premise led you?"

"Nowhere. I drew blanks, as we say."

"Tell me, is this woman alive, Mr. Macklin?"

"Yes, she is."

"Then why can't you ask her?"

"I can't. Perhaps we'll get to that later. For the moment,
accept the fact that I can't."

She nodded. "If you wish. May I ask what your third
assumption is?"

"That this woman had a hunger in her childhood—even
worse than her hunger for food—a hunger to know. A need
to know. And where else could she find the things that she
had to know, except in books? That's how I came to your library. My premise is that she made an impression of some sort
on some librarian. Yours was the ninth of the fourteen public
libraries here in Pittsburgh."

In disbelief she said, "Do you mean that you have been going
from library to library all day long, asking these questions?"

"That's what I've been doing."

"And——?"

"Nothing. So far, nothing."

"But why books? There are people with a need to know who
never come to books."

"I think she did."

"Another assumption?"

"Yes, but not without reason."

"I have never heard anything just like this," she said, shaking her head. "You're not at all what I think of as a detective. I don't even know that you're not having a joke at my expense."

"I am not," I replied. "I am very serious, Miss Olanski. I am trying to do a job that I have to do. And there's no reason for you to help me unless you want to. You can tell yourself that I'm a phony or a con man of some kind and just get up and walk out of here, and I'll understand that."

"I am not afraid of you, believe me, Mr. Macklin. I am an unimaginative spinster, and there is absolutely nothing that you could con me out of. Anyway, I think I believe you. How old is this woman today?"

"Twenty-seven."

She had finished her drink. I don't think she would have said what she did say if she hadn't finished the drink. I don't think she would have called herself an unimaginative spinster. She half closed her eyes now, as if she were counting the years and trying to find them once more.

"And her name, Mr. Macklin?"

"Sylvia."

The eyes were still shadowed, and then and there, in the half-light of the bar, Irma Olanski looked more beautiful than she had ever dreamed she could look. I suppose almost a minute went past before she said anything—enough for me to wonder whether she had even heard the name. Then she said, almost casually:

"Yes, I remember Sylvia, Mr. Macklin. I remember her very well. I don't think I shall ever forget her."

7

I recall exactly how I felt. I felt irritated and annoyed—
and full of confusion as to what I was doing there in Pittsburgh that night at the William Penn Hotel with a stiff, sex-
less, and desiccated librarian. I was angry. If I had put my
thoughts into words, I would have snapped at her that she
had never known Sylvia, that there was no Sylvia, that the
whole thing was a game and a fraud.

"Sylvia Karoki," Miss Olanski said. "Life is very strange,
Mr. Macklin. It is dull and strange and unexpected. But you
wait such a long time for the unexpected. I am afraid that the
manhattan has gone to my head just a little."

"Would you like another one?"

"Oh no—no, thank you. I don't drink a great deal, I am
afraid, Mr. Macklin."

"Then perhaps you would have dinner with me, Miss Olanski?"

She shook her head and told me that she had a previous
engagement for dinner. I knew that she was lying, and she
knew that I knew.

"Perhaps you could break the engagement, Miss Olanski."

"I thought you would be so much more pleased and excited
that I knew your Sylvia."

"Yes, of course. Yet it remains to be seen whether we have
the same person in mind, doesn't it?"

"No. I just feel this way. I just feel that this is your Sylvia.
I know."

Again I asked her whether she could break her engagement
and have dinner with me, and then she did something that
removed all my irritation. She looked at me for a long moment out of her gray-green eyes and said:

"I haven't any dinner engagement, Mr. Macklin. That was just a lie, because I feel ashamed and frightened. I believe everything you said, but I still feel like someone who has been picked up. And then I also feel that I wish I had just been picked up by someone like yourself, Mr. Macklin, because he wanted to be with me and not get something I know. So you can see how confused I am now, and I probably wouldn't talk so much except for the drink. But I haven't any dinner engagement. I don't have dinner engagements. I have a sister—she's married—she lives in South Hills, and I go there every week or so for dinner, and we have a dinner club at the library that meets once a month, but otherwise I have my dinner alone. So I would be happy to have dinner with you, if only to tell you about Sylvia."

"Was that also a lie?" I asked.

"What?"

"That you knew Sylvia."

"You didn't have to say that, Mr. Macklin. What do you think of me?"

"I don't know yet, Miss Olanski, but I like you. People like yourself who undervalue themselves don't seem to think things through. I could have asked you all the questions at the library. I asked you to have a drink with me because you're a good-looking and attractive woman. I didn't want to be alone tonight any more than you did, so will you have dinner with me, Miss Olanski?"

"Yes, I will," she replied. "I'm not dressed for dinner with just a skirt and blouse that I've worn all day. But if you want me to, I will. I'll be ready in a few minutes."

She went to the powder room, and I ordered a second whisky sour and drank it and thought about people, and God help us for what we are, and I thought about Sylvia West and Sylvia

Karoki—would it be Polish or Hungarian?—and Irma Olanski. When Miss Olanski returned to the table, she was wearing lipstick. She had one of those faces that are as good-looking without lipstick, but this helped her inside of herself.

"You look fine," I told her. "We sort of know each other now a little bit. My first name is Alan, but everyone calls me Mack."

"I like Alan. My name is Irma. Would it be all right if I called you Alan, Mr. Macklin—instead of Mack, I mean?"

"Yes, it would."

8

At first during dinner we just talked. I asked the questions about Irma instead of Sylvia. Irma existed; Sylvia was like something I had created out of my own need and whim, a slim book of poems, a few words scribbled on a card, a face on photographs. I was full of Sylvia without believing in her, and I am not sure that I wanted to believe in her.

Irma had been born in Pittsburgh. Her father had been an ironworker; he was dead now, as was her mother. A brother had been killed in World War II. Her sister, the only surviving relative whom she still saw, had married an insurance salesman. At least they had climbed out of the pit of bleak and desolate poverty. I felt the intensity of Irma's own struggle to be something other than the wife of a working man and began to understand the dry, dead trap that she had driven herself into. It made the connection with Sylvia when Irma said:

"Would you know what I meant if I said that your Sylvia was like myself? Not myself today—but long, long ago. I remember the first time I saw her; I think she was eleven years old then. How old did you say she is now?"

"Twenty-seven."

"I came to the library sixteen years ago, so eleven would be right, wouldn't it, Mr. Macklin?"

"You were going to call me Alan."

"Yes. Why is it so hard for me?"

"I don't think it's so hard."

"All right—Alan. What was I saying?"

"She was eleven years old. Hadn't she been to the library before?"

"Oh yes—yes. But I was new there. It was the first time I had noticed her. She had been standing around my desk, the way children do, you know, when they want to ask you something and they haven't enough courage to just come up to you and ask. Our children. Perhaps the children in Los Angeles are different. I don't remember too well why I noticed her—maybe the way she was dressed. Her dress was a hand-me-down, cut short to the knees and unhemmed. It was a grotesque fit. We were in a poor slum neighborhood then—most of the really bad houses have been torn down—but even in our neighborhood few children were as unkempt and as badly dressed."

"Unkempt?"

"Hair loose and unwashed, fingernails broken and dirty. Her neck was dirty, a ring of grime under her collar. I can see, Mr. Macklin—Alan, I will remember now—that you are thinking this is not your Sylvia, but believe me, I and many people like me have a fetish about cleanliness because of our childhood filth. There is an old saying in Pittsburgh—it goes a long time back—that the poor are dirty because often they choose between a cake of soap and a loaf of bread. I don't mean that was the case with Sylvia. Her father was an alcoholic, her mother a sick woman dying of lung cancer. But let me go back to that first time——"

"You were very young yourself then, weren't you?" I asked her.

"Yes. Only twenty, young enough to feel and remember. I finally went over to Sylvia and asked her if there was anything I could do for her. . . ."

9

"Yes."

"Are you looking for a book, my dear?"

"Yes."

"For school?"

"No."

"Then just to read yourself? Do you like to read?"

"Yes."

"What kind of books do you like to read?"

"Books. I read all kinds."

"Is there some special book that you want?"

"Yes."

"Do you know the name of the book?"

"No."

"Do you know the author's name?"

"No."

"Have you seen the book here?"

"I don't know."

"Well, what is the subject of the book? What is the book about?"

"A beautiful lady."

"Have you ever seen this book?"

"I just want a book about a beautiful lady."

10

"So you see," Irma said, "she simply wanted a book about a beautiful lady. What does one do? I was a young and enthusiastic woman on a new job. I gave Sylvia *Pride and Prejudice*."

"Did she read it?"

"Yes, she read it, and she understood a great deal of it. To her, it was a fairy tale. Mr. Bennet was a very beautiful person to Sylvia. You see, Sylvia's own father had raped her a week before this time of which I speak. I didn't learn that until later."

"What the devil are you talking about?"

"Sylvia."

"What do you mean?"

"I am the cloistered librarian, Alan, and you are the man of the world, aren't you? These things happen. Don't you know that?"

"I suppose they happen. How did you find out?"

"Not for a long time—not for a whole year. Do you think I remembered Sylvia out of ten thousand children because she was just like the other ten thousand?"

"I didn't think she would be just like the other ten thousand, Irma."

"You don't believe it's the same person?"

"I don't know what to believe," I said. "We sit here and we seem to have the two ends of a life between us. I want to connect them, don't you understand? This is the biggest job that I ever touched, and the least likely. I want to bring it off. I'm not used to big jobs or real money, Irma."

"I never asked you where you're from," she said.

"Chicago. That's where I was born and where I grew up."

"Is it a nice place, Mr. Macklin?"

"No. You can't break out of that, can you? Can't you accept the fact that you're eating with a man and that he might find you attractive?"

"You're not interested in me, Mr. Macklin. You haven't said a really kind thing to me since we've been sitting here. You just make me feel like something—I don't want to feel like."

"What? A woman?"

"There it is!" she cried out, almost in tears. "Why didn't you leave me alone? I'm perfectly happy just as I am. I get along. I get along very well."

"Irma Olanski," I said, "please believe that this is the first good evening I have spent in a long time, and it's a good evening because I am sitting here with you. For a little while I am not lonely and you are not lonely. Can't you just accept that? You don't have to like me very much."

After that there was a minute or two of silence. We had finished eating; we sat over our coffee, facing each other but not looking at each other. At last I asked her if she wanted a brandy. She nodded without glancing up from her coffee cup. I asked her what kind of brandy, and she shook her head again. I ordered cognac for both of us and said to myself, "The hell with Mr. Summers. He's getting more value for his rotten expense money than he knows." I wasn't proud of Alan Macklin. I suppose there are people who on and off during their lives feel a glow inside themselves, and this tells them that they are good men and of some small benefit to humanity, but it was hard for me to guess what that feeling was like.

Then I took out the photographs that Summers had given me and I handed them across the table to Miss Olanski. "These are pictures of Sylvia today," I told her. She took them and began to study them, each one long and carefully. At last she looked at me and nodded.

"Yes," she said.

"You're sure?"

"Yes."

"How can you tell from a child of eleven?"

"Not from a child of eleven. You couldn't tell from the way she was at eleven, Alan. But I knew her three years. She was almost fourteen when I saw her last, and then you could tell. This is Sylvia."

"Sylvia Karoki?"

"Yes, Sylvia Karoki."

"What kind of a name is that, Irma? Hungarian?"

"Her father was Hungarian. The mother was Polish."

"Something happens to you when you speak of her father."

"Yes, something happens to me," Irma said.

11

That day, about a year after Miss Olanski had first noticed Sylvia, the girl stayed at the library until closing time. She helped to clear the tables and to place the books that were scattered around in their proper places. Miss Olanski had told her once that she didn't have to do that because regular library pages were hired to do it, but Sylvia said that it wasn't work or a chore, that she liked to handle the books and read the titles and put them in their proper places. Could she please do it? Miss Olanski replied that of course she could, and it was a great help in any case.

When Miss Olanski was ready to leave, Sylvia was standing at the doorway, and she asked Miss Olanski could she walk a little way with her. It was January and already dark outside.

"Don't you have to get home?" Miss Olanski asked Sylvia.

"No."

"Won't they be expecting you?"

"No." The girl wore a thin, cheap waterproof jacket over her dress.

"Aren't you cold, Sylvia?" Miss Olanski asked her.

"No." She was cold. She shivered as she said that she was not cold. "Where do you live, Miss Olanski?" she said.

"A few blocks from here, Sylvia. I walk home."

They walked together to Miss Olanski's little apartment. It was in an old frame house that had been renovated—within limitations—and converted into four small apartments. Miss Olanski's apartment consisted of a combination bedroom, living room, and dining room about fourteen feet square, a tiny wall-closet type of kitchen, and a bathroom with a shower but no bathtub. Miss Olanski had furnished it very simply: a few maple chairs, a studio bed that doubled for a couch, an old pine table that she had scraped down and refinished herself, and an old pine farm sink that had been converted to a chest of drawers and cupboard. At the windows were starched organdy curtains, and there was an old foot locker painted bright yellow and covered with Pennsylvania-Dutch decalcomanias. Miss Olanski had also picked up at a secondhand furniture store some old—but not old enough to be antiques—pewter candlesticks and a threadbare hooked rug, yet not so threadbare as to loose the big red rooster that decorated the center of it. Two walls of the room were white, and Miss Olanski, not without certain trepidation, had painted the other two walls bright lemon yellow. She had done all the painting herself, and the room bore witness to the love and care and delight in her first dwelling—all hers—that it had evoked.

At the entrance to the house Sylvia made her good-bys but lingered and looked at Miss Olanski in such a way that the

librarian felt compelled to say, "Would you like to come upstairs and warm yourself a little, Sylvia?"

"Would you like me to, Miss Olanski?"

"Very much, Sylvia."

When they entered the little apartment and Miss Olanski
had switched on her lamps—imitation white hobnail glass—
Sylvia stared at the color and furnishings with sheer delight
and exclaimed:

"Oh, how beautiful, Miss Olanski! How beautiful! I have
never seen a house as beautiful as yours!"

This delight in Miss Olanski's tiny apartment gave the librarian her first real insight into Sylvia's background. There
was no doubting the absolute sincerity of Sylvia's admiration.
The tall, thin, dark-haired girl of twelve moved around the
room, her shyness momentarily overcome, and as Miss Olanski watched her the librarian repeated to herself the careful
sentence that Sylvia, in all her excitement, had delivered: "I
have never seen a house as beautiful as yours." It was a remarkable sentence, as Irma Olanski explained to me so many years
later, a manner of speech not considered or calculated but something already innate in this underfed child with the broken,
grubby fingernails, the dirty hands, and the dirty neck.

Some impulse, some reaching out toward Sylvia, made Miss
Olanski ask her whether she would stay for dinner, but Sylvia
shook her head and said that she couldn't. "It's so warm and
pretty here," Sylvia added.

"Then sit down, my dear, and warm yourself a little. I have
a very simple dinner tonight—some rice left over from last
night—and I am going to open a can of tuna fish and break
some store cheese into it and have a casserole—I mean the rice
and the tuna fish and the cheese all together."

"What is a casserole?" Sylvia asked her.

"Just a baking dish with a cover, Sylvia. But I suppose it's come to mean the kind of thing you put together in a baking dish, like tonight, this and that and whatever might go well together. Then you have a casserole."

"How did you learn all the things you know, Miss Olanski?"

"Well, how does one learn, Sylvia? Some of it you pick up —I read a good deal, and then I went to normal school, where I studied to be a librarian."

"What's a normal school, Miss Olanski?"

"Well, it's sort of like a college, Sylvia—you can't get the same degrees as in college, but normal schools do specialize in forms of teaching."

"Do you suppose I could ever get to be a librarian like you, Miss Olanski? You're very pretty. I could never get to be as pretty as you."

Miss Olanski, who was already putting the casserole together, turned now to see whether this was a joke of some sort, but then she realized that Sylvia had nothing of this kind of humor. The child was staring at her with unconcealed admiration. When she turned away again, she was close to tears. She got hold of herself and said to Sylvia:

"My dear, I am a lonely person and it's a great treat to have someone at supper. Please eat with me. Please—as a favor to me, won't you, Sylvia?"

She turned to Sylvia again. The child was staring at her, speechless, and there, as Irma told me, she had the first realization of the latent beauty in that drawn, sculptured face.

"Will you?" Miss Olanski urged.

Still Sylvia could not speak, and as if the same spark had touched both of them, Sylvia began to cry. It was the first and the last time Miss Olanski had ever seen her cry.

12

"Have you ever watched a starving person eat, Mack?"

"You said before that you liked Alan, not Mack. Now you're calling me Mack."

"What difference does it make? I tried to call you Alan, but it won't work."

"Call me Mack then." I grinned at her.

"You're nice when you smile."

"And I've been hungry. I watched myself eat."

"Really hungry?"

"Enough. You're going to tell me that the kid was starving."

"She was. First she tried to hold back and be polite—but she couldn't. I had a French bread. She took a piece and bit into it, and then she stuffed her mouth full, faster than she could chew it. I filled her plate with the tuna fish and rice. She didn't eat it, she attacked it. I wasn't hungry myself, so I gave her most of the food. She didn't look up at me. She didn't say anything. She just ate and ate with an earnest, desperate ferocity. I poured a glass of milk for her, and she drank it—I had almost a quart; she finished it. She ate the French bread and the tuna fish. While she was eating, I opened a can of baked beans and warmed it; she ate that too— I don't even think she knew what I was doing. I had a raisin pound cake—you know, the grocery kind that comes wrapped. I sliced it for her. She ate four slices and finished the milk, and then she leaned back and sighed—and she smiled at me. It was such a smile. I didn't remember having seen her smile before."

"What does 'such a smile' mean?"

"A wonderful smile. Her face became beautiful. It was full of love and contentment."

I realized two things: first, that Sylvia was neither an invention nor a casual incident in Miss Olanski's life; and second, that this was my Sylvia. How I rationalized the second fact, I do not know, but it involved my own growing sense of what Sylvia was. I was coming to know Sylvia—to a point where a given action would be credible in her personality pattern or would not. This was neither a studied nor a factual knowledge; it was simply that the mind and body and life of Sylvia had begun to take shape for me.

As to the first fact, the color and power of Miss Olanski's recall was beyond doubt. She remembered what Sylvia had said and done to a degree that was improbable, if not uncanny, after all these years; yet somehow I had no doubts as to her memories. Only too clearly I could see the skinny, hungry child gulping the food. Only too well did I understand when Irma told me that she had asked Sylvia to remain overnight. How could she not ask her? The child had not eaten for a day and a half. The night before she had slept in the half-warm hallway of a tenement she had crept into, curled up under the stairs, her face and body in all the aging smells of garbage and urine.

"I told her she had to have a shower," Irma said. "You understand that, don't you, Mack?"

I did. I knew only too well what cleanliness meant to people like Irma Olanski, why those who had vanquished the dragon of unmentionable filth had to re-enact the fight again and again all their lives. But I also understood why Sylvia fought against it and tried to leave and how Irma finally managed to get her undressed and into the shower. Then Irma told me about the bruises, the yellow and purple splotches that covered her body from neck to buttocks and on both arms.

"Mack, it wasn't just a child hit," Irma said. "It was a child

beaten savagely and mercilessly. You said I don't like her father. Her father did that. He said she had stolen twenty-five cents from him and that he was going to take it out of her hide— and after he beat her up, Sylvia left and swore to herself that she would not come back, ever. She told me the rest of it in time, her father assaulting her and all the rest that I don't want to repeat. Anyway, I can't tell it the way she did. There was no self-pity in Sylvia, no bending, no bowing, no submission. She was like a piece of iron, and that must have driven her rotten pig of a father crazy. That's why you could give her things, Mack. She took without the guilts of taking, and she surrendered none of that strange, twisted pride that was somehow the best yet the most provoking part of her. Do you know?"

"I know," I said. I knew it only too well. It fell into place, just as everything about Sylvia would fall into place for me. I listened to Irma describing how Sylvia looked washed, clean, a pink flannel nightgown covering her from head to foot, and I comprehended what Irma meant when she told me that of all the evenings in her life this was somehow the warmest and the best.

It would be. Irma had so much to give, and it was there for the taking, and who else had ever needed what she had and wanted it? Although Sylvia remained with Irma for almost three months, that evening was engraved upon her memory in minute detail. She told me how after the shower she and Sylvia had talked. This was a new experience for Sylvia; never before in her life had she been able to pour out into words the misery and degradation of her existence, a pathological father who alternately beat her and made sexual advances toward her, a dying mother who quenched her pain with alcohol, an unheated—except for a kerosene stove—cold-water flat in a rotting frame house, not simply poverty, but poverty degraded beyond belief. I was no stranger to poverty. In Chicago, I had seen poverty as flourishing as anywhere in America. But this was something else. Sylvia's father worked more often than not, and he spent the money in the local cat houses and saloons. Her mother whimpered with the woes and pains of all womankind. And out of all this had come Sylvia.

Irma Olanski did not try to explain what she comprehended only imperfectly—the force and need that drove Sylvia. Knowledge—the need to know—is comprehensible when it is a desire, a need, an avocation, a means to an end; when it becomes a disease and a passion, as it sometimes does among those whose circumstances are indescribable, then it is more difficult for ordinary people to understand. But she did describe it.

Sylvia stayed with her, lived with her, for almost three months. During that time Sylvia went to school, and during that time she was decently dressed and fed. Irma remade some of her own clothes for Sylvia, and each morning she made lunch for Sylvia to take to school. Each evening they ate together. Irma took pains to describe Sylvia's attitude during that time. It was not a grateful attitude in such terms as we commonly reserve for gratitude. Sylvia neither fawned upon Irma, nor did she parade guilts. Yet she attempted to anticipate Irma's needs and emotions. She had what Irma kept referring to as an "uncanny" sensitivity to others. She did not intrude. Since she could not pay Irma, she never referred to regrets about payment. She helped Irma clean and tidy the place, but she never pre-empted the function. And she learned. It was much as if some inner compulsion pressed her to question anything she did not know—a word, a phrase, a motion, the use of a knife or fork, gestures—she questioned everything.

When Irma made it plain to Sylvia that she could not remain with Irma unless her parents knew where she was, Sylvia nodded and agreed that it might be a good thing to send them a note. Irma wrote the note and mailed it but never received any response. On the other hand, no police inquiries or anything of that sort were made.

The evenings these two, the twenty-one-year-old librarian and the twelve-year-old child, spent together were unexciting and not too varied. On half a dozen occasions they went to the movies. Sylvia adored the movies, and from the moment she sat down she was fixed in the world of enchantment the movies offered her. But most evenings they spent at home, either talking or reading. Irma liked to read aloud—something I could never abide myself—and Sylvia loved being read to. She would enter totally into the world and was thereby the type of audience readers respond to best. Particularly, Sylvia liked to hear plays read aloud. She had never seen a play, and it was hard for her to imagine what a stage performance was like. Until Irma had explained it in great detail, Sylvia thought of a stage as an opening into a literal world where the play was enacted in time and depth.

Irma recalled some of the plays she had read aloud to Sylvia and which they had subsequently discussed. There was the Brian Hooker translation of *Cyrano*, *The Importance of Being Earnest* by Wilde, *Golden Boy* by Odets, and *Watch on the Rhine* by Lillian Hellman. Strangely, *Cyrano* was the play she loved best, *Watch on the Rhine* the one that provoked the most discussion. Only in the vaguest way was Sylvia aware that a great war was being fought, and even less was she aware of the issues behind it and the nations involved. The word "Nazi" meant little to her; her notions of geography were foggy, and out of her own twelve years of existence had developed a certain dullness on the question of the cruelty of man to man. She lived in a world where extremes of cruelty were matter-of-fact; and what was horrible to Irma was a natural part of the life experience to Sylvia.

On the other hand, *Golden Boy* left her untouched. She thought it was a silly play, full of silly feelings. But when Irma read her the rather obscure *Trojan Women* of Euripides, she listened openmouthed and afterward was speechless with emotion and pity, this in spite of the fact that she knew nothing of the background of the play or the author.

On weekends they visited the museums. I could understand how Sylvia had become a focus of Irma's existence, how suddenly the world became alive for Irma because she could explain what she knew about it to Sylvia.

It was much as if Irma Olanski had already accepted her own defeat, even at the age of twenty-one, and had now discovered a second chance, a reprieve, in the skinny, long-legged, and strange child named Sylvia.

"And then," Irma told me, "she left, and that came to an end."

"She left?"

"One night I came back and she wasn't there."

"No word? No note?"

"Yes, she left a letter for me. A carefully written letter. I still have it."

13

It was a pleasant evening, cool and with a ripe-orange moon in the sky. In fact, everyone I spoke to in Pittsburgh seemed to dwell on the fact that the summer of 1958 was so cool and

pleasant. We decided to walk to Irma's place; it was a good night for a walk.

As we strolled along, Irma said, "We've talked so much about Sylvia, Mack—what about yourself?"

"What about myself?"

"You're a funny man for a detective."

"So is every private detective. Most of us became that way by some accident."

"What was your accident?"

"I needed a job."

"Well, what did you want to be before then?"

I told her, and she shook her head. "A history teacher," she murmured. "That's strange."

"No, it isn't. You only think so because I am what I am now. If I had met you as a history teacher, you wouldn't think it strange at all."

"And what do you think of me, Mack?"

"I hardly know you."

"I don't believe that. You're a sweet man, Mack, but I feel naked in front of you. You seem to just listen, without asking questions, and then I find that I have said things to you that I have never said to anyone else before."

"Is that so terrible?"

"No, I guess not."

Very little changes in the life of someone like Irma. They become timid and wary of change, until something explodes and everything is changed; but that had not happened to Irma yet. She still lived where she had lived when she knew Sylvia. I had a sense of walking into the reality she had described.

"Sit down, please, Mack," she told me. "You're a special man, the first one to be in here in four years— Oh, I wish I had never met you, Mack."

14

She gave me the letter from Sylvia. In all truth, I didn't know whether it was the same handwriting or not. I am no hand-writing expert, and much had happened to Sylvia since then. But Irma said that I could make a copy of it. I did. Here it is:

Dear Irma,

When I think of you, I feel good. I guess I love you better than anyone. I would read about good people in books and I would scream at myself that this is lies. But since I have lived with you I know this is not lies. You are so wonderful and kind I don't know what to say. But you are not my mother or my sister and I can't keep staying here with you, Irma. That is why I am going away because there isn't anything else. I can't stay here.

I love you so much, Irma,
Sylvia

I finished reading it, and I looked at Irma. Her eyes were wet. All the years had sloughed away.

"Do you know what I lost, Mack?" she asked me.

"I know."

"It wasn't homosexual or anything like that."

"I know."

"I just loved that damned kid. I loved her so much. I needed her so much."

"Did you ever see her again?"

"I saw her once, months later."

"Yes?"

"It was more than a year later, Mack."

"She didn't come back to the library?"

"No. No, she never came back to the library. The library was empty, like a tomb. I saw her on the street. She was wearing a rayon dress and lipstick, and the long black hair was cut. She was trying to look sixteen or seventeen—but she wasn't. She was a kid with a pair of little breasts budding out and her body hitched forward awkwardly from the high heels she wasn't used to."

I nodded and waited.

"Well, I saw her," Irma said.

"You didn't talk to her?"

"Talk to her? I stood facing her. I said, 'Hello, Sylvia.' She said nothing, just stood and looked at me for a moment, and then turned around and fled."

"Just that?"

"Just that. I never saw Sylvia again."

15

"Mack—you've had girls."

"I been married, Irma," I told her. "It lasted a few months. We were both equally grateful for divorce laws."

"What happened?"

"Who knows? It wasn't right."

"And now—you live with loneliness?"

"Most of the time."

"So do I. What's wrong with us, Mack?"

"What's wrong with this whole lousy world? Why is it full of filth and indecency and lies and dirty all over? I wallow in dirt, Irma. What do you think I am? What do you think my business is? To track down all the cheap deceits and dirty infidelities that will earn me a buck and see me a day closer to an end as meaningless as the beginning."

"I don't like to hear you talk like that, Mack. Anyway, it's not true."

"How do you know?"

"When did you meet me, Mack?"

"Five o'clock this afternoon."

"That's just time. In my life, time doesn't mean anything, Mack. A year goes by, and there's nothing. Just nothing. I feel I've known you so long—like a brother of mine."

"Now what in hell's name do you need with a brother, Irma? That's the goddamn trouble with you! Brothers!"

"I know you're a frustrated history professor, Mack, so why do you try to talk like a movie private eye?"

"I don't try. It's the price of my profession."

"I say 'brother' because I'm afraid. I'm not normal any more, Mack. I'm so frightened, I'm trembling. Look at my hand."

"Of me?"

"Of me," she whispered. "I want to make an advance toward you. I don't know how. It's one in the morning now. Since midnight I've been saying to myself, 'I want him to kiss me. What do I do to make him kiss me?' "

16

I lay in Irma's bed and watched dawn begin to wash the darkness from outside. Soon there was enough light to reveal the woman who lay next to me, the strong naked limbs, the full breasts, the broad thighs shaped to bear children she never would bear—the virginal nakedness of a woman of thirty-six years.

Even now I cannot put down exactly how I felt toward Irma Olanski. There are easy words for such relationships, and the fact was that I had picked up a neurotic spinster librarian and had gone to bed with her. It did not begin or end there. I had lived with a woman for a few hours of rare and true intimacy. We had between us no lies or illusions, and we also shared a memory of a little girl neither of us knew but for fragments. We were no longer young, but something of youth came back to us—and perhaps something more.

Irma was awake. Had I slept? she wanted to know.

"A little."

"I didn't sleep," Irma said. "It's funny to lie here like this in the morning and have you looking at me, Mack."

"It's not funny. You're a beautiful woman, Irma—strong and filled with life and beautiful too."

"I know," she replied strangely. "But it's too late, Mack, too late."

PART 3

LAWNOX

I TALKED IRMA INTO GOING OUT FOR BREAKFAST. WE WALKED through the early streets among the long shadows, among the workingmen with their print shirts and their tin food boxes, and we found a place where we could satisfy our hunger. We ate big breakfasts. We were tired but alive.

I asked Irma could we have dinner together that night, and she said yes, relieved, I think, and then she said that she had been afraid that perhaps this was good-by. I told her that we had plenty of time to say good-by, and then I left her, she to the library and myself back to the hotel.

While I was shaving, after I had taken a bath, the phone rang. It was Sergeant Franklin from police headquarters, and he said that he had something for me.

"Anything good?" I asked him.

"Look, Macklin, I don't know what's good. You were interested in Sylvias, so I had one of the boys here do a little additional work on it. He turned up something that fits into your dates, so I thought I'd let you know."

"Thank you, Franklin. It's very thoughtful of you."

"The hell it is! Thoughtful. You put labels on things, Mack-

lin. Anyway, this is a Sylvia Bennett—the last name's a phony
for sure. In 1944 a cheap little hood named Fiselli was picked
up on a petty theft charge. He had a girl with him when he
was picked up, and she was taken downtown and then released
for lack of any evidence to tie her in with Fiselli's work. Her
name was Sylvia Bennett, as I said—the name she gave, anyway
—and according to the file, she was about fourteen years old.
She gave her age as seventeen, but that didn't hold any water
with the cop who put down the facts."

"That's all, Franklin?"

"What do you want me to do," the telephone barked back
at me, "wrap up a case for you? No, that isn't all. They picked
up Fiselli about a year ago on a grand theft. He's living out
at Lawnox Penitentiary, and you could go out and see him."

"How far is it from here?"

"About twenty miles."

"Could I get in to see him?"

"You got all kinds of passes to such parties, Macklin. But
if you want me to, I'll go along."

"Could you get away?"

"I could."

I told him that I would hire a car and pick him up at eleven
o'clock. A few minutes after eleven we were on the road to
Lawnox. Franklin hunched into his seat and said to me mood-
ily:

"Why is it so easy to buy, Macklin? You're an educated
man—how about you should enlighten me? With a few lousy
bucks you buy me. I don't know what you shoved onto Inspector Garowski, but the way he says to me, 'Now whatever
this Macklin wants, help him along. Don't break no regula-
tions, but help him along'—the way he says that, I figure it's
a yard. Now we're going out to a lousy stinkhole of a jail, and

for fifty clams you can buy the whole place, lock, stock, and barrel. What is it, Macklin? Has it always been this kind of a world, where a kid is taught to be honest and decent and straight, and then he grows up and it takes him four hours to learn that the world is a shithole?"

"Some of it is, some of it isn't, Franklin."

"Yeah. Show me where it isn't and let me scratch. I'll find pus before you can say 'rubber duck.' "

"I suppose it's what we make it, Franklin." I shrugged. "You and me, we're no different, we're just talented. The whole human race is talented—the talent of exoneration. Maybe when we're kids someone tried to teach us to be honest and decent, but the first thing we learn is, 'I didn't do it.' That's before we even know what the word 'larceny' means."

"Yet I never saw a punk," said Franklin, "not the cheapest, dirtiest, lousiest punk who didn't want a little respect from somebody else."

"I'm no philosopher," I said, "but I went to school four years to learn history and I came out of it thinking that there is a little progress now and then. Maybe I'm wrong. Who do I pay the fifty clams to?"

"Captain Brady. He's top officer."

"And if I don't pay?"

"You maybe get to say a few words to this Fiselli because I'm with you, but not alone."

"And if I pay I talk to him alone?"

"That's right."

"What do I do with the money? Hand it to him?"

"Christ Almighty, Macklin—what the hell do you think you do with the money?"

"I just don't want to put my foot in anything."

"All right, I'm sorry. Maybe on occasion you have had a bellyful yourself, Macklin."

"On occasion."

"All right. So I got it. I live with the stink, Macklin—I don't just get to smell it incidentally."

2

About religion, I keep my ideas to myself for the most part. Not only because they are somewhat foggy and confused, but also because there is nothing I can add to what others have said and very little that I can take from them. But there are times when I am taken with the notion of a God who sees each leaf fall and notes the passing of every sparrow. Such a God would know about people like Joey Fiselli, not just a clinical awareness, but a knowledge compounded out of sympathy and love—and perhaps a little pity. He would also know about Captain Brady.

I once asked Jake Hoffman, the assistant warden at San Quentin and a man of some insight and intelligence, why he had to give prison work to the Captain Bradys of this world, and he said to me, "Use your head, Mack. What is a prison? You hear kids say, 'I want to grow up and maybe be a judge or a soldier or a cop or a pilot'—but you ever heard a kid say, 'I want to grow up and be a prison guard'? A prison—any prison—is society's means of forgetting and torturing its worst and sickest and dirtiest, so what do you want for prison guards, Harvard men?"

Maybe you could find someone like Brady in Harvard—I don't know. Brady was short and wide, and he must have weighed close to three hundred pounds, but not all of it was fat; and Franklin told me that he was said to have killed a convict with one blow of his hamlike fist. That could be or not, because when you have a man like Brady you have stories about him. And when you have a filthy, rotting, graft-ridden jail like Lawnox, you have such stories about the place, and there's no proving whether the stories are true or not. Brady met me and measured me out of tiny squint eyes, so pale blue that they were like pinholes in his head, and I didn't think about whether he was fat or looked like a pig, but only about a man with such eyes.

I didn't have to worry about how he took, either, since he motioned Franklin out of his office and came right to the point and told me:

"This is a hell of a note, Macklin. What do you think we run here, a reform school? Nobody who ain't counsel or family talks to the inmates here, so if you want to talk to Fiselli it's got to cost you."

"How much?"

"Half a yard."

I gave him five ten-dollar bills, and he counted them carefully and slowly, licking his forefinger and separating each bill from the others. Then just as carefully he added them to a roll from his pocket, snapping a rubber band over the whole. He walked out and I followed him, and he explained to me that Fiselli was in solitary confinement.

"What did he do?"

"You want to talk to him, Macklin, or you want to find out if we know how to run a jail?"

"All right. I just wondered."

It is a peculiar and perverted tribute to man as a social being that through the ages no worse punishment nor more delicate torture has been devised than to lock him up alone with no sight or sound of his fellow man. It is no tribute to his fellow man, but after ten or fifteen days in proper solitary the cure takes, and Lawnox was proper solitary. The cells were located in the sub-basement, down two flights of stairs to a wet and molding concrete rectangle. It was as dark and silent as the black pit of death.

Brady flicked a switch, and a light bulb hanging from a cord cast a sickly glow in the place. The pit was about thirty feet long, and in a row on one side were the doors to ten solitary cells. The ceiling to the basement was about seven feet high, but the doors to the cells were no more than four feet high, reminding me of a row of kennel closures or zoo fronts. I followed Brady to the door of a cell. He took a flashlight from his pocket, turned a key in the lock, and opened the door. The cell was three feet by six feet, and the ceiling was no more than five feet high. The walls were covered with the molding damp that permeated the whole place. The floor was wet. A tin chamber pot made the place reek like a public toilet in Chicago. The furnishings consisted of an old army blanket on the wet floor, and on the blanket a man sat, a shoeless, shirtless man whose whole wardrobe consisted of a threadbare pair of gray cotton pants and who blinked with pain as the light cut into his eyes.

"There's Fiselli," Brady said, "so go ahead and talk with him, Macklin."

"Here?"

"You want me to take him to the bridal suite? I said you could talk to him. Go ahead and talk to him."

"Have a heart, Brady. You've got visiting rooms. There's someplace where I can talk to him, isn't there?"

"He's in solitary, Macklin."

"I can't talk to him here, Captain."

"What in hell am I running, a county hospital? If you can't talk to him here, don't talk to him."

While this went on, Fiselli crouched and blinked and listened. I don't know that he looked more the animal now than he might have five or ten years ago. He was a man in his thirties, but he was more like fifty now behind his sunken face and his blinking, tear-filled eyes. Brady grinned as he watched him, and the pink tip of Brady's tongue moistened the edge of his lips.

"Talk or not, mister," Brady said. "It don't mean a goddamned thing to me."

"Let's you and me talk."

Brady locked up the cell door again and we went out into the corridor. I peeled off five more tens, and Brady licked his finger five times. "I like you, buddy boy." He grinned. "I'm going to let you talk to Fiselli in our nice visiting room. You tell him your whole life story and he can tell you his. That's because I like you, buddy boy."

3

"Why the hell should I talk to you?" Fiselli said.

"I got you an hour out of that stinkhole."

"You got me nothing, mister. They put me back and add the hour on. You don't get nothing out of Brady for free, not even the sweat off his motherfriggen gonads."

"All I want is to ask you a few questions, Fiselli. That's all I want to do. I'm not here to make any trouble for you."

"I got trouble. I got plenty of trouble, mister. Plenty."

"I just want to ask a few questions, Fiselli."

"You a cop?"

"I told you what I am. I'm a private investigator."

"Crap on that shamus deal. I don't have to answer any questions. Go fly a kite."

He had to be brave. He had to be defiant and arrogant and

proud of himself; it was the only way he knew how to cling to whatever tiny shred was left of his immortal soul. He had been squeezed too hard and too long. His left cheek twitched with a tic. Four days of beard made him as ugly as he was mean and empty, and he squirmed and shivered like a naked little animal at bay. You have to sit in a jail as I did, facing him, to know what freedom is—and I knew: didn't I represent the fine civilized forces that had put Fiselli behind the wire screen that separated us—the better to instruct him? His instructor came in as he finished what he had been saying, and Brady knew all the innuendoes of instruction.

"What's the matter, Fiselli?"

They looked at each other, and the tiny slits that were Brady's eyes were full of enjoyment. I didn't suspect, when I first met him, that Brady enjoyed so many things. They were odd things, but he enjoyed them.

"He's my buddy boy, Fiselli. Right, buddy boy?"

I nodded. For one hundred dollars I was his buddy boy.

"You got to tell buddy boy whatever he wants to know, you see, Fiselli?" He put his enormous ham of a hand on Fiselli's skinny shoulder. The hand swelled and contracted. The thumb and the fingers began to come together, with Fiselli's shoulder in between. "Because he's my buddy boy, Fiselli."

The hand squeezed and Fiselli's whole body reacted to it. He made whimpering noises. He moaned, "Ah—ah—ah—ah," and the tears rolled down his cheeks. When Brady let go, Fiselli fell forward with his head on the table, crying and moaning.

"Now Fiselli will talk, buddy boy." Brady grinned and he left us alone again. I sat and waited; it is no use saying what I felt; I found that what I feel in a case like this is better not said or thought about.

When Fiselli stopped crying and groaning, he felt his right shoulder with his left hand. "I can't move my arm," he pleaded. "He broke something."

"You'll be all right, Fiselli."

"I tell you, he broke something."

"Take it easy."

"I never said I wouldn't answer questions, mister. You never asked no questions."

"Take it easy."

"Sure. Sure. But you didn't ask no questions."

He was pleading to please me. In all the years since World War II, I had forgotten how much fear one man can inspire in another man. Now I remembered.

"All right, Fiselli," I said. "I want to ask you about a girl called Sylvia Karoki."

"Who?"

"Sylvia Karoki."

"Something broke. Look, I can't move my arm. Jesus, it hurts. I don't know no Sylvia Karoki."

"Just Sylvia. Try that."

"Look, mister—I don't know no Sylvia. Mister, my arm hurts. I tell you, my arm is broken. How would you like to sit here and try to think about things with a broken arm? I been twelve days in that lousy, stinking hole. How would you like to spend twelve days in the hole, mister?"

"Your arm isn't broken, Fiselli. I know he hurt you and I'm damned sorry. I wish I could have stopped him from hurting you. But I can't do anything about that or the hole, and the best thing for you is to take your mind off your arm and think about my questions."

"I am, I am. What are you going to tell Brady—I wouldn't co-operate?"

"No, of course not. Now listen to me, Fiselli. In 1944 the Pittsburgh police picked you up and charged you with petty theft. You had picked up the take of the Victor Dance Studio, and subsequently you were convicted——"

"Dance studio hell! A lousy run-down cat house! You know how many squares I steered in there? Maybe a hundred, maybe two hundred, and I'm supposed to get three dollars a throw. Lousy bitch who ran it never paid off—never—hands me a ten or a twenty and says, 'Go play, Joey, you're a good boy.' She pays the cop, all right. All right. The cop gets his. I get smiles and I should take it out in trade. Shit on their trade. I don't need to pay. I never needed to pay——"

"You remember being arrested."

"I'll tell you something else——"

"Hold it. When you were arrested, you had a girl with you. She was just a kid, fourteen years old. Her name was Sylvia."

"What do you know!" Fiselli peered at me sheepishly and pleadingly. "That's right. Mister, you got any cigarettes?" I took out my pack. "Light one," he begged me, "and put the end through the screen. Brady would break my back if he caught me smoking here, but if you hold the butt it's all right. Huh? What do you say? It's all right?"

I lit a cigarette and put the mouth end through the wire. Fiselli leaned to the screen and puffed deeply, coughed, and drew again and again. "First one in twelve days," he whispered, his whole body trembling.

"You remember the girl?"

"Sure I remember." Fiselli grinned. "Gimme another puff. Sure. But the funny thing is, it just slipped my mind. Forgot all about it."

"Remember her name?"

"Yeah. Yeah. Her name was Sylvia."

"Last name, Fiselli?"

"No—no, something. You can be sure it wasn't no real name. I never knew a hustler who lived with her own name."

"She was a hustler?"

"She tried. She was afraid of the streets because once she was picked up by a cop who took it in trade instead of running her in."

"You're sure of that?"

"That's what she told me. Another puff, mister? That's why she latched onto me. She wanted to make a deal."

I let him smoke the rest of the cigarette and then ground out the butt on the floor. My stomach was a pit, full of sickness and emptiness and tiredness.

"What kind of a deal?"

"What the hell—you know what kind of a deal."

"Maybe I do and maybe I don't," I said. "I want you to spell it out for me, Fiselli."

"She wanted me to bring her business. Look, mister, I ain't no pimp. Nobody ever called me a pimp and got away with it. Christ, no! All right—so occasionally a guy wants something and I steer him. Anything wrong with that? That's what I want to know. Just tell me if anything's wrong with that. What am I doing's different from what any cabdriver does? But I never carried no dames. I never lived off no dames. Not a dame like this one—so help me God!"

"What do you mean?"

"Well, look—she says she's seventeen years old. She's able to talk like she's seventeen years old. What am I—a patsy? I never seen a dame before? I says to her one day, 'You lousy little liar, I give you a buck for every day over fourteen. Just bring me your birth certificate and you can make yourself a bundle.'"

"Did she?"

"What do you think, mister? All you got to do is take one look at those skinny arms and legs—who's going to pay money for that? Goddamn crazy kid drove me nuts!"

"What happened to her, Fiselli?"

"Who knows? What happens to punk kids like that? Maybe she made it for some two-dollar dame in a cat house and got loused up with venereal. Maybe she became a junkie. Maybe she's dead. Who knows?"

"You can do better than that, Fiselli."

"What do you want, mister? I got nothing to hold back. That's fourteen years ago, so I can't take no rap, no matter what, because of the limitations. I got no reason to hold nothing back."

"There are things you forget, Fiselli. Nobody disappears. There's always a thread somewhere. Try to remember. Anything. Maybe you heard something."

"No—no—wait a minute. I ask Sonny Bissell once what happens to this jerked-up kid. She says something about her going off to El Paso with Peter the Priest. He had a 1940 Ford. I wouldn't want to ride that to no place like El Paso."

"Who was Peter the Priest?"

"A cheap con man, made his living out of turning his collar around. I do a lot of things, but not that, mister. That's the lowest."

"And Sonny Bissell?"

"An old pot. She used to hustle a long time ago when I was just a kid. She liked kids. She always said that kids were full of steam."

"Where is she now, Fiselli?"

"Dead."

"Someone else? Didn't Sylvia have any friends?"

"Friends? You make me laugh."

"Peter the Priest?"

"Never heard of him again. Like I say, I guess he went to El Paso."

I didn't want any more. I wanted to forget Joey Fiselli and Lawnox Penitentiary and Captain Brady and all that went with it, and maybe the human race too, and myself, which is the hardest kind of forgetting. I wanted to run a bath back in my hotel and soak in it and smoke a cigarette and think about nothing at all. Most of all, I did not want to show Fiselli her picture, but I am in a profession where the best part of it consists of doing things that a normal and decent human being would not do. So I took her picture out of my wallet and held it up for Fiselli to see, and he was impressed by the picture and grinned and nodded.

"Who's that?" he wanted to know.

"Could it be Sylvia?"

"Don't make me laugh, mister."

"Fourteen years is a long time."

"It ain't long enough, mister."

There was no more I wanted to say to Fiselli or hear him say. Brady was waiting for me outside, and he wanted to know did that lousy pile of feces, Fiselli, talk. I said that he had. "Nice and easy and polite?" Brady pressed me with a perfectly natural solicitude for money paid and value given. I told him that Fiselli had answered my questions and it was as good as I could have expected.

"Well, Macklin"—Brady smiled, his tiny eyes becoming pinholes in his massive face—"any time you want to talk to someone here, you come back. I like you, Macklin."

"Thanks," I said.

4

I bought Franklin some lunch and then we drove back to Pittsburgh. He had been mostly silent until then, but when we were in the car and driving back he said to me:

"Macklin, you're an educated man and you been around a little——"

"How do you know?"

"It rubs off here and there. You been to college?"

"Yes."

"That's right." Franklin nodded. "I remember you saying you went four years to learn about history. Me, I'm just a cop, and the only thing I really learned in my life is that if you don't expect too much you don't cry over it when it doesn't happen."

"I suppose that's as good as anything else."

"Like hell it is! I'm an ignorant slob, Macklin, and you can't make anything else out of it! What the hell do I know? You take Brady—they say he's got maybe fifteen, twenty grand soaked away, just out of a rotten rathole like Lawnox. What does it add up to? You meet a lot of Bradys in my line of work; you meet a lot of Fisellis too. What does it add up to?"

"They don't teach you that in college."

"You know about history. Was it always this way?" Franklin asked.

"More or less."

"Was it ever any better?"

"Mostly it was worse," I said.

"Did Fiselli know your Sylvia?"

"Maybe he did, maybe he didn't—I'm not sure." I didn't want to have to listen to Franklin and make talk with him all the way back to Pittsburgh. I was tired of him and his arthritis and his sleepless pain-filled eyes and his bitter resentment of little men who enriched themselves by scavenging the open sores of littler men. I had no pity left, not for myself and not for anyone else. In a few hours I would feel different and I would come back to what was normal for me. But right then I was without pity and without hate and even without anger. I wasn't angry at Fiselli. If I could have had him dead by wishing him dead, I wouldn't have bothered. At that moment I didn't care.

5

In my room, after a bath that left me feeling as dirty and unpleasant as before and a cigarette that tasted harsh and bitter, I sat down at the writing desk that hotels supply and wrote the following letter:

Mr. Frederick Summers
Los Angeles, California

Dear Mr. Summers:
You will wonder why a man whose daily run of work is nothing to detail in front of ladies should feel that this job is a good deal dirtier and nastier than anything he ever took on before. I am afraid that I cannot explain that to your satisfaction. I don't think you're the kind of man who admits any kind of sensitivity in others except the kind you yourself possess— considering that you do possess some kind.
There will be no report on Sylvia. I think your whole project and proposition is the project of a lousy little mind and a soul as twisted as a coil spring. As to whether or not you marry Sylvia, I don't give a damn. Buy yourself another boy to snoop for you or shove the whole thing up your can—whatever you decide.

As for the money, it will be returned. I am entitled to fifty dollars a day and expenses when I work, and I have been working. But I don't want to work for you any more.

I signed my name with a flourish, felt a twinge of comfort or relief or something, read it through again, and then tore it into tiny shreds. It was after five now. I went down to the bar to have a drink and wait for Irma.

6

My wife's name was Lucy—not my wife now, but once for a little while—and I met her at the Hollywood race track. I thought about her as I stood at the bar and waited, because during the two weeks of our honeymoon we had been happy and we had driven down to El Paso and beyond El Paso, the only time I had been in El Paso. Perhaps, also, the only time I had been happy with the simple, pure kind of happiness that came to me the moment I met her at the track. It was the first time I had ever been to the Hollywood race track. I went there with Frankie Meadows, the old silent-picture star, who had hired me for a small job and taken a liking to me and was determined to show me how the better class of citizens passed their leisure hours. In the old poshy days Meadows had saved his money and put it into real estate in the then uninhabited Pacific slopes. Now he had enough for a Bentley and a chauffeur and a membership at the Turf Club and a table along the first railing and all the steaks and crabmeat and airborne lobster he and his friends cared to eat. He was too old to do very much with women by that time, but he still liked to surround himself with the widest-eyed of each new crop of starlets; and Lucy was one of these, her eyes as wide as blue windows, her hair cut short in what was then the new French fashion, and her face the wonderful, bright boyish face that was currently enshrined.

I don't know how I turned the trick, but it was probably—at least in part—the totality of my worship. Or maybe she just had her mind fixed on marrying a private detective.

I stood at the bar, had two glasses of whisky and ice, and remembered. El Paso was the place where you went across the border to Ciudad Juárez in five minutes and ate some Mexican food and bought some souvenirs and wandered through the dirty streets, the Canco houses, the honky-tonk joints, the little markets and peddlers of sticks and dirty pictures—and if you were young enough and in love enough, it was as wonderful as anything of the kind anywhere in the whole world. And then we drove out of El Paso along a concrete thread down the border until we came to mountains called the Sierra Blanca, which were piled up to the sky as white and pure as the clean wash of the lady in the ad—the one who has three child-actor-type children but loves better than all else her white, white wash as it comes out of her new agitator washer. Where the road hangs in the sky at the top of the pass, we parked the car and got out and stood on the summit of that white world, the wind whipping her short, sun-silk hair and pressing her thin dress to her body, and myself filled with love and adoration and immortality.

When you have gotten over that sort of thing and finished it and put it away, you are always a little less than you were before. I guess that I, now, standing at a bar in Pittsburgh, was a lot less, and even two drinks couldn't buy a little esteem in myself for myself.

7

It was almost seven o'clock before Irma appeared. She had gone home first to change her clothes, but more had been changed inside her; she had the tight glow and eager smile of youth; her arms were widespread for tomorrow. She wore a plain black dress and a single strand of imitation pearls around her neck, but she was full of warmth and desire, and she could see on my face how pleased I was with her appearance.

"I didn't feel like a librarian today," she told me.

"What did you feel like?"

"Pretensions and a great ego. I was sure that everyone was watching me."

"Maybe they were."

"Oh no, they weren't, Mack. I'm still a librarian in a black dress. But very happy. Mack, did your mother tell you that it's bad luck to talk about being happy?"

"I seem to remember."

"Then I suppose it's part of the folklore of all poor people. Don't mention it or it will go away."

"Something of the sort, I guess."

"What's the matter, Mack?"

"Nothing—nothing," I said.

"I feel so good." She smiled, shamefaced, like a little girl caught doing something wrong. "I want you to feel good."

"I'll try," I said.

I made a try at it. I had not planned for Irma Olanski to like Alan Macklin or to want to love Alan Macklin, but I should have known what it means to be hungry for so long. It was not simply that it had happened to Irma in terms of myself alone; we were bound together by the thin, distant thread of a strange skinny child whose name was Sylvia. I was seeking something that Irma had lost. I was not someone she had met thirty hours before; I was part of a life so lonely and empty that the two most important people she had known, Sylvia and myself, had become a single thing for Irma. I took Irma to dinner and tried to be as charming and as interesting as it was in me to be, and I talked about everything else—Los Angeles and my youth in Chicago and the war and how it felt to be a private detective—but not about Sylvia.

And finally Irma said, "You don't want me to talk about her either."

"Who?"

"Sylvia," Irma said.

"What gave you that idea?"

"Where were you today, Mack? What happened?"

"I went out to the jail in Lawnox with a cop called Franklin. That's why I have a car tonight, and I can take you for a ride later if you want to. I hired the car to go out to Lawnox."

"You don't want to tell me anything about it, Mack?"

"What is there to tell?"

"I don't know," Irma said. "But something happened to you since yesterday——"

"Yeah."

"About Sylvia——"

"Yeah—there's a cheap, dirty little hood doing time there, a pimp and junkie name of Fiselli——"

"Why do you talk that way, Mack? It's not you talking."

"How the hell should I talk with the company I keep?"

"I'm sorry, Mack." Suddenly she was frightened and bewildered, and I put my hand on hers and shook my head and smiled at her.

"Irma——"

"Oh, Mack," she said, "I don't want to push myself into what you do, but I feel so close to you. It's a crazy way to feel, but that's the way I feel." She looked at me searchingly. "I don't know enough to keep my mouth shut. I don't know anything, do I?"

Then I told her about Fiselli. I told her about Fiselli and

Brady and the hole at Lawnox, and I told her what Fiselli had said about Sylvia. And when I finished, she sat for a while and said nothing at all.

"There it is," I said, because her silence irritated me.

"A man like that Fiselli you describe," she said slowly, "well, he could be lying."

"Mostly he would be lying, but he would have to have some reason to lie. That wasn't the case here. Also, with a punk like Fiselli—he has forgotten how to dissemble. When he lies, you know it."

"It could have been another Sylvia."

"Could it?"

"All right, Mack," she said softly. "Why don't we go for a ride in the car?"

Not what she said just then, because the few words were nothing at all, but the way she said it and the tone of her voice cut through all the long distance between us. Suddenly I knew her a little, because all my smart, quick, wise-aleck knowledge of her was dissipated; and not knowing her at all, I knew her a little—if that makes any sense. I don't know of another way to put it. I saw Irma Olanski then as a tender and wise and wonderful woman, and I was sick with myself—who had gone to bed with a woman, a quick one, look at the way I knock them over, laddies!—and would get out of Pittsburgh tomorrow or the next day and never come back. Be grateful, Irma, as the custom has it; and if I wanted to hate the race, I could just as well begin with Macklin as with two more obvious brutes called Fiselli and Brady. A swift look at myself.

She said to me, "Mack—Mack—cheer up. There's a moon in the sky and just as many stars as there were yesterday."

But it wasn't until we were in the car and driving through the hills above the city that I asked Irma, "Why does a woman do it?"

"Do what, Mack?"

"Do I have to spell it out? Become a whore—just in so many words—become a whore."

"Mack!"

"All right, I asked you."

"You're the one who's been everywhere, Mack. I'm just a librarian."

"You're a woman."

"Yes—and what's a whore, Mack?"

"You never heard the word before?"

"Don't be clever with me, Mack, because I don't know how to be clever with you. Only sometimes I wonder how many men wouldn't be whores if there was a market place and women were buying."

"What does that mean?"

"You know what it means. What do you do when you're trapped and frustrated and lost—look in garbage cans? A girl sells the one salable thing left, and she wouldn't sell if you were buying."

"Let's drop the subject," I said.

"Oh, sure, Mack—sure. And when do you go away? When do you leave Pittsburgh and not come back, now that you have what you came here for?"

"You knew that, Irma?"

"Yes."

"What can I do?"

"All day long I was thinking of things that you could do," Irma said, not sadly and not angrily, but just because there it was. "I'm too old to fall in love, Mack, and it's all too quick. But I think I'd go anywhere in the world for you and with you—and I'm not pleading and not boxing you in and not trying to make you feel rotten. That's just the way it is, and I'll cry a little about it, but I'll be all right. You won't. Even if you wanted to, you couldn't remain here or be around me—or be any good for any woman."

"You've got that all figured out?"

"Is it so hard to figure, Mack? You're in love—not sanely, the way I suppose it happens to most people, but it's a sickness with you."

"And who am I in love with, Irma?"

"Sylvia," she said, "and I think I knew it the first time you mentioned her name."

8

I had no trouble locating John Karoki. I dropped in to see Franklin the following day, and he drew a respectable make on Karoki: three drunk arrests, two disorderly conducts, one assault, two impairing of morals, one carnal knowledge, and one petty theft. Altogether, there were three convictions and two years eight months in the Iron City Jail.

"It's the constant association with this kind of upright citizen that makes it a pleasure to be a cop. What do you want with him, Macklin?"

"Just a few words."

"Well, you sure select your associates—first Fiselli and now this lousy crumb."

"Do you have his address?"

"The last we have is 207 Peabody. That's about a mile from here. Go up Liberty and bear left. It's a little alley. Ask a cop if you need help."

"I'll ask a cop, Franklin."

"You don't need to be so touchy," Franklin said. "I did what I could to help you."

I said good-by to Franklin and I apologized to him as best I could and I gave him ten dollars, the better for him to loathe himself and myself too. You meet someone like Franklin and you go away from him. Two people touch each other; you touch Franklin, Fiselli, Brady, and Irma Olanski—and with the high and the low and the clean and the dirty, you leave the same unfulfilled threads of yearning that give human beings the common sense of missing the reason and purpose that put them on earth.

Then I went to John Karoki, who still lived at 207 Peabody. It was a wooden tenement, four stories high, as desolate and maggot-eaten a structure as you will find, even in Pittsburgh. He lived on the top floor, in the rear, and when I stood in the hallway and knocked at the door I didn't know what was worse, the unbearable heat under the tin roof of the tenement or the mixture of obscene smells that cooked in the boiling air. After a few moments there was a shuffling of feet and a thick voice asked who was there.

"John Karoki?"

"Who are you?"

Trying to keep down my stomach, my breakfast, and my unreasonable—for the past was made apart from me and could not be unmade—hatred for the creature behind the door, I replied blandly and smoothly, "My name is Harrison, and I represent the Allstate Surety and Recovery Association. We are a service organization for twenty-seven insurance companies, and one of the things we do is to place out-of-state claims. We held a policy for one Sylvia Karoki. She put in a claim for a lost wrist watch, and after the deductible we allowed her thirty dollars. But we cannot locate her. Since you were mentioned in the policy as the closest surviving relative, namely her father, we are forced by law to pay the money to you and clear our books. Providing you can prove you are John Karoki."

Through the door the thick voice said, "You mean you want to pay me money?"

"Yes, sir. If you are John Karoki."

"How much money?"

"According to the order which came from Southwestern Surety to our Pittsburgh office, thirty dollars."

"Thirty dollars?"

"Yes, thirty dollars."

"I'm John Karoki," he said, and he opened the door.

I was surprised that he was not a tall man. My impression of Sylvia was of a tall woman, but there I may have been right or wrong. This man was shorter than I, in his late fifties, bent, brutish, and smelling of liquor and the unwashed excrement of his own body. He was barefooted, wore a pair of dirty brown chinos, a dirtier T-shirt, and displayed a two- or three-day beard on his loose, fleshy face. His bloodshot eyes were full of suspicion, greed, hunger, and animal cunning.

"I'm Karoki," he said. "You don't believe me—ask the super. Wait a minute, I got a letter somewhere addressed to me."

The door opened into the kitchen of the flat, a kitchen full of disorder, dirty dishes, bits of uncollected food, flies, and cockroaches. He hunted through the kitchen, pulling out drawers and dumping their contents into the general chaotic disorder, tipping and emptying a garbage pail, searching through a pile of rubbish that lay in one corner, until at last he found the letter and showed me his name upon it.

"Then you're Sylvia Karoki's father?"

"That's right."

"Do you know her present whereabouts? It won't change

your receiving the money. My instructions are to deliver it to you. But we would like to have an address for her if you can supply it."

"Mister, I don't know where that lousy floozie is and I don't want to know."

"I'm talking about your daughter."

"So am I, mister. Look at me. Look at the way I live here. That's the reward I got from my daughter—don't care I'm alive or dead."

"When did you last hear from her, Mr. Karoki?"

"Maybe fifteen years ago. She walked out on me and her dying mother—and that's the last I ever hear of her."

"All right, Mr. Karoki. Now about the money—you want a check or cash?"

"I'll take cash. Yeah—cash. But how do I know you're telling me the truth? Maybe that watch was worth two hundred dollars."

"You'll just have to take my word for it, Mr. Karoki—the way I'm taking yours."

"What do I get—a lousy thirty bucks? Sure, you say to yourself I'm just a bum. Look at the way I'm standing here. So what is it, a hundred bucks for you, thirty for me?"

I took a twenty and a ten out of my pocket, handed it to him, and left. As I went down the stairs he screamed after me:

"Cheap, lousy crook—you'd rob the dead, wouldn't you?"

9

I met Irma outside the library at a few minutes after five o'clock, and after a word of greeting we walked silently toward her apartment. It was such a late-summer afternoon as one knows in memory—and in the memories of the generation before us—the whole world bathed in the golden glow of summertime and in a sighing warmth that slowed your steps without oppression.

At her house she turned to me and said, "Well, Mack?"

"I'm leaving on the midnight flight to El Paso, Irma."

"Yes. To find Sylvia?"

"A part of her."

"You know, Mack," Irma said quietly, "I never asked you why you had to learn what Sylvia was. I thought that if you wanted to tell me you would tell me. I know that someone hired you. Then I began to think that you were afraid to tell me what you were hired for."

"You were right, Irma."

"You don't have to tell me if you don't want to."

"I guess I want to tell you."

She nodded and asked me would I come upstairs with her and have a cup of tea. I followed her up to her apartment, and I sat quietly, watching her while she put up a kettle to cook and sliced a loaf of packaged pound cake—probably the same type of pound cake she had fed Sylvia here in this room. She set the table carefully and neatly, with all the precise and meticulous motions of a person who has lived a long time alone, and then she poured the tea and we sat down at the table. And I told her, more or less as it had happened, why I searched for the ghost of Sylvia.

For a while after I finished she made no comment. She looked at me during that time, but not with anger or annoyance. Then she said, "You must have wanted that money a great deal, Mack."

I said nothing. What could I say? Whatever goes for a soul in Alan Macklin sat there naked.

PART 4

EL PASO

IT WAS HOT IN EL PASO. I HAD AN AIR-COOLED ROOM AT THE Hilton Hotel, which was fortunate, but in the streets the thermometer did better than one hundred degrees on the days I was there. I wore a blue jersey sport shirt and a pair of gray flannel daks that Mr. Summers' fee had paid for, and I got to know El Paso a little—but only a little. You don't get to know a city quickly; it takes time. To make this a more meticulous account, I must also add that before I left El Paso I bought a pair of brown cotton slacks and I bought a sombrero in Juárez, but after an hour of pretending that I was a Texan and shattering the illusion with my Chicago accent I gave the sombrero to a small Mexican boy who was picking over a pile of peanut shells to find one or two that might still have peanuts in them. I also gave him a dollar, and I was frowned upon by a motherly, starched little American lady who looked like Whistler's mother and who told me that I was spoiling them and Juárez too.

I tried seriously not to spoil Juárez, or El Paso either, for that matter. I bought the cotton slacks—they were a mixture of cotton and dacron, to be perfectly accurate—because my gray daks were stained and torn in two places when I was thrown out of an important cat house in Juárez, a place that was partially owned by an Arab who lived in San Diego. He was an absentee male-madam-pimp of sorts and looked down upon by local management.

By that time I had talked to a great many of the local management and working girls in the red-light district of Juárez and of El Paso too. I drew a blank everywhere, and here and there some anger and annoyance, but it was only in the Arab's place that I was beaten up and thrown out.

There is an American legend to the effect that being beaten is a not unpleasant and sometimes rewarding experience, and this peculiar illusion is bolstered by television and films. Perhaps we live in an age when it is necessary to forget that the body is a delicate and fragile mechanism and to propagate the notion that it is indestructible, as witness an endless procession of cowhands and private eyes who neither break their fists in dealing out punishment worthy of a Neanderthaler nor have their own faces and innards broken by receiving the same. Myself, I have found that most sane men do not throw punches —if only because there are laws against assault and battery and because a lawsuit against a man too handy with his fists can be expensive.

But those kinds of laws are not effective in Juárez. All I wanted was to know whether a girl called Sylvia had worked in one of those places ten or twelve years ago; and in this particular place, maybe she had and maybe she hadn't. They didn't take kindly to my asking, and a Norwegian and two Mexicans gave me a going-over and threw me out onto the street and then kicked me in the belly and head a few times while I lay in the gutter and left me with my face in a pile of dung. Then they rolled me, but I was too far gone to care. In fact, I cared about very little until I woke up the next day in the county hospital out on Almeda Avenue on the American side.

A highway cop was sitting next to my bed, a big, well-fed, square-jawed specimen who greeted me with, "Hello, sweetheart—you back with us for good now?"

"Who are you?" I asked him, my jaw aching as I spoke, my head aching, my belly aching.

"I'm Sergeant Homer, sweetheart, and you're number-one patsy for today—right?"

"You got to call me sweetheart, I suppose."

"Right?"

"Right. I'm number-one patsy. Only it hurts when I talk," I begged him, "so go away now and come back when it doesn't hurt so much."

"It doesn't hurt so much, sweetheart. You just got a stiff jaw, not a busted jaw. In fact, nothing is busted on you except maybe your pride for having your face full of greaser dogshit, which was how they found you. You look better now."

"I don't feel better. Where am I?"

"County hospital. And you know who you are, don't you, sweetheart? You're not going to be one of those goddamned amnesia cases?"

"I know who I am."

"Tell me."

"Why don't you go away now and leave me alone?" I sighed. "You come back later and I'll tell you everything. I'll even tell your fortune, if that's what you want."

The big, round, square-jawed face that seemed to take up half of my area of vision split into a grin, and Officer Homer said to me, "You got slapped around by greasers, sweetheart.

Now you don't want to get yourself slapped around by big grown-up American boys, do you?"

"All right. Just don't call me sweetheart."

"You tell me your name," the grin said, "and then I call you by it. Right, sweetheart?"

"Alan Macklin."

"Alan Macklin? O.K., baby—no more sweetheart. I'll just leave the message with you. Where you from, Alan?"

"Los Angeles."

"And what do you do besides going into whorehouses and asking too many questions about a dame called Sylvia?"

"How do you know about that?" I whispered, my head becoming larger, thicker, and more painful with every word.

"Oh, what are we, Alan? Apes? Idiots? We can't ask questions? Nobody tells us nothing?"

"All right. So I'm trying to find someone called Sylvia."

"Sylvia what?"

"Sylvia Karoki."

"Karoki? What in hell is that? A Jew name? A Jap name?"

"A Hungarian name, I guess. Look, Homer," I begged him again, "I can't talk. My head hurts so damn much I'd just as soon die. If you have to slap me around, I guess you have to."

"Poor sweetheart." The square jaw grinned. "Poor little sweetheart. Tell you what, Alan, you get over that hangover of yours and you and me'll turn a bottle upside down. Just the two of us some quiet evening. I know games——"

I closed my eyes.

"So you're trying to find Sylvia. Why?"

"Because someone hired me. It's a job. I'm a private investigator."

"Oh? So you're a private cop, Alan? And all the time I

thought you were queer for talking to whores and getting slapped around."

The bright, brass-buttoned, leather-bound uniform was swimming before my eyes. The voice went on:

"I still think so."

"Look in my wallet——"

"You ain't got a wallet, baby. You were rolled. You got nothing but a shirt and pants and some cotton underwear. Me, I like the feel of nylon underwear."

"Ask Lieutenant Abbey—El Paso cops—ask him——"

The pain was slipping away, and I had that strange, wonderful euphoria that sometimes precedes unconsciousness. If I was dying, it was a relief and I didn't mind, so long as it removed Officer Homer. I floated off with Homer's vibrant voice reminding me:

"Pecos 4-6000—that's the number, sweetheart. I'll teach you games'll make football seem like potsy. Just curl up and get well, baby. . . ."

2

I remained in the hospital another day, and then the morning after that they signed me out and cashed a check for me for medication and the price of a cab back to the hotel. At the hotel I cashed a larger check, ate a steak and potatoes, drank two glasses of beer, and then went up to my room to smoke a cigarette and rest the pain in my belly. My head had stopped aching; the bruises were bearable and my hands were beginning to heal. But what they called "minor internal injuries" made me wince with pain when I took a deep breath, bent over, moved quickly, or tried to digest any food at all. The hospital food seemed to get along with my internal injuries; the steak kept me writhing and whimpering with pain for hours. The intern at the hospital had said that in another week I would feel like myself, but when I tried to pass a razor over the cuts and bruises on my face I wondered whether the process of shaving would ever be the same again.

After a shave and a hot bath I managed to sleep for a couple of hours. The telephone woke me. It was Lieutenant Abbey, the city cop whom I had dealings with, and he asked me to do myself a favor and come around to police headquarters to see him.

Abbey was what happens to a good many cops who give up and just play it for existence. He was about forty years old, with a hard face that revealed nothing and an attitude that pretended a total disassociation with humanity. He spoke to me in uncolored tones, without like or dislike. After he had motioned for me to sit down alongside his desk, he pushed my wallet over to me and asked me whether it was mine.

"It's mine." I nodded, going through it. Everything was there except the money.

"How much money?"

I told him about three hundred dollars, give or take a few.

"You always carry that much cash?"

"When I got it to carry."

"Well, an old Mex name of Tony Sandoz brought it here."

"Did he say where he got it?"

"Found it in the street. What should he say—that his mother-in-law gave it to him after rolling you?"

"All right. Thank him for me." I put the wallet in my pocket.

"Sure. It's a service he operates. Look, Macklin, people like Sandoz co-operate with us because there's a dollar in it. He expects a reward. That's only natural."

"It's only natural," I agreed. "How much?"

"Fifty."

"What?"

"Half a yard. Don't I talk clear?"

"Yeah, you talk clear," I agreed. I had paid a hundred already for a look at his files and index, three hundred more for the privilege of prowling through bordels in Juárez, hospital costs, and here was another fifty on top.

"Take it off your tax. It's deductible," he said.

"It's a big slice of nothing. Nobody in this town knows when to call it quits, do they?"

"Maybe you don't, Macklin. Nobody invited you here. I don't know nothing gives me such a pain in the ass as private cops. Take your lousy peepshow somewhere else. Go tour the cat houses in your home town. You got your wallet back; you got your papers back. Maybe you'd like to go back to Los Angeles for a new set."

I gave him fifty dollars and left the place, full to the ears with southwestern hospitality. I had been in El Paso eight days, and I had nothing, absolutely nothing—nothing out of the police files, the libraries, the old newspapers—nothing, no trace or indication that anyone called Sylvia Karoki had ever set foot in this city.

3

I remained in El Paso because, short of returning to Pittsburgh and starting over again, there was nothing else I could do. Except that I could quit and give it back to Frederick Summers, but that was also something I could not do—for reasons that became much clearer to me later.

It was too hot to roam the streets on foot, and the headaches continued. I hired a car for eleven dollars a day, which I considered a justifiable expense, and I had a better look at the city and the country around it. If I was short on facts, I would at least look for the nuances of the place and talk to some others than cops and pimps. I drove past ranches and oil wells and broken Mexican huts, and I pulled in for lunch but lost my appetite quickly without eating anything at a roadside place that said, "No dogs, niggers, or greasers wanted." I drove to the Rio Grande to see the green cotton growing on the edge of a trickle of muddy water, and then one day, when the headaches were gone and most of the pains too, out to the Sierra de Cristo Rey, where the great Jesus of Urbici Soler stands on top of its mountain.

Only three miles out of El Paso, Mount Cristo Rey is still a lonely place, and if you are alone they advise you not to embark on the two-hour climb up to the top where the giant statue stands. It was very early in the morning when I got there, and I was alone, except for a Mexican boy of twelve or thirteen years who sat on a rock in the morning shadows and picked his teeth gravely and thoughtfully. He had the fine white teeth of so many Mexican youngsters, a serene manner beyond his years, strikingly handsome features, and a shock of black hair that stood up and out like a firm, strong toupee. He wore old faded and patched blue jeans, a white T-shirt surprisingly clean, and no shoes; and he greeted me with:

"Good morning, señor. You are going to climb to Cristo?"

"They say don't do it alone because you can be knocked over the head on the way up."

"With me you are not alone, señor."

"Oh?"

"My name is Pancho—Frank in English—Pancho Guzman. I was named after Pancho Villa, may he rest in peace. That doesn't offend you?"

"No."

"Good. We will get along. I know all of the bandits, cutthroats, and cheap hoods on the fourteen stations up to where the Holy Jesus himself stands."

"Do you have television?" I smiled.

"Because my speech is interesting? Other tourists tell me so, and I try to cultivate it. We are too poor to have television, but my friend's grandmother has a set which she won in a lottery. I listen to the gangster shows, because the old lady was raised on the old Rancho Running Bar when her father was a vaquero there, and she says that the western shows on the television are all lies and foolishness. Because she listens to gangster shows mostly and private eyes. It will cost you a dollar."

I handed him the dollar and asked him what the fourteen stations were.

"You are not a Catholic, señor?" he asked bluntly.

"No."

"I see. A Christian?"

"That's open to question. You don't mind personal questions, do you?"

"I have an open mind, señor. I am not narrow-minded, like so many are. In Durango, from where my father comes, he says there are plenty of poor Indians who are not even Christians and just as happy as we are, but that always starts a fight with my mother, who is a very good Christian. For myself, I am not narrow-minded. Among all sorts of people I get along very well, señor. I will tell you that in our faith there were fourteen stages of Our Lord's Passion, from the house of Pontius Pilate to the mountain of Calvary. You have heard of these things?" he asked me patiently.

"Yes, I have heard of them."

"Now, señor, as we climb up the mountain to the great

Cristo, there will be fourteen resting places, each with a cross, and they are called the stations."

We began the climb. As we went along through that wonderful still morning, climbing from cross to cross all the long distance up the mountain, Pancho Guzman held forth on Urbici Soler, informing me that he was one of the sculptors who had worked on the great Christ of the Andes, on José Arturbi, who would fight this coming Sunday in the Plaza de Toros and who was wasted on the undersized and inferior bulls they ran, on the way to avoid being cheated in the market place, on whether it was preferable to be a Mexican north or south of the Rio Grande, and on the validity of numerous television programs and movies. He also informed me that he hoped to earn over a hundred dollars before school opened, that he had paid seven dollars for a half interest in the best fighting cock in Juárez, that I would be a fool to miss a cockfight, and that he had won eleven dollars betting time on the killing of the bulls.

We climbed on among the bare rocks and the occasional mesquite, and we met no one, and about two hours after we had begun the climb we stood on the wind-swept top under the great stone figure of Christ, with His patient and sorrowful Mexican face. From here one looked down upon all of El Paso and Juárez and Fort Bliss and its airport, on the brown ribbon of the Rio Grande, on the green patches of cotton field, on parched brown and white mountains that shone with the fire of the morning sun. In an airplane one is removed from the earth and remote from it, but on a mountaintop one is supported by the earth, a part of it, yet above it; and there comes out of that a feeling of peace and fulfillment unlike anything else. I let the peace become a part of me, a desperately needed part, thinking how natural it was that in the ancient times man

made the high places the home of his gods and built their altars there and offered up sacrifice there.

I sat down on a rock beside Pancho, who was watching me with interest and who asked me presently whether it would be too personal a question to inquire why I had climbed this long, weary distance.

"Since when does the degree of a personal question trouble you?"

"Texans are sometimes sensitive."

"I am not a Texan," I told the boy. "I am from Los Angeles."

"I see." The way he said that made it the same thing. He admitted no virtue to California but watched me gravely with his dark eyes. "You are troubled in soul, perhaps?"

"That is very interesting speech." I nodded. "Do you also do therapy?"

He asked me what "therapy" was, and when I had explained he said, "I like that word and I will remember it. I never forget a word in English. However, señor, I can tell you something. I am sometimes of assistance because I know El Paso and Juárez very well indeed."

"I bet you do. And if you wanted to find someone in El Paso, how would you go about it, Pancho?"

His eyes roamed over the distances spread out beneath us, and suddenly I envied this small Mexican boy whose memories of childhood would be washed through and through with the vistas of this mountain. Then he looked at me shrewdly and said:

"Who do you want to find, señor?"

"A woman."

"Ah. You are in love, señor?"

"Someday someone," I told him, "will put you over his knee and clobber you for asking such questions."

"Ha! Just let him try, señor. I got friends on this mountain. What did you say—clobber? Well, they know how to clobber good, you take my word. Tell me, you went to the police?"

I nodded.

"You look in the telephone book?"

I smiled.

"You be surprised—people are not as smart as they think they are. In this town the police, the priests, and the pimps know most about everyone. The pimps are liars, the police you have been to, and the priests keep their mouths shut. Me, I think a lot of trouble comes from looking for people. In Juárez there are always Texans looking for people. I think it is an Anglo trait."

"Are there many priests in El Paso—Juárez?"

"You can be sure."

"And you know some of them?"

The boy shrugged. "What can I tell you about priests? You are not a Catholic, so you can't possibly understand about priests. I would try to make it simple by saying that, as with other people, there are all kinds of priests."

Then he added, "But they will all keep their mouths shut."

"Pancho," I said to him very seriously, "tell me this. Suppose a Catholic is dying and wants to be absolved of his sins. Let us say that this is a man with plenty of sin, a cheap con man, a petty thief, a total punk and two-bit hoodlum—worse than that. I don't know what kind of a sin it is for a man to impersonate a priest as part of a con game——"

"A very important sin." The boy nodded, his eyes wide with interest now.

"Well, he did it—all of it. If he were dying, what priest would be called to give him the last rites?"

It was as wide and as woeful and random a shot as I had

ever tried, and it made the boy grin with derision, whether at my question or my assumptions of the details of his faith, I don't know. I felt that he was laughing at me politely and internally. I took another dollar out of my pocket and placed it on his knee. He fingered it, turned it over, and then folded it carefully and placed it in his pocket.

"In Juárez or in El Paso?" he asked.

"Either or both."

"Does he die in two places, señor? No—I will explain with seriousness. If such a man dies in El Paso, maybe they call the police chaplain, maybe they run to the closest Catholic church, maybe they just let him die—who knows? In Juárez, if such a man is dying, they will try to find Father Gonzales."

"Why?"

"Ah! How can I explain? Father Gonzales is a very poor priest for poor people, and full of patience. They say that in his own youth he was not without sin himself. You hear all kinds of things. But he is special in such things, with—what do you say?—yes, understanding. He is priest for the old, old mission on Chihuahua Street. It is not a very successful place. Even the tourists do not come there. But it would be interesting to talk to him about your problem."

"It would be interesting," I admitted.

4

A live oak had survived and grown to a good girth, so that it threw its dappled shade over the whole front yard. The early-evening sun gave it a piebald trunk. It was old and patient and deep-rooted. Underneath it the ground was yellow and devoid of even a blade of grass, and the walls of the mission were the same dry mustard color. I sat on a wooden bench with my back to the mission wall and listened to the sound of Vespers through the open door. It was a cool and restful place to sit. The bench itself was handmade, a thick slab of hand-hewn wood three inches thick and about seven feet long, with four legs pegged through it and a patina of great age over its surface. It felt cool and smooth under my fingers.

Vespers finished, and the priest came out and stood by the door while about a dozen people filed past him. They were old peons, plain Indian people, bent and tired from their day's labor, men and women. The priest looked upon each of them tenderly and thoughtfully. He himself was Indian, with a broad brown face, every inch of which was seamed and lined with a maze of wrinkles. In his long, shapeless black coat he might have been fifty or a hundred years old; I had no way of knowing.

Ordinarily I do not look with a kind eye on priests or any other kind of clergy, but about this particular man there was an air of compassion and humility that made me suspend any judgment. When his people had gone, he walked slowly over to me and nodded and said with only a trace of a Spanish accent:

"I am Father Gonzales. Are you waiting for me?"

I stood up and replied that I was waiting for him and told him my name, and then we shook hands. His hand was rough and hard and very strong. Then he sat down on the bench and indicated for me to sit beside him. For about five minutes we sat there in silence. I waited for him to speak, and when he did he said:

"This old tree, Mr. Macklin, is a live oak."

"I know. It's a fine tree."

"I think it gives us a little bit of distinction. There is no use pretending that this old church of mine is anything else than exactly what it is—a poor little dobe building that has seen all of its best days. But the tree gives it character, and the sunlight repairs my walls better than any mason could. You are not of my faith, are you, Mr. Macklin?"

"No."

"And you do not approve of my faith, do you?"

"How do you know?"

"Your attitude toward me, sir. You are somewhat suspicious. 'Who is this old Mexican priest?' you are asking yourself. You intend to suspend judgment. I also suspend judgment, Mr. Macklin. As I grow older I find that my talents for judgment decrease."

"I am sorry," I said. "The last thing in the world I desired was to offend you."

"Ah!" The old man smiled; an old man, no doubt about it now, and when he smiled, the broad, flat Indian face lost all of its bitter memories. "Have I said that you offended me, sir? No—no—it may be that I am more garrulous than an old man has any right to be, but you can look at it another way too, yes? I don't have the time it takes for one human soul to approach and know another, and it may be that I forget that in your country a man builds a wall around himself. When I see a man, I try to find him—and do you know, Mr. Macklin, I am even pleased when one of your people comes to me. For any reason. We are hardly more than a mile from the border of your country, but we are also a great, immeasurable distance apart."

"Yes, I suppose we are," I said. "You haven't asked me what I want with you, Father Gonzales."

"In your own good time you will tell me. As far as I know, my work is over for today. Unless your time is limited?"

"I have nothing else to do."

"Good. Have you eaten?"

"No. But I'm not hungry."

"Is that to be said—even to a poor man? I think that hunger is like grace; we should never be without a little bit of it. I live alone here, but there is a pot of our good brown beans in the stove and fresh tortillas I buy down the street here. I also have cold beer. If you don't mind plain Mexican food?"

"I would be pleased and honored."

He rose and said, "Then I will go for the tortillas now. Do you wish to remain here or come with me? We can talk while we eat and after we eat."

I went with him, down the street and into the next street, where, in the old Mexican manner, there were only dobe walls broken by doorways but not by windows. I followed the priest through one of these doorways, through a bare poverty-pinched room that contained a bed, a chair, and a wooden trunk, into a little back yard. There a tiny and withered Indian woman knelt in front of a low stove made of a sheet of metal supported by rocks. A fire of glowing coals burned under the metal. As we entered, the woman turned her head to see us, nodded, and said something in Spanish to the priest. He smiled and replied in Spanish, and she took dough from a pan beside her, rolled it into a ball, tossed it from hand to hand with speed and dexterity until it took the form of a thin pancake about seven inches in diameter. She placed it on the hot sheet and made another and then another. While she was doing this, the old man said to me:

"You see less and less of the tortilla made this way, Mr. Macklin. We now have machines. But they never have the taste and the flavor when they come from machines—nor the delicacy. This is the old, old bread of Mexico, the bread of the Mexican people in the countless generations before the Spaniards came here—so it is a little bit sacred"—he said this almost apologetically—"in the way that all bread is a little bit sacred. Perhaps you are surprised that I call it bread. But you know, in the beginning all the people of the earth made their bread this same way, as flat cakes—yes, in Europe and the Middle East, and Asia and Africa too. So you see that we people of the earth have something most profound in common. The bread of man's life is very profound and very true."

I stared at the old man, and something in my face must have made him wonder whether I believed him. I think he was hurt a little, as if I had betrayed some confidence or as if he had misjudged me.

"Oh no," I said. "It is perfectly true. You see, I was trained to be a teacher of ancient history."

"But you are not a teacher now, Mr. Macklin?"

"No. I'm a private detective."

"Oh? I think you are an unusual private detective, no?"

"As much or as little as you are an unusual priest."

He shrugged his shoulders and laughed. The tortillas were ready now. The woman wrapped them in a piece of paper, and the priest paid her. Then we went back to the mission. The mission itself was only a square, almost unadorned room, the simplest Catholic church I have ever seen: an altar, a crucifix and a confessional and a few other ritual elements, plain wooden benches on a brick floor grooved and polished by the bare feet of generations of peons. At the back of the church was the priest's room—a cot, two chairs, a table, and a clay stove where the beans warmed over embers. I sat in one of the chairs while the old man put the tortillas on a clay dish next to the beans. He then took two onions from a box in one corner, peeled them and sliced them onto a plate—hoping meanwhile that I would not object to onions raw, which were very good with the beans. I told him that I liked onions, and he was very pleased. He had a childlike pleasure reaction to simple and unimportant things. He set the table with brown clay dishes and mugs and then went out through the back door of the mission, to return a moment later with two bottles of beer, explaining that he kept two bottles cool in the well, for the enjoyment of his occasional guests.

"Tortillas, beans, onions, and beer—there is the food of my people, except that the beer would be for a saint's day. It is very plain food, but also very good food. Do you think so, Mr. Macklin?"

He had set out no table utensils, so I followed his example and spooned up the beans in pieces of hot tortilla, with a slice of onion and a mouthful of beer to wash it down. I had eaten pinto beans and tortillas in Los Angeles, but not like this, and the beer was cold and pale and clear. I was also very hungry, and I ate ravenously until the tortillas were gone and my stomach was full and comfortable and myself at least a little at peace. While we ate we exchanged only a few words, and when the beer and the food were gone the old man said to me, smiling gently so that there would be no edge to his words:

"Well, Mr. Macklin—what do you think now? That I am an old fraud with a cellar full of fat chickens and good wine—but I bring out this plain Mexican food for tourists?"

I admitted that such a thought had crossed my mind.

"Because our church is fat and rich?" he asked me. "Because we are full of devilish superstitions and we worship idols and we propagate such lies as hell and purgatory?"

"I'm no anti-Catholic," I said. "I leave religion alone—and I only ask that it leave me alone." The priest nodded, but without rancor. "I came to you because I heard good things about you."

"And who said these good things, Mr. Macklin?"

"A little boy I met out at Mount Cristo Rey—name of Pancho."

"Yes—yes. And what good things did he say, if I may ask?"

"Of course. He said that when here in Juárez an evil man lies dying, a man almost beyond redemption, they will call you if there is time to call you."

The slow smile appeared on the old man's face again, but this time it was contemplative and full of memory. He wondered why I should consider these things as good things said about him.

"Because you have to love people a good deal to give comfort to that kind."

"Or know them, Mr. Macklin? Have you ever thought about how hard it is for a good man to deal with evil?"

I replied that I hadn't—nor was I certain what he meant by a "good man."

"One who has not been tempted, Mr. Macklin."

"I'm afraid I don't look at things that way."

"No, you would not," he agreed. "How old do you think I am, Mr. Macklin?"

I shook my head, and when he waited I ventured that he was perhaps sixty-eight or seventy years old. Now his smile was quick and impish, like a small boy tricking adults. "Eighty-eight, Mr. Macklin," he said. "Eighty-eight years of watching the few joys and many sorrows of this earth. I was born in 1870, Mr. Macklin, not thirty miles from here, on the old Hacienda Grande. My father was one of three hundred peons who belonged to Señor Fortez, the master of the hacienda. I was one of eleven children, one of three who survived past the tenth year. And never, between my birth and his grave, did I see my father smile or my mother smile. My mother died when I was six. I ran away and got across the river, and first I was a candy-wagon boy and then vaquero on the Triangle Ranch in the Guadalupe country. Then I fought a cowboy who, as I felt then, had insulted me and my people, and when he drew his gun I killed him with my knife. But then I learn to use the gun, and by the time I am nineteen I have kill five men who will not believe that a Mexican can carry a gun and use it too. I am outlaw, with a thousand dollars on my head, and I ride and hide from here to Santa Fe and then across into California. I am vaquero sometimes, but always full of braggadocio and swagger and primed with hate of everything and using women to build my esteem and my gun to maintain it. Do you wonder that I who am a priest can talk about all this? Well, Mr. Macklin, because I knew and experienced so much of evil, because I broke every law of man and God—for that reason, I do not judge. I say to myself that if I am permitted to remain so long on this earth it is because I have work to do that must be done. Perhaps I am well fitted to hear the confession of evil men—for most of them are not evil, only lost and full of frustration and hatred of themselves. Did you know such a man, Mr. Macklin? Did you come to me because you think that I might have given him absolution when he lay dying?"

"Do you read minds too?" I whispered. He shook his head and smiled sadly and replied:

"No—no. Why else should you come here? I am an old, old man whom the Church permits to do his work—maybe because who else would come to such a poor old mission? So why would you come to me otherwise, Mr. Macklin?"

"I'm sorry."

"For what, Mr. Macklin? Because you made the mistake of thinking me a good man? That is not such a bad mistake. Very soon I go to where they will weigh my many sins against my few virtues. Will it hurt for Mr. Macklin's praise to be remembered?" His smile became impish again. "But of course a civilized North American like yourself does not believe such nonsense as heaven and hell. No—I am sorry now that I tease you, but this too is a sign of regard. My heart must go out to a man, especially a gringo, before I will dare to tease him. Tell me why you have come to me?"

I told him. I told him that I was a poor detective who worked with long notions and flights of fancy—and because a young punk from Pittsburgh who lived by a church con and called himself Peter the Priest had possibly come to El Paso, where there was no police record of him or anyone like him, wasn't there also a thin long shot that he had gotten into something in Juárez?

"Not such a poor detective, Mr. Macklin, for isn't it true that we all look for the part of our world that is hidden, and who ever achieves it without dreams and fancies and desperate guesses? When was this?"

"Ten or eleven years ago."

"And why do you feel that this man—Peter the Priest— why do you feel that he died in Juárez?"

"The truth is," I said, "that I can't even be sure that he was ever in Juárez or El Paso. I am just going by the supposition that in El Paso such a man would get into trouble with the cops. He didn't. Well, then either he never got there—or he went over into Juárez. And if he didn't die in Juárez, then why didn't he come back to El Paso? Of course all this is the wildest kind of supposition."

"Did you go to the police in Juárez?"

"I went. But this was a long time ago, and your police don't keep what we call MO records, the details of a man's habit of crime. It was a question of a name. Whatever his real name is, I don't know it."

"I know it, Mr. Macklin," the old man said calmly.

"What?"

"I know the name of this man you call Peter the Priest. He lies buried in the cemetery behind my church. And later, if you desire, I will take you to his grave. But meanwhile, do you want me to tell you the story of how he comes to lie there?"

Wordless, I could only nod.

"Then come with me to the bench where we were sitting before, in front of the mission," the old man asked me. "The sun is setting, and it is pleasant there."

5

A decade before, the priest had sat in the same place, resting his body, allowing the fatigues of age to slough away from him, and perhaps searching through his many memories for answers to questions that can't be answered, not even for a priest. He had lowered his eyes to the yellow soil. When he raised them, the girl stood under the tree. She stood in a dapple of passing sunlight, with her rich dark hair falling over her shoulders. Her dress? The priest would hardly remember, but a plain dress that hung loosely. Bare legs and bare arms. Mexican sandals —the kind that are made far in the south, in Oaxaca, and shipped to the border for the tourist trade. No paint on her face, but it was a high-boned sunburned face that needed no paint. How old was she? Sixteen—perhaps seventeen years old. Particularly, he had noticed the way she stood, relaxed very straight, like the Indian women in the south who carry their burdens on their heads. He had a fleeting notion that she might be Mexican; but she was tall, taller than a Mexican girl.

"Was her name Sylvia?" I asked the old man.

"Yes, Mr. Macklin."

"Sylvia Karoki?"

"I believe that was her family name. It was a long time ago, so I might be mistaken."

"But not about the name Sylvia?"

"No—no, Mr. Macklin. Her name was Sylvia."

6

"*Yo necesito ayuda. Por favor——*"

Her Spanish was accented but understandable—the kind that one picks up quickly by ear if one has the ear for it. The old man said to her:

"Please—speak English, my dear. I am at home with English."

"You are Father Gonzales?" She came closer to him.

"Yes, I am Father Gonzales."

"Will you help me—please?"

"If I can help you, child. Come over here and sit down and tell me what troubles you."

She sat on the bench, at the other end from the old man, but never taking her eyes from him.

"You are a priest?"

"Yes—yes, of course. Are you a Catholic, my child?"

She shook her head woefully. "No. I am no religion. But over in the morgue a Catholic is lying dead. He died without grace or absolution——"

"Who is he? A Mexican?"

"No. An American."

"How did he die, my child?"

"He was murdered. He got into a fight, and two of the men he was fighting with used their knives against him."

The priest nodded. He had compassion for her and for the

dead man—compassion for the travelers on every and any by-path of violence. "But he is dead now?"

"Yes."

"Then what can I do for him, my child? It is too late for me to hear his confession."

"You understand, Father, he is lying in the morgue. I asked the captain of police there—what will he do with the body? He said that for such scum there is the city cemetery and slaked lime. I come to you to ask you to take his body away and bury it in your consecrated ground. And then to do whatever you can for his poor damned soul."

"But you don't believe in immortal souls."

"No!" she cried fiercely. "No, I don't! Not in your God, either, Father! Not in any God! I am being truthful!"

"Be truthful, please." The priest nodded. "That is always the best way. But if that is how you feel, why should you come to me with such a request?"

"Because he believed."

"I don't understand you, my child," the old man said. "Are you his widow?"

"No!"

"Then you loved him?"

"I hated him!"

The old man spread his arms hopelessly and looked at Sylvia. He said nothing but waited, and presently Sylvia said to him:

"Be truthful! All priests are the same."

"No more than all men are the same," Father Gonzales answered gently.

"I asked you to help me. What difference does all this make?"

"No difference, my child."

"Then you will bring him here for burial?"

"He has no relatives, friends?"

"No one. No one in the world except myself."

"Then I don't think it should be too difficult to have his body brought here for burial. What is his name?"

"Frank Paterno."

"I see." The priest rose and took her hand. "Now, my child, we'll go to the police and talk to them."

7

It was twilight now, and the sky was a mantle of fading roses. The priest stood up and motioned for me to follow him, and without asking any questions I went after him into the cemetery, where Frank Paterno (alias Peter the Priest) was buried. His grave was marked with a wooden cross upon which were his name and the dates of his birth and his death. I looked at the words and dates and then stood there in the deepening twilight, lost in my thoughts and speculations. After a few minutes I nodded at the old man. We went into his room, and he lit an oil lamp and invited me to sit down.

"If I am not mistaken, Mr. Macklin," the priest said, "it is not the man but the woman that you care about?"

"Is that why you tell me a story without meaning or substance, Father Gonzales?"

"Well, Mr. Macklin, how much meaning and substance is there in this world of ours? When you are very young, you lock hands with the earth, and together there is a great and unshakable structure to stand up for all eternity. But with age it shimmers a little, doesn't it, Mr. Macklin? Its form becomes less certain—less enduring. You have seen that begin to happen with yourself, haven't you, Mr. Macklin?"

"What has it got to do with the case in question?"

"I have seen it, Mr. Macklin—to the point where truth and falsehood, real and unreal—it blurs and changes constantly. Is it just the meandering of a foolish and senile old man?"

"You are not a foolish and senile old man, Father Gonzales," I said, watching him thoughtfully. "You are a Mexican who talks English with all the authority and easy vocabulary of a scholar trained in the language. You are the priest of perhaps the poorest church in all the Southwest—and yet I think you are one of the most worldly men I have met. You served me the food of a plain peon, but you invested it with all the trappings of an epicure."

"Then, God help me, I have much penance to do."

"Have you, sir?"

"You are a very discerning man, Mr. Macklin," he sighed. "But I have no mysteries. Remember that, like so many of my countrymen here on the border, I was raised with two languages. I have spoken English since I was a child. I studied in the seminary in the Distrito Federal and then in Rome—and I have lived a long, long time. If this little church of mine is a poor place to you, it is a place of many riches to me, Mr. Macklin . . ." His voice trailed away.

"Enriched further with the body of Frank Paterno?"

"Perhaps. Who knows? He wanted only a few feet of ground."

"A thief, a pimp, a man who made his living out of the trappings of priesthood, a worthless——"

He interrupted me. "Who measures that, Mr. Macklin? Who holds the scales and puts a human soul in balance?"

"There," I said, "is the impossibility of argument with a cleric. You have a euphemism for everything."

"And you have a rationale, haven't you, Mr. Macklin?"

"I would like to have one. You have told me something and you told me nothing. Why was Sylvia Karoki exerting herself for the corpse of a man she had hated?"

"I can't tell you that, Mr. Macklin."

"You mean you won't tell me."

"Yes."

"Why?"

"Isn't it plain to you, Mr. Macklin?" the old man asked me, a forlorn note in his voice. "I am a priest. How can I reveal what was told to me when someone opened their heart to me?"

"Why can't you? It was not a confession, was it?"

"In that sense, no. She never confessed herself to me. She never attested to any religion or belief. She was a strange girl —or woman would be better, because she was no longer a child but a woman—and that is why the image and memory of her remain fixed so strongly after all these years."

"A prostitute! A whore in Juárez!"

"That is no worse than being a whore in El Paso, Mr. Macklin—and when you consider it, are we not all whores to one extent or another? I am old enough, Mr. Macklin, and you are worldly enough not to be taken in by the hypocrisy and cant that attend all this. We all sell ourselves—only with some the price for such sale is paid almost entirely by the seller. Do I talk strangely? I try to understand what we call sin, not merely to condemn it. My heart went out to this Sylvia Karoki—shall I tell you why?"

I nodded.

"Because she was full of pride and strength—not the pride that comes out of wealth or family or power or achievement— what we call in Spanish *soberbia*, a word that cannot be properly translated, and *ánimo*, which is also hard to translate and does not mean exactly the same thing, but the two of them, pride and courage and honor, for want of a better translation. How shall I explain? Long, long ago, on the hacienda where I lived as a child, a peon did something—raised his hand to an overseer, talked back, or did some small thing like that—and for punishment they tied him to the house post and lashed him to break his pride. With every ten lashes the overseer would look into his face and ask, 'Enough?' If he said, 'Enough,' they would have stopped. But he could not say this, and they whipped him until he died. Do you understand what I was trying to tell you?"

"I think I do," I said.

"Such a woman, a man meets once in a great long while——"

"Yes, once in a great long while."

"She stayed here with me," the priest said. "For five days. She had no other place to go."

"But you wanted her to stay."

"Yes, I wanted her to stay, Mr. Macklin. If I were a young man, Mr. Macklin, I would have said to myself that a woman like this one is all that a man can ask of life or fortune. I am not afraid to remember my youth or the passions that went with it, but those passions are cooled a long, long time. I was almost eighty when Sylvia was here. I gave her my bed and I slept on a pallet in the church, and I felt like a father whose child had come back to him—myself, Mr. Macklin, who never had a child of my own blood."

8

After the morning prayers, on the third day after she had come there, the priest walked around to the back of the church—to where Sylvia was washing his clothes in an old iron basin. He remembered the lithe shape of the girl in the morning sunshine, her black hair tied in back of her head, her strong brown arms buried in the pile of suds and clothes. She never entered the church during any of the offices, and during those times she remained either in the churchyard or the priest's room. After their initial meeting she did not again express any attitude toward religion, nor did Father Gonzales press the subject. Now he told her that it was thoughtful but unnecessary for her to wash his clothes.

"I eat your food, Father," she said, standing up from the basin and wiping back a strand of hair with one wet hand.

"Not my food, Sylvia. No food is *my* food. When there is food, I eat it, and I am happy for the good taste of it and the warm food in my belly. But when a stranger sits at my table, I am even happier when he eats it."

"Why do you keep doing that?" she demanded.

"Doing what, my child?"

"Parading yourself before me as a good man."

"Have I been doing that, Sylvia? I didn't mean to. But even if I do—what harm?"

"You told me that a lie is harmful."

"Yes?"

"There aren't any good men, Father Gonzales. You are very old. You have no passion left. It dried up. Do you think you can make a Catholic out of me by showing me how a man acts—when he has no blood or passion or anger left?"

"No—no, I don't think so."

"Then leave me alone!"

"Yes."

"And don't tell me how it makes you happier when someone else eats your food!"

"Yes, my child—if that is what you wish."

An hour later she was weeping and pleading with him to forgive her.

9

"Yet you tell me this," I said to Father Gonzales.

"As something that happened, not as her confession to me. In a strange way she was right. We become old, Mr. Macklin, and who is to say what is virtue and what is saturation and weariness? I never won even a nod for my faith, Mr. Macklin, but I think I won her trust and a little love. She was a very strange person, this Sylvia of yours."

"Of mine, sir?"

"I say 'of yours,' Mr. Macklin, because I think that you love her—more than that, I think your life is obsessed with her in a way that I don't understand and, I think, do not want to understand. She had something of the same quality—an obsession that precluded the world. She did things without pleasure—but because she was compelled to do them. Do you know what I mean?"

"I don't think I do."

"Well—my books, for example." He rose and went to a little bookshelf that stood against the wall. "I have only a few —my clerical books, a Bible in Latin, a copy of *Don Quixote* in Spanish, a copy of *Huckleberry Finn*—a book I cherish—a dictionary in English and in Spanish, *The Lives of the Saints* in Spanish, and a copy of *War and Peace* in English translation, which I have read many times for the great wisdom and repose I can take from it, just as I take a little laughter and some wisdom too and a better understanding of the gringo from *Huckleberry Finn*. Do you know that Sylvia read both English books, *Huckleberry Finn* in one afternoon, and then *War and Peace* in all its great length with a kind of driving need. Not with joy or repose, but with the ferocious hunger of a starving man who is given food."

I had followed him over to the bookshelf and examined the copy of *War and Peace* which he held out to me. I felt that I was handling a book that Sylvia had read, and I felt like a fool. He watched me and said:

"When she left me after five days, Mr. Macklin, she had finished most of that book, not all of it, but most of it."

"Why do you think she stayed with you five days, Father Gonzales? Not to read a book?"

The old priest nodded and said, "Both of you with the same hurt and the same need to hurt. When a person is filled with the need to love and the desire for love, and love brings only hurt and sorrow, then such a person strikes out wildly at the first sign of warmth and kindness."

"I'm sorry."

"What more can I do for you, Mr. Macklin? I can't tell you her confidences. I can tell you that she returned an obligation to this man, Frank Paterno, whom she hated, because he had done something for her. Her quality was not the quality of my people or my faith. It was puritanical. She composed her own morality, if you would call it that, very stern and very rigid. Life plays its tricks on ninety-nine people and they become broken, spiritless, and they bow their heads and accept. How many such people I have known, God help them! But then there is one who will not break and will not bow. I know. I know, Mr. Macklin, because I remember in myself——"

"And after she went away, did you ever see her again, Father?"

"One day—once."

10

On that day the old man had remained in the church after Vespers. He sat on one of the wooden benches, facing the altar, his mind full of memories, full of the sunlight and swirling dust and echoing movement of the past, full of the pageant of people he had known whose lives were a part of his corner of the Southwest. He sat there, lost in his own thoughts, and was not aware of Sylvia until she sat down beside him and put her hand upon his and whispered:

"*Buenas tardes, padre.*"

"*Bienvenida.*" His reply came as a whisper too, and he felt a glow of warmth, of comfort, of happiness. What could he have been thinking? he asked himself again and again in the years that followed. What had Sylvia come to mean to him? He told me that somewhere in his heart was the foolish dream and hope that she had come back to remain with him, that she would live here in the poverty-stricken nakedness of the mission, that she would care for him in his last years, as a daughter might—but he also added that such a flight of fancy was just that and no more. Yet his pleasure at her return was very great —even when she told him,

"I am going away, padre. I came to say good-by."

"That was very thoughtful of you, my child."

"No. I don't do thoughtful things, padre. But I also couldn't go away without saying good-by."

"Yes." He realized that she, like himself, was filled with emotion. "Where are you going?" he asked her.

"To New York. I'm leaving tonight—in just a few hours."

Now he saw that she was wearing a new dress, new shoes. She carried a purse. Her hair had been washed and set carefully. He asked no questions, but neither did she lie to him. She had never dissembled with him, and he had never reproached her.

"I met a man, padre, a salesman. He gave me some money and he is taking me to New York with him. I can't stay here."

"No, I don't suppose you can." The priest nodded.

brought Sylvia to me. Will you take my blessing for both of you?"

I said that I would. Somehow, for the moment, I had forgotten that Frederick Summers existed.

12

I desired only to get out of El Paso. The thermometer went up to one hundred and five degrees and remained there. The headaches that followed the beating returned again. I slept poorly or not at all, and I stopped counting the hours I spent in the darkness of my room, smoking cigarettes and waiting for dawn to break. I had a window facing east, and five times I watched the glorious southwestern sun rise out of the hills and desert and observed it sourly and wearily.

During the daytime hours I examined ancient hotel records. I bribed clerks and bookkeepers and expensively dressed, successful accountants; a little bit of tax-free money goes a long way. I pored over ledgers and deciphered hundreds of scrawled registration cards. I had the year, the month, the week, and possibly the two days; and men have been located with far less of a lead. I had to make a geographical presumption and, acting on the basis that a salesman who sells El Paso does not also sell New York, I granted my unknown traveler a base within fifty miles of New York City, and preferably the city itself.

I found nothing. In two hotels, records were maintained only for seven years. It might have been those hotels, but I found nothing. And then, after six days of searching, I recalled something—that Sylvia had come to the priest after Vespers and that she had come to say good-by because she was leaving El Paso that same night.

I added my first touch to my nebulous picture of my salesman. He was a respectable man, a married man, a family man.

Very likely the father of children. His hotel arrangements were made by the company he worked for and in that sense were public arrangements. Such a man thinks twice or three times before bringing a woman up to his room. My man was a careful man, a prudent man, a thoughtful man. He had finished his business and checked out of his hotel and made his preparations to leave El Paso before he consummated his arrangements with Sylvia.

He had been a thorough man, and I also became a thorough and careful man. I checked the bus, airplane, and railroad schedules of a decade before. If he had left El Paso for New York City after nine o'clock at night, he had driven his own car.

Why I hated him so unreasonably and malevolently, I did not know. I had no hatred for Fiselli or for the old man, Karoki; but this man I hated, despised, and desired to harm.

I manufactured him piece by piece. I became a part of his own eagerness with Sylvia sitting beside him. He would drive no more than two hours, less if possible—possibly no farther than the first decent motel. I hired a car, and on Route 80, less than half a mile outside city limits, I turned into the parking lot of the El Rancho. It had been built seven years before. The next mile yielded three newly built motels and one that reached back to 1947. It was owner-operated, and he poured me a drink before we sat down to bargain. We agreed that I would give him fifty dollars if I drew a blank, a hundred dollars if I found what I wanted. He left his wife to run the motel, and I drove him in to El Paso.

On the way he told me about his accountants, Peabody, Cohen and Sandoz. He stressed the fact that while many motel owners kept records for five or seven years, any client of Peabody, Cohen and Sandoz kept permanent records for the duration of their business lives. That way, there could be no mistakes, no fuzzy memories. He instructed me on the fact that the motel business was not like any other business, not like the hotel business, not in any way like the hotel business. He was a thin, pale man, completely bald, with a long, narrow head that kept nodding with his words. He licked his lips constantly; he nodded his head and licked his lips, and he had a strong, indecent body odor.

"You can't run a hot hotel, but nobody even blinks at a hot motel. All of them are hot—some more, some less. Even mine. You know that, mister, even mine. I like to be honest. Either you're a longnose or you ain't. I ain't. Anyway, what in hell could we do? Run them through a lie detector? I sign in guests at three o'clock. Two hours later they check out. Am I supposed to hold them there? It's a free country. You don't need no marriage certificate to travel. At least I run a decent place. Some of these places—they change their linen six times a day. Encourage kids. The hell with that. When I see them under twenty, then I want to see their marriage certificate. You agree with me, Mr. Macklin?"

I said nothing, and then he talked some more, and finally he shut up and kept quiet. In El Paso, at Peabody, Cohen and Sandoz, I went through more questions, and I had to show my license and then sign a waiver of some sort. I also paid a fee of five dollars, evidently for the time it took the clerk to dig out the box of cards for September of 1948. I sat down at a table with the cards, and with the motel owner and the clerk watching me, the motel owner fixed and intent on every move I made and blunt about it, making it plain that he wouldn't sit by and let me find the card and then see me wriggle out of the deal by claiming I hadn't found it at all.

"Go to hell," I told him.

"You can't talk like that to me, mister," he said. "I got a good mind to call the whole deal off."

"Go to hell again," I said.

The card was there. The first Monday in September of 1948:

Mr. & Mrs. Oscar Stevens
4500 Fort Washington Avenue
Philadelphia, Pa.

They had checked in at 10:40 P.M. The car Mr. Stevens drove had New York plates, and it had never occurred to Mr. Stevens that the motel man would carefully note the registration. Mr. Stevens had only a part of his mind on his deception. There is a Fort Washington Avenue in New York, but not in Philadelphia. He had begun to write Stew—and then had changed the *w* to a *v* and made it Stevens. I had a notion that Oscar Stevens might very well be Oscar Stewart, but in any case, I had the car's registration number.

I paid my one hundred dollars and then copied the information carefully. Then I told the motel man to go to hell, but I softened it with a smile. He stood up and told me that I had no call to insult him and treat him like a dog, and he was right. I admitted that he was right and apologized to him.

Four hours later I was on a plane to New York City.

PART 5

ENGLEWOOD

IN 1948, ACCORDING TO THE RECORDS OF THE NEW YORK State Bureau of Motor Vehicles, one Oscar Stewart, forty-one years of age, five feet nine inches tall, one hundred ninety pounds, brown hair, blue eyes, white, had been the owner and operator of a two-door Pontiac. In 1950 he bought a new Pontiac. In 1952 a four-door Buick was listed under his name, and in 1955 he became the owner of a Cadillac and transferred his registration to the state of New Jersey. The New Jersey bureau added the information that a second car, a Ford station wagon, was listed in his name in 1957. His address then read: The Gables, Cliffline Drive, Englewood, New Jersey.

Prior to his removal from the state, he had lived in two places since 1948. The first was at 322 Fort Washington Avenue, a downward-drifting, rather shabby street with remnants of a former middle-class gentility. From there he had moved to East Ninety-first Street, and then to Englewood.

In 1948 he had been a salesman with the fairly meaningless title of national sales representative for the Denning Glass Company. They specialized in glass and plastic containers for dairy and truck products and they did about three million dollars' worth of business a year. In 1951 his income had increased from seven thousand dollars annually three years before to over twelve thousand dollars, and he was vice-president in charge of sales. In 1952 Denning merged with Dexter Glass, one of the nation's giants in the field, and Stewart became a fifth assistant vice-president in charge of sales at eighteen thousand dollars a year. By 1958 his income was forty-five thousand a year, in addition to stock options, and he was first assistant vice-president in charge of sales.

He was born in Albany, New York, June 11, 1907, educated at Colby College, married Ann Richardson of Forest Hills, in Queens, in September of 1940, drafted in 1943, served two years in the armed forces, and was honorably discharged. Methodist by birth, but attended services at an Episcopalian church, his wife's faith. Three children, Robert, 1943; Joan Ann, 1946; Jeffrey, 1949. Member of the University Club in the city and the Five Oaks Country Club in Bergen County. Board of directors of the Community Chest in Englewood and the local hospital as well. His picture revealed a rather good-looking, round-faced man with a small tilted nose, gray hair, and light eyes behind spectacles.

Such was the life and success of Oscar Stewart, and the gathering of the above material was a simple matter of routine work. Given the solid substance of an automobile registration to begin with, a man's life is a good deal of an open book. Most of the investigation I carried out myself, finding it a pleasant change to work with facts instead of intuition and fancy. The bureau rundowns I turned over to Triboro Investigations, who were the New York correspondents of the Jeffery Peters Agency in Los Angeles. This is the kind of thing that is ninety per cent of the work of a private detective, and it is as run of the mill and as tedious as most research. I looked at the places where Stewart had lived. I found two pictures of him, one from a trade magazine and one from an annual report of his company, and at the end of three days my dossier on Oscar Stewart was as complete as I desired it to be. That was a Saturday.

It was almost five years since I had been in New York City, and however it may be considered as a place to live, there is certainly no other place like it to return to after five years away. I had a room in the Park Sheraton Hotel, at the corner of Seventh Avenue and Fifty-sixth Street, and when I stood at the window of my room I could see Carnegie Hall and a bit of Central Park and the unending streams of traffic and people below me—and feel something of the excitement that no other place in the world where I have ever been can quite match.

The summer evening was enough cooler than El Paso to remind me of Los Angeles weather. I walked downtown, had my dinner at Gallagher's Steak House, like any other tourist, and managed to get a single seat at *Two for the Seesaw*. I was alone, and I wanted to be alone. On and off during that evening I wondered why I felt that something in this job of mine was importantly different.

2

I decided to visit Oscar Stewart the next day, which was Sunday. Let me make clear how I felt about him: as I said before, I hated him—unreasonably and illogically—and I desired to do him harm. But the one was an emotion and the second was a childish petulance. I had no intentions of harming Mr. Stewart; I had every intention of making him as uncomfortable as I could; but it turned out that I couldn't sustain the hatred. I suppose that some people are well constituted for that sort of thing and others poorly.

At about ten o'clock on that Sunday morning, after I had

finished breakfast, I picked up a Hertz car and drove up the West Side Highway to the George Washington Bridge and across it. I had never been to Englewood before or, for that matter, to any town or suburb in the state of New Jersey, and I was surprised to find it so close to the city, stretching as it does to the top of the Palisades. My instructions were to turn off Route 4 at Grand Avenue, and I almost overshot the exit. Once off the main road, I doubled back and set out to find Cliffline Drive. I took a set of directions from a traffic cop, made a wrong turning, and then for about ten minutes drove back and forth through streets that reminded me of some of the older sections of Beverly Hills, large and imposing houses in the sixty-thousand or better class, broad lawns and old shade trees —with here and there a turn-of-the-century estate, set in its wire or stone walls, complete with gatehouse, greenhouse, and long driveway. By accident I stumbled onto Cliffline Drive, turned to my left, drove a mile, turned around and drove back, and a few blocks past my turnoff a sign told me that I was at The Gables.

It was stretching a point to name the place. My own observation has been that to attach anything else than the owner's name onto a piece of real estate is gauche unless the going price is at least a quarter of a million dollars, and I would guess that Stewart bought his spread for considerably less. But he had come up the ladder remarkably quickly, and the old gray stone house he occupied did sit in at least two acres of well-manicured grounds. It had a collie dog attached, and he properly galloped across the lawn and tried to get himself killed under the wheels of my car. Over to one side of the lawn a boy of about fifteen was practicing short shots with an iron. A woman stood in front of the house with a loaded golf bag at her feet. They were apparently a golf-conscious family.

I stopped my car within a few feet of her. She was in her middle forties, skinny but healthy-looking, her hair—which had about forty dollars' worth of silver tipping in it—making a nice contrast with her sunburned face. Her red station wagon sat in the driveway just in front of me, and as she walked over to my car I could see that she was still experimenting with just how one behaved to strangers when you were mistress of a place like The Gables. I got out of the car and told her immediately that my name was Macklin and that I was there to see Mr. Stewart.

"Really," she said. "Not this morning. You must be mistaken."

"This is Mr. Stewart's home?"

"Well—yes. But we're leaving for the club. We're late already. I can't imagine that my husband would make an appointment with you and then forget about it."

"What is it, Ann?" Stewart came out of the house, dressed for the club in gray flannels, gray sleeveless sweater, pale gray shirt, frowning at me and wondering what I was doing there. Across the lawn the boy went on practicing short shots. I introduced myself, and Mr. Stewart informed me that he had never heard of me before. He was beginning to become angry, and my own anger was fading. He was fat and older than his fifty-one years; he was washed, brain-washed and body-washed and belly-washed.

"What kind of a damn fool are you, sir?" he demanded at last, his patience going. "If you're selling something, come back another time! Or see me at my office!" He was frightened; he frightened easily. His wife was looking at her watch. "Really," she said in exasperation. "Really!" She looked at her watch again and said, "Really!" again.

"Could I speak to you alone, Mr. Stewart, just for a moment?" I asked him.

"I don't see why!"

"Why? Let's say to spare your wife's feelings."

His wife stared at me and then at him, and he looked at his wife and then at me. His line then was to tell me that anything I desired to say to him could be said in front of his wife, but he couldn't speak the line. His life was full of little peccadillos, but unknown, I would swear, to his wife. Her eyes met mine, and they glinted so hard and defiantly that I understood immediately how much afraid of her Oscar Stewart must be; and the whole summer sunshine display was backed by the monumental indifference of the teen-ager practicing his short shots. I always find myself pitying those I hate, and among the many luxuries a private detective can't afford, pity stands high on the list.

"This is a business matter, Mrs. Stewart," I said, "and I know that today is Sunday, but this can't wait; so the sooner I have a word with Mr. Stewart, the better off we'll both be."

Then I walked over to a manicured hedge of taxus; and he said a few words to his wife and she shook her head, and then he shrugged and came over to me and said:

"Now see here, Mr.—— What did you say your name is?"

"Macklin," I answered softly. "I'm a private detective from Los Angeles, Mr. Stewart, and I want to talk to you about a woman named Sylvia Karoki, whom you drove out of El Paso with just about ten years ago."

He stared at me, his eyes bulging, the blood draining from his face. A whole minute of silence must have gone by while he stood there staring at me, and then his wife said sharply:

"Oscar, for heaven's sake!"

He choked over his words as he told me that he had a date

at the club for golf and then lunch to follow. I told him that I was indifferent to his social engagements and that I intended to talk to him and, if he wouldn't talk, to his wife. Then he went back and spoke to his wife in a whisper. She did not bother to whisper when she answered him.

"If you let me go to the club alone, Oscar, I can only tell you that you will regret it!" He stood there mutely. She looked at him and she looked at me. Then she picked up the bag of clubs and strode over to the red station wagon, climbed in, flicked on the motor, and ripped out of the driveway. The teen-age boy continued his short shots without looking up from the green.

3

On the patio, at one side of the house in back of a wing, Stewart poured himself a drink and asked me whether I wanted one. I did not. I sat down in a wrought-iron chair. It was a big patio, red brick, iron chairs with pillows and cushions, two couches, a bar, and a ring of shrubs. A striped awning kept away the sun. Beyond the shrubs, the lawn stretched down to the road.

He was more of a man with his wife gone. "If this is a shake-down, forget it," he told me, trying to blow courage and defiance into himself. "I'm broke. Don't be fooled by this setup. I'm broke."

"It's not a shakedown, Stewart. I don't want a nickel out of you. I want information, and if you give it to me you won't have any trouble, and then you can tell your wife that I'm on the board of directors of Standard Oil and trying to steal you away."

He stood with the drink poised. "Is that true? On the level?"

"Yes."

"You're not trying to shake me down?"

"God damn it, I told you no. Here are my credentials. I'm a private detective." I gave him my wallet. "I want information."

"What kind of information?"

"About Sylvia Karoki ten years ago. We talk, and when we finish talking that's the end of it. You never see me or hear from me again."

"That's all?"

"That's all."

"Then why couldn't it wait?"

I replied unpleasantly, "Because I didn't want to wait."

"All right, Macklin," he said quickly, "it's not that I'm sore about being pulled away from the club on a Sunday. I can live without that, believe me. Now I get grief from my wife—that's all. You sure you don't want a drink?"

"I'll take a rain check."

"I mean, it's peculiar, the way you come out here to my place on a Sunday."

"Well, that's the way it had to be. Suppose we talk."

He sat down on the sofa, facing me, sipping at his drink. He nodded and said, "All right." He tried to smile. "You got me by the short hair, right? I have no choice."

"No, you haven't."

"She told you?" He shook his head. "Funny—I just haven't thought about that damn kid, not for months. I guess she told you. Wait a minute—how do I know she didn't hire you to shake me down?"

"You don't know," I said tiredly. "You'll just have to take my word."

"I could call my lawyer." He tried bluster in a small way.

"Oh, what in hell would you call your lawyer for? Talk sense."

"Well, you know what I mean. You come busting in here on a Sunday morning and tell me you're a private detective.

I'm an executive in a large corporation, Mr. Macklin. I can't afford any scandal, not on my job and not in my home."

"There won't be any scandal," I sighed.

"Well, you threatened me——"

"Like hell I did! I want you to talk about Sylvia Karoki. If you talk willingly, fine. If you don't want to talk, I'll use every trick I have to make you talk."

"Why?"

"Because that's my job."

He leaned back on the sofa and stared into his glass. "I shouldn't be drinking at this hour. I'm not a drinker. Two or three of these and I'll be tight. That was ten years ago, Macklin. It's funny to have something pop out at you that has been dead and buried for ten years. Anyway—what did I do? I found a kid in trouble in El Paso. She wanted to get out of El Paso like some women want a mink coat. So we made a deal. I was driving east and I took her along with me. She told me she was twenty-one years old, and I was damn fool enough to believe it. Then when I found out how old she was, I couldn't get out of it. All right—maybe I didn't want to. What's the crime?"

"Ask your wife."

"Sure—sure, Macklin. Be funny and hard-boiled."

"Why did she want so desperately to get out of El Paso?" I asked him, and he frowned and closed his eyes for a moment and then said:

"I don't know if I have it straight any more. I think she told it to me three different ways. She always claimed that she wasn't a hustler but was backed into it. Look, Macklin—I spent nine years selling on the road. I'm no babe in the woods, I'm no bluenose. Live and let live. Maybe she was a pro, maybe not. I had plenty of trouble with her——"

"About why she had to get out of El Paso?"

"I'm trying to remember. I think, the way she told it, some guy who came out there with her made a pimp arrangement with a big cat house across the river. Then they kept claiming that both she and this louse who was her commission man owed them money. They took away all of her clothes except one dress and some sandals. Then this friend of hers tried to get her out and started a fight of some kind and was knifed to death. She hid out with some old priest until things had quieted down—and then she got back across the river, but without a nickel. At least that's the way she told it and I remember it—a pretty lurid story. I met her across the street from my hotel, on the street. She came up to me with the old line about mistaking me for a friend. I knew it was a line, of course—but you don't see many girls like her, burned as brown as a Mexican, and beautiful. I don't know what she looks like now, Macklin, but so help me God, she was as long-legged and beautiful as any girl I've seen anywhere. Well, when she saw that I was interested, she came right to the point. I told her I was driving to New York. She agreed to come with me. In return I was to buy her some clothes and her meals and lodging. She didn't flirt with me or go into any routine. She was precise and matter-of-fact about the whole thing. Well, I took a chance and gave her twenty-five dollars and arranged to meet her later that night. Meanwhile I checked out of the hotel. I couldn't bring her into the hotel. I'd been coming there for years. I had to be careful——" He stared at me, then said, "I shouldn't be talking like this. What the hell, Macklin, I could just clam up and not say another word to you. I'm out of my mind talking to you like this!"

"Do we have to go through that whole routine again?"

He stared at me sadly. Then he put his drink down and

shook his head. "I'm not drinking. This is bad enough without drinking."

I nodded. "And then she met you later, and you drove out to the Rim Rock Motel and checked in for the night."

"How do you know that? I don't even remember the name of the motel."

"I do. I got your registration from the owner—so we can be clear on that. Sylvia didn't send me. I don't think that she knows you're alive or cares."

"What are you after, Macklin?"

"What's the difference? I told you, you won't be hurt. Did you sleep with her that night?"

All the gentleman in him bristled at that, and he replied with indignation that it was a hell of a question.

"Ah, don't be cute with me, Stewart. If I told you the one about the two boys who were in love with each other but couldn't get married because one of them was a Moslem, you'd have a fine sense of humor, wouldn't you? Don't be delicate. I don't intend to hurt you in any way, but I have no cause to love you—none!"

"All right, I slept with her. It happens, Macklin. You can take my word for it that it happens. I'm a lonely man, Mr. Macklin, then and now. I don't get along with my wife. It was all right when I could spend eight months a year on the road—now I'm in the home office. I turned to women. Yes— I turned to women. I like women. Why the devil shouldn't I? You saw my wife. I don't see that I did anything that the next man doesn't do——"

"Don't justify yourself, Mr. Stewart," I said wearily. "I don't care. I'm not interested in your morality. I just want the facts."

"I told you. I didn't take her along for company. The agreement was that she would sleep with me and I would pay her expenses to New York. And she kept it to the letter—not an inch more."

"Now what kind of a crack is that?"

"Just what I am saying, Mr. Macklin."

4

"Don't try to kiss me again," she said to him.

"Sylvia, I don't understand you. I swear I don't understand you."

"Don't try, Oscar."

"All I tried to do is kiss you."

"Don't try."

"I sleep with you."

"That was our agreement, Oscar. Our agreement was that you could screw me. There was nothing in our agreement that said that you could kiss me."

"I hate that kind of talk, Sylvia."

"Why? It's good English. You want me to say 'sexual intercourse'? But you didn't bring me along for sexual intercourse. You brought me along because I add up to a cheap lay between here and New York. So why can't you stick to screwing and be satisfied?"

"Because I'm not a hoodlum and I don't like to talk like a hoodlum."

"But I am."

"All right. I don't want to fight with you, Sylvia. I'm crazy about you."

"Thanks."

"I just want our relationship to make some sense. On the one hand, we have intercourse——"

"What does that do—make you feel respectable when you call it 'intercourse'?"

"I'm trying to say that it makes no sense at all for you to refuse to kiss me."

"Things make sense to me in a strange way, Oscar. I can't explain to you. Even if you could understand me, I don't feel like explaining. So if you want to call our agreement off, call it off. You're perfectly free to do so."

5

"I didn't call it off," Stewart said to me. "I never met anyone like her, Macklin. You can understand that—you know her. I don't want to offend you by anything I say."

"You can't offend me," I told him. "I have no interest in her—none. You say whatever you want to say."

"It's just that I never knew what to think of her. I never knew if she was lying or telling the truth. Her English was better than mine. I try. My wife corrects me. But sometimes Sylvia spoke like a Bennington girl and sometimes like a cheap hustler. She'd tell me that she went to Smith and that her real name was Cabot or Wentworth or something fancy like that and that she ran away from college and that her father was an old-family millionaire—and then she'd laugh at me and make me feel like a fool for believing her. I had the feeling that she kept trying stories on me. In Abilene she got into a conversation with a Mexican bartender, and her Spanish sounded as easy and good as his. Then she told me that she came from an old Mexican family down in the Valley of Mexico and that she had run away after a love affair with a wealthy Argentine— or some such nonsense as that. Then, in the next breath, she told me that she had spent three years in Juárez and learned her Spanish there, but the way she knew Abilene made me feel she had spent some time there. I never knew what to believe. She told me that she was twenty-one and seventeen and nineteen—the same way. It wasn't that she had to lie—she enjoyed it. She seemed to enjoy making me feel like a fool. Oh, I'll admit that there were times when she was feeling good and high and would be decent to me, but the next minute——"

6

"Why don't you shut up for a while, Oscar? I can't stand listening to you. It's bad enough to spend all day with you in this car——"

"I'm sorry. I didn't realize that I had said anything to bother you."

"You bore me to death, Oscar."

"That's gratitude, all right."

"You keep talking about gratitude, Oscar. What should I be grateful for—sitting here and listening to you for hours? Do you ever listen to yourself? Has it ever occurred to you how stupid and opinionated you are? You have an opinion on everything and you know nothing. You've been coming back here to the border for ten years and you've never troubled to learn ten words of Spanish. You look at the sun every day, but you couldn't even guess at its distance from earth. You've been to Abilene a dozen times—and you don't even know what its name means. Do you?"

"Of course I don't. Do you?"

"I do, because I took the trouble to find out. Abilene was a tetrarchy mentioned in Luke—and the town was named after that tetrarchy. But how would you know that? Have you ever read a book? Have you ever looked up a word in a dictionary? Have you ever asked anything but the way to the nearest cat house? Just don't ask me to be grateful again, Oscar."

7

I wanted to know why he stood for it—why a man stands for
that kind of treatment.

"I don't know, Macklin. After a while I began to need her.
I had never been with anyone like that before. In Kansas City
she walked out of the hotel room in the morning and didn't
come back until nighttime. I didn't know whether she was
ever coming back. I damn near went out of my mind."

"She came back?"

"Yes, she came back. I'll tell you something, Macklin—if
she had given two damns about me, if she had cared anything
at all about me, I would have—God damn it, I would have
divorced my wife! I don't know why I'm talking this way to
you. Maybe I've had a bellyful. You know what this lousy
place cost me? A hundred and ten thousand dollars. I'm up to
my neck in debt. I have a first mortgage of forty thousand and
a second mortgage of twenty-five thousand. I have a bank loan.
I would have gone bankrupt, but I sold every share of my stock
in the company—a thousand shares that was going to take
care of my old age. Shit on my old age, Macklin! I don't
give a damn what you think about me! You want to shake me
down—see how much water you can squeeze out of a stone!"

"I told you I don't want to shake you down," I repeated
again. "How many times do I have to tell you that? All I want
is information about Sylvia Karoki."

"Why don't you tell me why?"

"Use your head, Stewart. I'm a private detective. I'm being
paid to find out about her. That's all. I'm not here to make any
trouble for you. Let's get it over with."

"What else?"

"You brought her to New York?"

"Yes."

"Then?"

"She checked into the Hotel Pennsylvania. I took her there. I paid a week in advance."

"Why the Pennsylvania?"

"A big, busy place. I don't know people there. Suppose I took her to the Biltmore or the Belmont Plaza or the Commodore. I'd keep running into people I know, and that wouldn't help me, not in my business or at home. Look, Macklin—I'll level with you. I'm afraid of my wife. If she knew about this kind of thing, she'd cut my throat——" He picked up the drink now and drained it down. "That's right. She'd ruin me. She'd cut my heart out. I'm afraid of her and I hate her. I hate her guts."

I felt that I had heard all of that kind of thing that I could stand. I had no anger left for Stewart; I only wanted to get away from him and never set eyes on him again.

"Did she register under her own name?" I asked him.

"Who? Sylvia? I don't know what her name was. Maybe it was Karoki—maybe it wasn't. She registered as Sylvia Carter. She said that was her real name."

"And what city?"

"El Paso." He smiled ruefully for the first time that morning.

"You continued to see her?"

"I'm a sharp big-time boy, I am, Macklin. Sure. For the first four days—nothing doing. She was looking for a job, she told me. Then she saw me, had dinner with me. That was the last time. She said no more."

8

"Maybe I'm nothing to you," he said to her. "Maybe I didn't do anything for you to be grateful for. I'm not asking you to be grateful. I'm only asking you to let me see you now and then."

"What's the good, Oscar? Whatever I could give you, I've given you. And you paid me. You had your fun. I'm in New York. Let it rest there."

"Do I have to get down on my knees and beg you?"

"I don't set out to hurt you, Oscar," she said to him. "You force me to hurt you. You invite it."

"What harm——"

"Why don't you let it go, Oscar?" she interrupted.

"How much am I asking for? To like me a little?"

"You don't like anyone a little, Oscar. And I'm not sentimental about men. I had to learn early about men, Oscar—and I had good teachers. Very good teachers."

"I'm not to blame for that, Sylvia. For God's sake, you can't make every man responsible for——"

"If you only knew how boring this kind of an argument is, Oscar."

"Well, just see me once more."

"No."

9

He poured himself a second drink and gulped it hungrily. "No. There it was. That's the way the cards fall, huh, Macklin? A little eighteen-year-old floozie, and I could have got down on my knees and begged her. Oh, the hell with it! Why don't you have a drink? You loused up my whole morning. One drink."

I said I'd have a drink.

"Look at each other through Scotch-colored glasses. Keeps out the sun."

"You never saw her again?"

"Once. She got herself a job as change-maker in one of those honky-tonk penny arcades."

"Where? Which one?"

"I'm not sure that I remember—except that it was on Broadway somewhere between Forty-fifth Street and Fifty-first Street. A big one—you can't miss it. That was a few months later. I saw her from the street and went in there, and there she was sitting in the cashier's booth and reading a book between making change. Maybe the book is what made me look twice."

"She read a lot?"

"Everything. We'd go into a hotel, and if there was nothing else she read the Gideon Bible. She told me she read it more than five times—but sure as God, it didn't give her religion. She used to load up with those twenty-five-cent paper books, and sometimes when she couldn't sleep she'd go through three or four of them in one night."

"And it was Sylvia in the penny arcade?"

"It was Sylvia, all right. I went over to her and said hello. You think she said hello or gave me a smile or anything like that? Oh no! She looked up at me and said, 'Oh, it's you again, Oscar. Go away and leave me alone.' Just like that——"

A voice broke in and said, "Poor Oscar!"

We both froze into a long moment of sick silence, and then we looked up and to one side, and there at the edge of the terrace was the teen-age boy I had seen in the distance practicing short shots. Now he had his number-two iron with him, balancing it delicately against his hip. He wore basketball shorts, high and tight in the crotch, a T-shirt, and a gold bracelet. I would guess that he was fifteen, not much older, with long, round legs and a sulky, sunburned face.

"Poor Daddy-o." He grinned.

"Where were you?" Stewart gasped.

"Other side of the shrubs."

"How long were you there?"

"Long enough to read you. Every word. That Sylvia was some tomato, wasn't she? Bless your heart. I never thought you had it in you."

"God damn you—standing there——"

"Now don't get excited, Daddy-o. Please don't get excited."

"Get out of here!" Stewart fairly screamed.

"Where to?" the boy asked, swaying a little and grinning at him. "Where to? Do I wait for Mummy dear to come back from her golfing? Oh, she's going to be plenty miffed with you never turning up there, just sitting here on the terrace and getting yourself stinko. Do I tell her——"

"You lousy little bastard!"

"Oh, don't call me names. I love you. I'm going to cover for you."

"What do you want?"

"Shakedown, Daddy-o. That real nice private eye, he won't shake you down. But I will."

Stewart was greenish-white. He slumped on the couch, his cheek twitching, his breath coming hoarsely. For a moment I thought he was beginning to have a heart attack.

"What do you want?" he whispered.

"Live and let live. Double my allowance."

"You're crazy."

"Oh no. Or else, Daddy-o."

"Bobby, have a heart," he began to plead. "That's all I'm asking—give me a break, have a heart. I can't afford it."

"Yes you can. You're a big man. I'm only asking for a few lousy dollars a week—but the hell with it!" He turned and started to leave, but Stewart called him back.

"Bobby!" The boy stopped. "Bobby—let me think about it. Give me some time."

The boy swung the golf club over his shoulder. "Sure,

Daddy-o." He grinned. "Think about it. You got until she comes back from the club. I don't want to rush you." And he sauntered off, swinging his narrow hips from side to side.

Stewart watched him for a moment, and then he turned to me. His whole body shook, and tears ran down his cheeks, and through the tears he cried out shrilly:

"Screw you, Macklin! Screw you, you lousy two-bit stinking private eye! Get out of here! Get out of here, you lousy son of a bitch!"

I walked away from him and got into my car and drove out. As I left, I saw the boy out on the lawn. He didn't pay any attention to me or even look up at the noise of the car starting. He was bent over his number-two iron, practicing his short shots.

PART 6

NEW YORK (BROADWAY)

I MET A GIRL AT THE BAR IN THE PARK SHERATON, AND IN due time she informed me that she was waiting for her date—information which is time-honored and secure, because if the date doesn't show, it is nothing she planned and who is to say that she's not a nice girl after all. Her name was Joyce, and she had blond hair and blue eyes, and she might have been very good-looking a decade before, when she was in her twenties.

When her date did not arrive, we got onto the subject of food. She informed me that she was hungry, and I let her know that I had no one to eat dinner with. We agreed that Sunday night was an off night for both of us.

She had a good figure, hard eyes, and a plaintive projection of self-pity—and all the cunning intelligence of a homeless thirteen-year-old, and a wickedness that was equally innocent and unsophisticated. Thereby it was no wickedness at all. She was a girl who was trying to do the best she could for herself and not doing too well—but she was a person and a woman, and my period for the enjoyment of loneliness had passed. We each had two drinks, and then she said—in response to my question—that she would like to eat at the Hampshire House on Central Park South, because it was the nicest place in New York. She enjoyed the word "nice"; it was like a definition of her non-physical hunger. When I told her that I was a private detective, she said that it was awfully nice but offered me no information about herself, profession, marital status, or family. She said that the food was nice and that the dining room of the Hampshire House was nice, very, very nice.

Like the dining room and its pretentious décor, she was trying to be something that she wasn't and had probably forgotten whatever it was that she had ever desired to be. She talked on and on about all the things that were nice and some things that weren't nice. She was a compulsive talker who did not listen to herself; and I found all my resolves to be pleasant, to have a little compassion for another stray human soul—I found all these resolves melting and a desperate wish that I was back in a dirty and squalor-ridden Mexican town on the Rio Grande.

"The air conditioning is good here," she said to me. "Don't you think the air conditioning is good here? The other night we went to a place on Fifty-second Street where they said they had air conditioning—you know, one of them signs where they say 'deliciously cool and air-conditioned inside' and when you get inside you can die from the heat and can't even breathe, so you complain to the captain and he says, 'Madame, a little mechanical failure,' only I wish the people who owned them places would have a little mechanical failure and just drop dead, and anyway, Fifty-second Street has gone way down, way down if you ask me, except for Twenty-one, and I have been in places on Fifty-second Street where you wouldn't want to take a nice girl, if you understand me, because all they got is hootchie-kootchie and vulgarity, and I'm not narrow-minded but I can't stand vulgarity just for the sake of vulgarity, not that I mind a little spice or off-color jokes, but I just can't bear vulgarity for the sake of vulgarity and I don't mind if a girl can dance but when all she does is strip and stand there—well, you know the places?"

I said I did not and that this was only my second trip to New York.

"Well, Mack—this is what you like to be called? I know, because I knew a Frank Macneil in the record business. I don't mean he's a disk jockey or anything important like that, he's just a singer who never got to his station and forgot to get off the train and he always told everyone to call him Mack—I mean, anyway, how would you like to see one of them places, I mean if you never saw one before, because it's life and I think that anything that's life belongs just because it's life, don't you?"

I agreed with her and said that it would be fine, but first I would like to walk down Broadway—if she didn't mind?

"Why?"

"Just to look. I'm a tourist here."

"I would think that if you're a private detective you'd be here on business, I mean that you would be surveying someone or something like that. You know, Mack, I don't mean it as something insulting or anything like that, but you don't act like a private eye—I mean, you're nice, but not like a private eye, and anyway, there's nothing to see on Broadway. If you want to go down to the Village and walk around and look at the beatniks, well, I can understand that, but there's just nothing to do on Broadway—there's nothing to see, there just isn't."

Anyway, she could not walk—her heels were too high. We went to the place on Fifty-second Street, and at the bar there she met two men who were old friends. They began to buy her drinks, and she began to have a wonderful time. Their names

were Ben and Herb, and they were very polite and had no desire
to hurt my feelings, but they were old, old pals of Joyce; and
why didn't we all get together and go on a real tear and they
knew where some girls could be reached. I said that I would
love to but I had a sick aunt who was still waiting for me to
drop in. Joyce said it was just a cover-up, because all I really
wanted to do was to walk up and down Broadway. Can you
imagine? she said. Everyone was pleased, and Herb and Ben told
me that they would take good care of Joyce.

2

I frequently feel like the boy who hit his head against a wall
because it felt so good when he stopped. It felt so good to be
outside of a Fifty-second Street night club and amicably parted
from Joyce, whose last name I never learned, that I walked
down the street toward Broadway with a little less than my
usual distaste for myself and my company. For several hours
I had shared the feelings of Oscar Stewart about one Alan
Macklin. I was now ready to live and let live. It would at least
be tomorrow before I had to contrive additional lies, engage
in suitable duplicities, and degrade myself to the level that
Frederick Summers had purchased. I strolled along and took
simple pleasure in the quality of midtown New York on a
late summer evening. It is a quality like no other in the world,
the behemoth of all cities subdued without being abashed, almost sultry, its turbulence controlled and paced, its streets full
of people like myself, who had come from far away to taste and
look at what no one would admit was the first wonder of the
world.

I was there by the grace of Frederick Summers, might the
gods reward him. The kind of man who is myself has always
walked in the near and far places of the earth with such grace

—employed for all the varied arts of degradation. Our philosophy and rationale are simple: we try to turn a buck, and if we don't take it someone else will. Our total integrity consists of devotion to the person who hires us, otherwise we get a bad name in the trade and are hired less.

All of this I turned over in my mind, and then I put it away. Tomorrow I would work for Mr. Summers; the latter half of today was my day off. I crossed Broadway and started downtown, and after I had gone four blocks south, I saw the neon sign that said: *Lotus Amusement Arcade.* It was my night off and I was not working for Mr. Summers and I was also not sure what I was doing. I took out a twenty-five-cent piece and flipped it onto the back of my hand and said to myself, "Tails, I go ahead; heads, I take Mr. Summers' expense money and a plane to Europe." It came heads. There was an old woman selling pencils on the street, and I gave her the quarter. What I most wanted in the whole world was to spend six months in Greece and Turkey. I dreamed of hiring a power launch about the size of a deep-water game-fish trawler and following the coast of Greece through the Hellespont and into the Black Sea, and then on the Turkish coast to see all that Jason had seen when he led his Argonauts to Colchis for the Golden Fleece. There were other things that I wanted to do almost as much, such as a year in the city of Rome or a year wandering through the diggings and excavations of Israel— and minor things, too, like a special course they were giving on Toltec civilization at the University of Mexico. But a flip of a coin never decided anything important in anyone's life.

I went into the Lotus Amusement Arcade.

It was a big, garish, brightly lit place, and it offered a whole bonanza of delight and delectability for your pennies and nickels and dimes.

There was a case of plain, cheap, growing-boy pornography, playing cards with half-clad bathing beauties on them, hand-painted neckties with misdrawn nudes cavorting on them, rings with a peephole so that you didn't have to strain your neck looking into your neighbor's window, cards of suggestive verses, rubber nudes with a bowl you squeezed to animate them, sweet little toilet seats with filthy pictures under the lid, and a great deal more of the poor, degenerate japes that civilization and mass production have substituted for the ancient and frequently noble worship of the fertility goddess.

While I regarded all this, a small man with an enormous, wrinkled, scarified red nose and a heavy apron full of pennies and nickels and dimes came over and asked me what I liked.

"It isn't here," I replied.

"No?" He took private stock out of his apron and handed me a little booklet, which I opened and read:

> *The minstrels sing of an English king,*
> *Who lived long years ago.*
> *He ruled his land with an iron hand,*
> *But his morals were base and low.*

> *He loved to hunt the royal stag*
> *Within the royal wood,*
> *But most of all he loved to sit*
> *And pull the royal pud.*

He said, "Wait a minute—you want to read the whole thing on the cuff? A dollar lets you carry it away."

"Take it," I said, giving it back to him.

"Do you know what that is, mister?"

"It's a poorly rendered, distorted version of *The Bastard King of England*, which is attributed to Rudyard Kipling. It's not worth a dollar. It's not worth ten cents."

"All right—look, mister. I pick you out for a smart man. I give you something choice. You don't want something choice? O.K. Live and let live." He turned away and washed his hands of me.

The place was full of music and culture. Johnny Mathis sang from one end of it, Pat Boone from the other, and nobody minded that the blaring recordings were different. Down the rows of hand-crank films, pinball machines, and coin games wandered a throng of tourists and natives, sober married couples, grinning couples, venerable couples, teen-agers, kids, and twenty-year-olds. The crank movies at the front end were exotic items of the nineteen-twenties, where for a nickel you could see the vamps of the flapper era start disrobing but never complete their jagged performance; the twenty-five-cent machines in the back were less jerky and more revealing, but still the good clean sport of skee ball had more takers.

I wandered through the place, down one aisle and up another, and then I took a dollar's worth of change from the main cashier, an enormously fat woman jammed into a little cage in the middle of all the hoked-up excitement. I tried this and that, wanting only an excuse to remain there and look at the place. It might not have been the place I wanted, and after I had finished demonstrating my lack of skill with pinball machines, I left and went on down Broadway. It was the only place that matched Stewart's description.

Then I walked back to my hotel. It was almost midnight now. At the newsstand I bought three or four magazines and some cigarettes; but I was in no mood for reading, not even magazines, and I sat at the window that gave me a view of a slice of Central Park and smoked and brooded and composed sermon-letters to Frederick Summers and acknowledged the sick, longing feeling within me, the desperate and hungry desire for a hard, cynical, and ambitious lady of easy virtue.

It was not Sylvia West of Beverly Hills and Coldwater Canyon, but a skinny, dirty-faced kid, Sylvia Karoki, whose life I was reliving and whom one day I would find.

3

Just as Samuel Johnson once held that nobody but an ass writes for any reason but money—or words to that effect—I have never heard of a good private detective or Wall Street broker who was motivated by other reasons. Jack Fenney, the manager of Triboro Investigations, was a good private detective, and he once commented to me on the nature of a society where nobody admits to doing anything for money and nobody does anything for any other reason. He held that when a point of legality was stretched it ought to pay a little better than an aboveboard job.

His price for supplying me with a full set of credentials as a qualified employee of and investigator for International Finders Co., Ltd., of New York, Chicago, and London, was five hundred dollars. When I held that this was a considerable bundle for a dozen calling cards, he pointed out to me:

"I don't think it is, Mack, if you only stop to think about it. You can go to a printer around the corner and have those cards made up, but what have you got? The point is that International Finders exists. It is incorporated in New York and in London. It is a wholly owned subsidiary of Triboro, but it maintains its own offices here and in London. Suppose you get picked up with a set of phony cards. You know what follows: you lose your license and a lot more."

"I've used insurance cards on the Coast."

"That's kiddie stuff and you know it. A Finders operation is something else, and I'm drawing this goddamn thin as it is. If you get into trouble with the cops, I have got to back you up all the way down the line. Who the hell are you trying to trace, anyway? Not that Stewart character?"

"A woman."

"I'd be better off if I had her name."

"I can't help you," I said.

"All right. But be careful—please. I run a big operation and a clean operation, and if you didn't come here with all the blessings of Jeff Peters I wouldn't even talk to you."

"I'm always careful," I said.

"Do you carry a gun?"

"No."

"That's good. A shiv, a sap, brass knuckles?"

"No. My father and mother were both born in Scotland. We're a quiet and civilized people."

"All right. Now you have to tell me what deceased you're planning and what we're holding—so that we can set it up in London."

"I'd rather not."

He shook his head and said, "Hell, no! I don't play that way. It's got to be in the records of the company. It's got to be there to be found if the cops want to find it."

"All right—all right, I'll give it to you. Stefan Karoki. Born in Hungary, 1896. Died in England—you pick the place—1957. No known relatives. Give him whatever history you think best. His estate ought to be about four hundred thousand dollars in whatever currency you can work with——"

"That'll be escudos—a bit over three cents, I believe. We'll say ten million escudos, give or take."

"Why escudos?"

"Because we have a nice working arrangement with a Portuguese bank, and the Portuguese are very flexible about these things."

"Make it fifteen million."

"All right, Mack—since we're playing with stage money. Drop in tomorrow and we'll have your credentials and a complete dossier on Stefan Karoki."

"One thing," I said. "What happens when my job's done?"

"If you keep your nose clean, everything disappears—records, money, and all."

4

A penny arcade, like a saloon, is far from its best during the working hours of the day. There was an acrid smell about the Lotus Amusement Arcade. It was tinny and cheap and old in its tawdry pleasures, and the few tourists who moved in it were shamefaced about being there. The man with the enormous red nose looked more tired than the other night. He leaned against an automatic photography booth and leafed through a copy of the *Daily News*. The fat woman in the cashier's booth appeared to doze.

I asked red-nose where I could find the boss, and he glanced at me with immediate and remarkable recognition and said:

"So it's the scholar! So you know every goddamn line Kipling wrote!"

"The boss?"

"What's your business, mister?"

"The boss."

"You're some kind of a cop. You know, there's a cop smell, a cop look, a cop taste. What are you—one of them private cops from some suppression-of-vice committee? Process server?" He folded his newspaper and laid it aside. "I'll tell you something else, Jack—maybe you don't know all there is to know about Rudyard Kipling. Maybe you think he liked to turn out that garbage—like *The Road to Mandalay?* Why do you think they never made him poet laureate?"

"Tell me."

"Because he wrote *The Bastard King of England.* Don't look at me like that. You think because I work in a craphole like this I can't read a book?"

I took a dollar out of my pocket and handed it to him. He took the booklet out of his apron and gave it to me.

"The boss?" I said.

"What's your name, mister?"

"Macklin."

"What do you want to see the boss for?"

A man came in from the street, handed a five-dollar bill to red-nose, and said to him, "Butterfly in the third. Across the board."

"How?"

"Two and two and one."

Then the man left and I said, "You make change, peddle dirty poems, and book bets. What else?"

"Ah, I don't make book. Lousy little penny ante betting. I take it and pass it on and I get five per cent off the top. What do I do? I do the best I can."

The fat woman called out to him, "Hey, Chesty—how do you feel for nickels?" He went over to her booth and poured nickels from his apron and then came back and said:

"Why don't you give it up? Who owns a lousy penny arcade?"

"Let the boss tell me."

A six-foot-two-inch man in his twenties, dressed in a bright sport shirt and green pants, walked over and asked, "What is it, Chesty? Is this joker giving you trouble?"

"Nobody gives me trouble. Take your muscle somewhere

else. Go watch the customers." And when the young man had gone, he said to me, "Lousy muscle. All that's wrong with this world comes from the guns and the shivs and the muscle."

"Why do they call you Chesty?"

"You don't have to make conversation. I'm five feet two inches and I weigh a hundred eleven pounds, so they call me Chesty. Big sense of humor. What do you want to see the boss about? He pays his bills and he keeps to himself."

"It's not him. I want to ask some questions about someone who worked here once."

"Ah, what the hell!" He shrugged. "Go tell Mrs. Argona," nodding at the cashier's booth.

I went over there. She filled the place and flowed onto the change counter, staring at me from under heavy, mascaraed lids. Then, from a tiny rosebud mouth, she shrilled:

"Chesty—this all right?"

"All right."

She picked up the phone in the booth, pressed a buzzer, and said after a moment, "Man wants to see you. Chesty says all right." Then she replaced the phone and shrilled to the young man in the print shirt, "Muscles—hey, Muscles!" Muscles came over and stood next to me, and the fat lady smiled at me as sweetly as my mother might and said, "You see, mister, Muscles does what I tell him to. He's a good boy. He'll throw you on your goddamn ass right out on the street, you start any trouble. So take him down to Mr. Ling, Muscles, hear me?"

"I hear you, I hear you," Muscles said, and nodded at me. "Come on." And as we walked toward the back of the arcade, he told me that I could relax. I thanked him. "That fat dame," he said, "she been here so long she thinks she owns the place. One of these times she's going to order me around once too much and I'm going to slap her and that change booth all over the place. Nobody orders me around," he informed me, "nobody. Nobody. That includes Ling."

"Who's Ling?"

"He owns the place," Muscles said. Then he led me down a flight of stairs at the back of the place. At the bottom of the stairs there was a small lounge and three doors. On one of them it said *Men*; on another, *Women*; and on the third, *Office*. He knocked at the door of the office, and from inside a high-pitched, mild voice asked us to come in.

The office was air-conditioned, about twelve feet square, with a desk, a few chairs, some lamps, a filing cabinet, a bookcase, a typewriter, and an adding machine. The only thing that distinguished it from any run-of-the-mill small-enterprise office was the man behind the desk, who was Chinese, about sixty-five years old, and wore a pale yellow lounging robe and a set of long, dramatic mustaches. He greeted me with a smile, in faultless English told Muscles to go and asked me to sit down. I introduced myself and exhibited my license and my credentials from the International Finders Co., Ltd.

"I see." He nodded, placing the information on his desk in front of him and studying it thoughtfully. Then he looked at me and said, "My name is Ling Tu Cheh, and it would be quite proper for you to call me Mr. Ling—as most people do. I shall call you Mr. Macklin, and if we start on a basis of mutual respect and maintain it, then possibly whatever conversation we have will be both a pleasure and a benefit."

I smiled and agreed. He was an ingratiating little man.

"Now what can I do for you, Mr. Macklin?"

"First—if I may take some of your time, I would like to tell you what International Finders is."

"I have been wondering."

"Our main office is in London—and we have offices in New

York, Chicago, and Los Angeles. I say 'we'; I am less than literal. Actually I am a private detective hired by International Finders to find someone. That is the function of International Finders—to find missing people, for a fee, of course. In this case we are concerned with an inheritance. About a year ago a man called Stefan Karoki died intestate—in London. This Stefan Karoki had been born in Hungary in 1896. Subsequently he engaged in business in England and on the Continent and eventually established a substantial import-export business with offices in London and Lisbon. He had no known relatives and no friends apart from his business associates. His estate in London was small and was absorbed to a large extent by taxes and funeral expenses. He had a fifty-thousand-pound insurance policy—with the business as the beneficiary. But among his papers was found a bankbook of the Grand National Bank of Portugal, with deposits of something more than fifteen million escudos——"

"And how does that translate into American money?" Mr. Ling asked gently.

"About six hundred thousand dollars—more or less, depending upon the current rate of exchange."

"I see. A very substantial sum for anyone who is fortunate enough to be the beneficiary. But what has all this to do with me, Mr. Macklin?"

"Not in terms of yourself, Mr. Ling, I am sorry to say," I told him in what I considered the polished, professional tone becoming to an employee of International Finders, a note of regret mingled with a note of hope, "but in terms of someone who was possibly employed by you at one time. You see, many continental banks work closely with International Finders, and the Grand National Bank of Portugal commissioned our organization to undertake an investigation that might uncover an heir."

"And have you?" Mr. Ling asked politely.

"The possibility exists. We traced Mr. Karoki's family to America and subsequently narrowed the search down to one single surviving member, a woman, Sylvia Karoki. We believe that she changed her name to Carter, and certain evidence indicates that she was employed by you—oh, let us say nine and a half, ten years ago. That is—if you owned this arcade as long ago as that?"

"I have owned and operated this amusement arcade for more than twenty years, Mr. Macklin. But even if such a person did work for me so long ago, what purpose can the information serve today?"

"It will provide us with a step—a clue toward her whereabouts today."

"I see. A long and patient search. You are a patient man, Mr. Macklin."

"I have to be in my work," I agreed gravely.

"Of course. Of course."

"And, if I may ask—do you recall Miss Sylvia Carter?"

"I really can't say, Mr. Macklin," Mr. Ling smiled apologetically. "That is so long ago. I would have to refresh my memory, as the lawyers say."

"I see."

"But I am sure that if you are willing to wait a short time— say until this time tomorrow—I will be in a position to comment on your inquiry."

"I see."

"Our people regard patience as a virtue." Mr. Ling smiled. "As a virtuous man, certainly the delay will not be too burdensome."

"Of course."

"Then until tomorrow, Mr. Macklin. And may I keep your business card?"

"Please do." I nodded.

He returned my credentials, and I left the office and went up the stairs and out of the Lotus Amusement Arcade. I had a sinking feeling about the five hundred dollars I had invested in International Finders, and I also tend to mistrust Chinese who speak faultless English and are inordinately polite. I have felt that such people read too many novels about people like themselves.

Nevertheless, I permitted myself to be modestly hopeful when I returned the following day. Muscles was waiting for me. I realized that Muscles was a very handsome young man. He had a square face, a square chin, square brows, and a square nose; in fact, his face was like a stock painting of the young American male by an unimaginative magazine illustrator, and as devoid of any glimmer of intelligence; but then again, my distaste for his face might have been increased by the enormous spread of his shoulders. He led me downstairs, and when I went into the office he followed me and stood with his back against the door. Mr. Ling sat behind the desk, smiling politely and diffidently.

"Good morning, Mr. Macklin," he said.

"Good morning, Mr. Ling," I replied.

He was writing something on a slip of paper in front of him, and now he finished, placed his pen in its desk stand, and studied what he had written. Then, without looking up at me, he said:

"I am an unassuming Oriental, Mr. Macklin, but not wholly without means and resources. Not only is this place quite profitable, but I have a substantial import-export business of my own. Unlike your Mr. Karoki, I *am* in the business. Why did you feel that you had to devise that shabby trick and attempt to make a fool of me?"

"What shabby trick?" I demanded, summoning up all the indignation I could manufacture with Muscles breathing down my back.

"International Finders, Mr. Macklin. A dummy corporation to dupe children and genteel ladies. Such a shabby little trick! What did you take me for, Mr. Macklin? Did it never occur to you that I might have connections in England and that these connections might be available by telephone? Did it not occur to you that the British records would show that no one named Karoki had been in the import-export business, that no one by that name had died in 1957? Did it not occur to you that I might also have connections in Portugal, and that the Portuguese government might be troubled by the fact that a foreigner had died intestate and left fifteen million escudos on deposit in the Grand National Bank? And that this was not reported? Surely you know enough about the Portuguese government to realize that it would hardly remain indifferent to such a sum. Now would you like to explain all this to me, Mr. Macklin?"

He did not raise his voice or even allow more than a note of impatience to creep into it, and when he finished he smiled again to show me that all this was between two men of the world.

"If I did explain it," I suggested, "would you be willing to talk about Sylvia Karoki?"

"I have never heard the name before yesterday, Mr. Macklin, so I would be poorly suited to the task."

"Sylvia Carter?"

"An equally unfamiliar name, Mr. Macklin."

"Then I can't see that an explanation would serve any purpose," I told him.

"Perhaps so," he sighed. "Then there only remains my bill." He took the slip of paper he had been working on before and read from it: "Telephone to London: fifty-two dollars and thirty cents; telephone to Lisbon: sixty-nine dollars and eighty cents; my own time, which I value conservatively at fifty dollars an hour—I have given three hours of it to your little deception—one hundred and fifty dollars. In short, Mr. Macklin, you owe me two hundred and seventy-two dollars and ten cents.

"What?"

"Precisely, Mr. Macklin."

The long arms of Muscles enveloped me, slid over my body and under my arms, and then dropped away.

"He's clean, Mr. Ling," Muscles said.

"Do you seriously expect me to pay you two hundred and seventy-two dollars and ten cents?" I yelled.

"I do—and before you leave this room. If you are short of cash, I'll be delighted to take your check." Mr. Ling smiled and nodded.

"Like hell I will!"

"Well," Mr. Ling sighed, "then you will force me to do what they always seem to do in those silly films—to tell Muscles to work you over until your mood changes."

"You wouldn't dare."

"Oh, of course I would, Mr. Macklin!" Mr. Ling revealed just a trace of asperity. "We are a floor below the street, and my door is soundproof. Really, you have been annoying and childish. Please don't provoke the situation any further. Unless, of course, you are one of those film detectives who could take on the two hundred and thirty pounds of Muscles and beat him to a pulp."

"No," I admitted quietly. "I am not that kind of a detective, Mr. Ling."

"So much the better." Mr. Ling nodded.

I took out my wallet and counted out two hundred and seventy-two dollars. Mr. Ling reminded me about the ten cents, and I added a dime. Mr. Ling smiled. I didn't smile. Muscles smiled as he took me by the arm and led me upstairs, through the arcade, and out onto Broadway.

I walked back to my hotel in a daze and went up to my room and sprawled out on my bed. As I have admitted, my opinion of myself was nothing to write home about, but I had always considered myself brighter than the average.

5

It did me no good to blow my top at Jack Fenney, nor could I permit myself the luxury of blowing off in a manner suited to my frame of mind. The only foothold and helping hand I had in New York City was Triboro Investigations, and there was no anticipating when I would need them and how much. But I did go downtown to their offices and take what pleasure I could in telling Jack Fenney exactly what I thought of International Finders.

"Look, this wasn't set up for no Chinese businessman," Fenney admitted. "I been through this. No matter what precautions you take, you do business with a Chinese and you come out on the short end. He won't cheat you and he won't take you, but as sure as God, you're going to come out on the short end."

"He didn't take me, Fenney—you did. And for five yards. Do you know, back on the Coast I'd put in a month's hard work and be damned lucky to get five hundred dollars out of it?"

"Mack, take it easy. It comes out of expenses—didn't you

tell me that yourself? And what did you expect me to do—put a fix in on the Portuguese government? They got a dictator there. You know what it costs to pay off those cookies?"

"But you could have managed some kind of death cover in England."

"Ah, Mack—for five yards? Look, don't hold it against me. Stay away from Chinese. You want to use this setup, use it on a plain, straightforward American millionaire."

"And how about the two hundred and seventy-two dollars? The least you could do is split it with me."

Fenney looked at me and grinned, and that was all the satisfaction I got from him.

6

I spent the morning and afternoon of the following day doing one or two things that I wanted to do, and thinking too. I went to a couple of large bookstores on Fifth Avenue and I bought four books. I ate lunch at a high-class hamburger stand on Madison Avenue, and then I saw a French film in a theater opposite the Plaza Hotel on Fifty-eighth Street. Then I walked down to Fifty-third Street and spent two hours at the Museum of Modern Art. I was trying desperately to prove to myself that I had slightly more than average intelligence and that years of carrying out stupid and degrading jobs in a worthless and degrading profession had not removed me entirely from the fraternity of civilization—that is, considering that there was a fraternity of civilization.

At four o'clock in the afternoon I stopped in at my hotel and wrote this on a piece of hotel stationery:

"I would like to buy you dinner tonight. I will pay you one hundred dollars—the dinner thrown in—for two hours of your company and conversation. I am at the Park Sheraton, and I will be waiting in my room between six and seven o'clock. The twenty is a token of my trustworthiness and trust."

I signed my name to it, wrapped it in a twenty-dollar bill, and made my way down Broadway to the Lotus Amusement Arcade. As I entered, Muscles spotted me from the back of the place and started toward me. I made the change booth first, shoved the folded bill at Mrs. Argona, and told her to keep the change. Then I stepped aside so that Muscles could take hold of me with no inconvenience to himself. As we moved toward the entrance, I attempted to maintain my dignity and assured him that I was leaving. He agreed that I was leaving. "Why do you want to throw me out and create a disturbance?" I said to him. "I told you I'm leaving." Chesty joined us and said the same thing and pointed out that we were attracting a crowd and that a crowd did nobody any good. He convinced Muscles, who let go of me with a final warning that I was marked lousy at the Lotus Amusement Arcade.

"Take your pennies somewhere else, Jack," he said. "Next time I work you over. Ask Chesty how I work someone over."

"He works them over good," Chesty agreed. "In your line of work why don't you learn judo or something, mister?"

"Judo!" Muscles grinned. "That's right, Jack, you learn judo and then come back."

"It's an art," the little man said enthusiastically. "You wouldn't believe what a little Jap can do with that art."

I thanked them both and walked uptown to my hotel. After I had taken a bath and dressed, I put in a call to Mr. Frederick Summer in Los Angeles. It was only three o'clock in Los Angeles, and Mr. Summers had not yet returned from lunch. I told his bright secretary—the one who knew all about Miró —that I was at the Park Sheraton Hotel, on Fifty-sixth Street and Seventh Avenue in New York, and that I was making fair progress, and that I would appreciate it if Mr. Summers would wire me some expense money. She asked me how much, and I said I would leave that up to Mr. Summers, but that he might as well know that what I had started with was practically gone.

7

You never know about people. I waited until seven o'clock and had about given up on Mrs. Argona and on my own intelligence and intuition, when the phone rang and there was Mrs. Argona. She told me that if I was really serious about a good dinner and the two hours of conversation for one hundred dollars I should meet her at the Colony Restaurant at eight o'clock. In case I didn't know it, she further informed me, the Colony was not cheap and I would do well to wear a suit instead of the sport jacket I wore at the Lotus Amusement Arcade. In addition, she wanted the hundred dollars in advance. She was a woman of her word, she said, and for one hundred dollars she would tell me anything she knew, including the history of her own sex life, if that was what I was interested in.

Then I called the Colony. They were very dubious about the possibilities of a table at eight o'clock, but they felt certain that I could be seated before nine.

At eight o'clock I was at the restaurant. At eight forty-five Mrs. Argona, wrapped in yards of black satin, swept in, gave me a queenly nod, offered me a shapeless hand, and thought it unimportant to explain what had kept her. Her black hair was piled up on her head; false eyelashes curled out from her natural ones and up to meet the heavy bands of mascara that enveloped her lids; her great cheeks were wild and glowing with rouge, and the lipstick, magenta in color, lay thickly upon the tiny rosebud mouth.

"Hungry, sweetie pie?" she said to me.

"Yes, I'm hungry," I whispered, and followed the headwaiter to our table. At least when you walked with Mrs. Argona you were neither unnoticed nor unimportant; every head in the place turned to watch us, and Mrs. Argona was neither disturbed nor flustered. She swept through the place as if she had just purchased it, and as the waiter placed the chair under her enormous bulk she smiled benignly upon him. I had to admit to myself that she won the first round; the people there that night may have considered her unusual, but I don't think there was one of them who would have dared to consider her unimportant. She leaned over the table toward me and said softly:

"You see, child, I'm a fat old beat-up tramp, and nobody's taken me to dinner in a place like this in ten years. I don't know what you're after, but whatever it is, I'm going to enjoy it."

I nodded.

"You're a nice boy," she added. "You just relax."

"I'm relaxed," I said.

"That's good. Now suppose you buy me a martini. Tell him to make it dry. And do you know—I want something to nibble on. Do you know what I want to nibble on?"

"Caviar," I said.

"How did you know? You know, you're sensitive. I like sensitive people. I like sensitive boys. I want Beluga caviar, and I don't want any of that nonsense with chopped onion and chopped eggs—just plain Beluga caviar and a half of lemon and some toast to spread it on. I hope you like Beluga caviar?"

"I don't think I've ever tasted it," I said weakly.

"Then this is going to be a treat. You know, I think tonight's going to be a treat. You know, I love this place. It gives me a feeling—you know what I mean?"

I told her that it was the first time I had ever been there. "Sweet boy, wait and see."

She had three martinis and three orders of Beluga caviar, and she swore on her holy honor that ten years before she had weighed one hundred and nineteen pounds. I didn't doubt it, but she swore to it anyway. I had asked her if she had worked at the Lotus Amusement Arcade ten years ago. She replied that she was hungry. "Dear boy," she said, "I eat like a pig. That's the fat lady's secret and the fat man's secret. It's the only pleasure remaining that fills me with a sort of sick guilt and horror. Would you like to go to bed with me?"

"I hardly know you, Mrs. Argona," I managed to say.

"Dear boy, there you are. Neither would anyone else. So I eat. And don't call me Mrs. Argona. Argona was a little louse I married twenty years ago, and it's almost twenty years since I have seen him and I don't want to see him even in hell. It's better to be Mrs. when you got my figure—I mean, it gives you a little dignity and it's proof that someone wanted to marry you, even a little louse like Argona. But I don't want to think about that tonight. You call me Gracie. Try it."

"I'll call you Gracie." I nodded. She grew on you; she grew on me. I don't know how she did it, but with her own curious magic she called for respect. I found myself beginning to like her. "Yes, Gracie," I agreed. "They call me Mack."

"And what can I do for you, Mack?"

I took out a picture of Sylvia, the portrait bust, and I handed it to her. She looked at it—a long and thoughtful look.

"You know her, Gracie?"

Still she studied the picture.

"Do you know her, Gracie?"

Without glancing up: "I know her."

"Who is she?"

"Sylvia Carter."

"You're sure?"

"I'm sure." Her face was in motion now. Her cheeks quivered. The little rosebud mouth contorted, and suddenly she began to cry. One of the false eyelashes came loose; the mascara began to run.

"Gracie—can I do something?"

"Give me your handkerchief," she whimpered.

"The last thing I wanted to do was to make you cry."

"You didn't make me cry." She wiped at her face, and rouge and mascara and pancake make-up blended into a viscous mass. "Sweet boy," she whined through the handkerchief, "you didn't make me cry. It's just that goddamn picture—she's so stinking beautiful and look at me—a fat old whore!"

8

Frederick Summers had been right in one thing, in his interdiction of Sylvia, the flesh-and-blood Sylvia, in terms of myself. I suppose at the time his had been simply a defensive gesture; he was engaging in an unforgivable and unexplainable course of action, and he desired to bolster himself where he could. But beyond that, the whole game would have been lost had I ever spoken to Sylvia—perhaps if I had ever laid eyes upon her.

As it was, the more deeply I became involved with the deepening shadow of a woman I did not know, yet knew better than any other woman in the world—the more deeply I became involved, the more necessary it was for me to continue. Like the act of creation, the act of discovery can have a very profound effect upon a human being, and neither creation nor discovery had ever been a part of my life. The energy of my life that had not been directed toward the biological necessities of existence had been applied to the salving of my own hurt; but like so many people who are very much alone, the real awareness and fear of my loneliness came through another person.

Perhaps it is most plainly put in this way: I had never been required to comprehend or understand another human being; now my existence depended upon it.

I had to understand why Sylvia worked on the night shift, from 6 P.M. until 2 A.M., at the Lotus Amusement Arcade for nine months, and why during all of that time she never had a relationship with a man. She reached her eighteenth year there. She passed into the full flower of her womanhood there. And she was virginal there.

But perhaps of all the things men saw and remembered in Sylvia, the quality of her virginity was the most striking. I know of nothing in all man's recorded history that is more tinged with mockery and idiocy than his concepts of virginity and his categorization of women on the yardstick of a physical act. Six hundred years ago Boccaccio wrote the story of the princess who, on a roundabout trip to her promised prince, went to bed with a very considerable number of men—yet finished as a virgin bride. A hundred years later Malory extended the concept of virginity to men as a source of strength. I have known immaculate sluts; the face on Sylvia's pictures was the face of a woman without evil or guilt; but I had seen that expression on the faces of too many women to be impressed. But I was not afraid, and Frederick Summers was—and cursed with the infantile worship of one of the major lies he had lived with. Otherwise he would not have employed me to discover whether Sylvia was a good or bad woman—something I was no more enlightened upon than when I had begun my search.

Still, I knew that people lived easily with the lies and hated the truth, and not the least of the beloved lies is the book version of good and bad. The idiocy of our existence is tempered with a sardonic reasonableness; and there is a strange sanity in the fact that Sylvia took certain vows in a cashier's cage. She stood there, tall and beautiful and immaculate, and around her the pinball machines clattered, the tired sex films were cranked, the automatic picture booths blinked on and off, and the skee balls bounced.

Outside, the shabby, tawdry rubberneck life of Broadway poured back and forth. The days shortened as winter came. Rain and snow and sleet fell, and winter passed into spring and summer.

This was nine months of Sylvia's life.

9

"Why do you want to know?" Mrs. Argona asked me.

"You never asked me for the hundred dollars." I took out my wallet and pushed two fifties across the table toward her.

"The hell with your lousy hundred."

"She was a friend of yours, Gracie?"

"What do you think? We lived together—maybe she was the only good thing ever happened to me. Sometimes I wish I was a dike, the lousy luck I had with men. So now I should cut her heart out for your rotten hundred."

"Suppose I tell you that, as much as I know how and can do it, I won't let any harm come to her."

"When a man says something like that, Mack, it's ninety per cent bullshit."

"All right. I'm not lying to you, Gracie."

"Where is she now?"

"I'm trying to find her."

"Why?"

"Because I have to."

She sighed and took the hundred dollars and folded it up in her purse. "What do you want to know?" she said sadly. We had finished dinner. I ordered two brandies. She tasted it with a delicate tip of her tongue through the rosebud mouth.

"How come you lived with her, Gracie?"

"I lived in a furnished-room place on West Fifty-first; she was living in a hotel downtown. Ling pays good. That place is a gold mine. We took home about seventy-five dollars each, I think—let me see—yeah, something like that. Then they put up a new building on Eight Avenue and Fifty-third, and we took a three-room apartment for a hundred and twenty dollars a month. Unfurnished. We bought stuff for it. Funny, I was twenty years older than Sylvia then, but we were like a couple of kids. There was some dame she knew in Pittsburgh, where she was born, and she wanted this place to look like that. Oh, what the hell—that's water under the bridge. You don't want that. How about another brandy, sweetie pie?"

I ordered two more.

"I had no steady then," Mrs. Argona said. "I took on a guy once in a while, mostly some guy I knew, and I leveled with Sylvia about it. Funny thing about Sylvia—she never told you what to do for your own good. So we got along. I was only thirty-eight. I had a good figure; maybe you wouldn't believe it, but I did."

"I believe you."

"Sure . . ." Her voice trailed away and she stared at the brandy. "You're a smart guy, Mack. You talk like a smart guy, anyway. What does it all add up to? I haven't got a friend in the world. I'm just a fat old whore, sitting here and selling you information worth twenty cents for a yard. Maybe you're crazy. What kind of sense does any of it make?"

"I don't know," I said.

"I used to tell Sylvia it's the same. It's a rap you can't beat. It's like that stinking cashier's cage; it holds up your tits and makes you think you got the world licked for eight hours. That's an illusion."

"Did Sylvia take men on?"

"No! I told you before—she had nothing with anyone! She didn't want it. She was as pure as my mother then. You hear me? As pure as my mother!"

"I know that, Gracie."

"You know that! What the hell do you know? You don't know a goddamn thing! How I pleaded with that girl! I pleaded with her to take advantage of some things. Ling wanted to set her up. Maybe you don't like Ling. Maybe you got feelings about a Chinese. But Ling has millions. . . ."

10

Or perhaps Ling was attracted by the dark-eyed purity of the girl—as he saw it. He was a strange, complex, and romantic person, as many like him are behind the so-called "inscrutable" mask, and he could not accept so simple an explanation of Sylvia's presence as the plain fact—that she had been walking up Broadway and saw a "Girl Wanted" sign in his window. It had to be more than that—it had to be some complex of fate, as he afterward told Sylvia and as she had told it to Gracie. His morality, like his thinking and philosophy, was a garbled combination of China, America, and Broadway. In the light of this, he said to Sylvia once:

"I would be most pleased to see myself as you see me—to

look at myself through your eyes. How do you see me, Sylvia?"

"What a strange thing to say!"

Her answer was deliberate, and he was flattered. The core of Sylvia's innocence was her understanding of men, but that was an understanding of a segment. The whole, she never understood.

"Not at all strange," Ling protested. "Unusual, possibly—but not strange. It is a perfectly natural thing for one to desire to know, and it is an indication of my feelings about you, Sylvia, that I should put it to you so straightforwardly."

But as to what those feelings were—this was something of a puzzle to both Gracie and Sylvia. Ling had taken it upon himself one Sunday—the arcade was closed until five o'clock on Sunday—to invite himself to their apartment, arms loaded with Chinese delicacies and gifts. He was very formal and very correct, an attitude toward Sylvia which had never changed. His conversation on that first occasion, as he sat and drank the tea they prepared, was about the weather, about the various delicacies, about the difficulty those days in importing anything really lovely from China, and about the books he saw there. They were Sylvia's—and Gracie explained to him that Sylvia accumulated books just the way that other people tend to accumulate all sorts of trash and magazines. Sylvia said nothing—only watching him intently as he examined the books. He was very well read and made a number of appropriate comments. When he remarked on the three novels by Jane Austen and Sylvia replied that she kept them to reread rather than read, since she had read them so many times before, he glanced at her as if he had not actually seen her until now.

Gracie offered her opinion later, when Ling had gone, to the effect of his being greatly taken by Sylvia. Gracie wanted

to feel that there was some great tragedy in Ling's past, but Sylvia laughed and said he was no different from any other man. "He may have been terribly hurt by some woman," Gracie said, possibly to explain his aloof and restrained manner, but Sylvia said that in her opinion no man had ever been terribly hurt by any woman.

The day after that a package from Ling arrived at the apartment, magnificently bound editions of the four great Chinese novels: *All Men Are Brothers, The Golden Lotus, Money,* and *The Dream of the Red Chamber.* They were in English translation, and they were new to Sylvia, books she had never heard of by authors she had never heard of. Gracie, who tried to read one of them, drawn by the manner in which Sylvia buried herself in them, found little to excite her. She also discovered that Sylvia's delight in the gift made no difference in Sylvia's feeling about Ling.

A week or so later Ling fell into the habit of asking Sylvia to share a late dinner with him in his office; here, too, his manner and attitude toward her were exemplary in every way —that is, he made no move to touch her or kiss her or make love to her in any fashion. I asked Gracie what they did during these suppers, and Gracie told me that Ling taught Sylvia Chinese. This relationship between Ling and Sylvia went on for almost five months. At the end of that time Sylvia had absorbed a working knowledge of Mandarin Chinese and a good deal of Chinese knowledge and culture.

It was also at the end of this period that Ling asked Sylvia to clarify his image in her eyes.

"You are very kind," Sylvia finally replied, "very kind, very earnest, very sincere. I have learned a great deal from you."

"Not from me," Ling protested modestly. "My contribution was a humble one—just as my humble abode here was lightened and made lovely by your presence. You are a remarkable woman, Sylvia. You are the only woman I have ever known whom I wanted and needed."

Sylvia told Gracie that when Ling said what he said, not only the words but the manner of his saying it, she was afraid of a man for the first time in her life. While I doubted this and imagined that Sylvia had been not a little afraid of men on various other occasions, I understood what she meant. I had also seen the expression on Ling's face; it was not difficult to be afraid of him.

"I'm sorry it has to be that way," Sylvia said. "I wish I could say that I feel honored and touched, but I feel damn silly. I should have known that it always works out this way."

"You don't understand me," Ling said evenly. "I do nothing lightly—least of all say what I just said. There are women whom you take and women whom you honor and revere. There are the sluts and the goddesses. There are the tramps and the virgins. I have built an altar to you and burned my offerings upon it. . . ."

For weeks Sylvia had carefully rehearsed what she intended to say on this occasion, aware that this occasion had to arise. She had planned exactly how to handle it, how to develop it, how to finish it; and now, faced with it, all her intentions went down the drain, and she said to Ling bluntly:

"That's pure shit, and you know it!"

He went over to her and spit in her face. She slapped him. He caught her with a solid right into her abdomen, and she doubled up on the floor. He stood over her, saying, "Lousy ungrateful bitch," when she staggered to her feet, grabbed a chair, and broke it over his head. He fell to the floor unconscious, and she left him there, convinced that she had killed him.

When Gracie walked into the apartment around midnight of that day, she saw Sylvia sitting in a chair, with blank, hollow eyes.

"I killed Ling," Sylvia informed her. "I have just killed a decent Chinese gentleman who didn't do anything to me except spit in my face and belt me one. What should I do when the cops come?"

Then Gracie went over to the Lotus Amusement Arcade, where she saw Ling, a lump the size of a pigeon egg on his head. She returned to the apartment to tell Sylvia that Ling was alive and that she, Sylvia, was presently without employment.

11

"The funny thing," Gracie said, "is that Ling was right."

"How do you mean?"

"The virginity and all that crap."

"Oh?"

"For nine months this kid had been a virgin," Gracie explained. "I don't know why. You got to have a measure for people, ain't that right, Mack?"

"I don't follow you."

"Well—someone'll ask me about you. So I'll say—well, Mack's like that professor type, you know, Dick Powell or something."

"He's not a professor type and I don't look like him."

"Sure—sure, I know. But you're a private cop. So I say you're like a private cop, or Bogart or someone, only you're not tough."

"I try."

"Sure you try, sweet boy, but you're not tough. I mean, I

can say you're like someone. I got a measure for you. I say you're a nice boy. You sit here with a fat slob like me and treat me like I was a queen or something. See? But about Sylvia—I didn't read her. Who was she like? No one. Why was she a virgin like a damn queer or something like that? I don't know. I don't know what she had to get out of her system or into it. Maybe Ling saw something that wasn't there, or maybe it was. I talk to her and I'm talking to the wall. I say to her, 'Look, kid, what do you want out of life?' Then she just looks at me as if she's trying to understand what I'm saying to her. She looks stupid at me, but she ain't. She's the smartest kid I ever knew, not wise-guy smart, not sharp smart like the two-bit little tramps, not mean smart like the new crop of little whores with the hard pussies who train themselves to have no feelings at all—not that, but smart the way you're smart, Mack, only a lot more. You follow me?"

"I follow you," I said.

"But where to? It's smart in a circle. You think because I'm a fat old bag and getting tight in a fancy restaurant on your expense account that I don't read you a little, Mack? Let me tell you that I do. No wife, no family, nothing, just you alone. Right?"

"Right." I nodded.

"Don't get mad, sweetie. I'm just making a point. Where do you get on and where do you get off? You ever think about it?"

"I think about it," I said.

"That kind of smart—that's your Sylvia. Like you. She reads a million books. You know that Chesty, that little horny son of a bitch with the big red nose, the one who peddles the dirty poems out of his apron?"

I nodded.

"He's French. Never think so, would you? He came over here when he was a kid. Sylvia pays him to come to the apartment every morning on his way to the arcade and give her French lessons. Do you get that? French lessons. Do you believe me?"

"I believe you."

"What kind of smart? It's a crazy smart! Here's this kid eighteen years old and been through every goddamn thing that can happen to a kid, out West and in Mexico, and not enough brains to come out of the rain when it's raining, but all of a sudden a virgin and taking French lessons. You know what I mean?"

"I know what you mean," I said.

12

"He was here again," Gracie said. "He stinks! I swear to God I can smell the little son of a bitch when he's been here."

"Gracie, forget it."

"What do you pay him for these lessons?"

"Two dollars."

"Two dollars. Forty-five minutes. Two dollars. Jesus, honey, you're out of your mind!"

"Forget it, Gracie. When he's here, you're not here."

"I tell you, he's all horn. That little son of a bitch is a tool. He'll strangle you someday."

"No, he won't, Gracie. I don't want to talk about it."

"Sure. Sure. Just tell me one thing—you talk spick already. Now it's Chinese and French. What in hell are you going to be, a goddamn interpreter at the UN?"

"Interpreter—no. You know what I am."

"What are you, a floozie? Is that where all the smart and the books get you? I tried it. Look at me, and I'm not smart, not even bright enough to know the way home. I'm twenty years older than you—look at me!"

"I'm sorry, Gracie."

13

"I didn't even know what I was yelling at her for," Gracie said. "No connection. Oh, Jesus God, how I loved that kid! Not queer. You just got to look at me and see I'm no dike. I don't have to prove that, do I, Mack?"

"No, you don't have to prove it," I said softly.

"Don't love anyone, Mack," she said dismally. "You live longer, if you want to live longer. I don't know why anyone should want to live longer, but they do."

I asked her gently, "Gracie, could Sylvia love anyone?"

"What do you mean, sweetie?"

"You know what I mean."

"She was never in love, sweetie."

"Could she?"

"Why, honey?" Gracie was dozing, her head nodding forward. I paid the check, ninety dollars with the tip. It was the biggest check for two people I had ever paid and one I minded paying the least; and I was about at rock bottom with my expense money.

"Why, honey?" Gracie whispered again. "You love her? Go take the torch somewhere else, sweetie pie. There's no percentage in loving Sylvia—none at all——"

I took her home to a tenement between Ninth and Tenth avenues on Fiftieth Street, an old-law building that reeked with the smell of age and rot and urine and garbage, and I helped her up a flight of stairs and used her key to open the door of the two-room apartment where she made her life. She must have weighed three hundred pounds, and when I finally got her into an armchair every muscle in my body ached. Then she sat there—legs stretched, a vast shapeless mass of black satin and puffy white flesh—in a room of untidiness and aimless disorder as aimless as her own poor life. Now, under the bright overhead light, the colored paint on her face was grotesque yet pathetic, and her little rosebud mouth pouted as she begged me not to look at her.

"I know what I look like," she sighed. "Dear boy, make me a cup of black coffee."

I went into the kitchen, and among the smells and dirty dishes I found the percolator, washed it, and put up coffee to cook. When it was ready, I poured a cup for each of us, cleared an end table, and sat down beside her.

"You're a dear boy, Mack." She nodded. "What time is it?"

It was one in the morning.

"I know what I look like at one in the morning, sweet boy. You know, I had a fine time. I had a ball. Just imagine—an old slob like me having such a ball with you, sweetie!"

"You didn't have a fine time," I said. "I dragged up ghosts. Someday, Gracie, you and I will go out to dinner again, and no goddamn ghosts, not one of them."

"Sweet boy——"

"You want to tell me any more?"

"If I can stay awake, sweet boy. If I was ten years younger, you wouldn't leave here tonight. Oh no—no, you wouldn't!"

"I wouldn't want to, Gracie."

"Sweet boy . . ." She drank the coffee, her head nodding, her eyes blinking in the dark pits of mascara. "You want to find Sylvia, don't you? Sweet boy—I got one thing you ain't got; I won't fall in love with anyone, ever—not even you, sweet boy. What else can I tell you about Sylvia? I don't want to hurt you. You're too nice."

"I don't hurt easily, and I know Sylvia a little. A little, Gracie."

"I'm a floozie. I used to tell her, 'Look at me——' Ah, I'm tired, sweetie."

"What happened to her?"

"What difference does it make now?"

"Tell me, Gracie," I said.

"You heard of Molly Banter?"

"The madam?"

"No other. Well, she came by on Broadway one day when Sylvia still worked at the arcade, and she seen her through the window and went in and got to talking with Sylvia and left her card. That's it."

"You mean Sylvia went to her after she lost the job?"

"That's it."

"What happened?"

"What happened! We had a fight over it and Sylvia moved out, and I let a month go by. Then I phoned her at Molly Banter's place. Then I went over there. No Sylvia. That's all."

"What happened to her, Gracie?"

"Ah, sweet boy—I'm so tired. Why don't you go home? I can't think any more."

"Just tell me what happened to her, Gracie."

"I can't tell you, sweetie. She went. I don't know where or how or why. Gone. Where does a floozie go—good floozies, bad floozies? Go home, Mack."

I got up to leave, and for the first time I realized how hot it was in that apartment. My shirt was soaked through and through. I walked down the stairs with the feeling that they were bottomless, and I got a cab back to my hotel.

There was a wire from Summers waiting for me. He had sent me a thousand dollars more.

PART 7

NEW YORK (PARK AVENUE)

I NEEDED THE FOLLOWING DAY FOR MYSELF. I NEEDED A DAY in which I would not speak or think of Sylvia Karoki Carter West, a day without strong-arm men or cheap hustlers or broken-down prostitutes; and I planned to spend it in the Central Park Zoo. I had seen the zoo from Fifth Avenue, and I planned to wander through it slowly and rewardingly, to sit on the wooden benches in the sunshine and watch the kids play, to feed pigeons and elephants and whatever else there might be in the zoo that one could feed, and then to have my lunch under one of the umbrellas that made such bright spots of color on the cafeteria terrace.

It was a mild and modest desire, but when I woke up at about ten o'clock it was pouring a steady, dismal rain outside —an earnest rain that showed no sign of slackening. I showered and dressed and went down to the drugstore for my eggs and morning paper, and then it was still raining. So I called Jack Fenney and made a date to have a late lunch with him. We met at Lüchow's, an old German restaurant on Fourteenth Street, and we ate bratwurst and lentils and talked about Jeff Peters, who was a legend in the private investigation business, and about what would happen to the Brooklyn Dodgers and the New York Giants on the West Coast; and then we got to talking about baseball when we were kids and the difference between baseball then and baseball today. We decided, after an analysis of Christy Mathewson, Bill Keeler, Tyrus R. Cobb, George H. Ruth, Carl Hubbell, and a number of others—no less immortal than the heroes of Homer's time—that baseball was no longer what it had been when we were kids, nor was anything else, for that matter. We remembered the rosy glow of hope and sweetness that lay upon the whole world then, but I imagine that is an act of remembering and also a rosy glow common to every generation this world has ever seen. In the course of this, we each of us had three whisky sours, and I had temporarily stopped thinking about what a lousy cutthroat Fenney was and about what a patsy I had been for almost a thousand dollars out of his smart Finders setup; and I suppose he forgot for a little while that I was a country boy in the big city.

I asked him what he knew about Molly Banter.

"When you and I were kids, Mack." He grinned. "They don't do things any more the way Molly Banter did them. She goes way back to the twenties. Today a floozie's a floozie, but back in the days of Molly Banter a floozie was a real lady of pleasure and she lived in a real house of ill repute, just like the books say, and Molly Banter was a madam like they don't have no more, no sir, and believe you me, Mack boy, she entertained some great ones—and some live ones too."

"She goes that far back?"

"Sure as hell—way, way back. Just take a walk up Fifth Avenue someday, Mack, and look at some of them old citizens in the fancy clubs, and you can make it ten to one that most of them cut their teeth in Molly Banter's palace of pleasure. Way back. Yes indeed."

"Is she still alive?"

"The old bitch'll never die, Mack. Only the good die young, or so they tell me."

"You don't mean she's still at it?" I asked him.

"No. She kept trying, but eight or nine years ago she threw in the bag and retired with maybe two or three million. They say she never spent a nickel, except on the business. She wrote a book then——"

"She wrote a book?"

"Don't you remember? Hell, I don't mean she wrote it. She hired Artie Felson, who used to work on the *Journal-American* here, and she told him her story, and maybe he added a little piss and vinegar on his own, and the goddamn thing earned them both a fortune."

"What does she do now?"

"She's retired, my lad," Fenney said. "Enjoys the fruits of a life of sin and infamy—as much as an old bag of maybe seventy-five or eighty can enjoy things. She's got an apartment on Park Avenue, and they tell me that she throws some high-class parties and gets a lot of the celebrity crowd."

"You can go a long way in this town."

"All the way to hell and back, my boy. You know, when she tried to move into this place on Park Avenue, they didn't want her. The landlord thought it would run the place down to have a notorious old whore and madam living there, so Molly got some of her old clients together and formed a syndicate and bought the goddamn place—what do you think of that?"

"I think you can do better as a pimp than a gumshoe."

"That's no lie."

"Jack," I said to him, "can you get me an appointment with her?"

"Molly Banter? I told you she's retired."

"Stop clowning. I want to talk to her."

"You know"—Fenney nodded—"you might do yourself a favor, Mack, if you'd tell me what the hell you're after."

"You asked Jeff Peters, didn't you?"

"Sure I asked him!" Fenney was indignant at the thought that I suspected him of doing something behind my back. "You know I talk to Peters two, three times a week. Wouldn't I be a sap not to ask him?"

"What did he say?"

"That he didn't know."

"So let it lay. If I could tell someone like you, then the man who hired me would have given it to an agency like yours, and then you could clear the whole thing up in three days, just sitting on your behind and giving orders."

"Who hired you—the FBI?"

When the check came, I took it. It was a hard thing to do and I would have preferred to stuff it down Fenney's throat, but I wanted something from him and I would probably want other favors too.

"Well," I said, "will you set me up with Molly Banter?"

"Why don't you just walk in and use the International Finders stuff?"

"All five yards of it at once?"

"It might work."

"If what you say about her is true," I said, "then she can give plenty of odds to a Chinese businessman, and she'll see through that idiotic gimmick we cooked up just like it was glass."

"I never seen anyone cry over a little expense money the way you do."

"Seven hundred and fifty dollars is not a little—maybe in your time, but not in mine. Anyway, if I'm any judge, there's only one way to move a flint-hearted old floozie like that who probably has a trap of steel to begin with."

"How?"

"Sentiment. I want to be someone's brother, Jack. Can you fix me up with a Pennsylvania driver's license or something that looks like one and make it fit the name of Alan Carter?"

"It will cost you."

"Oh, Jesus God," I said, "hasn't it cost me enough? Have a heart! Have a little pity!"

"It's got to cost you twenty-five bucks."

"And you make the connection with Molly Banter?"

"That I'll throw in free," Fenney said with a big grin.

2

The rain stopped the next day, and I went to the zoo and had lunch at the cafeteria terrace. I fed the pigeons and the elephants and then gave it up because it was almost as hot in El Paso. The driver's license arrived, duly made out in the name of Alan Carter, and when I called Jack Fenney he told me to be patient and he'd have something for me within twenty-four hours. I tried an English movie this time, enjoyed it only moderately; mostly, I imagine, because I found it exceedingly difficult to concentrate upon what was going on in the film. After that I walked down Fifth Avenue to Brentano's bookstore at Forty-seventh Street, where I bought a paperback edition of Molly Banter's book. I took it back to the hotel, had sandwiches and coffee sent up to my room, and read through until about 2 A.M., when I finished the book.

It was neither a good nor an informative book. It was written in pedestrian journalese and as packed with clichés as a squash is with seeds. Lust had been replaced by titillation, and putting their heads together, the reporter and the old whoremonger made the business of prostitution sound like the functioning of a classy finishing school. Oh, it was a great big lark, and old Molly was a mother to the wayward girls, and there were enough leers and innuendoes to make it a big gossip item at the country clubs and at Schrafft's, but no names were named. The old lady had principles and was out to prove that there was as much honor among floozies as among thieves.

I learned nothing from it, and I was full of that frustrated and angry feeling I always have when I put hours into a poor and profitless book or film or show. I don't know why I should feel that way, because the time I earn my dollar with is just as rotten and just as wasted, but there it is.

I wasn't sleepy. I sat at the window, smoking and looking at the city—moonlit and silent and devoid of all motion but an occasional car. The first hint of sunrise was already in the sky when I crawled into my bed and fell asleep.

3

It was midday when I awakened, and after I had showered and dressed and was going into the problem of whether I had sufficient appetite to eat breakfast or lunch or whatever one might call it, the phone rang and a voice asked for Alan Carter. I had slept away the small amount of alertness I am endowed with, and I told the voice that my name was Macklin. The voice said that he knew that, but that Jack Fenney had informed him he would find Carter at the same number. Then I remembered, and I was very cordial to the voice, who informed me that his name was Fred Swanson, that he was a friend of Jack Fenney's, and that Jack Fenney had asked him to introduce me to Molly Banter. He, Swanson, just happened to be going along to have cocktails with Molly Banter that evening, and he'd be happy to take me along with him and make the introductions. I said that would be fine, and he suggested that he stop by at about six and we could share a cab over to Molly Banter's place.

At five-fifty that day he called my room again and said he would be waiting at the newsstand in the lobby. I came directly down and we shook hands and said the things that people say. He was a tall, thin man, perhaps a few years older than I, good, regular features and Brooks Brothers clothes. He looked like what I had always imagined a Madison Avenue account executive would look like, but it turned out that he was a partner in the brokerage house of *Aylesworth, Beale and Gray* and only a step away from having his own name added to the list. When he told me this, he added somewhat uneasily:

"Really, Carter, I owe more than I care to talk about to Jack Fenney, and I suppose that if he asked me to clean out the office safe and bring the contents to him I'd feel obligated to do it. At the same time, and not wishing to offend you in any way, it would seem that Carter isn't your real name?"

"That's possible. In New York State it's no crime."

"Well, that's none of my business, but Molly Banter is one of the firm's better accounts, and I hope none of this bounces back."

"I can promise you that."

He appeared to be considerably relieved, and in the cab going over to Park Avenue and Seventy-ninth Street he told me that Miss Banter's cocktail parties were a regular weekly institution and that in the winter months one might count two hundred people going in and out, and among them some of the most important names in the city. Now in September, with so many people still away, there might be no more than fifty or sixty present, but most of them would be interesting people. He put that in quotation marks and went on to say that they were not the kind of people he generally met, although, he admitted, he found them unusual and entertaining. He said that he thought he might introduce me as an old college classmate of his.

"What college?"

"Yale?"

I shook my head and suggested that I would do better as an account in his Pittsburgh office with a large bundle to spend on stocks and bonds. "If you have a Pittsburgh office?"

"We have one." He nodded. "I can do that—yes." He was disappointed, but whether in the fact that I wasn't Yale or that he would have to manufacture a little white lie, I didn't know.

We reached the house as part of a converging group and shared the elevator up to Miss Banter's terrace apartment with half a dozen others. It was the only apartment on the landing where the elevator stopped, and the door was open. A maid and a butler took care of hats and other odds and ends, and then we walked through a foyer paved with black and white slabs of marble into a vast living room, one whole side of it open to a terrace that overlooked the park, two avenues away.

I had always been under the impression that movie sets built to simulate Park Avenue apartments were grossly exaggerated, but this one could have been moved to a sound stage with no improvements required. The walls were done in white, with a gold trim and gold dado, and the floor was covered with dusty blue carpeting at least an inch thick, and the furniture was pale blue and ivory. The bar was built behind and around a faded triptych, and the religious note was carried on by two ivory-and-gold cherubs floating on their wings from the high ceiling. Perhaps thirty or forty people were sitting, standing, or ambling about the room and a dozen more were out on the terrace, and new arrivals averaged about half a dozen to the elevator schedule. No one paid any attention to who came in or out; no one greeted anyone or took tickets or anything of that sort; and the way the gate was building up, I felt that Swanson's guess had been an underestimation.

"She hasn't come in yet," Swanson said to me, glancing around the room. "You know, she's an old lady—about an hour of this is her limit." He might have been talking about a duchess or a Nobel Prize winner or Whistler's mother. "Why don't you find a drink and just look around? You'll find it interesting." He was all for you go your way and I'll go mine until I do what I promised, and how could a country boy not be thrilled just to be a part of all this? "Or would you like to meet people?" he asked as an afterthought.

"I'll get drunk," I said, and smiled to show that I didn't really mean I'd get drunk and not be my best before the great lady. We both moved to the bar, but then he drifted off. I stayed to have a straight Scotch quickly and then a double with soda to hold in my hand. A lady who was having her own refilled submitted that I was not an American because of the way I had gulped the first one. When I asked whether it was un-American, she laughed and laughed and had to repeat it to someone because it was so clever.

"I mean," she said, "you can almost spot a person's nationality by how he drinks. You're not an American, are you?"

I said I was a New Zealander.

"And you write books?"

I said I did, and she said that my name was on the tip of her tongue. She and the man she was with or who was around her took me to meet another writer, but she begged me not to tell her my name because it was on the tip of her tongue. The writer was out on the terrace, part of a group of seven or eight people. He was a little man with a gray waistcoat and pearl buttons and a wet cupid-bow mouth, and he was listening to a tall, bronzed, healthy specimen on the subject of a Broadway show.

"I don't mind the fact that it stinks," said the man with the sunburn, "but I mind it when a critic cons me into paying thirty dollars for a pair of seats. If I want art, I go to a museum. I don't go to a musical for art."

"Only murder is an art today," offered the writer, licking his lips and hanging onto the words of the bronzed specimen. "The other arts are decadent—the theater like a dog biting its own tail."

"We can't interrupt them," my guide whispered to me. "How I love to hear good talk!" I told her to listen and that I'd be back. Then I moved in the direction of the bar, working my drink as I went.

I started the fresh drink when Swanson motioned to me, and I joined his cluster, where he introduced me as Mr. Carter. A good-looking woman hoped I wasn't also in the market, and a man who looked like Adolph Menjou said that everyone was in the market and challenged me to contradict him. The good-looking woman asked me what I did, and I said that, aside from a bundle of money my father had left to me and which Mr. Swanson invested for me, I was a teacher of history.

"History? What period?" a tall, white-haired man in the group asked me.

"Ancient history."

"This should fascinate you then." He nodded. "Aside from the fact that we're thirty stories or so above the ground, this could be ancient Rome, couldn't it?"

I said that I hadn't thought of it that way. I didn't see much resemblance to anything in ancient Rome, but I wasn't teaching history now. Anyway, I was beginning to be a little tight, and when that happens I trust myself to talk less. The man who looked like Menjou told the story of the customer in a new and expensive restaurant called The Forum who asked for a martinus. When the waiter corrected him and suggested that he meant a martini, he snorted that when he wanted more than one drink he would ask for it.

On my fourth drink I don't smile out of politeness. The good-looking woman giggled and made another point, and the man of the party who was likely her husband said, "For Christ's sake, Bunny—martinus, one; martini, plural, Latin." Swanson was a smoother-over and confessed that he had missed the point as well and stopped a waiter to find the lady a new drink.

For all its size, the room was filling up. Behind me a shrill masculine voice was consigning the city to doom. "Already," he said, "there are too many cars for any given block. They stick out, and the crosstown traffic stops. This lousy city is dying, choking to death on its own blood."

"He was late to his analyst," another voice behind me.

"Lewis Mumford spelled out the whole thing twenty years ago."

"There you're wrong. I'm the last holdout against the couch. You'll never find me there."

"Alone."

"I was late to rehearsal, if you must know."

Swanson said to me, "She'll come in any minute now, but I think there are too many people here for an introduction to make any sense at this point. Can you stick around until the mob goes?"

"I'm yours, Swanson."

"Fine. There's a girl wants to meet you, a very talented young actress."

"Meet me?"

"She pointed to you, and I told her not to point, because you have money."

The white-haired man said, "Come now, Carter, doesn't this point a moral to a historian—the so-called cream of our city paying homage to an old whore?"

"That's a hell of a thing to say," an addition to the group put in.

"Inaccurate. A madam's no whore."

"I want Carter's opinion," the white-haired man insisted. "How does it look to a college professor?"

Swanson was not as dull as I imagined. He saw me grinning thinly and malignantly and grabbed my arm and steered me away, throwing excuses over his shoulder. "I told you not to get drunk," he whispered. "For God's sake, just talk to this girl. That shouldn't be too hard."

Then we found her, and Swanson told her to take care of me. She was very pretty, with brown hair and blue eyes, and she looked like all the pictures of pretty girls in Miss America contests and everywhere else they print pictures of pretty girls. "Don't you want a drink, Mr. Carter?" she asked me, and I said yes, I wanted a drink and would she please make it a double. At the bar she said, "Don't you think it's cute the way they used those old pictures under the bar? It gives it such décor."

"It's cute the way you're cute——" I said to her.

Afterward I was glad that Molly Banter came in at that point, because at least I never finished what I started to say. There was a kind of hush, and even though there was no band or music, you heard it strike up as a small, plump, old, old lady wrapped in about a thousand dollars' worth of gold-brocaded satin walked into the room.

4

Even Swanson had gone. I was alone in the immense room, drinking black coffee, with the butler and maid cleaning up and an old lady in a white dressing gown sitting facing me. When she talked, it was with a faint and unidentifiable accent, and the voice was tired and defeated.

"You feel better, now?" she said. "All right. Why do you stinking moralists always get drunk? In the old days, when I would see one of you come into my place, I warn the girls— there's one of them. Beware. Lechers and drunks. I don't think I love anything, Mr. Carter, but most of all I hate the moralists, the righteous ones, the purifiers."

"I'm no moralist," I muttered.

"Ha, ha, ha! No? You are a breed. I know you. How many times you been drunk like this in five years, let us say?"

"None."

"No. Of course not. You save it for Molly Banter's place, and you are going to teach that old whoremonger what she is. Ah—you make me sick, such people like you. In my bed-room you vomited on my bedspread, and my bathroom, it stinks like a sewer. Anyone else but me would throw you into the street. And don't think I am so sentimental and you are so good-looking—neither of them. I am curious. Curious. I am also lonely. Look around you. Where are they? They come here for—what is that word?—today your slang is as emasculated as the little homosexual boys who have taken over the theater and the books and everything else—kicks, that is the word, kicks. They come here for kicks, so they can talk about how they were at that old whore's house and who they saw there, but nobody wants to be caught with the old whore herself, and they clear out like Cinderella after the ball. And don't think I am feeling sorry for myself. I am not sorry for myself or for you or for anyone else. Also, remember something else. My butler was once middleweight champion of the world, so I don't stand for any nonsense here. And he doesn't fight clean. He carries brass knucks in his jacket, and when Fats Mc-Gowan, the big-time hoodlum, started to make a scene here one day, my butler, Joey, broke his jaw in two places. I am telling you all this because I don't like people who try to fool me. I don't fool people. I don't pretend. I am a fat old madam, and I am not going to talk about what I give to hospitals and orphanages and how my girls still come to me whenever they are in trouble or need a dollar, because all that is for the birds. I am what I am. But you are not any Mr. Carter, like that phony automobile license in your pocket says. You are a private dick from Los Angeles and your name is Alan Macklin. I also think that you are a stupid young man, and I don't know how someone like yourself can make a living out of anything, even being a private cop. Also, I didn't go through your pockets; Joey did. Such a private cop!"

I nodded feebly.

"It's a wonder someone like you keeps a head on your shoulders."

"It is," I agreed. "It certainly is."

"Now I want to know what you are doing here and why you got that stupid Mr. Swanson to introduce you to me as a Mr. Carter. That's a name! There is something you should know, Mr. Macklin, if you are going to continue to be a private detective. When somebody like yourself wants to take another name, he doesn't take Smith or Jones—no, that would be obvious. He takes such a name like Carter or Cohen or Fulton. Do you want another cup of coffee?"

I nodded, and she poured it for me. She waited a decent interval then before she said, "Well?"

Then I told her. I told her the truth. In the course of the whole business she was the only one I told the truth to, aside from Irma Olanski in Pittsburgh. I didn't tell her Frederick Summers' name or that Sylvia was Sylvia West or where she lived or about the book of poems, but beyond that I told her the truth. She listened to all of it and never took her eyes off my face while she listened, and when I finished she sighed and said:

"You are all the same, aren't you, you righteous ones?"

"I'm a private detective. I took a job."

"And without the job you would have starved?"

"No. I wouldn't have starved."

"Plenty of girls, they came to me, they would have starved," she said.

"I'm not condemning you. I'm not accusing you of anything."

"No?" She still studied me with those small black eyes of hers. "And when you have all the information—then you are ready to destroy Sylvia, yes?"

"No."

"Oh? Then you destroy the information?"

"No."

"Then please forgive a stupid old lady, Mr. Macklin. I don't understand you."

"I'm looking for Sylvia, Miss Banter. I don't know how else to say it to you. I'm looking for her."

"But you already know where she is." The old lady smiled thinly.

"There's no other way I can find her."

"What kind of sense does that make, Mr. Macklin?"

"I don't know if it makes sense. I don't know if it makes any sense that I would die before I would hurt her."

"I am surprised, Mr. Macklin. There is nothing in the world that is such a lie as a man saying he would die before he would hurt a lady."

"I only tried to say what I felt."

"For Sylvia? Are you trying to tell me that you are in love with her? With someone you say you have never seen?"

"You're not impressed."

"Should I be, Mr. Macklin? With such love?"

"I don't know what kind of love it is," I said hopelessly. "I guess I'll go now."

"And you don't want to hear about Sylvia?"

"I don't want to ask—it makes no sense to ask."

"What makes sense, Mr. Macklin? Does it make sense that all these rich and famous people come up here to drink my liquor and to favor a wrinkled old madam? Is there any part of our life that makes so much sense, Mr. Macklin? And does love make sense? Ask yourself that. Will Sylvia find happiness with her California millionaire? That's the way they put it on the soap opera on television, but for myself, I am not concerned about either Sylvia or you. I will not waste my time on it. I don't care—any more than you care about an old whore, Molly Banter. But don't come here any more with your righteousness and your drunkenness."

PART 8

SCARSDALE

"WHAT I CAN'T UNDERSTAND," JACK FENNEY SAID TO ME, "IS why Jeff Peters insists that you're a smart feller. I spoke to him only this morning, and he said that, no matter how different it might look, you got brains. I'm not hurting your feelings, Mack?"

"Oh no—no," I said to him. "Go on and make me feel good."

"What I mean is, it's not just a goof. I like you, Mack, and if you wanted a job I'd still give you a job, because to get a gumshoe who can spell his own name is an achievement. But I can go out on a limb for you and what happens? This ain't a Chinese businessman; this is a nice guy like Swanson."

"A prince."

"Sure, sure, so he has his habits. You got yours. I got mine. Maybe if we grew up any other place than the gutter we'd have good manners too. I don't hold that against anyone. The point is that his firm is one of my clients. They pay me a retainer of three thousand dollars a year, and I charge them for taking a couple of bearer bonds across the street or for collecting from a phony or anything else, and on top of the retainer.

It would be nice to lose that kind of an account, wouldn't it, Mack?"

"Go to hell," I said. "You can always fall back on International Finders."

"Still beefing about that? Why don't you tell me what kind of a deal you got cooking? Then I can help you. Now my hands are tied."

"All I want is to get to someone who worked at Molly Banter's house nine years ago."

"Anyone?"

"The way I feel now—yes, anyone."

"Well, there's one way," Jack Fenney said. "I think it was just short of nine years ago they closed Molly up for good. She did six months in the Women's House of Detention, if I'm not mistaken, and when she came out she retired. Now the way I remember it, about a dozen of her girls were brought into court with her. It was a long time ago and I don't recollect all the details, but if you were to go around to the New York Public Library you could read up on it and maybe latch onto one of the girls." Then he added, "I'm not charging for this one."

I thanked him.

I spent the rest of that day in the public library, running the microfilms of the back-date newspapers. It was a juicy case with all the regular and expected paraphernalia of high-priced sin in the big city, the little black books, the two young-men customers out of the top levels of society, the highly placed political figure, the military men whose names were not to be divulged—it being a matter of national security when a general gets fingered in a fancy bordel—the under-age prostitutes who sell their personal stories; everything was there except the plain fact that the same people who were so outraged over it were those lucky enough not to be caught or written down in one of the little black books. But as I had expected, there was no mention of any Sylvia Carter. I was already beginning to understand that when Sylvia moved from one place to another she broke connections clean and left as few loose ends dangling as possible.

Because the story was what it was, the newspapers clung to it for better than three months, and out of this vast coverage I was able to piece together a complete and detailed picture. Eleven girls had been arrested aside from Molly Banter. Three of these girls had been in the Banter entourage only a matter of weeks when they were arrested, which left eight. Two of them were aliens and had been subsequently deported on charges of moral turpitude. This left six. One of the six had jumped bail during the case, and since the police had not been able to find her I wrote her off my own list as well. A follow-up story informed me that, of the remaining five, one had gone to Houston and another to Chicago. Presumably three were still in New York, and of the three, one of them rang some sort of bell in my memory.

Her name was Shirley Digbee, and while she was very beautiful and very shapely, she was also six feet and one inch tall, which, among other things, made her desirable to a great many small men. Also, from what I could glean from the newspapers, she was not overbright, even in terms of her own area of operation.

I called Jack Fenney and caught him just before he left his office for that day.

"Of course," he said, "I should have remembered about Shirley Digbee. I could have saved you some time."

"You could have."

"But that was a nice case, you got to admit," he said. "You

don't often get to read about anything as nice and interesting as that case."

"What about Shirley Digbee?"

"Have you seen *Sweet Talk*, the musical?"

"I haven't."

"Then get a ticket and see it tonight. Shirley Digbee's in it. She's been with it since it opened, which is almost two years now."

I thanked him.

2

I don't know why thousands of people will pay anything between seven and twenty dollars to see something like *Sweet Talk*, but I suppose they had reasons as valid as my own. For all I know, they also came to see Shirley Digbee play the role of Paralyzing Pauline and sat patiently through a dull and tasteless first act in which she did not appear at all and in which the lyrics were banal, the music imitative, and the costumes as brief as city ordinances allowed. In the second act she did come onto the stage and for some twenty minutes she stood there in a G-string and rhinestone brassiere and never said a word and didn't move much except her eyes.

Yet I have to admit that the effect was overwhelming. In her high heels she was the largest thing on the stage by at least a foot, and I can imagine the effect she had on the type of man who stops short in his tracks when a tall woman passes by. I also had to admit that she had a beautiful figure, well proportioned, and when there was no one alongside of her for contrast, she appeared no different from any other woman.

When the curtain came down for the end of the show, I walked around to the alley and backstage. I looked like someone who knew where he was going, and no one bothered to

stop me, and when I asked for Miss Digbee's dressing room
one of the girls pointed it out to me. I knocked on the door,
and Shirley Digbee, in a dressing gown now, opened the door
and wanted to know who I was and what I wanted. In the
process she looked me up and down; literally, she measured me.
"I'm five feet eleven inches." I smiled. "With shoes. Without shoes, I'm maybe three quarters of an inch less."

"Oh, come on in," she said, nodding for me to enter the
tiny, cluttered cubicle that was her dressing room. "You think
it's a big joke—you should know the grief I have from the little
men. It's the same thing all the time. I have to knock them
down to keep them from climbing over me. Tonight's an off
night—I mean, tonight's a benefit and they're here with their
wives. Who are you, anyway? You a cop of some kind?"

"I'm a private detective from Los Angeles."

She squeezed behind a little screen in one corner of the little
room. "I'm going to dress while I talk to you, just the same
as they do in the movies," she said good-naturedly. "Otherwise you'd have to get out. Anyway, I like to get dressed with
a man in the room. I'm queer that way—neurotic. I got maybe
twenty neuroses, maybe thirty, who knows? They all come from
being so goddamn tall. The funny thing is, I like being tall.
I'm crazy for it. I wouldn't have it any other way. I went out
for a while with an analyst—a little one, maybe five feet two
inches. They get the most bang out of going out with me.
Bang—that's an understatement. I could write a book about
the little ones. But this one, the analyst, he was always trying
to convince me that I hated being tall. Finally I said to
him, 'Look, buster, why are you always calling me up twenty
times a day if all you got on your mind is to chop me down to
your size? There are plenty your size running around in the
grass. Go rope yourself one.' But believe me, when I say that

was all he had on his mind, that's the understatement of the year. If I knew you better I'd tell you what he had on his mind. But this one, all the time it was my neuroses. I said to him, 'With you, nobody can do anything because they like it. It's got to be a neurosis.'"

"Don't you want to know my name?" I interrupted.

"Sure. You know, it's a pity you're a private cop; I mean, since you are from L.A., you could just as well be in the movie business. But then you'd just be like all the others. You know what they say—all of them?"

"I suppose they say you're too tall."

"How'd you know?" Her dress was on now. Instead of coming out from behind the screen, she folded it in one motion and leaned it against the wall. "Sit down and make yourself comfortable. How do you like it?" She spun in the dress, a bright green. She moved easily and gracefully, for all her size, like a child. "But that's just a cover-up," she went on. "The too-tall business, I mean. I mean, look at James Arness in *Gunsmoke*—he's maybe seven feet tall, but it don't keep him standing still in a lousy musical like me. You'd think they'd give me one line—just one line. Oh no. No. It's not that I'm too tall. I got a stigma. That's my trouble."

"A what?"

"A stigma. Don't you know what a stigma is?"

"I think so."

"Well, that's what I got. I used to work for Molly Banter. It's no secret—everybody knows it. My goodness, they didn't have that kind of newspaper coverage for the Korean War, if you know what I mean. I mean, when someone like yourself comes in here, right away I say to myself it's Molly Banter all over again. That makes it kind of exciting. What is your name, anyway?"

"Alan Macklin."

"You married?"

"I'm not married," I said.

"Anyway, I got a date tonight, so I'm in a hurry. So what can I do for you, Mack? I'll bet everybody calls you Mack."

"Mostly."

"That's from having a name like Macklin. You got a lousy name like Shirley—what are they going to call you? So what do you want, Mack?"

"Were you working for Molly Banter in September of 1948?"

She knit her brows and considered it and then nodded. "Sure."

"Do you remember another girl who worked there whose name was Sylvia Carter?"

"Sylvia Carter?"

"Little taller than average, slim, good bust, long legs, dark eyes, dark hair, narrow nose with just a slight flare at the nostrils——"

"Ten years is a long time, Mack."

I took out the pictures and showed her a couple of them, and then she remembered—and somehow I had a feeling that now it was over and all the rest was simple, straightforward and direct. Even when her memory led nowhere, it didn't change that feeling.

"Yeah," she said, "yeah—sure. A quiet kid. Good-looking. She didn't stay long, maybe five, six weeks. Didn't have much to do with anyone—I mean the girls. Then she went."

"Where?"

"God knows, Mack. She walked out, exit, finish. I never saw her again. I wish I could help you, but I can't. I got to go now."

"Just give me a moment more," I begged her. "She must have had a friend there, someone. Just try to think."

"You don't know what you're asking for, junior, because I think like a broken record player. But I'll tell you what. There was another kid there—I think she left about the same time. I remember that because I met her about a year ago at a party at Lefty Meyer's house, and she was there with her husband. I mean Lefty Meyer put up half the money for this vehicle—he's not her husband. This kid had it made. She married Herbert Phillips and they live in Scarsdale and she's got everything right side up, which I give her credit for a hundred per cent."

"Who's Herbert Phillips?"

"Some kind of big wheel in the stock market or Wall Street or something, but he's loaded. Look, I don't know how this connects or any of it. You want to know about this Sylvia kid. This other kid—I think her name was Jane Bronson or something—she got out of Molly's place the same time. That's all——"

It was enough.

3

October 1 was a Wednesday, and it finished a week of talking to myself and finding no answers. There was one day when I began the report; that was Wednesday, the week before. I rented a typewriter and sat down to do what I had been hired to do, and by evening I had written twenty-two pages. It was the considered and thoughtful typewriting of an educated man who had made himself comfortable in a sewer. When I was a kid I stole apples and bananas because I was hungry; when I finished the first twenty-two pages I wasn't hungry, and I went down to the street to a liquor store, bought a fifth of Scotch, and got drunk in my room by myself. It was exactly seven years since the last time I had finished a bottle by myself, but seven years is not a very long time for a man to avoid an inspection of himself. Some people manage a lifetime and remain sober.

That was the twenty-fourth of September. It gave me a sense of accomplishment. A child had been born Sylvia Karoki and had lived and grown as no child should ever be made to live and grow on this earth. I had no tears to shed, because I was earning my dollar.

I didn't want to go to Scarsdale, but my single virtue was that I had no enthusiasm to do the things that I went ahead and did anyway. It was a small virtue and frequently invisible.

On Thursday, the twenty-fifth of September, I made up my mind to go to Scarsdale. It rained a little, and then I said to myself, "The hell with it. The hell with it all." I went to the movies. Then I called Jack Fenney, not because he was a private detective but because he was someone in New York whom I knew, and I desperately wanted to be with someone I knew and talk to someone I knew. But his day was filled and he had no time for me.

There was the day that I thought about Irma Olanski and Alan Macklin and tried to formulate in my mind some concept of the good man and the honest man. The major loss was in my observations upon myself. It is true that I had not found the good man and the honest man, but I was not looking for him. I was looking for the life of a whore, which is a wonderful word, if you think about it. A whore sells herself and thereby is a symbol in a society where men and women sell a pot or a pan or an automobile. I let my thoughts go no farther than that, because I did not want to start drinking again.

That was Friday, the twenty-sixth of September, and I decided to go out to Scarsdale. It was a warm, pleasant day, and the car I hired was a convertible, so I was able to put the top down and enjoy the drive up the parkway alongside the river and then into Westchester. In Scarsdale I stopped at a drugstore, looked up Herbert Phillips in the local telephone book, and copied out the address—44 Chadworth Road. It was a loose way of working, but I had lost all my pride in how I did what I did. I just wanted to do it and get it over with—and at that, most of it was done. I had exposed eighteen years of a woman's life; the seven years that elapsed before Sylvia West appeared in Los Angeles were of less consequence. It is true that I had been hired to reveal not only the meaning of a woman's soul but also the origin of her bank account; and also that as a competent professional I was obligated to deliver what I had been hired for. But these were the niceties of my profession; in a larger sense, I had already been magnificently successful.

I drove through at least twenty Scarsdale streets before I located Chadworth Road, and while I could have asked the way in the beginning, I chose not to. Aside from this, the drive was rewarding and informative. I had thought that such residences in multiple numbers were confined to places like Beverly Hills, but now I could lean back and drive here and there in Scarsdale and have the nice, poshy feeling that I was back in Beverly Hills. I also enjoy seeing the front lawns of seventy- and eighty-thousand-dollar homes, and it makes me feel cultured to say to myself, "That's Georgian and that's French Provincial and that's a sort of bastard Cape Cod, only no cottage, and that's Tidewater Colonial and that's Spanish Colonial." And there were even a few modern homes, but not on Chadworth Road.

On Chadworth Road each house nestled in its own two- or three-acre plot, and the prevailing style was a combination of Southern Plantation and Georgian two-story structures sitting behind half-circle driveways and fronted by pillared porches.

Number 44 was the kind of house that provokes you to say, "Well, I wouldn't want to live there," knowing damn well that you would. Next to being President, it was at the top of the American Dream.

I drove up to the door and knocked at the door via a large brass knocker that tinkled a bell at the same time; and a maid in a black dress and lace collar opened the door, listened politely to my request, and then informed me that Mrs. Phillips had gone to New York for the day, that she was meeting Mr. Phillips there and would be late in getting home.

Then I drove back to New York to my hotel, went into the bar, and had a drink and talked to the bartender. Bartenders are neither wise nor witty—by my limited experience—and neither have they got the kind of characters people like to think of them as having; but they preside over the loneliest club in our society and they provide what a man can hunger for more than almost anything else—the sound of a human voice directed at you.

Saturday, September 27, I slept late, dressed slowly, and walked in Central Park. It was a wonderfully beautiful day— the kind of day, they tell me, that happens only occasionally in New York, and then mostly during September and October. A dry, sweet wind blew out of the west, and the air was full of all the honey of youth and love. It was such a day as makes a man alone feel sick and lost and wanting; and it came home to me, sharp as a knife cutting at my insides, that there was only one woman in the world I truly wanted, one woman that I would want and always want—and no substitutes and no other. I was able to face it and recognize it and admit it fully to myself; and if I had nothing else in my life, neither a feeling of dignity nor self-respect nor accomplishment of any kind or worth, I at least had this: that I was in love. In a world where the dirt is deep and the decencies rare, it is something to have, you may believe me, even if you have to wait for it for thirty-six years.

Sunday I did one thing and another, and a day went by.

Monday, September 29, I rented a car again and drove up to Scarsdale. It was eleven o'clock when I got to Chadworth Road.

4

The same maid answered the door. I asked for Mrs. Phillips, and she said, "Please come in." It was a fine entranceway, with a double staircase spiraling up to the floor above, an Aubusson carpet on the floor, and an appropriate selection of Ginseburg and Levy antiques to set off the rug. There were Sheraton chairs against the walls and a grandfather clock next to an eighteenth-century gentleman who may or may not have been one of Mr. Phillips' ancestors.

I remained standing, having never been comfortable on a chair that cost more than most of my worldly goods, and I kept my hands in my pockets, which is a way I have of facing the accusing finger of large wealth and posh; and presently Jane Bronson, now Mrs. Phillips, came into the hallway or entry or foyer or whatever something of this sort is called, and she regarded me and I regarded her. She used the coldest and steadiest pair of pale blue eyes to do the regarding that I have ever seen in a woman. Otherwise she was strikingly good-looking or impressive, depending upon how you react to cameo features, a straight mouth, pale, fine skin, and a stance as statuesque as if she had an iron ramrod driven up her trunk in the traditional fashion.

Myself, I do not react with any warmth or pleasure to the combination, but I will admit that I was facing the grand lady and that she damn near brought it off. As much as I might try to remember that she had once been an employee of Molly Banter, I kept losing the recollection to an attitude that said plainly that I and all my type and breed were dirt. Mrs. Phillips inhabited the body of Jane Bronson superbly; there was no question about that.

"What can I do for you, Mr.——?" she asked me, but asked it as if I had no name and she expected none.

"Mr. Macklin."

"Mr. Macklin," she repeated. I had never heard the name sound so unimportant, so tasteless and vulgar. I wondered briefly how she could be convinced of my presence as an intrusion. After all, I could have been a necessary component, a gas meter inspector, an actuarial investigator, a tax assessor, or even a long-missing Phillips. Either she read men better than anyone I had ever met, or she treated every unidentified caller in precisely the same fashion. However it was, she was gracious enough to ask coldly what she could do for me.

I knew this: I knew that this was no time for International Finders or any other little-boy gimmick. I said the only thing I could think of saying:

"You can talk to me about Sylvia Carter."

I had expected any reaction and was prepared for any reaction. There was no reaction. Not a muscle in her face flickered. The beautiful Nordic mask preserved its sheath of cold and aloof insulation, but there was a long, long moment of silence before she said to me:

"I think you have come to the wrong place, Mr. Macklin. I don't know you and we have no business. Please go."

She was cool and collected and able to think on her feet, but I knew that I was in the right place. Her response was good, but it was not natural. It was the kind of thing she had put together out of books, plays, and films; but it was not the kind of thing that a woman who had never heard the name of Sylvia Carter would say.

"If you don't want me here, I'll go," I said. "Let's be clear about that. I'm not a hoodlum, and this is no shakedown or anything like that. At the same time, let's put our cards on the table. You are not going to call a butler or a chauffeur and have me thrown out. You are not going to call the police. You are going to handle this yourself, and I think you are entirely capable of handling it yourself."

She considered this for a while before she replied, and she also considered me. She appraised me as coldly and meticulously as a cattle breeder takes note of a prize bull he is ready to make an offer on. I had a feeling that in those few seconds she priced my shoes, suit, and shirt, dated my tie, noted my fingernails, and decided when I had my last haircut. Then she said:

"I agree with you, Mr. Macklin. I am."

Silence again. I waited. She waited, and outwaited me. I said, "Well, Mrs. Phillips?"

"I don't think we have anything to talk about, Mr. Macklin. If I must handle this myself, so must you. But I think we would approach the problem differently. The moment you declared your decent intentions, you threw in your hand. Either you have no cards or you're a cheap hoodlum. Which is it? Who are you?"

"I'm a private detective from Los Angeles. Here are my credentials." I handed them to her, and she examined them carefully and thoughtfully and then returned them to me.

"What is your interest in this person you mentioned, Mr. Macklin—this Sylvia Carter?"

"I want to find out where she was during the years between 1949 and 1956."

"Why?"

"So that a certain party on the Coast can decide whether he wants to marry her or not."

"And when you find out what you would like to know, then this certain party will decide not to marry Miss Carter. Is that the case?"

"I would imagine so."

"And what about the years before 1949, Mr. Macklin?" she asked me, quieter now—and colder, if that was possible.

"I know about those years."

"Then don't you know enough, Mr. Macklin?"

"I was hired to know about all the years. I take my pay and I do my work."

"I don't want to misjudge you, Mr. Macklin," she said slowly and reflectively, "but you sound like a complete louse. Do you suppose there are many men who would do what you are doing?"

"A great many." I nodded.

"How do you feel about men, Mr. Macklin?" she asked curiously.

"About the same as you do, I suppose. That includes myself."

"That's an interesting approach, Mr. Macklin."

"Yes? I don't know. I don't feel interesting, and I am not imaginative enough at this moment to manufacture interesting approaches."

"Then you amaze me, Mr. Macklin. What on earth are you up to? Just for the sake of argument, consider that there was such a person as Sylvia Carter and that I had some knowledge of her. After saying what you said to me, can you think of any reason why I should talk to you for even a moment longer?"

"Yes, I think so."

"Oh?"

"I don't think that Sylvia Carter should marry the man who hired me."

"No? He must be a rich man if he can afford such an expensive way of resolving his doubts."

"He's a rich man."

"But Miss Carter should not marry him?"

"No."

"And why not, Mr. Macklin?"

"Because he hired me. That's reason enough."

"Oh. You're judge and jury?"

"If you look at it that way."

"How should I look at it, Mr. Macklin?"

"My way," I said tiredly. "I think there is only one man who will ever know Sylvia. As much as you can ever know a woman."

"One man?"

"Myself," I said. Suddenly I was very tired and I didn't care, and I was empty and the whole world around me was empty. "That doesn't matter," I told Mrs. Phillips. "I think I made a mistake. I think I came to the wrong house." I started toward the door then.

"One moment, Mr. Macklin," she said.

My hand was on the door and I didn't turn around. "I'm only a two-bit hoodlum, Mrs. Phillips," I said. "You can put your mind at rest. I think my job is over, and I'll take great pains to forget that I was ever here or that I ever saw you."

"Why? Because it will take guts to finish your job, Mr. Macklin?"

"If you want to call it guts."

"Or is it because you're afraid to know any more about Sylvia?"

I let go of the doorknob and turned back to her. She was a self-possessed lady. She stood there and appraised me again.

The silence became full and frightening and overwhelming.

"Yes, I'm afraid," I whispered.

"Then God help you, Mr. Macklin," she said with no change of expression on that cold, smooth face of hers. "I may appear cold and withdrawn to you, Mr. Macklin, but whatever faults I have, I am not righteous and I married a man who was not righteous. Do you think you could have shaken me down, Mr. Macklin—even if you wanted to? Don't you think someone else would have tried, and someone else and someone else? Could I live that kind of life, Mr. Macklin? I married a rich man, a very rich man, and he knew what I was when he married me. Or what I was not. You see, Mr. Macklin—that was the difference between Sylvia and myself. I could face what I was. She couldn't. And I don't think you can face what she was either. Now you understand this situation, Mr. Macklin. I am not afraid of you. I am not even troubled by you. I think I only—pity you."

My hands hanging by my side, my body full of old and tired emptiness, I stood there and looked at her. I had nothing to say. Then she turned to the grandfather clock and, her back to me, pointed out that it was twelve o'clock.

"I'm hungry, Mr. Macklin," she said. "Would you like to take me somewhere in your car, and we could have lunch and we could talk about Sylvia."

"I would like that," I said.

"As a matter of fact, I am meeting my husband in town tonight. I was going to take the train in. You can drive me in if you'd like to, and we could eat in New York."

She had turned back to me now. "If you're hungry——" I began.

She smiled for the first time. "I can wait, Mr. Macklin."

PART 9

NEW YORK (FIFTY-SECOND STREET)

I DROVE MRS. PHILLIPS, WHO WAS JANE BRONSON ONCE, TO New York, and while we were sitting in the car I told her what I had to tell her sooner or later, that I had never seen Sylvia or spoken to her. "Does that make sense?" She said that it made sense in its own terms—and did I follow her? I said I didn't know. It was only six weeks since I had been with Irma Olanski in Pittsburgh, and six weeks wasn't long enough for a man to change.

It was easier to talk driving the car. I didn't have to look at her, only to watch the road. When she said that the barrier in talking to a man about a woman lay in the fact that no man who wasn't queer really desired to be a woman, I smiled thinly and nodded.

"Envy would help," I said.

"When I knew your Sylvia, she and I—well, all of us—it was a running gag. What species is most different from man?"

"Woman."

"So if you had met Sylvia first, that would have been the end of it, you know. You know that?"

"I think I knew it at the beginning."

"Sylvia was cursed with it. That was the way we were different. Maybe because I never had the brains Sylvia has, I could look at myself and live with myself. Sylvia couldn't—and she lived only for the time when she could stop being what she was. Then she would wipe it out of existence and destroy it. Then she would be free."

"I'm free that way," I said.

"And do you hate yourself as much as Sylvia hated herself, Mr. Macklin?"

"Most of the time—yes."

2

We had lunch at Twenty-one on Fifty-second Street, and I watched the way she walked into the place, where she was no stranger, and the way people looked at her—the way two men at the bar looked at her and whispered about her. She lived with it. She was proud and stiff as a ramrod, and she had trained the flesh of her face into a mask that was as invulnerable as ten-inch armor plate, but what was inside of her was not hard at all, and I began to have some notion of how it quivered and hurt. She had once been a kid in a little prairie town called Jericho in North Dakota. Her father had been kicked to death by a sick horse when she was seven years old, and she had seen and remembered. Her mother committed suicide a year later. Like Sylvia, she had never pleaded with the world for a living—it owed her nothing—and if the county orphanage where she lived her childhood was kinder to her than the lousy tenement was to Sylvia, it was not such a tremendous difference when all is said and done.

The waiter deferred and scraped as he took our order, but it was a little too much; and she was shrewd enough to realize that I noticed.

"You never forget." She nodded. "You grow up. It took me a long time. I don't want to forget. I thank them, the stinking bastards."

"Couldn't there be another way?" I asked her.

"You tell me, Mr. Macklin. How many times would the doorbell ring for a shakedown? How many times on the telephone? Have you ever listened to that dirty, degenerate, anonymous voice that comes over the telephone? I have. And every time my husband looked at me I'd be asking myself—no, it wouldn't work. There's no other way—no place to go, no place to run. You always take yourself with you. We haven't solved that one yet."

"And Sylvia knew how you felt?"

"She knew. You have to understand how it was with Sylvia and me. She came into that damn cat house of Molly Banter's —the rottenest cat house of all because it pretended to be something else, with that old bitch talking it up that she was our mother for her cut of twenty dollars each time one was banged —she came into it like a damn duchess. No, that isn't it. She came in as if her eyes were bandaged, only they were open. I've trained my face, Mr. Macklin; she trained her mind and soul to be somewhere else. She would sit in the living room, reading a book, and then Molly would have what she liked to call a 'client' for her, and Sylvia would close the book and go through it, and if he left early enough she'd go back and pick up the book again—as if she had never been interrupted. You can imagine how the other girls reacted to that. For a week they tried to cut her heart out, but they couldn't reach her. No matter what they said, they couldn't reach her."

"And how did you reach her?" I asked.

"She needed a place to live." Mrs. Phillips shrugged. "I had a two-room apartment on East Fifty-seventh Street and I told her she could share it and we'd split the rent. But the girls gave up on her. Maybe I was more like her. Maybe I had some notion then that if you waited and timed it properly and learned not to say 'ain't' and 'don't' when you mean 'doesn't' and not to throw the four-letter words around—then you could escape. Go to sleep and wake up, and it had never happened."

"But Sylvia believed it?"

"When she was awake. When she was asleep, she would whimper and cry—and oh, maybe two, three times a week she'd wake up out of a nightmare and scream as if the devils were tearing her apart. There were nights when she was afraid to go to sleep at all, and she'd sit up reading all night—not sleep until she was dropping with fatigue. That was no good when she slept with a man—she'd wake up the worst way—and there was a Brazilian millionaire who beat her half to death because she woke up that way and he went out of his head because she was screaming and he had to make her stop. But that was long afterwards. And she'd scream in her nightmares about the things that had happened to her in Mexico—she'd been in places in Mexico, oh my God, yes. How well do you know her, Mr. Macklin? Tell me."

I looked at her but said nothing. The food came, but I had no appetite.

"Do you think she's so tough, Mr. Macklin? Hard? Able to take anything, do anything, survive anything? That was her largest lie, Mr. Macklin."

"Why did you leave Molly Banter?"

"You'd ask Sylvia that too, wouldn't you?"

"I suppose so."

"Oh, why do you suppose we left, Mr. Macklin? We didn't enjoy being call girls. Enough was enough. I know what you're thinking, Mr. Macklin—why in the first place? Why did we start? You'll have to work that out yourself—or ask yourself why you take the money from the man who hires you."

"I have asked myself." I nodded.

"And what do you come up with, Mr. Macklin?"

I shook my head.

3

They found jobs as waitresses in one of a large restaurant chain, ten o'clock to eight o'clock, a ten-hour day, on the theory that there would be a staggered two-hour break between three and five. But it never worked out just that way; between three and five there were the lady shoppers, the afternoon soda drinkers, and the quick snacks for the hungry ones. Between the base pay and the tips, they took home about fifty dollars each, and they were able to eat on the job. Rent for the two-room apartment was a hundred and twenty-five dollars a month. They talked about another apartment but did nothing about it. This was hard work, and they worked six days a week. Frequently it was almost nine o'clock when they got home, and they would sprawl out on their beds. Jane Bronson would turn on the radio and listen to pop music. Sylvia would read and fall asleep after a few pages. They saw almost no one. They had almost no dates.

They had been there almost six months before a man called Herman Seeman, who managed the place, learned that they had worked in Molly Banter's house.

(How, I wanted to know. How would a thing like that get out?)

It always got out. It was seepage, uncontrollable seepage—it was osmosis—it was an act of pride to nod at a girl and whisper that she did it when the price was right. Also, the Molly Banter scandal was beginning to break, and everyone was aware of it.

They weren't fired. Herman Seeman knew a good thing when he saw it, and they were both beautiful women. A man's mind breaks down—as Jane Bronson put it—when he is faced with continuing proximity of not one but two of Molly Banter's girls. He had to try, and he caught Sylvia alone in the pantry in the break hours, when business was slack.

As it came out again and again in the delineation of Sylvia, she never screamed or shouted for help when something like this happened. She fought back silently. But Herman Seeman was a strong man, and he was getting the better of it when Jane Bronson came in and broke a catsup bottle over his head. There was less blood than catsup, but they were both without jobs and without the chance of a snowball in hell for a reference.

For five weeks they were jobless, and then they gave up the apartment and got jobs in a road show that was described as variety and was mostly a second-rate strip tease. The show moved south, and in Fort Lauderdale, Florida, they were picked up by the police. The show's manager took off with the money, and the girls got out of it with a suspended sentence and all the money they had going for fines.

(I had thought that in show business that sort of thing was over with, done with, a part of the past.)

They stuck together, but a part of it was the desperation of facing their separate loneliness. They found work as waitresses in a Palm Beach hotel, and when they returned to New York four months later, they had seven hundred dollars between them. They got another apartment, on Fifty-eighth Street this time. Three weeks after they moved into the apartment Jane Bronson had found a way for both of them to go to work at the Galeries Français' Fifth Avenue store—which was something they had schemed for and planned for. Jane was crossing Sixth Avenue on her way back to the apartment, when she was hit by a drunken driver and taken to the hospital with a compound fracture of the leg and a broken pelvis. It was a bad and dangerous situation, and she was in the hospital for eleven weeks. Internal injuries were found, and after that there was a constant danger of embolism. She was placed in a private room, and for three weeks she had nurses around the clock. But when she left the hospital eleven weeks later, she had no worse reminder of the accident than her memories of the pain and a thin scar on her thigh.

4

"The world, Mr. Macklin," Mrs. Phillips said, "buys friendship between two men. In the best of all possible worlds, man-made naturally, it has the best of all possible promotion. How does that line go—'Greater love——'?"

"I think—'Greater love hath no man than this, that he shall lay down his life for his friend'—or something like that."

"Greater love hath no woman than that she should scratch her best friend's eyes out. That is a mountain of shit, Mr. Macklin, but too large to be moved. You'll forgive my language. It happens when I get out of Scarsdale. Any doctor will tell you that for a hundred fags there is no more than one dike—and even then it's different. We are not the sex that suffers from perversion, homosexuality, and all the nice obscenities that Krafft-Ebing catalogued, but let two women feel for each other something that's a bit more than skin-deep, and the snicker societies work overtime on it. Oh, the hell with that! The plain fact of the matter was that Sylvia and I were two kids out of nowhere and nothing, and we did the best we could and we liked each other. Love in the big male promotion has become a sick and dirty word. If I said we loved each other, you'd write us down on the queer list, wouldn't you?"

"No, I wouldn't," I said. "Sylvia paid the bills—took care of you. That's what you're trying to tell me?"

"I'm glad you're bright."

"I'm not bright, Mrs. Phillips. I am just sitting here and listening. If you would get the chip off your shoulder, it would be better."

"You're right. I'm sorry."

"I was just wondering how much of your stake was left by then."

"About sixty dollars," she said.

5

Lolo Diamonds' place was called "the calculated risk," and it was known fairly widely but still discreetly by the crowd in New York that was in the know about such things. It was on Madison Avenue in the Sixties, and it looked like a cross between a small bar and a quiet saloon. More often than not a policeman was within half a block of the place. It had no name. Printed on the window in the front of the curtains was the word *Bar*—nothing else.

Sylvia went there and asked for Mr. Lolo, who was called "Diamonds" because he liked them. He wore three large diamond rings and a diamond tie clasp and a wrist watch set in diamonds. He was a very short, fat man with a discolored right ear, and he always dressed meticulously in an oxford-gray suit, white on white shirt, and a narrow blue silk-knit tie. It was noised around that someone had once convinced him that in such a costume he would commit no vulgarities of dress and that, having assimilated this fact, he never tampered with it. But he could not give up the diamonds. He was a man of about fifty then when Sylvia went to him. He had an old reputation with the beer mobs in the twenties and he had done some time here and there, but now he was in a legitimate business in a town where pimps and madams were not poorly regarded, so long as they did not cut their prices or mess up the so-called dignity of the streets.

Sylvia went there during the afternoon, as she had been advised to—having made some inquiries on the subject—and Lolo interviewed her at the table in the corner of the bar which he called his "office." He looked her over carefully and professionally first—something Sylvia had experienced before and was not particularly bothered by—and then he said to her:

"Now I want to hear you talk, sister."

"Well—that's what I thought, that we would talk about it, Mr. Lolo."

"Sure. That's it, exactly." He nodded. "I am trying to make a point with you, sister. We have had in here girls who were stacked enough to make a man come in his pants, but when they opened their yaps it came out like a third-rate Grand Concourse floozie. I am not running a place here for Grand Concourse floozies. Where you from, sister?"

"El Paso," Sylvia said.

"Texas?"

"Yes, Mr. Lolo—Texas."

"What are you? Spick? Greaser?" He turned to the man behind the bar and called, "Hey, Charlie—what is this El Paso out in Texas, a spick place or American?"

"I hear it's a border place, no?"

"So what are you, sister?" he demanded of Sylvia.

"Half Mexican."

"Half Mexican. Hey, Charlie—how about that? I put my finger on it, huh?" And then to Sylvia, "Only don't lie to me, kid. I catch you lying to me, I boot you out of here on your ass. Out on your ass. You're a good-looking kid, and I can use somebody talks spick. You talk spick?"

Sylvia nodded, and Lolo said to the bartender, "Charlie, try her out with some spick, huh?" The bartender held up his glass and grinned. "*Me hace daño la leche*—hey, cutie? I drink it anyway. It settles my stomach."

"What'd he say?" Lolo demanded.

"Milk doesn't agree with him."

"Then what the hell you drink it for—huh, Charlie? Tell you what," he said to Sylvia, "you tell him the story of your life in Spanish. Go ahead."

(It was here and now, as Jane Phillips made me understand, that Sylvia realized she could not go through with something that she had to go through with; and in the end she went through with it. She did something she was no longer capable of doing—and that made it a dangerous thing to do, and she knew how dangerous it was.)

Now she stared at Lolo thoughtfully, and it made him uncomfortable. He repeated his demand. Sylvia said:

"*He existido—he vendido—he permitido—he leído—he comprendido—he sufrido—he vivido . . .*" She said this slowly, thoughtfully, almost inwardly, and then asked the bartender softly whether it was enough. He stared at her and then nodded. "Enough," he said. "She is speaking good, Lolo. The hell with it. Don't bring me into your damn problems."

"All right," Lolo said. "You work anyplace before?"

"I was at Molly Banter's—about five weeks."

"You were picked up there? I don't want anyone was picked up in that place."

"I left before it happened."

"Where'd you go?"

"I went to Florida. I got a job in a hotel waiting tables."

"But you come back, huh? You get a taste of the easy money—no more work, huh?"

"That's right," Sylvia agreed. "I need money quickly."

"All right—all right, sister. Now let me tell you something about this place. It ain't no cheap cat house or pickup joint. Twenty, thirty girls work from here—they get a hundred dollars a night. No more, no less—one hundred dollars a night, no clipping and no rolling. I got an international place here— the best trade in town. Ten years ago there wasn't no such place like this in New York. No. This is like the UN, like a part of it—a prime minister of some country, an ambassador, a German millionaire—this is where they come, and they stand at the bar like gentlemen, and if a girl comes and says hello to them and they like her, there it is. That's all. They know it is straight and the city watches. That's why I got a cop outside. This place is quiet and straight and honest. You don't ask for money and you don't touch money. That I take care of. Once a night. You shape up here between nine and nine-thirty. Just walk in and go to the bar and order a drink. That dress you're wearing—how much you paid for it?"

"Eight dollars."

"Garbage. You got a good dress?"

Sylvia nodded.

"Wear it tonight. Take a bath. Look like a lady when you come in here—not like some cheap floozie. I don't mean without sex. Look like a lady with sex."

"How much of that hundred do I keep?" Sylvia asked evenly.

"Fifty. An even split."

"It's not enough."

"No? Excuse me, Lady Godiva—maybe we're two other people. Just who the hell do you think you are?"

"I need sixty dollars a day."

"What you need, I don't give a damn, sister. You take the split or go."

"Very well, I'll take the split," Sylvia said. "When do you pay?"

"End of the week. You come in on Sunday and I pay off. Now I want to tell you what I got for you. We got a Brazilian millionaire. Damned ignorant bastard don't speak a word of English. Last night I give him a blonde—big, tall stacked blonde like all them spicks want—no, it's no good for him. Wants a dark girl can talk his language——"

"Brazilians don't speak Spanish. Their language is Portuguese."

"What?" He yelled to the bar, "Charlie—what the hell is this, a Brazilian don't talk spick?"

"Portugee."

"God damn you, why don't you tell me?"

"Why don't you ask me?"

"Stupid! All them Ricanos—stupid! Why didn't I ask him? Stupid! Well, sister—you talk Portugee?"

"I'll get along," Sylvia agreed. "I'll get along. He probably understands Spanish anyway."

"All right. Go ahead and change your dress and take a bath and come back here nine o'clock."

(I was beginning to understand what Sylvia felt at that point, or have it that I was beginning to understand a little bit about Sylvia; and as always when something like this was told to me, my thoughts went back to the skinny kid in Pittsburgh who had spoken to Irma Olanski. I have heard it said that when a boy and a girl know each other as kids and grow up together it doesn't usually work out; but I had grown up with Sylvia in another way, and if I had never seen her, the breath and motion of the girl were with me and around me always—day and night.

It had become a part of me. Later, during this same day that I was having lunch with Jane Phillips and listening to what had happened that other day, years ago, and seeing it and feeling it—later this same day, I went up to Madison Avenue and found the bar and went in and ordered a glass of beer. The cop, or another cop, still hovered around outside the place, and Lolo Diamonds was still inside, sitting at his table and going over his careful books that told him how much his fifty per cent of service to the finer types amounted to. If Sylvia had somehow managed to block all this out of her mind and memory, it was now being printed on mine indelibly.

Sylvia did as she was told. That was another part of her; along with the violence and passion and life that suffused her, there was the talent for resignation. I think that if Sylvia was told that she had only a day to live she would accept it without protest or anger. She fought what could be fought; what she created deliberately, she did not resist or fight, and this was something she had created, the whole of the situation and the circumstances.

She came back to Lolo's place a few minutes after nine. She wore a black jersey dress that set her fine strong figure and her dark beauty off to wonderful advantage, and it doesn't take much imagination to guess what effect she had on the Brazilian millionaire. His name was Anton Fugillo Perez, a very large and important coffee exporter, with millions of dollars' worth of real estate holdings in the best residential section of Rio de Janeiro. He was about five feet four inches tall, but widely built and strong as a bull, a hairy man with long arms and an underslung chin.

He insisted upon taking Sylvia to dinner, and she agreed to this, and he took her to the Chambord and ordered a gluttonish mass of food, enough for five, but she hardly tasted it. Then they went to the Harwyn, which he had heard about, and he had three crème de menthes on ice, a drink he was extremely fond of, and then he wanted to go to the Little Club, another place much favored in the circles he moved in; but by now Sylvia was physically tired and emotionally exhausted, not able to face what was coming unless it came quickly. They went to her apartment.

Until now—not the point of its happening but the moment of my learning what had happened—I had not been able to face and deal with, so far as I myself was concerned, that fact that Sylvia sold her love and body and caresses for money. Now I could face it, and whatever it did to me was far less than it had done to her. I could bring into my mind the picture of that hairy bull of a man making love to this woman and Sylvia earning the money she had been promised for the night in the only way she was capable of earning it. As she had planned it, it had to be, it happened, and it was done with. He lay on her bed, naked and content and immersed in whatever dreams Brazilian millionaires indulge themselves with.

Sylvia dressed herself and went into the kitchen and made coffee. She was agonizingly tired, exhausted to the point where every nerve in her body pleaded for oblivion, but she was afraid to sleep, not afraid of the Brazilian—she didn't fear men, and they had talked easily enough in Spanish—but afraid of her own nightmares. The coffee was very strong, but as is so often the case with coffee, it had a reverse effect and made her even sleepier; and finally she went into the living room, where they had a foam-rubber couch-bed, and lay down there and was asleep in moments.

That was about half-past one in the morning. An hour later Sylvia began to scream in her sleep. She awakened almost immediately, not only to her own screams, but to the fact that two massive hands were throttling her.

Evidently Perez had his own automatic reaction to the sound of a woman screaming, and his immediate, crazy need was to stop the sound. Stark naked, he was on top of her and choking her, and Sylvia realized that unless she could break his hold he would kill her in a few moments. So she clawed at his eyes and he let go of her neck, and with a desperate show of strength she got a foot and bent leg under him and managed to throw him off her. He then leaped to his feet and caught her with a blow on the side of the head that sent her flying across the room, and she struck her head on the edge of a cabinet. It made a deep scalp wound but did not knock her out, and as the blood ran down her face, she reached out for the telephone —within grasp—and dialed the operator.

During all this she had not screamed or wept or lost her head, and her action of taking the telephone broke Perez's fit and brought him to his senses.

"What are you doing?" he cried out in Spanish.

"Calling the police."

"No! No! Please!"

Sylvia covered the mouthpiece and said calmly, "The operator is on here now—so don't make a move toward me, you crazy bastard."

"Not the police," he begged her.

"Let you kill me instead?"

"No—please understand. I would not harm a hair of your head. Believe me—to me you are like a sweet, beautiful flower. But I wake up like that and I go crazy. I don't know what I am doing. Look at me. Would I hurt a fly?"

"I'm calling the police," Sylvia said, knowing suddenly just what she intended to do.

"No—oh no—no, my sweet Sylvia." He dropped to his knees, his hands clasped in front of him. "Do you understand? I am here on an economic mission. Official. Only think of the scandal—not myself but my family. I have a wife. I have five children——"

"You bastards always have wives and children," Sylvia said coldly. "I've never known it to fail."

"What am I asking for, my sweet Sylvia? What am I asking? A little pity? A little hope? Is it too much to ask?"

The blood from her head wound was soaking the front of Sylvia's dress now, and she was suddenly shaken with the fear that she might faint from loss of blood before she finished what she had started. She touched her face and held out her bloodied hand.

"And what do I do with this, Señor Perez?"

"I will make it up to you, Sylvia."

"How?"

"With money. Money is sweet. It will smooth over these things. It will place everything in a proper perspective. Money is like medicine—it can heal everything."

"Not everything, Señor Perez," Sylvia said coldly.

"A thousand dollars?"

Sylvia managed to laugh at him. She replaced the telephone now, then put her fingers on it and informed Perez that she only had to lift it up. "There isn't a newspaper in New York that wouldn't pay me five thousand dollars for the story of what happened here tonight—and for a few pictures of a girl soaked with blood." She ripped down the front of the blood-soaked dress. "It makes a better picture now, doesn't it?"

The fear went out of Perez's manner. This he understood. He relaxed and asked sourly, "Very well. How much?"

"Ten thousand dollars," Sylvia said.

"You are out of your mind!"

"I won't even repeat the sum," Sylvia said coldly. "And you'd better make up your mind quickly. If we don't stop this blood, you'll have a corpse on your hands. That will be one to explain."

"Name of God, agreed! Only let me sign a check and stop that bleeding!"

"On what bank?"

"My bank, of course—the Brazilian National Bank."

"Don't you have an account in the Chase or the National City?"

"In the National City—yes."

"All right. We remain here together, and tomorrow morning we both go to the bank. You can wire Rio and confirm a certification."

"Impossible!"

Sylvia reached for the telephone.

"All right. I agree."

Then he got dressed, and Sylvia went into the bathroom and washed the cut and pressed the flesh together and held it that way with Band-Aids. It was not that Sylvia was indifferent to pain; she reacted to pain as she did to danger—with an acceptance of the fact that there was no one to help her but herself.

The next morning she went with Perez to the bank, and the transaction was completed.

6

The waiter took away my untouched food. "You haven't eaten anything," Mrs. Phillips said, and watched me shrewdly out of those cold, clear eyes as I muttered something or other about having no appetite. "Love"—she nodded—"is a peculiar thing at best—don't you think so, Mr. Macklin?"

"I've never had it at best."

"At worst?"

"Was it Mark Twain," I wondered, "who said that Christianity is a very good thing, only it has never been tried? I guess love is in the same category, Mrs. Phillips. It's a large item in this civilization of ours."

"Yes, that has occurred to me."

"And like all these large items, it gets so worn and dirty and rotten that you don't enjoy talking about it."

"You don't, Mr. Macklin?"

"I don't—no."

"And Sylvia?"

"You forget that I've never seen Sylvia, Mrs. Phillips."

"Why? Was it because the man who hired you told you to stay away from her, Mr. Macklin?"

"You're very perceptive."

"Oh no—I'm not perceptive, Mr. Macklin. I am precisely what I am, and I have been luckier than Sylvia. I had a friend like Sylvia. Would you like me to judge whether she was right or wrong in rolling Perez for ten thousand dollars? No, my point of view is not colored by the fact that she used part of the money to pay my hospital and surgery bills. It is a long time, and I can be objective. I would have done the same—if I had the guts for it. I don't have that kind of guts, Mr. Macklin."

"Don't ask me to sit in judgment on Sylvia."

"We don't sit in judgment on those we love—to use a word you don't like. My husband taught me that. I met him at a time when I needed to be taught a great deal, Mr. Macklin. At the hospital when I was recuperating. His wife died there of cancer—not someone he ever loved or had any real relationship with, but a human being—and the guilt is worse that way. How much do you know about people, Mr. Macklin? Did you know me when you met me this morning? Or could you only think of a cold and hard-faced bitch who would not co-operate in your effort to earn a buck the hard way? Or is it the easy way?"

"The easy way," I said. "I never took the hard way."

"Why, Mr. Macklin?"

"Guts. What Sylvia has and I lack."

"That's a trick too, Mr. Macklin. That's the man's trick—— Oh, see what a noble bastard I am, because I can look at myself with open eyes and say forthrightly that I am a bastard. But I don't buy that, Mr. Macklin. I wouldn't give ten cents for it."

I shrugged. "All right then—why tell me anything?"

"Because I don't think you're as bad as you would like me to believe, Mr. Macklin. I think you've got brains and you've got heart, and I think something else."

"Go on."

"I think you love Sylvia."

"Is that important?" I asked.

"Is it? You tell me."

"Other men have loved Sylvia."

"Do you think so?" she asked me almost sadly. "That's the love you were talking about before. 'He's so cute—I'd like to marry him.' It starts that way with the sixteen-year-olds, and most of them never grow up—or the men. The men go gray at the temples and they're forty and fifty, and still they haven't grown up—and are you going to sell me their love, Mr. Macklin? You have the wrong party. I sold love. I have been in the business. It stinks from Canarsie to Kalamazoo, it stinks like carrion. Who loves Sylvia—who knows her, who ever will, God help her?"

"And you imagine that I know her now?"

"A little. It's better than not at all."

"And the man who hired me?"

"The hell with the man who bought you! There have been whores who stopped being whores. Or don't you believe that, Mr. Macklin?"

"I am trying to believe it. I'm a private detective with a few dollars in his pocket and the first decently paying job in five years. Your Sylvia is a rich woman."

"And you think that whores become rich? Is that all you know about it, Mr. Macklin?"

"Just about. I don't know a hell of a lot."

7

During the year that followed, Sylvia held three jobs. She worked in a department store on Fifth Avenue and left the job after four months. She never told Jane Bronson why she left the job, but the pay was nothing to write home about, and Jane knew that she was uncomfortable in it. She then worked five weeks at a language school with a manufactured set of college references. The references were checked and they collapsed, the job with them. There was an interval of some time then, perhaps seven or eight weeks, and then Sylvia found a job in a large East Side store that specialized in prepared foods. After six weeks on this job, the manager of the store fell ill and had to stop working. Sylvia was offered the job, took it, held it for about two months, and then quit.

During this time and afterward she studied finance and market movements. This was the result of Jane Bronson's growing relationship with Herbert Phillips, then a man in his early forties. When Sylvia was with them, she listened with great interest and curiosity to anything Phillips said about his own

work at the brokerage house in which he was a partner. She had the ability to draw men out, and she managed to overcome Phillips' reluctance to bore two good-looking and young women with what he considered a dull and mundane subject—the technical movement of securities. But Sylvia listened well and asked questions adroitly.

Without informing Jane Bronson or Herbert Phillips, she enrolled for several courses during her evenings, two of them at New York University and two others at the New School. She had no dates with men and wanted none. She had never gone back to the bar on Madison Avenue. On the occasions when Jane Bronson tried to arrange some sort of date or foursome, Sylvia put it plainly but firmly:

"I don't want it. Just try to think about me as someone who is sick in that direction. In time I'll heal up."

"Not this way—you won't," Jane argued. "You can't blame the whole world of men for what happened to you, Sylvia."

"I don't blame anyone," Sylvia said. "I told you that something inside of me is sick. Either it will get well or it won't—but men won't help me now. I don't want men now."

Occasionally, perhaps once in a few weeks, she would be persuaded to spend an evening with Jane Bronson and Herbert Phillips, but only on the condition that it was a dinner in Phillips' apartment. She would not go out with them or be seen anywhere with them. It was on one such occasion, after dinner, when she was pressing Phillips on some point of his own work, that he said to her:

"Why, Sylvia? Where does this take you? You're not like the women who play the market with their dream of the great kill—but using it like poker and the races to try to make something that's dead in them come alive. These are ravenous, hungry women, and the market never satisfies their hunger."

"Maybe I am as ravenous and hungry." Sylvia smiled.

"No—that's no answer. What do you want?"

"Money," Sylvia said.

"No—really, no." Phillips smiled politely at an awkward joke; he lived in a world where people had money and none of them admitted how much they wanted it. "Really," he said, "you are the last person in the world, Sylvia. I've hardly known anyone as indifferent to money as you are."

"It's not hard to be indifferent to something you don't have and can't have."

"Well—that can be argued. But the point is, Sylvia," Phillips went on, "the market is not a diamond mine. You can't simply strike it rich and make a fortune."

"I think you can," Sylvia said calmly.

"I wish you'd tell me how." Phillips smiled. He was a large, heavy-set man, as Mrs. Phillips described him, bearlike in his manner and movements, and with that gentle earnestness that some big, awkward men have.

"I'll try." Sylvia nodded seriously. "You were telling us about these transistor things the Telephone Company people invented. You say it's only a matter of years before they replace most radio and television tubes—and that the Bell Company had to license out the manufacture. Now this company you spoke about before—Transiton?"

"Transistoren Incorporated."

"Yes. They're selling half a million shares of stock—most of it through your house. The stock will be issued at five dollars a share. Now you yourself said that it should double its price within a month."

"I said it should, Sylvia. What does that mean? It's my guess against someone else's."

"I like your guesses."

"Thank you, Sylvia. It still won't make any of us rich. We specialize in underwriting issues of this sort—you have no idea how many we put through. And each one of them is investigated and approved before we accept it. If it were as simple as you suggest, I'd be the richest man on the Street."

"They're not all for the manufacture of transistors, are they?"

"Just what do you know about transistors, Sylvia?" Phillips asked, unable to keep a note of condescension out of his voice.

"Only this—that they are small and that people will be able to put a radio in the palm of their hand. I think people will enjoy that and buy it."

"You may be right and you may be wrong, Sylvia," Phillips said. "I wouldn't argue the point. I wouldn't even try to talk you out of buying a few hundred shares of their stock—because I don't think you could be hurt very much. But I wouldn't urge it. If a person in your position decided to buy stock, I would recommend some of the outstanding and time-tested blue chips, let us say Jersey or Du Pont or Dow Chemical or Corning—a solid, investment-quality security with strong growth possibilities. At best, Transistoren is a speculation. If you should decide to speculate——"

"I have decided," Sylvia said.

Phillips smiled at Jane Bronson, who had not said a word until now. She nodded slightly, knowing something of what went on in Sylvia's mind, and Phillips said:

"Think about it, Sylvia, and if you still want a hundred shares tomorrow, call me at my office. Five hundred dollars is a reasonable sum to risk on a thing of this kind—if you insist."

"I have thought about it," Sylvia replied evenly. "I've thought a great deal about this sort of thing before you ever brought up the matter tonight. I don't want a hundred shares—I want twenty thousand."

Phillips smiled, but Jane Bronson didn't. Instead, as she told me, it came with a chill—a cold chill that cut into her. Yet even if she had desired to, she couldn't have stopped it, and she was not certain that she wanted to stop it.

"I'm quite serious," Sylvia said.

"Come now, you're talking about a hundred thousand dollars, Sylvia. I have never questioned Jane, much less you, about your background or finances or anything of that sort. I have no desire to. But I know that you both work hard for a living, and—now I don't want to hurt your feelings—but I know you don't have any money. A hundred thousand dollars is a great deal of money—an enormous sum. An impossible sum . . ." His voice trailed away, and he looked hopelessly at Jane Bronson.

"I know how much it is," Sylvia said. "I'm not a fool, Herbert. I'm not penniless either. I have about six thousand three hundred dollars. Understand me—I know you are a broker, and I am not taking advantage of your feelings about Jane. I am talking to you as a broker. I want to turn that money over to you tomorrow, and I want you to buy me a six-month option on twenty thousand shares."

"What?"

"You heard what I said."

"I wouldn't think of it," Phillips declared.

"Then you would force me to go somewhere else."

"For heaven's sake, Sylvia," Phillips said with some asperity, "this is speculation twice compounded. I wouldn't do this for a stranger—much less you. What has gotten into you? There's no way to become rich overnight. It just can't be done. I can imagine what it meant to save that much money——"

"No, you can't," Sylvia said sharply.

"Really, I——"

"I didn't save it," Sylvia said evenly. "I don't give two damns about it, and this is what I intend to do with it."

"I won't permit it," Phillips insisted.

("He should not have said that," Mrs. Phillips told me. "Not that. Anything else—but then at that time no man could say a thing like that to Sylvia." I asked her whether she, Mrs. Phillips, could have stopped it. "Perhaps. I don't think I wanted to. It had to come. I just told myself, 'Let it come.'")

"You won't permit it?" Sylvia repeated. "Herbert—what do you think I am? Look at me. What do you think I've done with my life? Just go past the fact that I talk any way I want to talk and have learned not to dress like my life. I'm a whore, Herbert—a plain, unadorned prostitute—and I've practiced that profession since I was thirteen years old. Do you know where I got that six thousand dollars? From a Brazilian millionaire who almost killed me in a fit of insanity and who paid me off to keep a scandal out of the press. So don't dare tell me what you will or will not permit!"

(I think I remember Mrs. Phillips' exact words as she said to me at that point, "You must understand, Mr. Macklin, that the apotheosis of a man in the eyes of a woman is not quite the same as in the eyes of another man. Perhaps once in a lifetime of a relationship a man will do something that is wholly admirable and wonderful in the eyes of a woman—and most often, seemingly, a very small thing indeed. Herbert did it that night.")

Herbert Phillips appeared neither shocked nor perturbed. He looked at Sylvia thoughtfully for a long moment and then he said:

"I think I owe you an apology, Sylvia, and I am not quite sure how I should make it. I am doing my best. I am sorry for what I said, but not for what you said. I would like you to come to my office tomorrow morning and bring the money with you. We will see what we can work out."

"Thank you, Herbert." Sylvia nodded. It was harder for her than for him. If he had never known a woman like Sylvia before, neither had she known a man like Herbert Phillips.

8

I paid the check, and we left the restaurant and walked slowly toward Fifth Avenue. It was about half-past three on the afternoon of September 29, and I had spent over four hours talking to Mrs. Phillips, but the cold fact of chronology was meaningless. To my own awareness, a long, long time had gone by. My search was over and the job was finished.

"What happened with the options?" I asked. There were a few threads. I didn't care too much about them, but I had habits of neatness.

"Do you know how a stock option works, Mr. Macklin?"

"I have a very vague notion."

"Well, in this case Sylvia wanted a call option. And a time period of six months and one day—which would put the profit into the area of capital gains, if there was a profit. It's done this way—the call merchant selects a price over the original price, and the option is to buy at that price. My husband got the best option he could—but it remained a wild speculation. For six thousand dollars Sylvia bought the right to purchase twenty thousand shares of Transistoren at fifteen dollars a share. In other words, within the time limit the stock had to appreciate from five dollars a share to fifteen dollars and thirty cents or so for Sylvia to get her six thousand back. A three hundred per cent rise."

"It doesn't sound likely."

"It wasn't. My husband's partners raised the very devil with him, because that kind of thing isn't good for the integrity of any house, but he went ahead with it, nor did he ever again warn Sylvia against it. Do you understand?"

"I think I do." I nodded.

We turned off into the Plaza, and for a while we leaned against the stone wall, watching the fountain in the sunken area.

"It wasn't luck," she observed.

"No?"

"I just felt that luck played a small part in Sylvia's life. She did the best she could. This crazy gamble was the same thing."

"What happened to the stock?"

"Sylvia sold out at the end of the time limit. The stock was then selling at thirty-six dollars a share. It was the kind of thing that happens on the Street—more often than you imagine, but very few are in it like this. Sylvia's profit was four hundred thousand dollars—and after taxes, three hundred thousand. You see, it worked, and Sylvia broke out. That was what she had dreamed of, and she did it."

"It's hard to believe," I said.

"I know."

"And after that she disappeared, didn't she?"

"About four months later, Mr. Macklin, she went to Europe. We said good-by to her, and we knew how it was and so did she, but it was no use talking about it. When your single passion in life is to destroy yourself, to wipe yourself out of existence, and to prove that you never existed, then there can't be any exceptions."

"She could have trusted you."

"It wasn't a question of trusting us or anyone, Mr. Macklin. Sylvia had to finish and start again. It had to be complete. That's all. . . ."

We stood there in silence for a little while, but I couldn't go away without asking her why she had told me all this.

"Because I loved Sylvia," she said. "Not queer, Mr. Macklin. She was the only human being I ever knew until I met my husband who never reproached me and never betrayed me."

"You didn't answer my question."

"I think I did," Mrs. Phillips said. "I don't know any other way to answer it."

Then I thanked her and said good-by to her; and the last thing I said to her was this: "If I should see Sylvia and talk to her—should I tell her about you?"

"It isn't necessary, Mr. Macklin. Sylvia knows about me. It's up to her, you see."

9

I walked north on Fifth Avenue and then to Madison, where I saw the bar and went in and saw Lolo Diamonds. It was something dead and entombed and encrusted with the dust of centuries. It was like digging in the tomb of some old, old infamy—and the infamy was tired, used up, and wretched. I was full of pity, for myself and for the society of man of which I was a part.

Then I walked back downtown and picked up the car from the parking lot, drove it to its home garage, and turned it in. I went to my hotel from there and bought my ticket to Los Angeles—on the night flight on Wednesday, October 1. I left myself the time until then to complete my report.

On Tuesday evening I finished the report—a single typewritten copy and no carbon. On Wednesday I sat in my room for hours, trying to think through it and find out about Sylvia and about myself as well. That was unprofitable, and I was relieved when at last it was time to go to the airport.

PART 10

SANTA BARBARA

THERE WAS DUST ON THE DESK IN MY OFFICE, AND I BEGAN
to take it off with a handkerchief before I remembered that it
was a habit I had never liked. I found some cleaning tissue and
wiped off the desk, the chair, and the filing cabinet. That did
the house cleaning, more or less.

There were some bills to be paid, and I still had money in
the bank. I paid the bills. My pile of mail was mostly composed
of that increasing American institution called Direct-Mail
Advertising. I separated that and threw it into the wastebasket.
Then there were five personal letters.

Two were from prospective clients—not an overwhelming
tribute to the solvency of my business, but on the other hand,
most of my business came by telephone or on foot. A man in
Ventura wanted me to find a pedigree boxer that his small son
adored. It must have had a considerable pedigree, because he
offered fifty dollars for quick results. The letter was dated
August 19. I threw it away. Either the boxer had been found
or it had strayed beyond redemption. The second prospective
client was what is called a "regular" in the trade. He was convinced that his wife was two-timing him, but not sufficiently
convinced, because he offered one hundred dollars for total

conviction. That letter was dated September 1. It also went into the wastebasket.

Both letters elicited modest reflection on my part. As my thoughts went, I was not much of a private detective and I didn't get much fun out of it. The third letter was from Frederick Summers, and it was dated September 24. Would I telephone him as soon as I arrived in Los Angeles? Since I had been in Los Angeles only about four hours, I felt that he could wait a while longer.

The fourth letter was from Professor Cohen at UCLA. It was dated September 29. His department was being enlarged, and he had been granted permission by the department head to take on another assistant. It was not much of a job and it paid only four thousand dollars a year, but if I could work out any scheme for survival on that much money he would be happy to talk to me about it. His inverted phrasing was polite and intriguing, and my immediate response was such a flood of desire and relief that I reached for the telephone. My second thought was to stop reaching and think about it. I sat there for a good fifteen minutes thinking about it and then I put the telephone away and opened the fifth letter.

It was from Lucy Richards, my ex-wife. I knew that she had remarried, but I had not known that the marriage was such a dismal disaster as the letter indicated. Her husband was a civilian employee at the naval base in San Diego. They had separated about a year ago, and as it so often turns out, he had stopped his payments and she had gotten a lawyer who was not much of a lawyer. She had a job for a while and she had paid the lawyer a hundred dollars. Now she was sick and desperate; she had to be desperate to ask me for help.

I sent her a check for two hundred dollars, which practically finished my account; but I still had some expense money and I would get along all right. I felt rotten because I could not send more, and after three attempts to write a letter to go along with the check, I gave it up and sent the check by itself.

That completed my personal business, and now the few fragments of my life were in some kind of order. For a while then I stared out of the window at the blue rim of mountains in the distance. I had slept only fitfully on the plane and I was tired. Putting my feet up on the desk, I closed my eyes. I must have dozed that way for almost an hour. It was 1 P.M. then.

I called Frederick Summers' office, and the blonde who knew a real Miró from a fake one answered. She had the kind of voice that you remember, a neutral voice spotted with fancy accents—until she knew who you were, and then the voice fitted the caller. I was low man on the scale of voice effects. She said, "Oh?" but she invested the word. Then she said, "The private detective."

"Yes, the private detective."

"Well, Mr. Summers wants to see you as soon as possible, Mr. Macklin. I can tell you that."

"When is that?"

"He's out of town now," the blonde said. "He won't be back until Tuesday or Wednesday of next week."

"Then I can't see him until Tuesday or Wednesday."

"You're very perceptive, Mr. Macklin. I suggest you call us Tuesday morning. Unless Mr. Summers telephones me, in which case he may call you at your office. Can you be reached at your office?"

"Sometimes."

"And when is sometimes, Mr. Macklin?"

"When I'm in my office."

"I see. Don't you have a secretary?"

"I can't afford one. I'm not your boss, just his private boy."

"Don't you have an answering service?"

"I had one, but I cut it off to save money when I left town. Why don't you tell Mr. Summers to wire me if he can't live without me for a few days?"

"Mr. Summers wouldn't appreciate that."

"He'll live," I said, and hung up.

Then I went downstairs and down the block to Googie's, where I had a hamburger and a glass of milk and a piece of apple pie and a cup of coffee. I was home. My days of high living and travel were over.

2

Places cultivate local guilts, and in Los Angeles guilt fixes on sun and weather, the former beneficent and the latter admirable. The calumnies come from New Yorkers, puritans, and other people with pleasure inhibitions, and if they are forced to admit to anything admirable, they always fall back on smog. There was little smog in the city today and none of it in Beverly Hills. It was a warm, clean day, a pleasant and desirable day.

I walked without giving much thought to where I was walking and after a while I found myself on Santa Monica Boulevard, and up the street I could see the sign of the Dryden Bookshop. No human voice had as yet granted me even a small welcome back to the place I called home, and I thought that it would be as gratifying to say hello to Ann Goldfarb as to anyone else. I walked over to the bookstore and went in, and Ann was there behind the little counter where she wrapped the books, and she looked up and grinned and said, "Hello, stranger."

I felt better than I had felt in a long, long time.

"Been to far places?" she asked me.

"Near and far."

"Glad to be back?"

"It's home," I said. "What are the bright folks reading these days?"

"Not very much. It's almost as bad as detection."

"What do you recommend?"

"I've got stacks of them, Mack. Look around. When do you want to come by for dinner?"

"The next time I'm hungry."

"I like you." She smiled. "Find a book, and I'll give you twenty per cent off."

I browsed. That's a fine, healthy word. My father once told me what it meant—that in the old country, when the first tender shoots of green appeared, the cattle were turned out into the fields to eat the *browse*. It seems to be ironically proper that in a country where books are regarded with suspicion and often with alarm the act of looking at them should be equated with the feeding of cattle. It's a singular movement—short steps and a taste of this and of that. I looked at the fiction and found nothing that excited me or made me want to read, and then went through the new packaged journeys into antiquity, wondering why, suddenly, so many people were concerned with their beginnings. Was it because the end was close or ominous —or because we had all been uprooted too hard and too much and had a great need for connection?

I was leafing through Professor Bertram Cohen's new book on the Etruscans and had made up my mind to buy it, when Ann came over and nudged me and said:

"Still interested in poetry, Mack?"

"I never was very much, Ann."

"You were interested enough to buy a copy here once. Do you remember? A *Moon without Light* by Sylvia West."

"That was something special, Ann."

"So is Miss West, I think."

"That's right. You did say she came in here."

"Two or three times a week. This is one of them. I thought you might like to meet her, Mack."

I turned around and looked at Ann—and then beyond her to where Sylvia West stood at the other end of the store. She was standing half away from me—I saw only the edge of her cheek—but I knew her and, strangely, I felt no excitement, no surge of delight and expectancy, but a certain relief. I had known that it would come, either this way, by chance, or through my making it come about. This way was better, I decided.

Yet I must have looked at her more intently, more deeply than I knew. She wore a pale gray suit and a white blouse. No hat. Her dark hair was set in a bun at the back of her head. She carried a black pouch bag and wore black shoes. And then as I looked at her she turned her head toward me, and it was like seeing again someone I had known and seen a hundred times before. It did not occur to me then to ask myself or tell myself anything concerning her beauty. The fact that she was beautiful was beside the point—the whole point being that she was Sylvia.

"Yes, I want to meet her," I said. "I want to meet her very much, Ann."

I followed Ann across the store. There were a few other customers in the place, but who they were and what they were doing, I do not know. Sylvia noticed us coming, and she waited, a book in one hand, her brows slightly raised in normal curiosity—and her eyes upon me with the speculative appraisal of a woman who has had much to do with men and to whom men are meaningful.

"Miss West," Ann said—she could do a thing like that, simply and directly and with no offense to anyone concerned —"this is Mr. Macklin. He asked to meet you. He was most interested in your book, and he bought a copy here a few months ago."

Sylvia smiled, put down the book, and held out her hand to me with no hesitation. I like a woman to offer her hand as a man does. "I am pleased to meet you," she said. "I'm delighted to meet anyone who bought a copy of my book. I live in the certainty that only my closest friends buy it. So you see what a pleasant surprise it is to find a total stranger doing it."

"I read it and I liked it," I said. Ann was watching me narrowly. "Also, I haven't met enough authors of books not to be very impressed when I meet one."

"Thank you, Mr. Macklin. It's nice of you to say that. But I'm afraid mine is a very small and unimportant book."

"No book is unimportant."

"Oh? You like books then?"

"Enough to buy them occasionally," Ann said. "He is an old and good customer, Miss West. He is also an old and good friend."

"That's a very high recommendation, I think." Sylvia nodded, at the same time reaching almost unconsciously for the book I held. I offered it to her. "You like ancient history, Mr. Macklin?"

"He lives it." Ann smiled and then said that she had a customer and left us alone. Sylvia was looking at the book and then she glanced at me inquiringly.

"I majored in ancient history at college. I wanted to teach it. That was a long time ago. It never became more than a hobby."

"That's a pity," she said unexpectedly.

"I think you're right, Miss West. But why do you say so?"

"You make me feel that you wanted to. A man should have a chance to do what he wants to do."

"So should a woman, Miss West. You're fortunate."

"You're sure I'm doing what I want to do?"

"I can't think of any other reason to write poetry. Can you?"

"No—unless you have to."

"I can understand that," I said.

"Can you?"

"I read your book." I took a deep breath and said, "Miss West—we're not complete strangers. Your book and—well, I come with Ann's recommendation. I mean, have you had lunch yet?"

She smiled and shook her head. "Not yet—no."

"Neither have I," I lied. "Would you—please have lunch with me? Please. I want to talk to you. Unless you've made other plans?"

"I have no other plans," she said simply.

"You will then?"

"All right."

3

Outside I asked her whether there was any special place she would like to eat, and she said that any place I chose was all right. My own garage was three blocks away, and when I suggested that we walk there she pointed out that her car was parked in front of the place and why couldn't we use it. I agreed to that and suggested an Italian restaurant on the Strip where they had a patio in back and the food was plain and good. Her car was neither a Thunderbird nor a Jaguar, but a 1956 Plymouth convertible, and she drove it without tricks or mannerisms, just watching the road and seemingly lost in her own thoughts

—almost as if she had forgotten that I was with her. I was able to look at her without being too obvious, and now for the first time I specifically related the high-boned profile and the clear, sunburned skin, the wide, full-lipped, brooding mouth to the woman whose past I had relived and whose image I had created. Except for a touch of pale red on her lips, she wore no make-up, but it achieved none of that innocuous innocence that many women evidence when they leave their make-up off. Her face relaxed was neither youthful nor innocent, though it was unlined and the skin was clear as a child's.

I was also able to reflect on the fact that I had leaped without looking or thinking particularly, and here I was and what did I do with it now? Did I become a cheat and a liar as easily as I had been all the things that marked me before?

"There is time," I told myself, "and sooner or later this will work out the only way it can work out—however that is."

At the restaurant we ordered our food, myself as little as possible, and then looked at each other as people do in a situation like this, and she reminded me that I had wanted very much to talk to her and asked me why.

"I read your poems," I said, "and at first I didn't understand them too well—not as well as I wanted to."

"Why did you want to—Mr. Macklin?"

"I'll be able to explain that sometime, I think. I wanted to. I talked to Ann Goldfarb about you, and she said you came in there sometimes. Then I saw a man called Gavin Mullen, who is professor of modern literature out at UCLA, and I spent an evening with him, and your name came up, and we spent the best part of the evening talking about you and your poems——"

"I don't believe that at all." She laughed.

"We did. As a matter of fact, I could bring you there. Mullen would be delighted to meet you."

"Well——" She looked at me and said, "You're not artful, Mr. Macklin, but you make me feel wonderful. My day started wretchedly. Must I ask you what Professor Mullen said? You see, I don't even believe that there is any Professor Mullen——"

"Call UCLA——"

"—but I still want to hear what he said. Did he like the poems? Did he think they were any good?"

"Don't you know?"

"I don't know. You really do live in a world where people respect poems. Don't you understand, Mr. Macklin, that the least of all in this land of ours is a poem? The very least. Books like mine don't sell. The publisher brings them out at a loss. And they are reviewed in very few places—and for the most part by people who haven't the vaguest notion of what I am saying or why. And the question of whether they are good or bad or mean anything at all is never decided. Oh yes, there was one critic in a college quarterly who tore everything to shreds and thought that I was a threat to the whole world of letters, and there were one or two others who said that I was a bright young talent—which is about the nastiest thing I have ever been called. But none of it added up to anything."

"Mullen liked your work. Do you want to hear something he said? I mean as nearly as I can remember. That was almost two months ago."

"You like him—Mullen?"

"I like him fine, Miss West—a tiny, shrunken man with wonderful eyes and a beautiful wife and a houseful of kids—does that add up to a good critic? I had asked him something or other about your poems—what he thought of them—and he said that he would not say to another person whether Sylvia

West was a good or bad poet. He was indignant that anyone dared to ask. He said that first your poems should be listened to—and that the listener should feel—I think his words were 'the wild hatred' and 'the burning hurt' inside of you——"

"He said that?" she asked very softly, watching me out of her dark, thoughtful eyes.

"Yes."

She was silent for a while after that. I lit a cigarette and smoked and watched her as she ate. Then she glanced up and caught my eyes.

"You're not eating," she said.

"No. I ate before. I lied about it."

"Do you lie frequently, Mr. Macklin?"

"Frequently." I nodded and smiled at her—and she smiled back, and I knew it was all right. I hadn't known until then.

"They call you Mack, don't they?"

"Alan Macklin. They call me Mack mostly—yes."

"And what do you do that gives you time for two lunches and picking up a woman in between?"

"I'm a private detective."

"Oh?"

"I didn't pick you up. We were introduced."

"I suppose so."

"How do you feel about private detectives?"

"I haven't formed any opinion about them, Mack. Do you want me to?"

"You will in time," I said.

4

At three o'clock that afternoon we sat in her car on the edge of Mulholland Drive, where the embankment is cleft and there is a little parking space, and all the world to the north of us was visible, the blue mountains washed by the golden California haze, the cool sea breeze only beginning to blow. The long brown grass swayed and rustled with the breeze, and two hawks slid down into the valley, like leaves tumbling on the wind.

"Mack," she said, "have you ever been to Mexico before the rains, when the hills are brown and dry and dead and the land is so old it frightens you?"

"Yes."

"You like it?"

"I like it because I've felt that way, old and dry and dead."

"When you say something," she asked strangely, "how do you know what I'm thinking?"

"I don't."

"I think you do. You can't tell me the truth about very much, can you?"

"I try. About some things—yes. It was true about my mother and father both being burned to death. It happened that way. Funny, I tell myself it is something I invented, it couldn't happen that way. But it did. I get over everything except that. I got over the war. I got over the days and nights of this lousy way I earn a living. I got over my wife. There was a letter from her today about how she and her husband separated, and one rotten break after another, and could I help her. I sent her some money, but nothing inside of me wept for her——"

"Mack?"

"Yes?"

"You say something like that. One moment you talk like a punk from downtown and then you say something like that——"

"My father was born in the old country, Sylvia, in Scotland. I picked up some of his habits of speech—— No, I won't go into that. I tell the truth about most things, I suppose, not about what you think."

"So you know what I think." She smiled.

"Sometimes I do—or I think I do."

"You're a funny guy, Mack. You know what I like about you?"

"No. I'm glad you like something about me."

"I like other things about you too—the sound of your voice and the way you look at me, and I like your face, which is plain and filled with whatever you happen to think at the moment—I don't know how you could play poker or be a good detective——"

"I'm a third-rate detective." I grinned.

"—but I like best about you, I think, that you haven't asked me one thing about myself, who I am—who I am besides writing some poems—and am I married or do I have a guy and where do I live and what do I do for a living—none of those things."

"You'll tell me if you want to—when you want to."

"Why do you say that?"

"Because it's so."

"Mack," she whispered, "who the devil are you?"

"I told you——"

"All right. Was it a lie about Professor Mullen?"

"No."

"Then you and I are going to see him tonight, and if you were lying, then so help me God, I'll cut your throat."

"I believe you would," I said.

5

We drove down to Ventura Boulevard and stopped at a drugstore, where I looked up Gavin Mullen's telephone number and called him. It was four-thirty now, and I caught him at home, and it was good to hear the warmth in his voice as he said, "The private eye—why, of course I remember, and I was hoping that I would hear from you again, me whose life is condemned with boys and girls and the bloody scholars." I told him about Sylvia West then, and he was delighted and said that nothing would please him more. "But it cannot be tonight, Macklin. I have a class tonight. Tomorrow evening? Will the two of you come for dinner?"

"I think so—I'd love to. But I'll have to ask Miss West. I don't know what her plans are for dinner tomorrow night." She was at the counter, drinking a coke. I opened the door of the booth and called out to her, and she said that it would be all right, and I told Mullen we'd both come. I told him, "Mullen—Mullen, do me a favor."

"A small one, Macklin. I am no damn good with big favors."

"Then forget about my literary gumshoeing when we first met. I was just someone who liked her poems enough to talk about them."

"I can do that."

I thanked him and went over to the counter and Sylvia, who looked at me and said, "Of course it was a dirty, rotten way. You trapped me with Mullen. You'd know what I'm talking about, Mack, if I talked about writing—what it is with me?"

"Maybe I would," I said. "I'd try."

We went out to the car, and she drove west, toward the sea, and for about ten minutes neither of us said anything. I waited for her. I didn't know where I was going—perhaps she did.

"Writing," she said at last. "I've known you a few hours and I make you a goddamned father confessor. The hell with you!"

"The hell with me," I agreed.

"Don't be bright with me, Mack."

"Something rubbed you the wrong way. Even if you hate men, you get along with them."

"Don't analyze me."

"Just a poor try."

"It's easy and glib with all of you amateur gods. I hate men. That answers everything. There's a lot I like about you, Mack, but I also think you're a louse."

"You're right. Most men are, more or less. Maybe a little more in my case."

She smiled just thinly and went on with her driving and said, "That's so—I won't withdraw it about your being a louse. I'll wait and see. Why do you say I hate men?"

"Just a guess."

"You're not as bright as I thought."

"No, I'm not."

Then after a few minutes she said quietly, "I'm sorry about what I said before, Mack. I used to lose my temper and say things, but I haven't for a long time. I don't know why I did now."

"I provoked you."

"No, Mack—oh no. You're very sweet and gentle."

So it began that way, and I rushed headlong into it, full of it now and not thinking anything else but that it was the way I had known it would be from the very beginning, and this was the one woman in the world I ever had this feeling for—the one woman who was mine. Not in a belonging sense, because she would never belong to anyone, because her hate and her sickness were rooted deep, deep within her—and even if I were not Frederick Summers' boy, bought and paid for, there would never be peace and contentment with Sylvia, not for myself or for Frederick Summers or for any other man. . . .

We turned down the shore road and parked at the hot-dog stand opposite where Sunset Boulevard cuts through to the sea. The night chill had come now, the cold wind rolling in from the ocean, and suddenly we were both hungry, ravenous with some kind of emptiness that we both shared. We sat in the car, eating frankfurters and drinking orangeade. It was what we wanted and needed, and it was here, not liquor or people, but just the sufficiency of ourselves, of each other. Sylvia pressed close to me, shivering a little, her shoulder and arm touching me. It was the first physical contact we had experienced. I had not tried to kiss her or taken her hand or touched her until now—only this. And after we had eaten the frankfurters, I lit cigarettes for us, and we leaned back and smoked and looked at the beach houses and the stream of cars on the shore road and the houses perched on the cliffs beyond the road and, southward, the great, rounding swell of the Pacific. And Sylvia said:

"What I meant about writing before——"

"I know." I nodded, because she let go of it and couldn't say what she wanted to say. "You wrote a book, and you were going to prove that all the hurt and anguish of a woman's life was rational and made sense and had meaning—you were going to prove it to yourself, and suddenly whether the book was any good or no good became the most important thing in the world, and it had to be good and make it possible for you to go on living—but the whole theory is impractical and wrong. Can't you see that, Sylvia?"

She shook her head.

"The book can't change what you are, Sylvia. Not this book or ten books."

"How do you know what I am?"

"Do you think that any human being can look at another human being the way I'm looking at you—and not know something?"

"I'm tired," she said. "And I'm beginning to be bored."

She had turned into something hard and alien and very cold. She put up the roof of the car and asked me where I lived. I told her, and then not another word passed between us until she dropped me at my apartment house in West Hollywood. She drove off without even saying good night.

6

I was numb, locked in, and I specified to myself that all was for the best. Then I added to my arguments that it was compulsive, adolescent, and neurotic on my part to select for love one woman whose cause for hatred—of myself—would be both severe and justified. A long time ago I had ceased to believe that the act of love between a man and a woman simply happened. One did not fall in love, as the romancers would have it; one performed the act of falling in love as a voluntary process, and the choice of the impossible in so doing was a particular sickness. I have known women who chose only married men as the recipient, men who chose only married women, and specimens of both sexes who singled out a variety of other complexities and impossibilities.

What else had I done? I asked myself. And why couldn't I be intelligent enough and objective enough to allow Mr. Frederick Summers to get what he roundly deserved? "Who is Sylvia and what is she" was finished; I had played out my little game; and if the art of the private cop was in all truth a shade more respectable than the conniving of a hungry pimp and worthy of definition as a profession, then I was a fair pro and had done my job. Starting with a picture, a poem, and a few words of writing, I had unfolded the life of a woman. I was talented and I was a hero, and when I turned in my report to Frederick Summers and he wrote out his check for me I would be four thousand dollars richer than I had ever been, and Mr. Summers would be possessed of the following information concerning the woman he loved, according to his lights, which the odds held were every bit as good as mine:

She was a liar, start to finish.

She was the daughter of an alcoholic and half-insane bum of Hungarian origin.

Her name was Sylvia Karoki, not Sylvia Carter or Sylvia West.

Her profession, during her formative years, had been an ancient one—the art of prostitution.

She was possessed of worldly goods because she had won the basis of a fortune through blackmail—namely, the tired con of the shakedown.

Her experience with men, which began when she had hardly entered the stage of puberty, had built into her personality, her brain, and her soul a deep-seated hatred of men, a distrust of men, and most likely an abiding fear of men.

And, likely enough, she was frigid, every normal reaction and emotion either beaten or blocked.

As a footnote, this was the woman I had selected to fall in love with; and I brought to this exercise of passion a series of qualifications in no way inferior to hers, namely:

I was broke, or almost broke.

I was a liar, start to finish.

My future, economically speaking, depended upon a report I had written which would not only destroy this woman's dream of marrying an eligible millionaire but would very likely destroy her in the process.

I had chatted with her and grinned at her and at least by word made love to her, while all this hung on my neck a good deal more lightly than the albatross on the neck of the old gentleman in the poem.

I was a fraud.

I earned my dollar sometimes as a whore and sometimes as a pimp, but with the difference that I had the nod from society and I could watch the so-called reflection of my ways in the antics that a dozen idiots performed on television—a half-witted and brutal gibbering that had made the trade of the private eye a part of American folklore—or so they say.

I didn't care to balance any scale. I had performed, and the hell with the applause! The hell with everything!

I smoked a cigarette and watched the lights in the black bowl of Los Angeles beneath me. Then I went to bed. I was tired, physically and emotionally exhausted, and I think I was asleep the moment my head touched the pillow.

7

I was shaving the next morning when the phone rang, and it was Sylvia. "I didn't wake you, did I, Mack?" she said easily, conversationally.

"No. No, you didn't. I was shaving."

"Will you do me a great favor today, Mack?"

"If I can, I will. Of course."

"I'm showing some of my roses at Santa Barbara, and I'll be too tense to drive sensibly—and maybe you'd like to drive me there—if you have nothing better?"

"I'd love to," I said.

"I feel like a pig. You have your own work."

"I haven't. That's not unusual in my line. Anyway, I would lie about it if I did have work, Sylvia."

"You're sure?"

"Very sure," I said. "When shall I come by for you?"

"Would ten o'clock be too early? We don't have to be in Santa Barbara until two, but I don't want to rush. And I won't cut the roses until you come—I mean, until we're ready to leave."

"Ten is fine."

"I'll give you coffee—toast? Eggs?"

"Anything."

"You're a dear and considerate person, Mack."

"Sometimes. Tell me where you live."

She gave me the number in Coldwater Canyon, and then I put away the phone and finished shaving and reviewed my position relative to life.

I kept reviewing it all the way to Coldwater Canyon, and then I drove slowly and guessed about the houses. I can't pretend that I knew which one it was; there were half a dozen I felt she might have lived in—and finally, at the number, an unpretentious one-story cottage of brick painted white. She must have been watching for me, because when I turned into the driveway she came out of the house. I think I had made myself forget, as they say, how beautiful this woman was— or perhaps because I had not seen her before in the morning sunshine, with the yellow light on the grayed pink cotton she wore. She was tall, long-limbed, and all that there was in the whole wide world. She held out her hand to me as casually as if I were her oldest friend and took me to the patio at the back of the house, where breakfast waited on a wrought-iron table, with a backdrop of such a rose garden as I had never seen before.

8

The peculiar deference that is frequently called "honor" comes to those who make the journey in several generations, whether it is Beacon Street in Boston, Park Avenue in New York, or the harborside in Charleston—or any one of ten places that serve a similar function. In California it is more loosely arranged for the moment. Sylvia's journey to Coldwater Canyon had taken a quarter of a century, and I had followed the path in a matter of weeks; and we had similarly invested the matter of existence in a substance that might be called refrigerated dreams. Both the marten and the wolverine bite off their limbs when they are caught in traps. On Sylvia, the scars were invisible. She offered the cottage as testimony and the garden in the line of the same, and her relaxed manner and impeccable security rested upon various questions of taste—none of it, so they say, acquirable in a handful of years. The limbs she had bitten off, torn off, or bent or broken—and not a revealing scar on a sunny morning.

She was a fraud so wise and calculating and skillful that I could have sat down and wept for the first time since childhood, and what I felt for her is my own and not to be spelled out in any words I know. We each of us have our own way to love and knowledge about it and ineptitude and squeezed dream of what might be or ought to be between a man and a woman.

Only it wasn't a fraud and neither was she. It was Sylvia's house, and not changed a great deal since she had first walked into Irma Olanski's little apartment in Pittsburgh and seen that there were people who did not live in a cave of their filth, as animals did. The walls in the house were painted white, the windows were big and wide, and the place was drenched with clean air and sunlight. There were organdy curtains, white in one room, pale yellow in another. There was no tradition, no fake background, no odd bits of furniture to underline anything, no manufactured portraits or photographs. The tissue of lies that she had presented to Frederick Summers was not implemented in any way, as if she could not bear to concretize the hazy legends that she had spun for a particular need. The furniture was either local California, Mexican cottage type, or Breton farm stuff that she had bought herself in Europe. The floors were tiled, except for the floor of her study, which was of broad, pegged planks of redwood in the paler luster of its natural color, and the walls of this room were lined with bookshelves of the same wood.

The books had gone with her and remained with her, used and read and reread. In this room there was a long California table upon which she worked, a desk chair, two modern contour chairs; and the whole thing faced glass sliding doors opening on the garden. On the walls of the other rooms were modern paintings, the kind of thing that is done so well now at La Jolla and Carmel, possibly art and possibly no more than line and color put together, but divorced from everything but the moment of today and reminding of nothing and asking no more than its color and motion commands.

Everywhere in the house the colors were bright, and light poured in. Like all of Sylvia, it was the aching truth behind the lie. Enmeshed in the fabric of her own inventions and fears, she had to cry out that she had nothing to hide, nothing to conceal.

9

The rose garden was in a half acre of space between the back of the house and where the slope of the canyon began, and it was divided into three levels, each separated from the next by three steps built of red brick, and in it, as borders and formal beds and hedges and climbing bowers and hoods and sprays and fans, were over eight hundred roses. A small and very old man, a Mexican, was working among the bushes when we came into the garden. He had evidently just finished watering and spraying, for the whole place glistened with moisture, and the scent of the roses was heavy and all over it. He spoke to Sylvia in Spanish, and she answered him easily and casually in the same language. I know enough Spanish to know that hers was very good and fluent, and just enough to catch the drift of what they were saying: that he had been rooting and propagating the miniatures as she had instructed, and did she want the old roses cut yet. She answered that she would cut them herself and he should bring the basket and the wet moss.

"Old roses?" I asked her.

"Then you do know Spanish, Mack. How nice!"

"A little and poorly. I caught the words—'old roses.'"

"But do you like my garden? Tell me."

The bees were out now, lustful bits of gold in the warm morning air. We moved past the old man onto the first terrace, which was separated from the part below by a rose hedge. The red brick path that wound through the terrace had shoulders of sweet alyssum. On one side a stone retaining wall hung under a weight of red and white roses. I didn't know what to say. I told her that I didn't know what to say—because what could one say about a place like this? Suppose she had asked me whether I liked her. This place was like her; it filled you full of desire.

"I'm glad you didn't find any name for it," she said. "That's the best way to like it—not the way some come here, and they

say, 'My dear, how pretty!' I hate that word. This isn't pretty
—it's full of heat and primacy and it aches for something—do
you feel that?"

I nodded.

"And most of it I made, Mack—that's why I'm greedy and
proud about it. Oh, there were roses here, the big climbers
and some of the floribunda hedges and a few others—perhaps
forty or fifty roses. I put in the rest—that is, myself and Estan,
my gardener. Do you know about roses?"

"Not about any flower, I'm afraid, Sylvia."

"You asked about old roses——"

"It sounded strange in Spanish."

We stopped by a square bed of a dozen plants, all of them
with heavy and wonderful blooms. "Old roses are something
else. I'm showing them because they seem to do best here.
Mack," she said suddenly, "I learned all this in a few years. I
never even knew that a rose grows in the ground, and then
it did something to me——" I was watching her, and she
turned away and touched one of the flowers. "These are hybrid teas——"

Anything she learns, I thought to myself, she has to have
all of it and live it like it existed for no one but herself.

"—well, you see them everywhere. They're very beautiful and
showy. This is Chrysler Imperial—they have silly names, some
of them, and some are incredible names. I mean—do you think
the Chrysler people paid them? Oh, I don't know. But you see
it's so red it's almost hateful. Then I put the Pink Radiance
and the Charlotte Armstrong in with it, and they blend
into something, and the Chrysler red isn't so bitter any more.
Supposedly, they are three of the most beautiful roses in the
world. These in here are all right but not very good. I've seen

these roses in the gardens at San Jose—enough to make me
very jealous. I can't grow the hybrids like the professionals do
—you have to know too much on the chemical side—but I do
well with the climbers and floribunda, and the old roses.
You see, they're not just old plants, Mack, but a kind of rose
that we call 'old roses,' a whole category that goes back to before
all the professionals and scientists began with the hybrid teas
and the floribunda and all the other beautiful things they've
made, but with not much smell or strength—and I suppose I'm
trying to prove something. Do you think so?"

"We all are, all the time, I think. Where are your old roses?"

"On the top terrace," she said, leading me there. "They were
here—well, two thirds of them were—when I bought the place.
I bought the others at La Canada, and they were supposed to
have been developed from the Descanso Gardens; they say
that's the very best old-rose garden in America. So now I have
eighteen roses here, but I do have a feel for them, and I was
thinking that this whole terrace should be in the old roses."

The old roses were in a circle in the center of the terrace,
placed around a weathered and chipped bowl piece of an old
mission fountain. The path around it had a patina of ancient
blue glaze on the bricks, and the roses were rather strange to
me but striking in their beauty and their difference. There was
a tiny red flower that did not look like a rose at all—which
Sylvia had not been able to identify and which she had named
Irma. The place was old and full of the past, and I began to
comprehend how Sylvia related to it. A bush of delicate yellow flowers, each with five single petals, she identified as Father
Hugo—and made the first remark she had ever made to me
concerning her past.

"It reminds me of an old priest I knew in Mexico," she
said, "and somehow when I look at it I always think of his

mission. He had no roses there, but in my memory the place seems to be pervaded with a yellow glow."

I nodded and pointed to enormous flowers of translucent pink. "Those are magnificent."

"Aren't they? Those are my beauties—I hate to tell you what they are. They're called cabbage roses—and some of them have over a hundred petals. I suppose they call them cabbage roses because of the shape, but I think there's nothing in the tea roses as lovely as these. I have been told that my Father Hugos are a better flower, but no one pays much attention to them when you show them, and they won't have any special category. It always comes down to the cabbage roses and the York and Lancaster—those showy red and white ones. You can have a red rose and a white one, both on the same bush. I guess they named it after the war, not the other way around—or do you suppose that the old gentlemen plucked these same roses? They could have, you know. Some of these old roses go back several thousand years. There was a Greek city in Italy in the olden times, and they say the whole city was like a rose garden— what was it called?"

"Paestum." I smiled.

"Mack, you're laughing at me."

"No—no, believe me, Sylvia. Only I never heard you talk before. Yesterday——"

"Yesterday I wasn't here with the roses, Mack. Anyway, we're going to be late if I keep talking. I'm showing five cabbage roses, and I have them picked out. I'll get Estan and we'll cut them. You wait here."

She went off to find the Mexican gardener. She was alive and beautiful and full of laughter and happiness; and all my judgments, guesses, and profound conclusions about her fell into a deep well.

10

During most of the drive to Santa Barbara she was silent, her head back against the seat, her eyes closed, the wind washing through her black hair. On the shore road, the fog had rolled away and the air was warm, the sun hot, the Pacific heaving and foaming lazily. The talk she led into was about small things, and when she talked of herself it was of California and the past two years. She told me how she had met Ed Lemmingwell, a director at Fox, and how he had insisted that she take a screen test. "But I can't act," she said, "and I don't want to. I can dissemble—I think you know that, but that's something else, isn't it, Mack?" I said that I thought it was, but how much acting ability a screen required, I didn't know. I had guessed that her life was not to be seen, not to be looked at, not to be lived beyond a small circle, and possibly it was so much that way that she was utterly conditioned to it. Sylvia Karoki could walk safely and relaxed at a rose show in Santa Barbara. But at the same time I held out the possibility that I was wrong.

She asked me about the Greek cities, such as Paestum, where the air always smelled of roses, and for about a half hour I held forth on how the Greek cities in Italy were settled, and how the settlers took with them their olive trees and their rose and grape cuttings, all of it very didactic, since until this morning I had never been in a rose garden; and I reflected on the fact that while I knew a reasonable amount of this and that, she had probably seen more with her eyes than I had and absorbed more.

Once we pulled off the road and stretched our legs and watched the Pacific churning among the black rocks and the white sand; and we talked about oceans and swimming and skin diving and boats—she knew a man who owned a yacht, she told me—and then she said to me suddenly, vehemently:

"Just stop me, Mack, if I keep on with it!"

"With what?"

"That kind of talk. Rich friends. Yachts. Millionaires. All the honey flowing from the honeybowl without end."

"You don't talk about it so much that I've noticed."

"Too much."

"Well—there's nothing wrong with liking a rich man or a yacht. I like yachts. I wish I had one."

"No, you don't," she said. "You don't give a damn whether you have one or not."

"I suppose so, Sylvia."

"You were poor, weren't you, Mack?"

"On and off." I nodded.

"I mean as a kid."

"There's always somebody poorer. You learn that, too, as a kid."

"It doesn't bother you?"

"Now?"

"Now."

"It does, Sylvia," I said. "Anyone who tells you such a thing doesn't bother him—he's either lying or he's pumped himself full of a position. I never bothered to. Poverty is degradation, and all the holy tales told to prove otherwise are for the birds, and when you grow up with this degradation it stays with you. There was a writer who made a big splash about twenty years ago telling little fairy tales full of fancy language about how gifted and happy the poor are, and Sinclair Lewis said the perfect thing about him once, that he writes about the poor for the rich. I don't buy any of that way of remembering, but I don't stay awake with it. The main thing is that we grow up, and a part of growing up is to stop being afraid."

"And you're not afraid any more, Mack?"

"Not that kind of fear. Other fears, yes. But not the fear of being a poor and hungry kid with the whole world closing in."

"Were you hungry?"

"I was eleven years old in 1933, and I was hungry enough to turn over garbage cans and separate the garbage piece by piece."

"Mack——"

"I lived."

"Is that all that means anything, Mack, that you lived?"

"Basically, yes. The rest is up to me."

"Mack?"

I looked at her, but she shook her head, and we got back into the car and drove to Santa Barbara.

11

In a vague way I had known that flower shows existed; just as I also knew about dog shows and horse shows and baking contests; but this was my first visit to the actual scene. I came as a friend. If Sylvia liked flower shows, I was prepared to have the same reaction. If people there were her friends, I was prepared to make them my friends. Nothing had changed or been worked out or resolved in any way whatsoever, but my life had come to its point and focus. Whatever Sylvia was or had been or would be, my life was fairly meaningless without her. I will confess that it had not been saturated with meaning or purpose before I knew her, but I was able to live with it then. This was no longer true.

I came to the flower show, thereby, with an open mind. I felt good—as close to happiness as I had yet managed—because

I could look at her and watch her; and I had stopped making a separation between what was a lie and what was not a lie. So far as Sylvia and I were concerned, the only lies had been on my part. Of herself, I had asked nothing and she had told me nothing, and there were no lies. Not even here. Whatever I might have felt about the place where the show was held, Sylvia graced it. The lawns were greener because she walked on them. The long greenhouses had meaning because she took me through them. The roses on display and entered in the various categories of contest were important and beautiful because she was interested in them and took the trouble to tell me about them. The people who were present existed in terms of a woman I loved deeply, unreasonably, and more than I had ever loved before.

When I could, I stood apart and watched her. I watched the way she walked and held her head, the way she greeted people and said a few words to this one or that one. I had never known that particular kind of pleasure and fulfillment before. It was a pleasant day. I have not been in Santa Barbara too often, but when I have been there, as now, it was cooler than Los Angeles. And we were high enough to see the top of the old mission across the rolling foothills. And Sylvia was there.

Among the people she introduced me to, there was a Mr. Leland and his wife. He was in his fifties, with the voice and manner of a rich man, and his wife, in pastel greens, tried to be queenly in all ways that she knew. I imagine Sylvia had forgotten that she had made a sort of date with them—at least to see them there—and when she introduced me to them Mrs. Leland said:

"But where's Fred?"

"He's out of town on business." Sylvia smiled.

"For today?" Mr. Leland asked.

"For a week, I believe," Sylvia answered. "Mr. Macklin was kind enough to drive me up here. I always find the drive alone too tiring."

"That's very kind of Mr. Macklin," Mrs. Leland said.

"Not at all. We're very dear friends. I think he enjoyed it."

"Oh?" said Mrs. Leland.

"We were hoping you and Fred would stay over at our place," Mr. Leland said pointedly. "Perhaps you would like to?"

It was pointed enough, and Sylvia smiled again and said, "I don't think Mr. Macklin made any plans to stay over. Did you, Mack?"

"No plans at all," I said.

"And we have a date for dinner in Brentwood," Sylvia added.

"Of course," Mr. Leland said.

"You will give our very best to Fred, won't you?" Mrs. Leland said.

"I'll be delighted to."

Sylvia won a second prize and an honorable mention, and by half-past three we were on our way back. We had gone at least half the distance back to Los Angeles before Sylvia said to me:

"Aren't you going to ask me who Fred is?"

"No."

"Or who the Lelands are?"

"I don't give a damn who the Lelands are. If you liked them, I would care about who they are. But you don't like them. So I don't give a damn who they are."

"And Fred?"

"That's up to you, Sylvia."

"Aren't you curious, Mack?"

"Yes, I'm curious."

"I like you, Mack," she said. "You're loyal. You also have brains. But that isn't the main thing, that you're like a kind of tough TV boy scout——"

I took my eyes from the road to look at her, and she was smiling. "I know," I said. "You like me because I don't ask questions like about Fred."

"Go to hell."

"Why do you like me?"

"You're not much to look at," she said, "but I feel comfortable with you."

"That's something."

"I don't have to be on my guard," she added.

"Are you always on your guard?"

"Most of the time."

"It's not a good way to be," I said.

"No. Mack?"

"Uh-huh?"

"How do you feel about me?"

"I love you," I said.

I didn't look at her now. She was silent for a while. Then she said to me, "Mack?"

"Yes?"

"You mean what you said before—about loving me?"

"I meant it."

"That's why you play it the way you do—no pass—no attempt to touch me or kiss me?"

"I'm not playing it," I said. "I'm afraid."

"You're a big boy, Mack."

"And you're Sylvia."

"We don't talk very clever to each other, do we, Mack?"

"I'm not clever."

"Mack—Mack . . ." She was only whispering now, and then there was silence again, until she said, "Mack?"

"I'm still here."

"About Fred . . ."

"It doesn't matter about Fred."

"It matters, Mack. He's the man I'm going to marry."

PART 11

BRENTWOOD

MRS. MULLEN MANAGED SIX AT DINNER AND PUT FOUR OF THE six children to bed at more or less the same time. A general air of chaos was leavened by Mullen himself, who kept our glasses filled with a red wine of Napa Valley out of a two-gallon jug, explaining that one of the minor blessings of poetry derived from a former student of his who had come into the operation of a winery in the north and remembered his old instructor with ten such jugs each year. A big clay bowl of *arroz con pollo* gave Mrs. Mullen a maximum of mobility. The kids howled and wet their diapers and fought the punishment of sleep, and with unruffled calm Mrs. Mullen moved from the kitchen to the children to the dining room. The other guests at dinner were Gerald Heintz, who was in the Literature Department at the university and had just published a novel about ancient Rome, and his wife Martha, who had been Mullen's assistant instructor but was now very pregnant—in fact, in her ninth month—and sat through all the madness of the dinner with that beatific and somewhat bucolic expression that so many women take on during the last months of pregnancy. Later in the course of the evening five of Mullen's students joined us to meet Miss West and talk to her. And at about ten o'clock Professor Cohen and his wife came by. Mullen had invited them for dinner, but they were unable to make it, and Professor Cohen asked to come by later, since he wanted to see me. I suppose he was the only one who did.

In Sylvia's life it was the first evening of this kind, the first time she had been exposed to a group of university people, instructor and undergraduate—people who were interested in things important to her, and perhaps the first time she had ever been in a home like this, where there was neither money nor luxury of any kind, unless a mountain of books can be regarded as a sort of off-beat luxury; yet neither was there the kind of squalid degradation that was defined in her mind as the quality of poverty, but rather a pervading warmth and a mental order contrasting oddly with the physical disorder.

That it could have been otherwise, I was well aware, for there can be nothing as cold and deadly as an evening of pedagogues frozen in their timidity of thought and multifold institutional fears, or pompous and irrational in their half-knowledge and their book-bound ignorance; but neither of these was the case tonight. The people there were not of great importance or reputation, but they were eager to meet a young writer who had written something different and alive, and when they met Sylvia they responded to what she was as Sylvia.

I watched how she responded. I don't know why I was afraid and had conceived some notion that a great deal might come out of this night—but perhaps that was only because I was afraid; and then the fear went away. At some time, when Gavin Mullen said something about her, the fear went away. Mullen said then, I think:

"I would eat out my heart with jealousy, Macklin, were it not that the gods, in their infinite wisdom, gave to a twisted little man like myself a woman not so different from your Sylvia West."

"You believe that?" I said.

"Do I believe it? Jesus God, man, notice the way she looks at you. Have you no sense for women whatsoever?"

"Not a hell of a lot."

"Then I pity you. In your place I would kill any bastard who stood in my way."

"I have felt that way," I said.

2

With Mrs. Mullen, it was two women who watched each other and I watched Sylvia. I watched her hold one of the kids while Alice Mullen handled the other. What does a woman say then? To myself, I begged Sylvia, "Don't say it's darling. Don't say it's cute." She said nothing. She was looking at the child, who was three years old, a fat-cheeked little girl, just looking at her. She handed the child to Mrs. Mullen, and I said to myself, "The hell with you, Macklin, and all your stinking, lousy little fears and doubts! The hell with you!"

3

At the dinner table Heintz made the point that Sylvia was not what he had expected. He couldn't hold it in. "You're just not what I expected," he said. "You don't write like that out of the imagination."

"Most of it has to come out of imagination, doesn't it?" Sylvia said gently.

Martha Heintz made the placid comment, "He means you're a stunning woman, Miss West."

"He's a damn prude, Miss West"—Mullen grinned—"and the child doesn't know what in hell he means. He's licked his lips over the symbols in your stuff, and now you have broken his heart with your innocence."

"That's sweet. I'm not innocent."

"Of course not. No woman is innocent," Heintz declared.

"Now what the hell do you know about women?" Mullen demanded. "Ah—be calm, boy. No man knows a damn thing more, but Heintz here has eyes in his head, and he can look upon innocence even if he doesn't comprehend a bit of it. The meaning of innocence is artlessness, not the act of closing your eyes to the dirty writing on the wall of a public john. You look like what you are, Miss West. Did you ever imagine that she would look any different, Macklin?"

"I knew what she would look like," I said. "But I think I know what you mean," I said to Heintz.

"The point is, you've written with a point of view," Heintz said. "That's what fascinated me. I don't go all the way. I think you've thrown away every tradition, and you can't do that——"

"Why the devil can't she?" Mullen put in. "Anyway, it's not true. What about the tradition of New Orleans? What about the singers in Oregon and Washington?"

"A point of view——"

"Now what does that mean? You keep on saying it."

"All I am trying to do is to explain why you took me by surprise. Now you and Macklin went to a flower show—you mentioned that. You don't write about flowers or flower shows, Miss West. You write about a side of our society that's raw and terrible and frightening. You put your words into the mouth of a woman who has been used and beaten and destroyed——"

"Not destroyed," Mullen said. "No one who is destroyed sings."

"But you see what I mean," Heintz said.

She listened thoughtfully. She was detached. They were talking about someone, and she was thinking about the person they discussed. She wasn't disturbed, and I realized that she wouldn't be disturbed by anything tonight—but nevertheless it was happening.

"I have read poems about roses," Sylvia said. "I don't think I would write one."

"Why not?"

"It would mean nothing," Sylvia said slowly. "The rose is there. I understand about roses. I don't understand about atom bombs. I don't understand about war. I saw a man killed once— and I don't understand that. I don't understand what a man does to a woman he says he loves. I don't understand all the hate and sickness and fear that we live with."

"But is that the meaning of poetry—to understand?" Heintz pressed her.

"Some of the meaning, I think."

"And how much can one understand?" Mullen wondered.

"I don't know. I think that if I showed a rose to your little girl—the one I held in my arms before—she would know about it and understand it and reach out for it. I never wondered about what a rose meant, because I knew. But about the things I wrote of—I know only a little and I have to know more."

4

During one of those moments that happen in a roomful of people, I was alone with her, and she said to me:

"You are a bastard, Mack. Why did you bring me here?"

"There are all kinds of ways to live. You might as well know about it."

"You don't live this way," she said. "You're a private cop, and you live with all the dirt that goes with the job."

"That was a living. I didn't give a damn how I lived."

"But you give a damn now."

"Now—yes," I said.

"Still, you're a bastard. You brought me here because you knew how I'd feel."

"I hoped."

"Like hell you hoped. You knew."

5

She sat with the undergraduates around her. Three were girls. The two boys were nineteen or twenty, and they adored her. They were in love with her; they never took their eyes off her face. In good time they would leave the university and go wherever they had to go, and they would never forget an evening they spent with Sylvia West. Nor would Sylvia forget the evening.

I sat to one side and listened and watched, and Professor Cohen, next to me, was saying:

"It's not her beauty. I'm not even sure she's beautiful. But she is alive—it's an old life, an ancient aliveness, do you understand me, Mr. Macklin?"

I nodded.

"It is almost an immorality in our terms. Where did this woman come from? Who is she?"

"She lives in Coldwater Canyon."

"I am not asking you where she lives. Where did she learn to hold her head the way she does? Where did she learn to look at one like that? Is she Spanish?"

"I doubt it," I said.

"My wife thinks she is. My wife lived in Mexico three years. She says only someone born to it talks Spanish like your Sylvia West."

"She has an ear for things," I said. I wanted to listen to

her, not to Professor Cohen's speculations about her. He, in turn, wanted to talk to me about being his assistant. My life had begun and finished—could I tell him that? He argued that I belonged in his department, and I wanted to ask him did he have any notion of what an acre of ground in Coldwater Canyon brought in today's market, or could he guess the price of the dress she was wearing?

One of the undergraduates was talking about Proust. Then another brought up the plays of John Ford. Then the conversation turned to *The Duchess of Malfi*. Mullen joined them and boomed that it was a great, great play. I got up and crossed the room and stood next to Mullen's wife.

"You have changed, Mr. Macklin," she said to me.

"Have I?"

"I think so."

"I wonder," I said.

"I mean that wherever you have been, you found what you were looking for. Was it Sylvia West?"

With someone else I could have said that it was none of her damn business. Now I was sorry I had come and sorry that I had ever seen the Mullens. Gavin Mullen joined us and asked me to stay after the others went. "I want to talk to her a bit," he told me.

I shrugged and nodded.

"You keep giving her up, don't you?"

"She isn't mine to give up," I said sourly.

"And everyone is putting his nose into your own precious business, is that it, boy?"

"I'm not sensitive."

"The hell you're not!" Mullen said. "Why don't you take the job Cohen is holding out to you?"

"I'm no teacher."

"Then what are you—a private eye? I have my doubts. Or are you sick with the dream of the big money because that plain and simple dress on her back cost a hundred dollars if it cost a penny? What in hell's name does it matter? Are you like Heintz, who expected her to be a snotnose delinquent because she had the guts to look at and face the pile of shit that men erect in the holy name of civilization? You were looking for her and you found her."

"Did I?"

"That's for you to answer, Macklin."

6

One by one they left, and then there were Sylvia and myself and the Mullens sitting down to a nightcap of a little whisky, and Mullen demanding of her:

"What did you think of the kids, Miss West?"

"I liked them."

"You see the small compensation for the mystery America faces, why we poor bastards in the colleges work for penny wages. There is now and then a bright gleam of compensation. Can your bankers and brokers and private eyes say the same?"

"Can they, Mack?" She turned to me.

"*Salut*," I said, and they joined me with the whisky, and Mullen told her that I couldn't be forced to an opinion. "You've had an evening of opinions," I said.

"You are a Scot on both sides, aren't you, Macklin?" Mullen said. "You see, we are both of great races and we could have turned this world into a goddamned garden, but my own folk are cursed with drunkenness and yours with sobriety, and I'm damned if I know which is the deadlier!"

"When our kids are a little older"—his wife nodded—"I will

put an end to all this swearing he does under the illusion that he is talking the Irish language."

"Keep on provoking me and I will take a stick to you."

"I wouldn't want that," she said seriously.

Sylvia watched them, smiling slightly, puzzled slightly. She had not been here before. It was my trick but, like all tricks, it had failed.

"I want a word about your poetry, Miss West," Mullen said.

"Please tell me," Sylvia said quietly.

"Anything?"

"It's no good if you're not honest with me," Sylvia said.

"That's the damn painful truth of making anything, isn't it? When Macklin here put it to me some months ago, he wanted to know if your poems were any good, which is the devil's own question to answer. Do you want to be a fine and beautiful poet, Miss West?"

"Yes."

"Then you want it a lot. Do you know that Heintz put his finger on it? He's shrewder than he seems to be, and if you can look at a rose, Miss West, then you can also look at that smoky pile of slag called Pittsburgh where you lived and were hurt as a kid and you can come out of it with some sense and understanding. I haven't been prying, my dear. You've put it down in your writing, but it's cloaked in such mystery and fear that you have made a fetish out of it, and you are lost in all the aching symbols of misery and slime. But do you think you're the only one? It is terrible and dirty for a kid to have happen to her what must have happened to you, but it is worse to grow to an adult's estate and not be able to regard what happened and face it with your eyes open. When you do, you will be a poet—if, damn it, you want to be a poet."

There was no reaction but fear and flight. I saw it, they didn't;

I saw it begin and spread over her and squeeze the muscles of her face and pinch her and clutch at her heart. Then Mullen and his wife understood a little, but there was nothing they could say, only the silence that stretched and stretched until she got up and walked out of the house.

7

In the car she began with a whimper. "Mack, why did you bring me there?"

"I didn't bring you there. You wanted to go."

"You knew."

"I didn't know."

"Why did he say that about Pittsburgh?"

"I guess because he felt that it wouldn't matter if he spoke about it, since it was in the poems."

"It wasn't. Wouldn't I know? He had to show me he was clever! He had to show me how clever he was!"

"You can look at it that way," I said.

"But I'm right, Mack. Why did he have to play games with me? I was never in Pittsburgh."

I shook my head.

"I tell you I was never in Pittsburgh, Mack. Don't you believe me?"

"It doesn't matter if I believe you."

"Well, don't you believe me?" she pleaded. "Do you think I'm a liar?"

"I told you it doesn't matter."

"Why doesn't it matter? Suppose he writes some kind of an article somewhere and says that about Pittsburgh. Suppose he gives it to one of the columnists."

"He wouldn't do that."

"How do you know?"

"I know the kind of man he is," I told her. "He wouldn't do anything of the kind unless he spoke to you first and got your agreement."

"Then you think I'm lying?"

"I didn't say that. It doesn't matter to me whether you come from Pittsburgh or Timbuktu. Can't you understand that? It doesn't matter to anyone."

"Go to hell," she whispered.

"All right."

But she couldn't let go of it. She was sick with fear. She was like an animal with her fear—a fear without reason or sense or rationale; and after a while she said, "Mack?"

"Sylvia, nothing happened. Stop thinking about it."

"Mack, would you see him tomorrow and make him swear that he'll never mention that again—to anyone?"

"What good would it do, Sylvia? He hasn't any magic powers. If he could make that guess out of your poems, then others can too. It's only a guess. It doesn't mean anything."

"It means something to me."

"He's not going to talk about it. I told you that."

"I don't come from Pittsburgh."

"I told you, I don't care."

"You don't care," she cried, and I was glad that it was dark in the car and that I couldn't see her face. "It doesn't mean anything to be lied about and slandered! Well, it means something to me! That man they spoke of today——"

She might have stopped there, but now I didn't want her to stop. "You mean Fred?"

"His name is Frederick Summers. Do you know who he is?"

"I know the name," I said.

"Mack——" She was pleading as a child pleads. "I'm going to marry him. He's a millionaire. He's one of the most important men in California. I know this won't impress you. Just try to think of what it means to me, Mack."

"I'll try," I agreed, "if you'll stop being frightened and get hold of yourself and talk some sense."

"I'm a fool to talk to you about this."

"No," I said sharply, "you're not a fool to talk to me about this. It's what you're letting it do to you."

"I can't help it."

"You can help it," I said.

"Why should you help me?"

"I'm only asking you to help yourself, to get hold of yourself. What are you trying to tell me—that Summers won't marry you if he finds out that you come from Pittsburgh?"

"I don't."

"If he thinks so?"

"Mack, Mack," she begged me, "try to see what I'm in. Let me tell you about myself—and you'll see what this means to me and to Fred."

"No!" I said.

Then she got hold of herself, and she sat there silently until we were back at her house.

8

"Do you want to come in?" she said to me. It was not too late, a half hour past midnight.

"If you want me to."

"Yes." She opened the door and led the way into the house. She asked me whether I wanted a drink or coffee, and I told her I'd have coffee if it wasn't too much trouble. We were both calm and even-voiced now. We went into her kitchen, and she put a pot of coffee on the stove. Then she turned around and looked at me. I had made up my mind. I suppose that when a person makes up his mind about anything of any consequence it shows and he demonstrates it in some way.

"Is it because I didn't tell you about Fred?" Sylvia asked.

"No."

"What have you decided, Mack? That you're going to walk out of here and never see me again?"

"That's up to you, Sylvia."

"I like you, Mack. That's all I ever said."

"I know."

"I like you," she said hopelessly. "What does it add up to? Would I be any good to you? Can you see me caught like Alice Mullen, with six kids in that madhouse?"

"There are all kinds of madhouses, Sylvia."

"I've been in them. Every damn last one of them, Mack."

"I know."

"The hell you know!" she cried. "What do you know about me? Sylvia West, the poet? The rose garden? Shall I go out there and cut you some roses, Macklin, so you can paste me into a Jane Austen book and tell me that you know me? You don't know one goddamned thing about me—so don't ask me to explain anything! Anything! I do what I have to do! The hell with you! I don't have to explain to you!"

"No, you don't."

"And don't be so stinking righteous about it!"

"I'm not righteous," I said. "I don't even have the surface decency to go with it. I don't even have a foot of ground to stand on. I'm Frederick Summers' boy, bought and paid for."

"What?" She came over, close to me, her black eyes fixed on me. "What did you say, Mack?"

Then I told her. She didn't interrupt me. The coffee boiled over and she was unaware of it. I reached out and turned the burner off. I was aware. I was aware of the smell of the coffee and the look of Sylvia, rigid as a piece of steel, and the white fittings of the clean, modern kitchen, and the dress she wore and the loose lock of hair across her forehead and the slight flare of her nostrils and the space between her full parted lips and the white edge of her teeth and her high breasts rising and falling as she listened—all of this. I had the lousy, rotten gift of awareness; I carried it with me.

She listened. I dwelt on nothing and I left nothing out. I made a summation of the life of Sylvia Karoki. I told her how I had put it together and how I was hired to do that and what I was paid and what was still to be paid to me.

I told her all of it, and I finished, and then it was cleared out of the way, and the air was just as hard and clear, and we stood facing each other, naked.

"You louse!" she said. It was sufficient comment. It was enough. No more needed to be said. I turned around and went out of the kitchen, through her dining room, and across the living room to leave the house. Her voice stopped me short of the outside door.

"Wait a minute!"

I waited with my hand on the knob. I didn't turn around because I couldn't turn around. I couldn't look at her now.

"Where is the report?" she asked me, her voice like ice.

"Why? What difference does it make?"

"I'm not poor," the icy voice said. "If Summers can pay, I can double his price."

"Go to hell!"

"Where is the report?" Her voice didn't change. It was cold and inhuman and completely under control.

"There is no report."

"You said you wrote a report in your hotel room in New York."

"I did."

"Where is it?"

"I tore it into small pieces and flushed it down the toilet in the same hotel room. There's no copy of it. There's nothing. There isn't any report."

"You're lying. You were lying from the beginning. You're a cheap tout and a dirty liar."

"Go to hell," I said again, and walked out and slammed the door behind me. I got into my car and drove, and I drove until my head was too thick and heavy to think. Then I stopped at a bar and had some drinks, and I drove again. But I was going nowhere, and finally I went back to the one-room apartment I called home and opened a bottle of Scotch and took a mouthful of it and spat it out. I was sick, and I hung over the toilet bowl, clutching my stomach, and vomited the way I hadn't vomited since my trip overseas in 1942. Then I sat in the stink and darkness of my toilet and cried some; I was drunk and alone, and who gave a damn if I did cry the way a man shouldn't?

Then I got to my bed and lay down with my clothes on and fell asleep and dreamed my dreams.

PART 12

LOS ANGELES

THE NEXT TWO DAYS, SATURDAY AND SUNDAY, PASSED. THEY were hard days, but they passed. I don't recall much about them; they were full of fog and they stretched through the timelessness of sheer existence that was without pleasure or comfort in anticipation or memory. I drove down to San Diego, thinking that I would see my former wife and make a sop to my conscience, but sanity eliminated that kind of thinking. I had some drinks at a bar. I sat on a beach above La Jolla and I slept at a motel. The next day I didn't drink at all. Having no desire to be back in Los Angeles, I stopped at the big amusement park at Anaheim and watched the kids. At sundown I drove up to the city and found a double-feature show that kept me sitting in a kind of daze until midnight. The two days passed.

It was nine-thirty on Monday when I reached my office, and at nine forty-five Frederick Summers' secretary called and told me that Mr. Summers had returned to Los Angeles on Friday night and had been trying to reach me all day Saturday and all day Sunday.

"Now you've reached me," I said.

"Can you be at our office in an hour?"

"I'll be there," I agreed.

I was in Summers' office in about an hour and ten minutes, but he decided to punish me by keeping me waiting another half hour before he informed me, through his secretary, that I was to enter his office. It was a week short of two months since I had last seen him, but he was the type who neither ages nor changes. His shirt still carried a twenty-dollar price tag, his brown suit called for brown alligator shoes, and his eyes were as coldly appraising as they had been the last time we had met.

He nodded for me to sit down, but I preferred to remain standing. He was standing. He offered me neither his hand nor his greeting, but faced me across the corner of his desk.

"You're back," he said, wasting no words on pleasantry or introduction, "so you must have finished the job."

"It's finished. For what it's worth."

"What is it worth, Macklin?"

"Not much."

"How much?"

"Not much. Not much at all."

"What did you find out?" he asked quietly.

"Nothing."

"Two months of dead end?" he asked, smiling thinly and with no humor.

"That about sums it up." I nodded. "Two months of dead end. I could not have put it better myself, Mr. Summers."

"Where is your report, Macklin?"

"What report?"

"The one I paid through the nose for, Macklin."

"No report. It was dead end, as you put it. No leads, no traces—no report. Why waste your time?"

"I have lots of time, Macklin."

"I see."

"Lots of money, lots of time. The time helps the money along, and when I spend the money I do so thoughtfully and carefully."

"I've noticed that as a virtue of the rich," I agreed pleasantly.

"I am pleased that you're observant, Macklin. If there's no report, then surely there's an itinerary—the cities you visited in your travels at my expense, the hotels you stopped at, the people you interviewed?"

"No itinerary. I don't make notes, and you were thoughtful enough to agree that I did not have to account for expenses."

"Under the assumption that I was dealing with an honest man," he said, his voice hardening.

"I suppose that was your assumption. You were dealing with a private cop—you should have thought of that too."

"I see." His eyes narrowed as he looked me up and down carefully and speculatively. "I'm ten years older than you, Macklin," he said, "but I'm in good shape. I think I could take you."

"You've been seeing too many films. When you use fancy literary slang that way, you're not being clever, only gauche, Mr. Summers."

"I'll take my chances on being gauche. What would you do if I worked you over, Macklin?"

"Sue you for every dollar you have." I shrugged. "Anyway, you shouldn't try. Beating up someone is not a question of weight or good condition; it's a question of attitude. You have to know how. I don't think you know how, and I don't think it makes much sense for you to get sore and talk about beating me up. We made an agreement. I didn't promise you anything. I said I would try, and you were willing for me to try."

"And you tried, Macklin?"

"I told you, Mr. Summers—nothing. That's what it adds up to."

"You're a liar," he said. "You're a goddamned liar!"

I dropped the "Mr." I was fed up with being his boy. Even for a thousand dollars and another hour, I was fed up with being his boy. Anyway, I didn't want the thousand, I had a shred of professional decency left, and it wasn't big enough to wrap a thousand dollars in. I was fed up with him.

"Don't call me a liar, Summers," I said. "I'm ten years younger than you and I know how to play rough. I like to think that I'm civilized, but I'll beat the shit out of you if you call me a liar again—and I'll spit in your face first. I don't like you. I think you stink. I think you stink like carrion."

I didn't raise my voice, but he shouted at me, "There goddamn well was a report—and you sold it to Sylvia West!"

"What?"

"You were at Santa Barbara with her on Friday! You made a deal with her! You sold out!"

I began to laugh, and then I knew that I was all right again. I stood there laughing at him while he screamed:

"Both ends against the middle—you lousy cheap crook! You won't get away with this! I saw the commissioner today! You're finished, Macklin! Your license is finished! You're through in Los Angeles, Macklin—through!" All his debonair graces had given way to the fact that he wanted to tear me in half and he couldn't, because he was afraid of me and of physical violence and of doing something he probably had never done before—fight a man with his bare hands. So he screamed at me, and when the secretary came running into the room, I said to her:

"Give him some water and a sedative, and when he calms down tell him I left."

Then I went out. I paused at the Mirós, because I would probably never be that close to Mirós again. He shouted after me:

"Don't come back, Macklin! I'll have you arrested if you show your face here again."

Then I went out. The job was done, and I breathed more easily. I took the elevator down, and outside the warm California sun was seeping nicely through the smog. For the first time in eight long and painful weeks I felt that it was all right with the world.

2

Instead of using the Freeway, I drove along Wilshire Boulevard all the way to Beverly Hills, and then I turned up North Canyon Drive to Coldwater Canyon. I wanted time to think it through, but there was not a great deal to be thought through.

When I rang the doorbell at her house, a maid answered and told me that Miss West was on the patio out back. I walked through the house. Sylvia sat in the shade of the garden wall, a bridge table in front of her and paper on the table. How much she was able to write, I don't know. She was watching me as I came out of the house, her face calm, her dark eyes direct, her manner neutral. She said nothing, only watched me. I stood there for a while, silent and a little foolish too, until she nodded at a chair. Then I sat down and said to her:

"Why did you tell Summers I sold you the report?"

"Why not? It's the kind of thing he'd expect you to do."

"He's been over to City Hall already. I'm washed up as a private cop."

"What should I do, Mack? Weep for you?"

"The hell with you," I said. "I don't want your tears. I don't want anything from you."

"What did you come for then?"

I shook my head.

"You were washed up as a private cop anyway, weren't you?"

"I guess so," I agreed.

"What did you do with the weekend?" she asked me.

"Why? Did you try calling me and figure I blew out my brains? Are you disappointed?"

"Yes. I'm disappointed."

"I drove down to San Diego," I said. "Then I went to Anaheim yesterday. I walked around and watched the kids."

"I was never there," she said.

"It's a nice place. For kids."

"I called you."

I nodded.

"It won't be good like they say these things should be good," she said. "We're not young—I'm not even sure we don't hate each other more than we have any real feeling for each other. What do I know about you—a private cop who never got a month ahead with his rent? I'm not even sure I can have kids—I'm not sure of anything——"

"It's a beginning."

"Of what, Mack? Of what?"

"Of being Sylvia Karoki. Of remembering about the skinny, wonderful kid who walked into the library in Pittsburgh and asked Irma Olanski about a book. Of touching life where it hurts most and bleeds most, because as rotten and sadistic and superstitious as our race is, we are also the only thing the world can promise, and not a bad promise at that."

"You're a funny guy, Mack," she said. "You're kind and you've got some kind of strength I don't understand, but I don't even know if I like you, and sometimes I hate you."

"I'll take my chances," I said.

"That's all it is, Mack." She nodded. "Chances. You know about Sylvia. You know what you're getting into."

"I know."

Then she said, "Well, you might as well kiss me. You haven't kissed me yet."

So I took her in my arms and kissed her, and she was crying then. But whether weeping for herself or for me, I don't know.